M☢NDAY AFTER THE AP👄CALYPSE

JESSIE D. EAKER

Jessie D. Eaker
jessieeaker.com

This is a work of fiction. Names, characters, places, and incidents are a product of the author's imagination. Locales and public names are sometimes used for atmospheric purposes. Any resemblance to actual people, living or dead, or to businesses, companies, events, institutions, or locales is completely coincidental.

Cover designed by MiblArt

Monday After The Apocalypse / Jessie D. Eaker — First edition

ISBN 979-8-9857335-0-1, Trade Paperback

To my children, who gave me the gift of insanity.

Contents

CHAPTER ONE

Mornings Suck

Sydney

SYDNEY ULYSSES CARRINGTON III put a hand to his aching head and studied the debris-choked staircase. The collection of broken boards, bricks, and chunks of concrete completely blocked the stairway from his underground shelter into his multi-million dollar mansion. Since the elevator refused to operate, and no one seemed to be able to hear his calls for help, he had decided to take matters into his own hands and dig his way out. Which was why he was trying to systematically extract the wayward pieces of debris and place them to one side of the stairs, hopefully without bringing the entire mess crashing down on his head.

Selecting a chunk of cemented brick, he carefully extracted it and heaved it to one side with the others in the growing pile.

The ensuing cloud of dust caused him to sneeze violently and once more set off his throbbing headache. His skull felt like a reverberating church bell. He put a hand on either side of his head and tried to steady it.

"This is not doing my hangover any good," he muttered.

He couldn't understand how he had missed whatever had caused all the mess. Sure, he had managed to overindulge during his solitary dusk-to-dawn pity party, but he should have heard *something*! He was quite a sound sleeper, especially when he drank. But he had been quite surprised to open his door and find it totally blocked.

Sydney smiled, perversely pleased with himself. Admittedly, his behavior had been deplorable for a Carrington. But his indulgences provided the only distraction from who and what he was. If it weren't for his *condition*, he wouldn't drink nearly so much. You can only tolerate something like that for so long without going crazy. Although from the looks his butler gave him, he was pretty sure James thought him well past the threshold of being insane.

Sydney removed a chunk of brick, and a draft stirred the dust around him. Although it was just after midnight, he could make out a dim light through the hole he had just created. With a cough and a cry of triumph, he shoved the remaining boards aside and emerged into the open air.

But his grin quickly faded as he looked around in shock. *What the hell had happened?*

Because of the rubble blocking the cellar, Sydney had expected to find his house damaged. But he was totally unprepared for complete annihilation. His once graceful mansion, with its two-century-old architecture, lay in scattered ruins as if some giant hand had simply swept it aside. A chill breeze, tainted with smoke, caressed his cheek and set a nearby piece of sheet metal flapping. In the distance, he could hear the gurgle of water running, likely from a broken pipe. Sydney shivered.

Hardly believing it, he stumbled through the wreckage.

What had happened?

A refrigerator lay on its side, speared with a leg off of his antique dinner table. The table had been an heirloom that had occupied the family dining room since his grandfather's day.

A picture frame, clinging to scraps of the portrait it once contained, sprawled across a toilet seat. The picture had been of his father's favorite sailboat, the *Good Weather Pride*.

The bust of a laughing cherub stuck foolishly out of a wide-screen TV like some sick comedy routine. The statue had guarded the driveway since Sydney, as a child, had broken its twin.

It was almost too much for his brain to process. His beautifully manicured grounds had been torn apart, hedges ripped up, flowers crushed, and the ancient family oaks, which had stood for over two hundred years, had been stripped of their leaves and broken in half.

It must have been a tornado.

Sydney wiped his sweaty hands on his pants and muttered to himself, "One thing's for sure, the insurance company's going to give me hell."

In a daze, he stumbled out into the wreckage. He picked up a broken chair arm and stared at it in shock. He could just hear his servants, James and Maude, complaining about the mess.

Sydney gasped in realization. "Oh, please no." *James and*

Maude had been in the house! Frantically, he began scrambling through the wreckage, calling them, and pulling at every patch of cloth he found. But there was no trace of them.

He felt an overwhelming sense of loss. He knew they didn't particularly care for him, but they had always done what he had requested, no matter how strange. But more importantly, they had been his last contact with humanity as he slipped further into his self-imposed isolation.

Realizing he would need help to find them, he ran back into the cellar, emerging moments later with his mobile phone. It was thankfully at full charge. He didn't normally use it since it couldn't get a signal within the shelter—not that he had anyone to call or text with anyway.

He immediately dialed 911 but was only rewarded with a message stating he had no service. He climbed on top of a broken fountain to get higher, but there was still no signal. He stared at the device in frustration. The towers must be down. From the destruction he had seen so far, it would not be surprising.

Thinking he might be able to flag down someone passing by, Sydney stumbled numbly along the driveway toward the gates of his estate. But he stopped cold at the mounds of rubble the gates had become. He looked out in shock and despair.

His house, built on a hill just outside Rhidnesburg, commanded an excellent view of the city below, especially at night. But the only light visible came from streaks of lightning in the distance and sporadic fires dotting the darkness.

"Damn big tornado," he muttered to himself. It must have knocked out the power lines.

To the north, a strange, ominous green glow caught his eye. It reflected eerily off the overcast sky. Sydney searched his numbed brain for an explanation. D.C. was in that direction, but not much else. Then a disturbing thought occurred to him. "No." He shook his head in denial. "They couldn't have."

He ran back inside the shelter and emerged with an old handheld radio from his father's day, which he just so happened to have batteries for. He quickly donned the earphones, fumbled with its miniature controls, and tuned it over the entire range of frequencies. But there was nothing, only static from the nearby lightning.

Still unbelieving, Sydney ran back inside, and after a longer delay, emerged with a Geiger counter. Hoping the batteries still worked, he turned it on. He grew wide-eyed when the needle swung into the red—not immediately lethal to people, but not exactly healthy either.

"Those bastards!" He shouted. "Those stupid bastards! They went and blew up the whole damn world."

The realization of his plight slammed into his brain. He had survived the big blast. The last war.

The apocalypse.

"DAMNATION!" he cried into the night. "Everything is gone! No more city, no more movies, no more electricity, and—oh no! No more *refrigerators*."

With one final burst of lightning, the rain started. Sydney held his head. *My condition!* No more bottled meals. I'll have to survive as they did in the old days. I'll have to track down my own food. I might actually have to—ugh… He shuddered at the thought.

Sydney looked up as the falling rain beat on his face. The loss of his friends, his house, his... everything, was too much for him. He sank to his knees as the tears overwhelmed him.

Survival in a post-apocalyptic world wasn't going to be easy.

Especially for a vampire.

About an hour before dawn, the rain stopped, and Sydney managed to pull himself together. Standing, he wiped the tears from his eyes and pulled his shoulders back. He was a Carrington, and Carringtons were survivors. Since the first Carrington had bravely gone forth into the new world (that would have been Abraham Carrington), they had been survivors. Abraham had crossed the Atlantic in a leaky ship and secured a home despite sickness, starvation, and hardship. A true pioneer.

That was the situation he faced, Sydney told himself—alone in a new world. He would have to figure out something, and sitting in a mud puddle wasn't exactly constructive.

Taking one more look at the rubble that had once been his home, Sydney went back down into the basement and shoved the thick steel door closed. It creaked slowly shut, reminding him, not for the first time, of a prison door—keeping the world out and himself isolated from humanity.

Sydney surveyed the shelter's interior, not actually believing he had survived. Judging from the room, one would never guess that everything outside had been destroyed. Not so much as a picture frame had been jarred.

That was one thing Sydney could say about the shelter—it was well built. His grandfather Carrington—Sydney's namesake and his guardian for as long as he could remember—would have tolerated nothing less. The senior Carrington believed in being prepared for anything.

Long before Sydney had been born, during one of the missile crises popular at that time, his grandfather had converted the basement into a bomb shelter—reinforcing the walls, installing a generator, and stocking it with every item that a survivor could conceivably need, including food, booze, and toilet paper. He even made arrangements to have the shelter's stock rotated to ensure instant readiness.

The finished shelter was modest by Carrington standards, with only a living room, a recreation room, a combination dining room/kitchen, a couple of bedrooms, and only one bathroom. But it would do in a pinch.

Since it was possible they could be confined inside for weeks at a time, his grandfather had put in a pool table—which could also be converted for ping-pong—twenty-five decks of cards, every board game you could imagine, and a multitude of books. One might die of radiation or germs, but never boredom.

And so the shelter had stood ready but idle for the next fifty years. Then Sydney, after developing his vampire condition, rediscovered it, finding the shelter exactly what he needed—a dark place to sleep during the day and a refuge from people during the night. He installed a custom-made double-wide casket in one of the two bedrooms, turned the other bedroom into a study, and abandoned the rest of his house to the staff. Since the Carringtons had a long history of being slightly eccentric, this behavior was hardly noticed.

Shedding wet clothes along the way, Sydney toweled off and donned a robe and slippers. He stopped a moment before the mirror to comb his hair. Thankfully, unlike the legends had said, vampires could see their reflection. But he had an idea where the myth originated. The mirror tended to reflect strong light, which hurt his sensitive eyes.

Sydney smiled sadly as he remembered James scowling at him for wearing sunglasses in the basement. At the time, the butler hadn't commented on his sudden sensitivity to light. But shortly afterward, he discovered James had quietly removed a few of the lightbulbs to dim the glare. Not for the first time, he wondered what he was going to do without his trusted servants.

He sighed, continuing to stare into the mirror. Yet, Sydney still found his reflected image disturbing. On the outside, he didn't look any different than he had before. The same medium height, the same slender build, and the same angular face with light brown hair and blue eyes. No different from the nondescript young man he had been before.

But if he smiled, the two razor-sharp points of his canines completely shattered the image of normalcy. That was likely the real reason vampires avoided mirrors. It wasn't that they couldn't see their reflection. They just didn't want to.

Suddenly craving something to drink, he went behind the living room's bar and inspected his stock. Despite his heavy consumption over the last few nights, he still had a few bottles left, plus another couple of cases in the storeroom. No, alcohol was not going to be a problem for a while. He reached for a bottle, but his stomach started doing flip-flops, and he drew back. Even a vampire's stomach could only handle so much abuse.

Instead, he turned to the small refrigerator behind the bar to inspect his *other* stock—four plastic bags of whole blood. He shook his head. Supplies he had, but blood he did not. A need his grandfather had not foreseen. How could his elder have possibly dreamed that one of his descendants would become a vampire?

Sydney took a bag from the refrigerator and searched for a clean glass. None were behind the bar, so he tried the kitchen and found all the dishes in the sink were dirty. He sighed. Add another item to his growing list of concerns—he'd have to wash dishes.

He rinsed out a long stem wine glass that didn't have mold in the bottom and poured himself half a bag. Putting the remainder back in the refrigerator, he reclined on the sofa and took a sip. He winced—it still tasted bad. When he was just starting out as a vampire, drinking blood had made him nauseous. But now, he simply tried to think of it as tomato juice and choke it down. It did help a little.

Sydney leaned back in his chair and began to sort through his situation. He was safe in his basement—he felt sure of that. From what he had seen of the surrounding area, he doubted if many had survived the destruction, so he didn't expect hordes of people to come knocking on his door. The radiation, however, was another matter. He had no idea what effect it might have on him. His experience so far indicated he was immune to most diseases, so he had to assume he was unaffected by radiation, too. He glanced at his laptop on the kitchen table, thinking he could certainly use the Internet about now. But he had already established it wasn't working before opening the shelter door.

Sydney scratched his head and tried to remember all he could on surviving a nuclear apocalypse. It wasn't much. Most of what he knew came from watching old sci-fi movies—a habit he had developed from being up all night with nothing much to do.

Sydney grinned, remembering one movie about a nuclear war where those dosed with strong radiation were called 'the living dead.' He laughed. Somehow, he didn't think they were talking about him. In another movie, the hero had a dog to tell him what to do. Sydney could use one of those about now, fleas and all. And of course, there had been other movies where the radioactive mutants would seek out the normal people for their flesh, brains, or various other body parts.

That was all Sydney's overactive imagination needed—the hairs on his neck stood up. He looked nervously at the door. Would mutants try to get him?

He took a firm grip on his imagination and forcibly calmed his fears. The idea of mutants right after a nuclear war was ridiculous, he told himself. It would take generations for mutants to appear—not one day. Be realistic.

The vampire got up and stretched. It was almost dawn, time for him to get to bed. He put his glass in the kitchen sink and opened a supply cabinet. During his stay in the basement, Sydney had used very little of the supplies. It was well stocked with all sorts of food, both canned and freeze-dried. He pulled out a snack cracker and munched on it to get the bad taste out of his mouth. He estimated the food and water would last for months, and if he conserved it, enough natural gas to power the generator for three weeks. But as a vampire, he was still missing the one critical item he needed the most. Blood.

He had to have at least half a pint a day or face a gradual weakening followed by death. Once before, he had tried going without it, but on the third evening, he became so weak he couldn't even feed himself. He'd had a hell of a time explaining *that* to James.

With three and a half pints left in the refrigerator, and counting the four pints he had in the deep freeze, he could last fourteen days. Two weeks wasn't very long to find a new blood supply.

"Damn this curse," Sydney thought, not for the first time. "If only I didn't have it." He shook his head. "I'm a disgrace to the Carrington name."

Sydney sighed. He had no choice—he would have to go out tomorrow night and look for a new supply of blood. He would first check the blood banks and hospitals. But then if he found nothing—

He shook his head, trying not to think about it, but he dearly hoped he wouldn't have to track down some poor survivor.

And bite them.

CHAPTER TWO

Bad Luck

Allie

ALLIE MEDLEY AWOKE KNOWING something was wrong—she just wasn't quite sure what it was. But it had to be bad. Lately, bad luck was all she'd had.

She opened her eyes and glanced around in the total darkness she usually slept in. *What was it?* She couldn't put her finger on what had set her off. She groggily felt for her phone and thumbed it on, then blinked in the sudden brightness. As vision returned, she could see that the underside of her mattress was undisturbed. The white felt covering looked like it always did. Not a speck of dust. She might sleep under her bed, but she kept it spotless, vacuuming it every couple of days. While her clothes might be thrown about without a care, she was at least going to sleep clean.

She glanced at her phone's display—6:02 pm. She frowned. She would have to be at work in less than an hour, so she had better hurry. Hopefully, the bus would be on time this evening. She was already under the boss's eye for being late, and she couldn't afford to lose this job.

What was wrong?

She groaned and rolled toward the heavy quilts draped around the mattress to block out the light. While she didn't have to sleep in total darkness, she just felt more secure when she did. She imagined that someone more refined might have an actual coffin, but not her. She might be a vampire now, but she was still a girl on a budget. So it was under the bed for her.

She slid toward the edge, lifted the quilt—and immediately drew back in surprise. A chunk of ceiling blocked her path, one that hadn't been there the previous night. She sneezed in the sudden cloud of dust wafting toward her. She shoved her phone out from underneath the covers to illuminate her surroundings. *What the hell?* It looked like the ceiling's center had collapsed while still connected at the side, levering downward and landing at an angle, creating a sort of lean-to between floor and wall. If her bed hadn't been set against it, it would have been crushed. And she under it. She took back her comment about the bad luck.

Then she realized what was wrong. Her collapsed room certainly qualified, but that wasn't it. It was the quiet that was so wrong. She lived downtown, so there was always traffic, shouting, or just people moving. But now, it was deadly silent.

She had to get out.

She flipped around and slid to the foot of the bed. It was not blocked, so she managed to crawl out and into what was left of her collapsed room. She looked up to see that her basement apartment had suddenly developed a skylight. A big, open-air one. She wondered how she was going to explain this to her landlord.

Her second-hand sofa and the flat-screen TV that had been a fifty percent off clearance special were neatly crushed under the collapsed ceiling. But surprisingly, the poster of her professional wrestling idol, Clare Montare, was still attached to the far wall and was totally undamaged. The female wrestler was smiling encouragingly. *Get on with it, girl*, the image seemed to say. Allie had taken encouragement from the poster in the past, and right now, she could use every bit she could muster.

Allie rooted around and managed to find a pair of old sneakers, which she located only because she knew the approximate location of where she took them off. Then dressed in only what she had slept in—her Clare Montare T-shirt and jogging pants—she managed to crawl out of the basement.

As she stepped out onto the curb beside her building, she couldn't help but wonder how she had missed what had happened. Sure, she slept pretty soundly during the day, but to miss this? The entire neighborhood of old three-story apartment buildings was totally destroyed. It was as if a giant had decided to just sweep it away. She immediately dismissed the idea it was weather-related. The ground was dry. In fact, there was this gray powder everywhere.

Her eyes drifted toward the north, where an ominous green glow reflected eerily off the overcast sky. Normally the view of the horizon would have been blocked by all the buildings, but with the structures flattened, she had a pretty good view all around. She saw a flash of lightning off in the distance.

Her mother.

Allie jerked out her phone and hit dial. Her mom was living in San Fran with her washed-up rock star boyfriend. She might know what had gone on. But the phone immediately told her it didn't have a signal. She glanced around and spotted a leaning utility pole. It had been stripped of its electrical lines but was still standing. It was the old kind with foot supports sticking out of it. It would have to do.

She managed to leverage herself up onto the first foothold and then climbed as high as she could. When she could go no higher, she held her phone up to the sky. But still no signal. She sighed in worry. She and her mother weren't on the best of terms, which was why Allie had gone east while her mother had gone west. Having a continent between them seemed to work pretty well. But still, she was her mother, and they did care about each other in a broken family sort of way.

As she lowered her phone, she noticed the scene around her for the first time. A bolt of lightning flashed and illuminated the surrounding area. A numbness came over her as she took in the scene. It was like one of those black and white pictures in a textbook. One where it's nothing but complete and utter devastation. She swallowed and gave her head a tiny shake. *It couldn't be.* But then another flash happened, and she saw the landscape had not changed. Everything had been destroyed. Flattened. No one was visible.

Her eyes were drawn again to the green glow on the horizon. She remembered one of her coworkers at the hospital talking about Russia and the President getting into some kind of disagreement. Tensions had been high, but she had shrugged it off. Weren't they always disagreeing? Surely they wouldn't go that far. But with a sinking feeling, she realized it would account for everything she was seeing.

Nuclear war.

The apocalypse.

There was another lightning flash, and a few moments later, she heard the loud rumble of thunder. A cool breeze plucked at her hair and caressed her face.

What was she going to do?

Then she felt that familiar hunger. One that she could not deny. And another realization hit her. Where were all the people? Millions lived in the city, surely some of them had survived. Many of them would be injured, but they would be there.

Only, it was eerily quiet. The only sound was the rumble of distant thunder and the whipping of the wind stirring bits of loose paper. She blinked back tears as the loneliness of the situation hit her like a physical blow.

She needed people. Not only for the company, and not only for the security being with them provided. No, she needed them for another reason. She bowed her head and clung to the top of her pole.

Surviving would not be easy for a normal human. But it was going to be even more difficult—

For a vampire.

The approaching storm chased her back to the ruins of her apartment with frequent flashes of lightning and urgent booms of thunder. Thankfully, as a vampire, her vision was well adapted to the dark, and despite all the debris, she easily found her way back. But when she reached it, she quickly realized she couldn't stay there. It was basically a big hole in the ground now, and at the first rain, would likely fill with water. No, she was going to have to find somewhere else to stay.

A bolt of lightning, quickly followed by a deafening boom, highlighted the point. She needed to move—and it had to be tonight. So Allie set about searching for things to take with her. Important things.

Like jeans.

She realized this would not be an easy task, but she needed something more rugged than her sweat pants. Especially since she wasn't sure if she would be coming back. And while her sneakers were comfortable, they would not do for walking over all the debris. No, this girl needed boots.

Thankfully, the storm was all bluster, and after giving a little sprinkle, veered off to the west. Allie counted her blessings since it took her an hour of digging to come up with just the basics—jeans, some old hiking boots, and her faded school backpack to hold everything. And of course, underwear. Her mother had always told her to always wear clean underwear, reminding her that a good bra and panties were a girl's closest friend.

However, for some odd reason—likely because of putting off her laundry for the last month—shirts were a problem. She had finally settled for her special collectible professional wrestling shirts, which she had been saving for a special occasion. She guessed that surviving the apocalypse qualified. Besides, she drew strength from wearing her idol's picture—Clare Montare.

Clare was Allie's favorite. She was young, not much older than Allie herself, and a relative newcomer to the wrestling scene. And so strong. The other wrestlers didn't stand a chance against her. And she fought fair, too. Some of the other wrestlers would try some underhanded tricks and might even have her pinned with only a few counts left. But Clare always came alive at the last moment and turned the tides on them. She always came out on top. Allie sighed and wished she had Clare with her right now. She could use a little bit of strength and bravery.

Once clothed, Allie set about her next challenge. Food. Her tiny kitchen had been thoroughly crushed, so there wasn't much to pick from. Not that she kept much in her pantry anyway. She breathed a sigh of relief when her rooting turned up a candy bar (which she ate), a diet soda (which she gulped down), and two cans of chicken and rice soup. But delight quickly turned to anger when she realized she couldn't find the damn can opener. She threw them in her backpack anyway. Maybe she'd run across a hardware store or something.

But the food did not satisfy her real hunger. She needed blood. And soon. The cravings would become unbearable in only a day or two. Plus, the longer she went without, the weaker she would grow. So weak, she wouldn't be able to stand, little alone walk.

She glanced up at the sky. And she couldn't forget shelter. Dawn was still hours away, but she couldn't afford to be caught outside. She had found out the hard way that vampires and sunny days did not mix well.

She glanced over at the poster of Clare Montare clinging to what was left of her far wall. Clare smiled confidently at her, arms crossed, and her thumb held up in salute. She seemed ready for anything. 'Clare will dare!' was her tagline—one Allie had often repeated.

Allie had tried to emulate her hero but hadn't succeeded very well. She had saved her meager funds and joined a gym. In fact, she was just getting into weight training... when the unimaginable happened. It forced her to cancel her membership.

Hell, it forced me to cancel my life.

It was when she had been turned into a vampire.

That first month had been traumatic, to say the least. Her body had changed in subtle ways, her teeth growing, lights becoming extremely bright, and the most unexpected one... not having a monthly. Now that had panicked her. She had been afraid that on that fateful night, her date had taken advantage of her, and along with his name, wiped it from her mind. But that had proven not to be the case. It just seemed vampires didn't have them. She assumed it was to reduce the loss of blood.

But the worst thing was not being able to go out in the sun. She loved the sun, going to the beach, lounging in the park, even going to the zoo. All gone.

The changes forced on her had been devastating and made her sometimes wonder if this new life was worth continuing. But it was that picture that had given her the will to survive. Something about Clare Montare's confident smile warmed her. *You can do it*, her expression seemed to say. Just as it did now.

Allie finished the last of her soda and tossed it into the wreckage. Surely if she could survive being turned into a vampire, she could survive this. Piece of cake.

Her mother had always told her that you should never try to eat a sandwich all at once. No, instead, you took it a bite at a time. And this one was no different. One bite at a time.

So, she donned her backpack and grabbed her raincoat. Her

destination was her work—Staddard Circle Hospital. If there was anyone left, they would be there. If nothing else, it would be somewhere she could get out of the rain and shelter from the day. There might even be some blood left in the refrigerators. Assuming the generators were working.

So with a last look around, she turned to the poster on the wall and returned Clare Montare a thumbs-up. Then she turned to leave. More out of habit than anything, she brought up her phone and saw it was after midnight. Monday, in fact. She took a deep breath and let it out slowly before bravely stepping forward on this Monday after the apocalypse.

CHAPTER THREE

On The Cutting Edge

Sydney

THE NEXT EVENING, SHORTLY after sunset, Sydney made his way down the debris-scattered Carrington Hill and walked into town. He had spent the first hour of the morning packing and mapping out the most efficient route to visit all the hospitals and blood banks in the area. His intention was to stop at the nearest first and work his way outward.

Although he traveled light—carrying only a map, compass, and a backpack stuffed with sandwiches, munchies, and a thermos of his required beverage—the going was rougher than he had hoped. The wreckage was bad—the knocked over, crunched up, strewn everywhere kind of bad.

His own mansion had been hit the worst, since it was up on an exposed hill, but the city lay in a slight valley and so its destruction wasn't as severe.

But that wasn't saying much. Few buildings had been left standing, and those spared usually lacked a roof or had been gutted by fire. The streets were filled with bricks, glass, boards, and burned-out cars, which often made walking difficult. Sometimes, whole piles of wreckage would block his path, forcing him to scamper over or backtrack and find another route.

However, it was the silence that really got to him. Not a bird, squirrel, dog, or human. The only sound came from either a breeze or himself. His every step echoed off the battered walls. More than once, he whirled at a sound behind him, only to discover it to be some pebble that he had disturbed himself. Sydney tended to think of it as a dead quiet, kind of like being in a theater after hours or in a graveyard at night. Even though you knew no one was around, you could feel someone watching. Combined with his overactive imagination, it gave Sydney the creeps. He tried to ignore the feeling (as well as his overactive imagination) and concentrate on his journey. But he still kept looking over his shoulder.

To his surprise, his vampire traits helped him maintain a relatively rapid pace. He scrambled over piles of rubble and even moved heavy obstructions without becoming the least bit winded. Although he had been a vampire for almost two years, he had never truly tested his abilities. Living a solitary life in a fallout shelter, he rarely went out. Sure, he stayed reasonably fit, preferring to exercise on the shelter's elliptical and weight machine. But that was the extent of it.

Of course, he had managed to figure out a few things about his vampire abilities. For instance, some of the historical attributes of vampires simply weren't true. Yes, he did have to have blood, but no, he wasn't really dead. He ate and eliminated as he had before. His heart still beat, and he still breathed air.

But his heart did beat much slower than a normal human's, and unless he was exercising, his respiration was hardly noticeable. It was even less so when sleeping. For all intents, he would appear to be dead. Not to mention that he became unbearably tired at dawn and felt more comfortable sleeping in a tightly enclosed area. A casket was perfect for that very reason—and pretty comfy, too! He'd tried a coffin but found it rather uncomfortable. The odd shape left no leg room at all.

The one thing about vampires that the legends got correct was sunlight—direct exposure would give him third-degree burns in only seconds. Sydney's experiments led him to believe it has something to do with ultraviolet light. He'd proven that when he'd accidentally exposed himself to an ultraviolet LED. It had only been for a few seconds, but it had been enough to give him a terrible sunburn. He'd been sore for a week! So sunlight was definitely off his list.

Sydney paused in his journey and surveyed his surroundings, easily picking out the ruined buildings and debris despite the lack of illumination. Earlier, when he started out, he had used a flashlight but soon put it away. Although he didn't know why it surprised him, his vampire eyes were especially suited to the night. To him, it looked like an overcast day. He guessed the cloudy sky helped. It emitted a strange glow, which he hoped came from the moon's backlighting and not from radiation.

He had checked the area earlier with his Geiger counter, and it had read higher than normal but not exceedingly high. While not an expert, he didn't think it was an immediate concern.

He guessed that the blast that had destroyed Rhidnesburg was centered to the north of the city. Judging from the wreckage, he expected that almost everyone had been killed. But like him, wouldn't some people have survived? Then, where were they?

But it was the lack of bodies that puzzled him the most.

His only explanation was that everyone had been caught inside their emergency shelters. Although he had to admit—it was a lame explanation. Wouldn't a few people have been caught outside? It remained a mystery yet to be solved. Sydney remembered one movie he had seen where a comet turned everyone into sand. Could that have happened here? There was certainly an abundance of fine gray dust lying around. Could it be connected? Sydney shook his head. Surely not.

Despite the wreckage and his sometimes faulty navigation, he made it to his first stop in just under two hours—the Eastern Metro Blood Service. But he passed the building twice before he realized it. Sydney closed his eyes and shook his head.

The structure had taken a severe beating, practically leveled. The building had been one of the older ones constructed of old-fashioned red brick and decorated with ornate statues out front. Now, however, it was a pile of rubble decorated with scraps of wood and pipe. A still-standing street sign was his only confirmation that he was indeed at the right place. He climbed on top of the wreckage and searched carefully for access to the refrigerators buried inside, but he could find nothing. It would take a bulldozer to move all the debris.

Disappointed but not defeated, Sydney hopped down from

the rubble and pulled out his city map, taking a bearing on the next closest hospital. Since it was the area's largest, it seemed the most likely to have some blood that had survived.

As he considered which direction to go, a distant sound broke the deathly quiet. Sydney looked up. What was it? He held his breath, listening. He heard it again, a faint buzzing, like a bumblebee or a horsefly.

Sydney's overactive imagination kicked in, reminding him of some other movies he had seen. The ones where the radiation had done strange things to insects, turning them into humongous monsters. His imagination showed him visions of giant crickets shooting atomic fire, monster wasps with laser stingers, gargantuan spiders injecting nuclear venom. He shuddered.

With considerable effort, Sydney got his imagination under control and admonished himself for his lack of reason. Mutants just didn't spring up overnight. Besides, insects of that size couldn't support their own weight. They could only exist in his imagination.

"Then why are your teeth chattering?" he muttered to himself.

Listening closely, Sydney heard the sound again. As he listened closer, he decided it wasn't an insect but something else. Exactly what, he wasn't sure. His curiosity got the better of him, and he thought it might be worth investigating. At least he could prove to himself it was nothing. He turned towards the sound.

Rounding a corner, Sydney saw light coming from the open doorway and window of one of the few buildings still intact. The building's picture window had a gaping hole in it, ringed with jagged edges. It reminded him of a hungry mouth with long sharp teeth. Sydney picked his way to the door and peered inside. From the contents strewn about—hoes, rakes, and lawnmowers—Sydney guessed it had been a lawn and garden shop. The light he had seen came from a gas lantern sitting on the counter at the back of the room. But the shop's most amazing feature was that it was occupied.

A broad-shouldered man—much larger than the vampire in both height and weight—stood with his back to Sydney, bending over a counter at the store's rear. The man was bald and wore a loose-fitting gray uniform that was vaguely familiar. He appeared to be intently working on something, but his body was blocking Sydney's view of exactly what.

A breeze blew from the building towards Sydney, and he suddenly found himself suppressing a sneeze. His sensitive vampire nostrils were assaulted by the smell of exhaust and gasoline. But there was something else. Another odor much worse than the others. It smelled something like the B.O. of a junkyard skunk, but that was putting it mildly. He tried to breathe through his mouth.

Sydney was brought up short when the man stood aside, allowing the vampire to see what he had been working on.

A chainsaw?

The man stretched and rubbed his back. That must have been the buzzing sound he had heard. Sydney couldn't imagine what the man was going to use it for, but whatever it was, the man seemed to have been working on it for a long time. Maybe he had a friend trapped inside one of the buildings and planned to use it to free them. But Sydney didn't think so—the man's pace was too leisurely.

He bent back to the saw.

Quietly, Sydney entered and stood in the doorway—the man had yet to notice him. The vampire wondered how he could attract the man's attention without scaring him to death. None came to mind, so he took the easy way out.

He cleared his throat.

The big man jumped and whirled, presenting the chainsaw like a sword. When he saw Sydney was unarmed, he said, "You scared me." He lowered the saw, letting it swing in one hand. "I thought I had this whole city to myself."

The man smiled. But it was a strange smile and made Sydney uncomfortable. There was an almost predatory glint in his eyes. Sydney couldn't shake the feeling the man was watching him like a cat would a canary. Wasn't it supposed to be the other way around?

"Sorry I startled you," apologized Sydney. "You're the first person I've seen since everything went to hell." The vampire eyed the chainsaw uncomfortably. "How did you manage to escape all the destruction?"

The big man turned and placed the chainsaw back on the counter. "I was in the hospital," he answered simply. He continued working on his saw.

With his tongue, Sydney gingerly touched the razor tips of his vampire teeth. Although he didn't want to, a fresh blood supply was standing right in front of him. He stared at the man's back uncomfortably. And if he bit the man, it would also turn him into a vampire. He remembered his own horrid transformation. Did he want to subject another person to that?

Did he have a choice?

Sydney decided to talk to him a little more—maybe the man

was diseased or on drugs. He didn't think he could contract a disease, but one didn't relish drinking something spoiled. Besides, that awful smell seemed to be coming from him.

Quickly, he racked his brain for some way to bring the man's health up in conversation. "You know," Sydney said. "I just had a physical before all this happened. The doctor said I checked out okay. How about you?" Sydney winced. That sounded so lame.

But the man didn't seem to notice. "I don't like doctors," he said flatly. He continued his work.

"Oh." It occurred to Sydney that he was really just stalling, and he should just get on with it. But did he really want to?

The big man picked up his chainsaw and turned to face Sydney. He frowned. "Are you my friend?"

The question took Sydney off guard—what did that have to do with physical health? But the gleam in the man's eyes made the vampire nervous. "I'm your friend, of course." The vampire extended his hand. "My name's Sydney."

The man ignored his hand and continued to inspect his chainsaw. "At the hospital, they kept telling me—Rip, you shouldn't hurt your friends." The man nodded to himself. "But I ask you. What are friends for?"

Sydney didn't like the way this conversation was going. "Which hospital were you at?"

The big man placed a hand on the chainsaw's pull chord and looked straight at Sydney. "State Mental."

He pulled on the cord, and the engine flared to life.

"Isn't..." Sydney yelled over the engine. "Isn't that where they put all the criminally insane?"

The man smiled. "Yeah." He opened the throttle and swung the chainsaw at Sydney.

Only his vampire reflexes saved him. He jumped back, the whirling blades missing his stomach by mere inches. Due to the chainsaw's weight, the big man was slow to bring it back around. Sydney used those extra seconds to dance to the side.

Rip circled, and Sydney realized too late that his attacker had positioned himself to block the door. The man may have been crazy, but he wasn't stupid. Advancing slowly, Rip revved the engine. His chilling smile never faltered.

Sydney glanced around for an exit, and not finding any, faked toward the door. But his assailant blocked with his weapon.

How the hell do you fight a chainsaw?

The man walked slowly towards him and spoke calmly over the chainsaw's idle. "Did you know my nurses claimed they were my friends? But all they did was give me drugs and keep me locked up in a little padded room. The doctors also said they were my friends, but all they did was hook up wires to my head and shock me. So believe me when I say, I know how to treat a friend!"

Sydney held his hand out as he backed away. "I'm not your friend! I'm the most rotten guy you've ever met!"

The man continued to advance. "They kept me locked up in the basement. I was lucky the nukes opened the door to my room, or I'd still be trapped down there."

Sydney backed against the wall. "I'm not a nurse or a doctor. I hate doctors, actually. I can understand exactly what you feel."

The man looked puzzled. "You understand?"

Sydney nodded vigorously, grasping the thread of hope. "Yes! Yes! I understand."

The man suddenly reared back to swing. "My psychiatrist used to tell me that, too!"

Nearly too late, Sydney jumped to the side. The chainsaw passed uncomfortably close, ripping his shirt and leaving a gash on his chest. While Rip reversed for another swing, Sydney seized the opportunity and dashed for the door—

Unfortunately, his foot caught the last standing merchandise display, and he fell, throwing hammers, screwdrivers, and crowbars across the floor. Sydney caught himself and rolled to his back to find Rip standing over him. The man was grinning wide as he revved the engine of the chainsaw hovering over him and slowly began to lower it. Sydney was confident the whirling blades would kill him as easily as a stake through the heart.

The vampire tried to slide away when his hand landed on something long, cold, and metal—a crowbar? But he wouldn't have time to bring it up.

Sydney looked beyond the man and called, "Hurry with that straitjacket, *friends!*"

The man's eyes went up in shock. He glanced behind him. Sydney brought up the crowbar and hit him in the shin. The man turned back to him, slightly pissed but otherwise unaffected. "You tricked me. I hate tricks!"

Rip revved the engine and swung the chainsaw down.

In pure reflex, Sydney held up the crowbar with both hands. The chainsaw bit into it. Sparks blazed.

And the chain flew off.

The man held up the de-toothed chainsaw and blinked at it.

He began to sob. "You broke it!" He looked at the ceiling and bawled like a baby.

Seizing the opportunity, Sydney scrambled to his feet, and without looking back, fled like the devil chased him.

He quickly decided—

Insane people were definitely off his list.

CHAPTER FOUR

Saving A Cat

Allie

ALLIE CAREFULLY PICKED HER way through the streets headed toward Staddard Circle. She was beginning to worry she might not make it before sunrise.

When she started out, she had expected to reach the hospital in about an hour. After all, it was only five miles from her apartment, and she had walked it before after missing her bus.

But it didn't take her long to realize just how unrealistic her estimate had been. The wreckage and piles of debris forced her to backtrack constantly. Even worse, most of the street signs had been knocked down. And as for landmarks? Well, there weren't any. Thank goodness for her phone. At least the map she had stored there was still working. But she dared not use it too much. She wasn't sure when she'd get to recharge.

Obviously, there was no electricity and therefore no lights. Thankfully her vampire vision was excellent in the dark. To her, it looked like a cloudy day. She had never noticed before since she was always surrounded by electric lights.

As she traveled, she was not only amazed at the things destroyed but also at the things that were left. She passed an elementary school that had been flattened, but strangely, its playground swings stood untouched. A fast-food restaurant had been swept away, but the drive-through looked ready to place an order.

But where were the people? There should be bodies lying around. She assumed they were hidden under the debris, but that didn't seem right either. There were plenty of burned-out and turned-over cars. But all of those were empty too. No, something else had happened. Something that didn't affect vampires. And if it didn't affect them, then what else had it not affected?

She turned a corner and came out onto what she thought was Main Street. Her eye was immediately drawn to a light coming from around a corner a block away. It was dim, but in the darkness, her vampire eyes had no trouble picking it out.

And it was getting brighter.

Her immediate thought was to hide. She didn't want to encounter anyone without knowing what she was up against. But she didn't have time. A dark blur streaked around the corner, immediately followed by a dimly glowing object.

Allie blinked, thinking something was wrong with her eyes. But as the light approached, she could make out it was a tiny glowing figure.

And it was floating.

The dark blur bounded for Allie but slid to a halt just behind her legs, using them as a shield. It was a black cat. The first live thing she had seen since waking that morning. And there was a splotch of blood on one ear.

But Allie didn't have time to examine the animal more closely. The glowing figure floated closer, a high-pitched hum growing louder as it approached.

"Ah-ha!" it shouted in a deep British accent as it came closer. "I have you now, you coward."

Allie shook her head and rubbed her eyes. She must be hallucinating.

During her first year of college, she'd had a roommate that liked mushrooms. The illegal kind. She loved to brag about her trips and some of the hallucinations she had seen—talking pillows, melting walls, and people that weren't there. Her friend had even had a pink teddy bear discuss politics with her. But she had never mentioned anything like this.

What approached had to be a pixie. A rather determined one from the look of it. And he was armed too, with a nasty-looking sword. And now that he was closer, Allie could tell the approaching creature was wearing long brown pants but was otherwise shirtless. Despite being a deep green, he was quite the specimen of maleness with a physique that would give any of the wrestlers she'd seen a run for their money.

Only he was a foot tall and had wings on his back.

Allie couldn't help herself. "You're a pixie," she blurted out in utter shock.

The pixie alighted on top of a nearby pile of rubble, his wings suddenly stilling and revealing their dragonfly-like shape. He frowned. "Indeed I am. Now stand aside and let me deal with that monster. No one attacks me and gets away with it."

She looked down at the cat behind her. It was huddled in fear and stared up at her pleadingly. "You've got to save me, lady," it said. "He wants to kill me."

Allie blinked. The cat talked. She was sure she was hallucinating now. She had read somewhere that the best way to deal with imaginary things was to just confront them.

"You're a cat. You can't talk."

The cat looked insulted. "I am *not* a cat. Anyone can tell I'm a *familiar*. How do you think I'm talking to you?" He looked back to the pixie. "If you save me, I'll have my mistress grant you a wish."

"Your mistress?"

"Yes, she's...."

"Do not listen to that monster!" shouted the pixie, pointing his sword at the cat most dramatically. "He ambushed me, thinking I would be easy prey." He lowered his voice menacingly. "But he thought wrong."

"That guy is crazy!" yelled the cat.

Allie reached down and picked him up, holding him up so she could look him in the eyes. "Did you attack him?"

The cat shook his head. "No! Why would I do such a thing?"

"You lie!" shouted the pixie, his wings fluttering in agitation.

Allie looked back at the cat skeptically.

The feline rolled his eyes. "All right, maybe I did. But it was a case of mistaken identity. I thought he was a mouse. I haven't eaten anything all day."

The pixie gave a dramatic snort. "But he tasted my steel instead."

The cat huffed. "I don't know about tasting, but that thing hurt." He flicked his injured ear.

Allie muttered under her breath. "This is one very realistic hallucination." She pointed to the pixie. "I can't let you kill the cat. What if I make him apologize?"

The pixie frowned. "Death for that monster is the only compensation I will accept! He tried to eat a royal emissary."

The cat tried to leap away, but Allie held him firm. "I told you he's crazy," he said as he squirmed. "Now, let me go."

Allie hugged him to her chest and looked back to the pixie. "I can't let you kill him."

The pixie slit his eyes in anger. "You do realize the choice you're making. No one goes against a pixie. Especially one in the royal service."

Allie shrugged. "It can't be helped. I don't particularly like cats, but in this realm, we don't kill for things like that. We're civilized."

The pixie laughed and spread his arms wide, indicating their surroundings. "You're civilized? And I suppose all this *mess* is from a really good party?"

Allie grimaced. "Would you believe we're going through a difficult time right now?"

The pixie folded his arms over his chest. "That is irrelevant." His wings fluttered in agitation. "This is my final warning. Give me that monster."

"No," Allie said flatly. "I'll make him apologize…"

"So be it!" the pixie shouted. He quickly sheathed his sword and rose into the air. "Since you defy me, I will have you summoned to the royal court to face his majesty's judgment! And he will not go lightly on you! You should make peace with your creator and live in fear till then." He turned his back on Allie and launched himself in the direction he had come.

Allie watched as the faint glow receded, finally going back around the corner he had come from.

She held the cat up to eye level. "What was that all about?"

"Hell if I know. I told you he was crazy."

Allie cocked her head to one side. "Actually, I think I'm the one that's crazy. I'm talking with a cat."

She put him down. He immediately sat and started licking his paw, using it to wash his injured ear. "I told you, I'm not a cat. I'm a *familiar*."

Allie frowned. "I hope you appreciate what I just did for you."

"Believe me, lady, I do appreciate it. That guy was out for blood."

Allie pointed to his injured ear. "Speaking of which, do you want a bandaid? I have some."

The cat stood. "No thanks. The fur, you know. Hurts like hell to get them off." The cat extended its paws and arched its back in a very cat-like stretch. "If I ever find my mistress, I'll tell her to grant you a wish."

"And just where is your mistress?"

The cat glared at her. "If I knew that, I wouldn't be searching for her. We had a house out in the west end, but it got squashed when all this happened. She and her mate left to find another one while I got left behind." He flicked his tail. "She was going to come back for me, but I ran out of food and decided to look for her. I'm hoping she gives me tuna."

"So there are other people left?"

The cat walked on. "Depends on your definition of people.

Only those with magic inside them have survived. Like you, *Miss Vampire.*"

Allie looked at him sheepishly. "You can tell?"

The cat nodded. "A very distinctive scent. Not quite human and not quite... something else."

"Something else?" she asked. "What's that?"

The cat sat in the classic cat-pose with his tail wrapped around his paws. "My mistress can explain it better than me, but you're gradually transforming into something much darker than you are now. It's hard to explain. But the change is very gradual. You have at least a couple hundred years before you have to worry."

She sighed. "That's a relief." On sudden inspiration, she held out her hand. "My name is Allie Medley, by the way."

The cat gave her hand a 'you've got to be kidding' look. He turned up his nose and stood. "And my name is Schro."

Allie frowned. "Schro? That's an unusual name." She looked down. "Where have I heard that before?" Then she brightened. "You mean as in Schrödinger's Cat?"

She laughed in delight.

The cat did not.

He stared at her in disdain. "Yes, my mistress can be especially cruel." And with that, the cat turned and began to walk away.

"Hey," she called after him. "Do I need to be concerned with what that pixie said?"

He paused and looked back at her. "I'm not sure. I don't encounter royal pixies every day, but I doubt he was bluffing. They're probably here to see all the destruction for themselves. Everyone loves a disaster."

"So I'm going to be put on trial for saving a cat?"

"No, you saved a familiar. Big difference." And with that, he broke into a trot and was soon out of sight.

Allie stared after him in disbelief. She wasn't sure she believed what had just happened. Stuff like that just didn't occur in a normal world. She wondered if there had perhaps been magic mushrooms in her brand cereal.

But then she considered the cat's words about those with magic surviving. As she thought about it, it did make sense in a strange sort of way. What if the world actually had supernatural creatures, but they were hidden within the mass of humanity? Then if that mass was suddenly removed, wouldn't it expose all the hidden creatures?

Allie shook her head. There was no way that was possible. She had to be hallucinating. The stress of being a vampire in dystopia was evidently just too much for her. She snorted. The next thing she'd be seeing was a unicorn.

It took Allie much longer to reach Staddard Circle than she had expected. Fortunately, there were no more pixies or talking cats, but she did find several of the streets blocked with the most unsafe-looking piles of debris. In a couple of places, it looked like some giant hand had tried to shape the destruction into walls stretching for blocks. She was forced to backtrack several times to find a way through.

So when she arrived, she only had about an hour before dawn. Which meant this girl had to hurry.

The hospital turned out to be in better shape than the surrounding buildings. Structurally, it had survived the blast. But every window in the building had been shattered, and the front doors had been blown off.

It was dark inside, even by her standards, so she pulled out her phone to provide some illumination. The lobby was disturbingly quiet. Broken glass was everywhere, and it crunched loudly under her boots. The hospital was normally full of noise from the hurried movement of people and the calls over the intercom. But the deadly silence unnerved her more than anything she had seen so far.

And that strange gray powder was everywhere. She wondered where it had come from.

Allie shook her head. She was running out of time. She'd worry about it later.

Looking in the receptionist's desk, she fumbled through the drawers and gave a cry of delight when she came across the flashlight she was hoping was there. She would have to be on the alert for some way to charge her phone, but right now, avoiding its use was best.

She normally used the elevator, so it took her a few minutes to locate the stairs. Thankfully, these had survived intact, with only more of that gray powder covering them. However, she did notice an odd odor. It was faint but definitely there. *Could a skunk have survived?* She decided to worry about it later.

Exiting on the second floor, she quickly made her way to the refrigerators. She paused with her hand on the handle and took a deep breath. *Please let there be blood in here.* She opened the door.

She grinned as she spied the dozen or so plastic bags neatly labeled and filed by blood type. She couldn't believe her luck. It was much more than she expected. The hospital usually didn't keep much on hand, having an outside firm to provide them what they needed on short notice.

She held her breath as she touched the first one. But as soon as she did, she knew this was not going to work. They were warm. She shined the light across them and saw that they were already turning a dark brown.

With the mixture of chemicals in the bag, they should not be going bad so fast. Also, why were they warm? She didn't know much about refrigeration, but these were medical-grade units and should stay cool for at least a couple of days.

As she fumbled with the packets, she could feel the beginning of tears filling her eyes. *Why was this happening?* She didn't ask to be made a vampire, and she certainly didn't ask for this stupid apocalypse. Then her fingers touched one on the bottom. It was cooler than the rest and hadn't started to turn like the others. Gasping in surprise, she hugged the bag to her chest and hurried over to a nearby coffee station. The coffeemaker's carafe lay shattered on the floor, and the maker itself lay beside it in a puddle of spent coffee grounds. Looking under the counter, she found exactly what she needed—a stack of disposable cups.

Using her trusty nursing scissors, she carefully opened the blood packet and poured it into one of the cups. From the smell that drifted up to her, she could tell it was already losing its potency, but it would do. She took a sip and winced at the taste. It was just red cells, not whole blood, so it tasted bland. Kind of like eating soup that didn't have enough salt. She quickly chugged the rest and wiped her mouth with the back of her hand. She had been doing this now for over six months, but she still hated it. The taste disgusted her. She looked at the empty bag and grew sad at the thought that she had just drunk some-one's gift to save a life. Thankfully, it allowed her to survive a bit longer while avoiding turning anyone into a vampire. But for how long? Would she have to bite someone? Would her hunger overcome her reason? She shivered and prayed for the strength to not pass on her curse.

Her phone's alarm went off, and she silenced it without even looking. Sunrise was only fifteen minutes away. She wasn't sure why she set the damn thing because she didn't need it. She could feel the approaching sunrise an hour before it happened. But strangely, the alarm gave her a sense of normalcy. Although there was nothing normal about her.

She stepped out into the corridor and looked up and down it, trying to think of somewhere safe to go. Not much time was left, so she had to hurry. She could find a bed on the floors above, but with all the damage, she might accidentally be ex-posed to the sun. No, she needed somewhere dark and protected. She smiled. She knew exactly where to go.

Allie hurriedly ran to another set of stairs and went down two flights. She didn't usually come to the basement, but it only took her a moment to locate the morgue. It was protected with a badge reader, but a few whacks with a chunk of loose concrete took care of it.

The tiredness caused by the approaching day was beginning to creep up on her, leaving her with minutes to spare. She went to the wall of refrigerators and pulled out a body drawer. These were thankfully the single occupant kind. And even better, it was empty. While she had no fear of the dead, she didn't relish sleeping beside one.

She inspected the drawer latch. Not surprisingly, there was

no release on the inside of it. She grabbed a nearby sheet and draped it over the drawer's facing, experimentally closing it. It was just enough to block the latch, keeping her from being locked inside.

Satisfied, she lay down on the cool steel tray—feet first of course—and put her backpack across her legs. Then she pulled herself all the way inside and allowed the door to close. Over her head, she could see a very faint outline of light around the opening of her drawer. It would be enough.

She breathed a sigh of relief, and the deep sleep of day began to claim her. She hated this part almost as much as drinking blood. When the sun rose, her body just shut down. She had no choice about it and could only delay it for maybe ten minutes at most. After that, she would just keel over. She knew. She'd tried it. Had the bruises to prove it.

She was almost asleep when she heard cloth moving and then a click. She looked over her head and gasped when she could no longer see that thin line of illumination around the drawer.

It had closed.

Someone had locked her in.

CHAPTER FIVE

Singing Beauty

Sydney

AN HOUR LATER, SYDNEY finally felt safe enough to stop for a rest. He had been running in the general direction of his next stop, Staddard Circle Hospital, but more northward, just in case he had been followed. He breathed a sigh of relief.

Sydney examined the cut on his chest from the chainsaw. He had been really lucky that it was little more than a scratch. And it was already healing—something else he had discovered about vampires. In another couple of hours, all that would remain would be a slight scar. Being a vampire did have a few advantages.

Sydney sighed. His designer shirt was another matter. It was totally ruined. Later, he would have to change into the spare in his pack. *Always be prepared* were the words of his grandfather.

He pulled out his map from his backpack and tried to get his bearings. There were no street signs, and the landmarks were hard to locate, so it took him a few minutes to figure out exactly where he was. He had come further north than he had thought, so he set off due west.

Rounding a pile of rubble, Sydney saw a sign sticking out of its side. The building had once been a mortgage company, but its message now seemed comical in its present state. 'Come build with us,' it said.

This perked Sydney's attention, and he began looking for similar ironic messages. He passed an auto repair shop with its sign still visible. 'Cracked glass? See us today!'

He smiled at the one in front of an insurance office. 'We'll protect you against anything!' But the one that really got him was in front of the evangelical church: 'The end is near!' Somehow he didn't think the surrounding devastation was what they were talking about.

Sydney turned but froze in place. He strained his hearing to be sure, but there was no doubt.

He heard singing.

And it was definitely a woman's voice.

He turned towards the sound and considered. With the last such exploration fresh in his mind, he was reluctant to investigate. But then again, there couldn't be two chainsaw killers in the city, and he did need a donor. A female might make things easier. He had discovered, quite by accident, that he could exercise a hypnotic control over women. He had tried it once on his maid Maude and realized he could make her do anything.

James had interrupted them before things could have gotten out of hand, but he found such power was a heady drug. But evil. Sydney had not used it since.

Did he dare use it now?

Sydney overcame his apprehension of another encounter and turned down the street towards the sound. With his luck, it was probably recorded music from a store or a still working car.

Rounding another corner, he saw a distant figure standing in the middle of the street, singing *Ninety-nine Bottles of Beer on the Wall* very loudly and slightly off-key. She had a nice voice though—a deep alto, kind of sexy. Obviously, she had been singing for quite a while because she was on bottle number six.

He circled around so that he approached her from behind. She gestured dramatically as she sang. Her motions reminded him of some pop performer—her pile of rubble substituting for a stage.

As he quietly crept closer, he could tell she was wearing some kind of tight-fitting silver garment. It showed off her pronounced hourglass shape quite nicely. But he didn't see any hair.

When he got closer, he stopped in shock and depression. The *she* was an *it*.

A robot, to be exact.

In form, she had the appearance of a woman with a slender waist, full bosom, and wide hips. In fact, her proportions were almost exaggerated, like some idealized woman's body. But the resemblance to a female ended there. Her skin had the sheen of metal and the color of stainless steel. Her eyes were patches of black, and her hair—well, she didn't have any. Sydney stared open-mouthed. The robot reminded him of one of those blowup sex dolls.

While definitely an *it*, Sydney couldn't help but think of her as female. She suddenly noticed him and broke off in mid-verse. "Oh, hello. I didn't notice you coming. Uhh... Are you sick or something? Excuse me for saying so, but according to my sensors, you're almost dead."

Sydney sighed. Women had accused him of that even before he became a vampire. "No, I'm just fine, thank you." He paused. "Excuse me for asking, but... what *are* you?"

She thumped a metal fist on her ample bosom, which rang dully. "Name's SARGE. Stands for Sabotage, Attack, Ravage, and Guard Equipment. And as you can see, I'm not your normal woman."

"Oh, really."

"Yep, I'm in the marines." She leaned closer and said in a conspiring whisper, "You haven't seen any of the enemy around, have you?"

With the chainsaw incident still fresh in his mind, Sydney immediately took a step back and shook his head. "I'm not an enemy."

"I can *see* that," said SARGE indignantly. She folded her arms across her chest. "Well, have you seen any military personnel running around? I got separated from my escort on I-95 north of here. They left me in the back of a truck beneath an overpass, the jerks. Haven't seen them since. Probably got killed in the attack. But orders are orders. They told me to sing out if I ever got lost. But they didn't tell me which song, so I just chose one."

Sydney blinked at her in disbelief. He didn't think she was a danger, but there was something a little off about her. "No, I haven't seen anyone," he said, glancing around nervously. He took a step back.

"Well, it doesn't matter," she said. "I didn't like that crew anyway." She put her hands on her hips and moved suggestively. She stepped closer. "You know you're kind of cute, and we're all alone out here. Just you and me. We could generate a little action. You know, get *real* friendly."

Her intent was all too obvious. Sydney took another step back. "But you're a robot. You can't...."

She came closer. "I'll have you know, I'm the product of advanced government engineering, designed to meet all conceivable needs on the battlefield. Including *that!*"

No wonder she resembled a sex doll! Sydney held up his hands and backed away. "No, thank you... I mean, I can't...." He tried to sound threatening. "Stay back! I'm a vampire!"

The robot quickly closed the distance between them and took him in her arms, pressing his head to her breast. It was as cold as a doctor's stethoscope.

"Don't be afraid, honey," she said. "I'm a modern lady. I understand these things. It'll be my first time, too."

"No! You don't understand. I can't with you!"

Suddenly, she released him and held him at arm's length. "Oh! I get it. How stupid can I be? You're gay, aren't you?" She patted him on the shoulder. "I understand. Everybody's got their own style."

Sydney started to deny it but thought it might be better if he just played along, at least for now. "I'm sorry," he said, trying to keep the relief from his voice. "But I did try to tell you."

"Oh, don't apologize. It's not your fault. I just come on a little strong."

Sydney thought hyperactive was a better word.

She continued, "It's all because some smart-ass snuck in a

copy of *Secret Confessions* into my initial programming read. I've been oversexed ever since. I want to have those fireworks I read about. The big bang. You know?"

Sydney couldn't believe his misfortune. Here he was, a vampire after a nuclear war with no blood, who barely managed to escape a chainsaw killer, and now almost raped by an oversexed robot. And the night wasn't even *half* over. What next?

He tried to think of how to gracefully escape this hyperactive creature. "Well," said Sydney. "I've got to be moving along now. See you around." Sydney tried to walk by her.

"Wait!" she called.

He turned. The robot looked down and began smoothing the dust with one foot. It reminded him of his cousin Martha, who as a child, would do the exact same thing just before she got him into trouble.

"Can I come with you? I haven't got any place to go, and I'm not designed to work alone. Although I hate to admit it, I need human guidance."

His cousin Martha had pleaded with him in exactly that same tone of voice. "I don't know," Sydney answered. "I travel faster by myself."

The robot dropped to her knees. "Please!" she begged. "I don't eat much, and I promise not to slow you down. Besides, I'm hell on any of the enemy. Come on, give me a chance."

Sydney looked up at the sky. When he was six, his cousin Martha had gotten down on her knees and begged him to go behind the garage with her and play doctor. Reluctantly, he had agreed. Once there, she suggested that he go first. But as soon as his pants hit the ground, she grinned evilly and screamed, "Mommy! Sydney's showing me his thingie!"

Suddenly, the small area behind the garage filled with adults, including his own grandfather, who refused to believe his side of the story and punished him severely. That little incident had cost him three weeks of TV, two weeks of riding lessons, and one week of not being able to sit down. But he'd gotten her back—he put peanut butter in her shoes.

Sydney considered the kneeling robot. Could he trust her not to try to molest him again?

"Would you have really forced me to... you know," Sydney said. "Even if I hadn't wanted to?"

"Of course not," said the robot disgustedly. "But how could you resist a *woman* like me?"

That did it. Sydney shook his head. "I'd better not. I'm more used to being alone, and besides. How do I know I can trust you?"

She turned her head to one side. "Does this look like the face of a criminal?"

He had to admit, she didn't look like a criminal. A trifle obscene maybe, but not criminal. "No, I'd better go alone." He turned away. "I'm sorry."

Sydney could have sworn he heard whimpering behind him. He felt sorry for the robot, but he just wasn't sure he could trust her.

He traveled up the street, avoiding the piles of rubble. He checked behind him several times to ensure the robot wasn't following him, but there was no sign of her. He breathed a sigh of relief.

Sydney turned down Main Street and entered a section of town badly burned by uncontrolled fires. He could still smell smoke in the air. With a sudden sense of *Déjà vu*, he recognized where he was—Jackston Avenue, near Rommeao's Pizza. His childhood favorite. His grandfather would sometimes take him there, but not nearly as often as Sydney would have liked. His grandfather got indigestion easily.

Sydney counted the buildings. There was the adult lingerie store his grandfather would hustle him by, and beside it, the musical instrument store they would sometimes enter after eating. If Sydney was lucky, he'd get to try a saxophone.

As he came to the next building, he couldn't help but smile. Rommeao's Pizza. The place was responsible for some of his happiest memories.

The pizzeria had been on the bottom floor of a two-story building with some kind of insurance office upstairs. Now it was badly gutted by fire, with gaping holes in the roof and crumbling brick. But it still stood. Sydney stepped closer, glass and charred wood crunching beneath his feet. He looked in the front window.

Although the restaurant had changed hands since he and his grandfather had frequented it, its basic layout remained the same. He could still make out where the booths, tables, and the cash register had been. He could almost see himself, about ten, sitting with his grandfather in a booth at the front, near the jukebox. They always ordered a large, double-thick pizza, with double cheese, and double pepperoni. They had called it the triple-double. A smiling young girl would bring it to their table, piping hot, along with a soda for him and a beer for his grandfather.

Sometimes he and his grandfather would try to see whose strings of cheese would stretch the farthest. Sydney sighed. Those had been good times.

If only his grandfather hadn't been so hard on him, constantly urging improvement and nearly working him to death with his belief of always being prepared. Sydney had been forced to learn everything from trick horseback riding to playing the piano. He rarely had time to be just a child.

Sydney was called out of his memories by a hiss. He looked around and saw the robot SARGE motioning to him. He shook his head and started to yell at her, but she put her finger over where her mouth was supposed to be and even more emphatically motioned him to come.

He shrugged and walked towards her.

"What do you want?" he said. But as soon as the words were out of his mouth, he heard a loud crash behind him. He turned to see the pizza parlor had collapsed into a pile of bricks. Where he had been standing was completely covered!

The robot pointed toward the wreckage. "I didn't want you to be squashed."

Sydney gave her an accusing glare. "You've been following me, haven't you."

The robot shook her head. "Not at all. I just happen to be going in the same direction."

Sydney eyed her for a moment and then pointed to the wreckage. "I guess a thank you is in order. I would have been turned into pizza dough if you hadn't motioned me out."

She shrugged. "See? I told you I could be useful." She looked down and again smoothed the dust with her foot. "The offer still stands. I'm more than willing to protect your ass."

He stared at her a moment. Having someone to watch out for him might not be a bad idea. She had proven she could at least do that. He sighed, remembering his cousin Martha. He couldn't help feeling he was making a mistake. "If you still want to, you can come with me. Just don't give me any trouble."

SARGE flung her arms around him and swung him around. "Thank you! You're the best friend a girl ever had." She put him down.

Sydney straightened his clothes and wondered if this was such a good idea. "Call me Sydney."

"Right, Sid."

"It's *Sydney*," he spat. "I hate being called Sid!"

"Right, Sid."

Sydney threw his hands up. It was going to be a long night. "Come on. I'm headed toward Staddard Circle Hospital."

"Hospital! I knew you must be sick or something."

"No, I'm just going there to look for some blood."

"Blood!" SARGE exclaimed. "What do you need that for?"

"I drink it."

"Drink blood? Hell, I thought I was weird."

Staddard Circle Hospital turned out to be in better shape than the blood bank. Structurally it had survived the blast, but every window in the building had been shattered, and several sprinklers were dripping water.

Sydney led the way into the building through the emergency room entrance. He had to use his flashlight in the interior—it was too dark even for his night vision. The beam sliced through the darkness, making the broken glass sparkle. A crunching sound echoed through the halls, giving them a haunted feeling. Wheelchairs and beds filled the halls, some overturned and laying on their sides. He shoved one table out of the way, disturbing a thick layer of powder and filling the air with fine gray particles. He sneezed violently.

Sydney wondered where all the bodies were. He had expected the hospital to be full of corpses, but there were none, just that strange gray powder. He was grateful in a way since seeing dead people made him uncomfortable. He frowned and tried to shake off the feeling of shame. No, *terrified of them* was a better way to think of it.

After consulting a directory on the wall, Sydney and SARGE took the stairs to the next floor. From there, the signs on the wall directed them to the blood repository.

Sydney excitedly stepped to the refrigerator, and in joyful triumph, flung open its door—

And stared in disbelief.

All the plastic packets had turned an unappetizing brown, and when he touched them, they were surprisingly warm. While he had not expected them to be cold, he had thought the heavily insulated refrigerators would have at least kept them cool. He searched through the dozen or so packets looking for at least one in good condition, but he was disappointed.

He paused, his hand hovering over an empty space. From the way they were stacked, he could tell one of the packets was missing. He guessed that someone must have taken it just before the bombs went off.

Sydney closed the refrigerator door, and sighing, leaned against it. "None of it's usable."

SARGE placed a heavy hand on his shoulder. "Don't take it so hard. Maybe I could make you a Bloody Mary instead."

Sydney started to say something smart but didn't get the chance. The robot's head came up, and she cocked it to one side. "Did you hear that?"

Sydney glanced around the room. "Hear what?"

"I thought I heard moaning."

He shrugged. "It's probably just the wind."

"The air was still when we came inside."

Sydney listened, and presently he heard it too—a cross between moaning and crying which sounded strangely hollow, almost ghostly.

The robot pointed. "It came from over there."

They walked back into the hall and over to an air intake. Presently, the sound came again—drifting up through the vent.

SARGE shook her head. "It could be coming from anywhere in the building."

"Nope," Sydney said, remembering his instruction on air conditioning systems. For some strange reason, his grandfather had included it in his weird training regiment. "Look closely. That's a main feed, and it comes straight from the basement." The vampire pointed out the vent's direction. "Let's go see what it is." Sydney started toward the stairs, but the robot hung back.

"Why don't you go ahead? I'll catch up with you later." The robot's voice wavered.

Sydney looked back. SARGE seemed frozen to the spot.

"Not scared, are you?" he asked.

SARGE pointed to herself. "Me? Scared? Not on your life. Remember, I'm some of the finest military hardware ever constructed. It'll take a lot more than a ghost... I mean a strange sound to scare me." But the robot clearly acted terrified.

Sydney blinked at her in surprise. "You're afraid of ghosts?"

"Fear wasn't programmed into me," she stated.

Sydney couldn't help but grin. "And you're lying."

The robot shrugged. "I can't lie. It goes against the Laws of Robotics."

Sydney gave her a puzzled look. "The laws say nothing about lying."

SARGE crossed her arms. "But it does about protecting humans. I'm just protecting you from the truth."

He rolled his eyes and shook his head.

Sydney led, and SARGE followed at a distance as they took the stairs down into the basement. All the while, the moaning grew louder.

When they reached the basement, they stopped at a partially open door with the lock hanging loosely from a few wires. Someone had forcibly removed it.

SARGE grabbed his hand holding the flashlight and moved it up to illuminate the sign identifying the room.

It was the morgue.

He whispered to the robot, "Why would someone want to break into the morgue?" He didn't know why he whispered. It just seemed appropriate, like when at a funeral.

"I don't know, but it can't be good." The robot's voice shook.

He couldn't help but smile. "I doubt a ghost beat the lock off."

"You never know," the robot responded nervously. "Ghosts can do some strange stuff."

Sydney eyed the robot and shook his head in disbelief.

Turning back to the door, he gave it a gentle push, and it swung silently inward. He shined the flashlight into the room.

There were what looked like people-sized filing cabinets along one wall. Body drawers. The hairs on his neck stood up. Which meant there could be dead bodies in there. He didn't do well around those.

As if to demonstrate the point, a loud rapping came from one of the compartments, and a muffled voice called, "Let me out!"

Sydney jumped, placing a hand over his heart and wondering if vampires could have heart attacks. He turned to the robot but didn't see her. He had to look *down* to find her.

Hunched over, cowering behind him, SARGE moaned, "Oh hell! It's a robot demon. It'll either possess me or eat me!"

Sydney wasn't doing too well himself and was within inches of running out.

Dead bodies terrified him.

It all went back to his Uncle Jimmy's funeral. His older cousins, as a prank, had locked him in the parlor where his Uncle Jimmy lay in state. Standing outside the door, his cousins made scary sounds, and Sydney, only six, had been so terrified, he'd wet his pants. His grandfather finally rescued him from the parlor and scolded his cousins for their cruelty. He then spanked Sydney. Carringtons *did not* wet their pants for *any* reason.

The event left Sydney with an unreasonable fear of dead bodies, which would make him hyperventilate and pass out if he even came near one. Funerals were out of the question.

He hadn't even attended his grandfather's.

Sydney stammered, "Why don't you go see what's inside that thing?"

SARGE shook her head emphatically. "I may be crazy, but

I'm not *stupid*. You want it—you go get it!" The robot's knees began to knock together.

Sydney sighed. "I thought you had to protect me?"

"I *am* protecting you. I'm telling you not to go!"

He had trouble arguing with the robot's logic and suddenly feared for his own sanity.

Sydney was caught in a dilemma. Although he was terrified of bodies, he couldn't just back away. Sydney forced himself to breathe deeply while he thought. There had to be a perfectly logical explanation for this. After all, ghosts and zombies did not exist. But a nagging thought occurred to him—there weren't supposed to be any vampires either!

The banging came again. "Help me."

Sydney took a deep breath and tried to center himself. There could only be one explanation—someone was trapped inside— someone *alive*—and he had to help them. He would just make sure he opened no other drawers.

Steeling himself, he approached the wall and slowly reached out to grasp the handle of the noisy container. SARGE, outside the door, moaned.

Sydney swallowed, released the latch, and pulled on the drawer.

At first, it resisted, but as he strained against it, the drawer began to move.

The robot moaned again. "Oh hell! He went and did it! Oh hell!"

Sydney braced himself as the slab slid out—

And got the surprise of his life. Lying there was a pretty young woman dressed in jeans and T-shirt—and very much alive.

"Hello," she said, smiling up at him. "Nice to meet you. Now, if you'll excuse me, I've got to *go!*"

CHAPTER SIX

Finding A Partner

Allie

ALLIE SAT UP AND swung her legs over the side. "Thanks," she said, easing down to stand in front of the young man that had rescued her. He was a little closer than she liked. Not that she minded—he wasn't bad looking. But she had more pressing issues at the moment. She had not only spent the day sleeping inside, but once she awakened, had spent most of the night calling for help and beating against the door.

"Why do you have to go so soon? We just met." The disappointment on his face was almost comical. She hoped this guy never played poker. He wouldn't stand a chance.

Behind him stood a woman covered in what looked like

silver paint. Allie couldn't help but notice she had a very, very good figure. But as she looked closer, she realized the silver was actually her skin. Was she a robot of some sort? She looked like one of those blow-up sex dolls.

Allie placed a finger on the young man's chest and gently pushed him back. "Don't worry. I'll return in just a moment. I've been trapped in there since yesterday, and I've really got to *go!*".

She smiled as she saw understanding creep across his face. He blushed. She headed towards the restrooms at a brisk walk and prayed they still worked.

With a determined frown, he followed along after her. "I'm not going to let you out of my sight. You're only the second person I've seen."

She shrugged. "Suit yourself." And hurried on.

She gritted her teeth. She wasn't going to make it. She shoved on the lady's door, and the young man stopped as if hit by a wall. She grinned. Was he blushing again?

She started unfastening her pants and ran into the first stall she could find. She made it just in time.

After finishing her business, she discovered that the toilet didn't work. Not surprising, considering the destruction she had seen.

By habit, she went to the sink across from the stall and turned the handle. She rolled her eyes. Of course, it wasn't working. She took a wipe from her backpack and used it to clean her hands and face. She looked at herself in the mirror over the non-working sink. Staring back at her was a young woman with short blond hair and a pleasant face—more girl next door than beautiful. Her only distinctive feature was her green eyes. They had gotten a bit greener after turning into a vampire. And this girl knew how to use them.

Shortly after becoming a vampire, she had found out that she had a type of mental power over normal people. She had made this discovery when her landlord had come to collect the rent. She had looked into his eyes and pleaded for a few more days. This dreamy look had come over him, and he had readily agreed. He had never done that before. She next tried it on her female boss, but that almost got her fired. She quickly found out that it only worked on males, and she could make them do pretty much whatever she wanted. One look into her eyes, and they were toast.

And that young man just outside the door could be her next meal. Next several, in fact. Using her mental persuasion, he might even come to like it.

She shook her head. But it wasn't right. Making someone give you a few extra days for the rent or give you their seat on the bus was one thing, but it was something completely different to turn them into your snack.

She thought back to the night of her own turning and shook her head. Could she subject someone to what she had been through?

"No," she whispered to the mirror. "I can't do it."

"Are you all right in there?" the young man called through the door.

She was simultaneously both pleased and irritated that he was checking on her. Didn't he think she could take care of herself? It was only a bathroom, for heaven's sake. She'd been doing that since forever. In fact, she was almost convinced she'd potty trained herself since her mother was never home, always in pursuit of the rock band du jour. She glanced at herself in the mirror and ran a hand through her hair. Then again, she *had* been in the bathroom for a bit.

She paused. Could he have been the one that locked her in the drawer? But as she thought about it, she didn't think so. But it wouldn't hurt to find out. And for that, she *would* use her mental powers.

When she emerged, he looked visibly relieved. She had to fight to suppress her grin. There was something cute about him that she couldn't figure out. Unlike most of the men she came into contact with, he was just so open. Taking him would be so easy.

But there was something pleasant about him and the way he looked at her. She somehow knew that he was no threat.

But I could be one to him.

She decided to leave. She didn't want the temptation to become too much for her. After she asked about locking her in, she would give him a mental compulsion to not follow her. Maybe even that he should totally dislike her. It was sad to run someone off she'd just met, but it was the only way to keep him safe.

But when she tried to exert her control, it felt like it slid off. He wasn't being affected.

And then he got the most puzzled look on his face.

"Miss?" he asked. "Excuse me."

She shook her head. Not understanding what was happening. "What?"

He fumbled with his words. "Are you... are you by any chance... I don't mean to be forward, but... are you by any chance a vampire?"

She gave him a surprised look. "What makes you say that?"

The young man shrugged. "Just a hunch. It just so happens I'm one myself. A vampire, that is."

"Really?" Allie smiled, knowing her vampire fangs would be visible.

He returned it, and he had fangs too.

"How did you know?" she asked.

"I tried to give you a compulsion, but it didn't work."

"Were you going to bite me?"

He shook his head. "I'll admit I considered it, but no. You seem like a very nice person. I was going to have you keep your distance from me." He looked down. "I haven't been a vampire all that long, and I haven't bitten anyone yet. I don't think I can."

She smiled. "I'll be honest with you. I was trying to do a mind thing on you too. I was going to ask you a few things and then have you forget about me."

Then he smiled. "Then we're even." He held out his hand. "My name is Sydney Ulysses Carrington, the third. It is nice to meet someone friendly in this destruction."

Allie glanced at his hand but didn't take it. Could he have been the one that locked her in the body drawer?

When she didn't take his extended hand, he blushed and rubbed his neck. "Ugh..."

Allie took a deep breath. "Did you lock me in that drawer? I had fixed it so it wouldn't latch, but someone removed the sheet blocking it from locking."

He looked at her in utter shock. "It wasn't me. I just got here a little while ago. I was upstairs checking out the blood refrigerators when I heard a voice through the air vent."

Allie considered him. *Was he telling the truth?* The poor guy's face was an open book, so his shock had been real. And if she thought about it, him being a vampire made it unlikely. He would have been subject to the rising sun just as she was. No, he didn't do it. She was sure of it. Which meant whoever had was still out there. It was a chilling thought.

After hesitating a moment, Allie extended her hand. "I'm sorry I was rude. I thought you may have been the one that, you know, did that to me. But I can tell you're not. My name is Allie. Allie Medley. It's good to meet you."

He took the offered hand, and his whole face lit up. It was like he'd opened the biggest present under the Christmas tree. The glow of his smile warmed her inside.

But there was more. Maybe it was the vampire thing, but she could almost feel the loneliness behind his smile. Almost like she was reading his heart. She had time to wonder if perhaps he was doing the same to her.

The robot came up between them and pulled their hands apart. "That has to be the longest handshake in recorded history. I thought moss was going to grow on it."

Sydney seemed to catch himself. "Oh, and this is SARGE. She claims to be a top-secret military robot..."

SARGE shoved in front of him and pointed to herself. "I'm the best damn thing that's happened to him. I don't mind sharing, but I found him first. Even if he is gay."

"I'm not gay," Sydney objected while eyeing Allie.

The robot was unconvinced. "You have to be. There is no way you could resist my beauty. I'll have you know..." And she launched into a tirade on her construction and having been designed for every conceivable need.

Sydney stepped around the robot and motioned Allie to follow. They moved toward the stairs. "Don't pay SARGE any attention. I can't seem to get rid of her, but she's harmless. She did get me out of a building right before it collapsed, so she's been a bit useful." He licked his lips nervously. "As you can probably guess, I'm looking for a new blood supply. And I'd wager you're doing the same."

She nodded and gave a sad smile. "Right on the mark. I drank the only good bag left in the fridge upstairs. All the rest had spoiled. But even that wasn't too fresh. I'm going to need more soon."

He brightened. "Perhaps we could work together and split the profits, so to speak. Be sort of like blood partners or something."

She raised an eyebrow. "Blood partners?"

Sydney blushed. "It sounded better than blood friends. And definitely not blood brothers."

Allie thought for a moment. "But why would you want me? Wouldn't we be in competition for a limited resource?"

He gave a nervous glance over his shoulder. "I've found this new world to be a little dangerous. Having a second set of eyes could be the difference between life and death."

Allie sighed. "I have to agree with you. Having someone to help out would be nice."

Sydney looked at her expectantly. "So what do you say? Want to join up?"

Allie considered the offer. Did she dare trust this man? Trust was not something she was big on. She had seen her mother betrayed time and time again as she looked for that special boyfriend. Not to mention, Allie herself on her last date—

He had turned her into a vampire.

But then again, Sydney seemed different. And while she couldn't use her mental powers on him, There was still some kind of connection there. She was pretty sure she would know if he ever lied to her.

She sighed. *So, what did she have to lose?*

She stuck out her hand. "Then partner it is."

He smiled, and they shook hands again. This time she was more conscious of the gesture. His palm was warm and a little sweaty, but his grip was firm—not too limp and not too hard. She found it unusually reassuring as his big hand enveloped hers. She was almost reluctant to let it go.

Sydney indicated the corridor. "Shall we go then, partner?"

She smiled back. "Let's."

Together the pair made their way out of the hospital, leaving SARGE behind. A few minutes later, SARGE shouted after them. "Hey! How could you leave a poor defenseless girl behind?"

Sydney called out over his shoulder. "Easy, because you're not a girl."

"What!" the robot cried out.

Allie and Sydney exchanged a grin.

"How can you possibly say that!" SARGE put her hands underneath her metal bosom. "Look at these babies. I'm one hundred percent female." Then added under her breath. "He's got to be gay."

After they got outside, Sydney proposed they head to the next big hospital, County General.

Allie shook her head. "Wouldn't Pleasant Oaks Hospital be

closer?" She pulled out her phone and consulted the map. She held it out to him.

She expected him to pull the 'I am a man, and I know exactly where to go' routine, but instead, he set down his pack and pulled out a map. A paper one. Allie blinked. She hadn't seen anyone use one of those in ages. He unfolded it and studied it for a moment before asking to see her phone's map again.

After a few moments comparing the two, he nodded. "That sounds like an excellent idea. I had no idea there was a hospital there. My map must be out of date." He pointed roughly north-ward. "Then we should head in this direction."

She blinked at him. He had accepted what she said. While the sample of males she'd dealt with previously was seriously contaminated by her mother's flawed selection process, she was unprepared for his open acceptance. He was treating her like she had a brain. What a concept.

Sydney folded up his map and put it away. She couldn't help but notice he folded it back exactly right the first time. She didn't know of anyone that could fold a map back once unfold-ed. Someone had once told her that map folding was a black art known only to a few. She was impressed.

They started in that direction with SARGE trailing behind. The robot had been quiet since Sydney had accused her of not being a girl. That last exchange had seemed to quiet her. Allie thought she was sulking.

After an hour of silent travel, Sydney pointed at two steel picnic tables on the sidewalk that were intact and uncluttered by debris. "Let's sit for a moment and have a cup of our favorite beverage. I don't have much, but I'm willing to share what I have."

"You don't have to," she said. "It's in short supply."

He stopped dead in his tracks and turned to her. "What am I supposed to do? Drink it in front of you? That would be more than rude. Besides, I have to have some, so I assume you need some too."

Allie looked doubtful. "No offense, but I don't want to be obligated to you. I'm my own girl. I already owe you for getting me out of the morgue, and I will pay you back somehow."

He considered her for a moment. "I thought we were going to look for blood together. Which means I can't have you falling over with hunger when I need you to watch my back. I thought we were going to be a team." He shrugged. "And teams... share."

She sighed. He had a point. "All right. But we can't make this a habit."

He waved his hand toward the table and smiled. "I promise to let you pay next time."

She couldn't help but smile back. Damn! Why was he so good at making her smile?

They seated themselves, and Sydney pulled a thermos and two cups out of his pack.

She looked at the cups inquisitively. "Two? There's only one of you."

He sighed. "I always carry a spare. It was sort of hammered into me when I was young."

He poured a little of the blood into their cups before sitting down across from her. She had no doubt what it was. She could smell it. And it was whole blood too. What she had drunk the day before had been separated already. While the red blood cells would satisfy her, it just wasn't the same. She had to control herself to keep from snatching it up and draining it.

"Cheers," she said, picking up her cup and bumping it against his. They drank together. And both winced afterward.

"I'll never get used to the taste," Sydney said.

Allie shuddered. "Me either."

He pulled out a pack of crackers and a bag of sliced cheese, offering her some. She reached into her own bag and pulled out one of the vexing cans of soup. "You don't happen to have a can opener, do you? Maybe we can have some of this later."

He grinned and reached in his pocket and pulled out, of all things, a Swiss army knife. He plopped it down on the table.

She grinned back. "Then breakfast, or dinner, or whatever you want to call it, is on me."

He nodded. "You're on."

And then there was that smile again. The one that made her feel all warm inside. She could really get used to that smile. She quickly looked down and took another cracker. She was behaving like a love-sick teenager. She didn't normally act this way. She had seen what her mother's continuous string of boyfriends had done to her, and Allie had sworn it *would not* happen to her.

No, this must be a vampire thing. She had better keep a close rein on her emotions. Down that path lay only heartache, or even worse. She would not repeat her mother's mistakes.

Sydney leaned back and nervously nibbled on a cracker. He glanced around, trying to look at anything other than her.

"Nice weather we're having," he said matter-of-factly.

Allie looked up at the clouds over their head and their slightly green glow. In the distance, she could see another lightning bolt. She didn't think this qualified as nice weather. "It's a little cloudy," she said. "We might get some rain later."

He nodded and resumed his awkward silence. She noticed he snuck a hand under the table to wipe it on his pants leg. She then took in his tense shoulders and bearing. To her amazement, she realized he was nervous—

And clearly had no idea how to talk to her.

She couldn't decide if she was irritated or pleased. It was kind of cute.

Allie was never the shy one and decided to help him out a little. So with her elbow on the table and propping her head in her hand, she leaned closer and smiled conspiratorially. "What brings a nice vampire like you to a place like this?" she asked.

He couldn't help but smile at her corny line.

"Seriously," she continued. "How did you survive?"

He shrugged and got a faraway look. "I don't really know. I woke up and discovered the door to my shelter blocked with what was left of my house."

"Shelter?" she asked.

He gave a cute blush.

Stop it! She admonished herself. *Get a grip!*

He nodded. "After I became a vampire, I moved into the fallout shelter my great-grandfather had built back during some missile crisis. As I'm sure you know, we need somewhere protected to sleep off the day, and the shelter was just perfect for it." He took another cracker. "Apparently, it served its purpose and kept me safe from whatever had caused all this." He shoved the last of the cracker into his mouth. "What about you?"

"Pretty much the same story. I had a basement apartment

and woke up to an open sky. Quite the shock." She glanced at her phone. It was later than she thought. "I'm not sure we're going to make Pleasant Oaks today. We better get moving. Dawn is only in about an hour."

He nodded and gathered up his stuff. "Then we'll need to find somewhere away from the sun."

Allie thought for a moment. "I know where we can go."

He put his bag over his shoulder. "It's not a morgue, is it?"

Allie smiled. "No, I think I've sworn off those for a while." She put her own bag over her shoulder and pointed to their right. "I was thinking of Wellastone."

"Wellastone?"

"Yeah, it's a funeral home."

He froze. Then two heartbeats later, he nodded, but his expression was flat, uncomfortable even. "Not my favorite type of place, but we can't afford to be picky."

They both stood and started back down the street.

"So," Sydney said. "What did you do before all this happened? You seemed to know your way around that hospital. Were you a nurse?"

"Close. Phlebotomist." She paused to let him ask what that was. Not many people knew.

But he surprised her. "Really? Being a blood tech probably helped you as a vampire. Getting blood is not easy. How did you do it? I thought they accounted for every drop."

She nodded. "They do. The easiest thing would have been to draw an extra vial or lose one. But if that were to happen too often, they'd start asking questions, and I'd lose my job. So the best way I found was to dispose of what was left over when the tests were done."

He nodded. "Very clever. I had to take a more direct approach. I bribed a doctor to prescribe it for me."

The horizon was just beginning to lighten when they entered the funeral home. Allie couldn't help but notice that Sydney tensed up the moment they entered. She could sense some kind of disquiet about him. She couldn't see why though. Except for the blown-out door and windows, it looked just like any other parlor she had seen. It had two reception rooms, but they could not find a casket inside either. Apparently, it had been a slow day when the attack came.

They found a stairway down into the basement, but it was completely dark. Sydney stopped at the top and shined his flashlight down into the gloom. Allie saw him swallow hard and wipe his palms on his pants. *Was he afraid?*

"What's wrong, Sydney?" asked Allie from behind him.

Sydney swallowed again. "Nothing." He gave a quick shake of his head. He took a deep breath and started down the stairs. Allie was right behind him, and SARGE brought up the rear.

When he reached the bottom, Sydney turned to say something to her. But SARGE stumbled and knocked Allie into him. Sydney quickly caught her, pulling her securely against him. She looked up to find her face bare inches from his. As their eyes met, they seemed to lock in place. His body felt warm, and his arms reassuring. They only stayed that way for mere seconds, but for just that moment, she was surprised to discover she liked being so close to him.

Sydney blushed and helped Allie regain her balance. He stepped back and quickly turned to explore the basement.

It had been the perfect chance for him to kiss her. Or her to kiss him. Or even just kiss each other. But it didn't happen. And she found she was disappointed. *Get a grip, girl! You barely know him. You can't think with your heart.*

Sydney shined his flashlight around the room. It was filled with caskets of several designs and colors. Several were stacked in two-tier metal shelves, while others were in the middle of the floor on wheeled stands.

"Looks like we've got our pick," Allie said. She had to admit though, the room seemed creepy in the dark. She wished the electricity was still on so she could see them better. Placing a hand on one, she felt its smooth surface. Definitely an upgrade from where she normally slept. There had only been one occasion when she had slept in a casket, and it had been very comfortable.

Sydney stepped over to a black casket with ornate silver trim resting to one side, separate from the rest. "These should do nicely to sleep in." Sydney patted the top. "I think I'll take this one. Let's see what she's got under the hood." He raised the lid—and gasped.

It was already occupied.

Awakened With A Kiss

Sydney

SYDNEY STARED IN SHOCK. The elderly man inside was quite deceased, having that prepared look of one ready for the family viewing. He obviously had been placed inside before the disaster. Sydney's light illuminated the face, giving it a pale, ghostly quality. He yelped and immediately slammed down the lid.

Sydney faced Allie, trying to conceal his terror. "We don't want this one," he said with a pronounced tremor. "It's already taken." He stepped away from the casket. "I think I need a breath of fresh air." He made to go back upstairs.

"Wait!" Allie grabbed his arm. "Don't you realize this is the first dead body we've seen? I would have thought there would be plenty after all the destruction we've seen, but there aren't *any*. Haven't you noticed?"

He nodded. "I did. I assumed any bodies were buried under the rubble." He glanced nervously at the casket. "Not that I minded."

Allie walked over to the casket, a determined look on her face. "Hold the light."

Sydney hesitated but did as she asked, holding the flashlight so tightly he thought he might crush it. She opened the lid, and he moved the beam where she directed. She didn't seem to notice that his hand shook.

With clinical intensity, Allie examined the man—hands, fingernails, face, hair. But she could find nothing unusual. She started to undress him, but she paused at Sydney's gasp.

"Don't," he pleaded. "We shouldn't… you know… disturb the dead."

Allie glanced at him, ready to protest, but upon seeing his face, gave a resigned sigh and shut the lid.

She leaned back against it and folded her arms. "Nothing looks unusual about him. But why is he in the casket when no others are around? I don't get it."

Sydney was relieved the lid was shut. "Maybe it's because he died before the event happened. Which would mean something other than a nuclear blast made all the living things disappear."

In thought, Allie patted her lips with her finger. "But what could have caused it?"

Sydney shrugged, stepping away from the casket and using his chance to change the subject. "Let's talk about that later. We need to find a place to sleep. The sun will be up in only a few minutes, and I'd rather not share the room with this person."

Allie reluctantly nodded in agreement.

Looking behind a door at the basement's far end, they found a utility area and rolled the occupied casket inside. Then quickly, because time was running out, they selected two other ones, thankfully empty. By silent agreement, they placed them side by side.

Sydney turned to the robot, who had been watching them with interest. "SARGE, would you mind keeping a lookout while we sleep?"

"You'd rather me be on watch rather than sleep with you? Talk about a waste of resources."

Sydney blinked at her in surprise, and behind him, he heard Allie stifle a laugh.

He shook his head slowly. "I don't think that's a good idea. The casket is only built for one."

She stepped close and pressed her body against him. She drew circles on his chest with her finger. "Would that be so bad? We could be *really* close."

Sydney wasn't sure how she managed it, but she was colder than a block of ice. He took her by the shoulders and pushed her back.

"Not tonight. I have a headache."

The robot stared at him in disbelief. "Well, if you say so. Your loss." She shrugged. "Then I guess I'll keep watch." She turned and headed for the stairs.

"Thank you," Sydney called after her. He turned to find Allie smiling in amusement. He couldn't help but blush.

Thankfully she chose not to say any more about it. "Good-night," she said as she crawled into her casket. "Although it feels odd saying that."

Sydney grinned. "I know. Goodday sounds strange, too." He held up a finger. "How about pleasant dreams?."

Allie grinned. "Perfect. Pleasant dreams then." She lay back.

"Pleasant dreams to you too." He climbed in, and together they shut their lids.

Sydney lay staring into the dark as he waited for *the sleep* to claim him. Since becoming a vampire, he basically shut down when the sun rose. It was scary in a way, being completely unconscious until it set.

As he waited, Sydney thought back over the day's events. His lips curled into a smile. He liked Allie. She was an intelligent and no-nonsense woman. One that was determined to make it on her own. He really admired that. The women he'd encountered thus far usually fell into two camps—those that avoided him at all costs and those that were unavoidable because they wanted his family's money. He'd fortunately figured that out at an early age and learned to avoid the latter group. He didn't have to worry about the former since they took care of themselves.

No, there was something about Allie that was different. He wasn't even that embarrassed around her. True, it might have something to do with her being a vampire, but he didn't think so.

His smile faded. His grandfather had impressed upon him to never, ever trust a woman, saying they were nothing but deceitful gold-diggers. And once they got their hooks in you, your life would be hell.

Would trusting her be all right? She seemed nice. But would

he find out she was really just pretending and didn't really like him? He had just started dating when his vampire curse had forced him to shutter himself, so he didn't have much experience.

He settled into the padding. He was getting ahead of himself. There were more pressing things to worry about now. Unless they came up with some blood soon, they would die. Not to mention having to find their way in a world gone to hell.

As Sydney felt himself begin to drift off, he couldn't help but wish for the millionth time—

That he could just be normal.

At sunset the next evening, Sydney was abruptly awakened. He had been dreaming about Allie. She was bending over him, smiling, her blond hair gently caressing his face. She bent to kiss his lips—

They were colder than ice!

Sydney jerked open his eyes and stared into SARGE's metallic face. "What the *hell* do you think you're doing?" he yelled.

SARGE stood up. "I was trying to awaken you the most pleasant way I could think of." She sounded insulted. "Excuse *me* for trying to be nice! Next time, I'll throw ice water on you."

Sydney rubbed his lips. "It'd probably be warmer!"

Allie pushed open the lid to her casket and sat up. "What's all the commotion?" She stifled a yawn.

"I got tired of waiting for you two," SARGE said. "I've been waiting all day. That's a long time for a sophisticated female machine like myself. It's because my quantum brain is so much faster than yours. I'll have you know, I can count to a hundred zillion in less than a tiny fraction of the time it takes you to blink an eye." She crossed her arms across her chest smugly. "In fact, I can calculate to within ten decimal places the exact position of the earth with respect to the sun a hundred million years from now. I can calculate the number of water molecules in the ocean in three eye blinks."

Sydney ignored the robot and began climbing out of his casket.

SARGE had a good thing going and wasn't going to ruin it. "I can see you don't believe me. I'll prove it to you..." a slight pause, "See there, I just calculated the probability that an electron will pass through your body within ten microseconds."

Sydney stood beside his casket and scratched his head. Allie joined him.

SARGE continued. "I can see you still don't believe me. Well, give me something, anything. I'll work it out. Come on, don't be afraid." The robot looked upward. "Come on, give me a hard one!"

Sydney ignored the robot and turned to Allie. "What do you want for breakfast?" he asked.

SARGE, thinking the question was intended for her, put her hands over her eye slots. "Mmmm... That's a hard one. Give me a minute. Mmmm..." The robot went silent.

Allie gave Sydney a questioning look and pointed in SARGE's direction. He shrugged. He had no idea what the robot was up to this time.

They gathered up their belongings and started outside. The robot remained motionless.

"Do you think we should leave her?" Allie asked. "Is she broken or something?"

"I don't know what's wrong with her," he said. "But I'm sure she'll follow when she snaps out of it."

They left the robot standing in the basement.

Thirty-two minutes, forty-nine point zero five two seconds later (plus or minus a few milliseconds), SARGE suddenly unfroze.

"That was a good one," she announced. "I give up. What's the answer?" She uncovered her eyes. "Hey! Where did everybody go?"

Outside, Sydney and Allie sat on a clear stretch of sidewalk and had breakfast, splitting Allie's chicken and noodle soup and a sandwich from Sydney's pack. He pulled out his thermos and held it up. "Need more? It's not going to last much longer."

She looked at it longingly but shook her head. "I'm good for now."

Sydney stared at her. She was determined not to depend on him. While he appreciated that, he didn't want her to harm herself either.

He held the thermos out to her. "Why don't you hold on to this, just in case you need it. It's going to go bad soon anyway."

She looked like she was going to refuse.

He sat it on the sidewalk next to her. "Please. I promise to let you buy the next round."

She couldn't help but smile. She sighed. "I can't. I don't have any way to pay you back, and you might... *expect things* if I do."

He held her gaze. "Never," he said earnestly.

She held his eyes captive for a moment more and seemed to read something in them. Then she looked away. "What say we split what's left?"

He nodded and again pulled out his cups and divided the remainder between them. He held his up as Allie took hers. "Cheers." And touched his cup to hers.

She smiled. "Cheers." And they both drank.

Allie made a face. "I hate drinking that stuff. Even though I crave it, it makes me sick."

Sydney nodded and turned back to the rest of his soup. "Yeah, I've sort of gotten used to it, but I don't *like* it. As my grandfather Carrington used to say, you can get used to anything."

Allie took a bite of her sandwich. "Have you been a vampire long?"

Sydney shook his head. "Not really. Not quite a year and a half. How about you?"

"A little over six months for me." Allie pushed a strand of hair behind her ear. "How did... you know... how did it happen?"

"You mean how I got bit?"

She nodded.

Sydney leaned back and braced himself with one arm. "Well, it happened to me walking home from a party—I had drank too much."

He decided not to mention his over-indulgence had been caused by his date abandoning him for her ex. It was supposed to be his big return to the world after his grandfather had died. Only, it had been a complete and total disaster that left him utterly humiliated.

He sighed. "I was staggering down the street headed home when someone jerked me into an alley. They punched me in the face and took my wallet and phone. I don't remember much about it. It all happened so fast. But I do recall finding myself sitting propped up against a wall with no money, no identification, and, due to my over-indulgence, definitely no coordination. I thought I was somewhat safe since nothing worse could happen." He paused and took a deep breath. "As I sat there trying to figure out what to do, a dark figure appeared and bent over me. The last thing I remembered thinking was that something worse *had* happened." He shrugged. "After that, I'm not sure. I woke up at sunset the next day in a dumpster with no idea how I got there. The dumpster likely saved me from being fried. But when I woke, I knew something was different about me. Something more than the bite marks on my neck. I didn't figure out just how different until three days later when the cravings started."

Allie's eyes were large in amazement. "Wow!"

Sydney popped the last of his sandwich into his mouth. He had to admit it was nice to talk to someone who *understood*.

"How about you?" he asked.

Allie took another nibble of her sandwich. "It happened to me on a blind date. Gladis, my ex-roommate, set me up with this guy that wanted to date me. His name was Fritz. And from her description, he was movie-star gorgeous, rich, and had the brain of Einstein. She begged and begged, so to get her to shut up, I agreed to go out with him."

Allie glanced away, her expression troubled. "We agreed to meet at a restaurant downtown. I was early and got a booth to wait for him. I hadn't been there long when I looked up to see a man and a woman approaching my table. He was an older guy, kind of plain actually, but he carried himself with a cocky self-assurance. She, on the other hand, was drop-dead gorgeous, about my age, and stylishly dressed. To my surprise, they both slid into the booth across from me. Then Fritz smiled and apologized, saying there had been a change of plans. I remember getting angry. If he had another date, he could have just told me. But then the woman smiled. It was a smug one, as if she knew something I didn't. And when I looked into her eyes, I couldn't help but notice they were a deep, deep blue. So deep, I felt like I was falling into them."

Allie's expression turned sad. "And that's the last I remember. I awoke the next evening lying on my bed with a quilt covering me. I was even still dressed in the clothes I went out in. When I saw the bite marks on my neck, I wasn't sure what to think." She shook her head. "It was quite a shock—worse than finding out you're pregnant."

Sydney nodded. "I understand completely." Well, maybe not the pregnant part.

She sighed. "The strange thing was Fritz's number was missing from my phone. And when I asked Gladis where I could get in contact with them. She looked at me like I was crazy. She had no idea who Fritz was and denied knowing anyone by that name."

I tapped my head. "The mind trick thing."

She looked down, taking a sudden interest in folding her napkin. "I was afraid he had also turned Gladis, but he thankfully hadn't. Apparently, he'd only used her to get to me." She looked off into the distance. "I've often wondered why. I'm just a girl. Why go to all that trouble? Plus, who was she, and why was she with Fritz?"

Sydney nodded. "My turning was definitely one of opportunity, just being in the wrong place at the wrong time. But yours was deliberate. Maybe there's something special about us." He waved his arms around him, indicating the destruction. "We did survive the apocalypse, after all."

She smiled. "Indeed we did." The glow of her smile lightened his heart.

Realizing he was staring, Sydney looked away. "Have you ever... uh... bitten anyone?"

She shook her head. "No. Being a phlebotomist made it relatively easy to get blood, so I didn't have to. Plus, judging from the bite marks on my neck, I've been assuming that biting someone is how you transmit the curse. So I decided never to pass it along." She looked down. "No matter what."

He understood exactly how she felt. "I haven't bitten anyone either. I bribed a doctor into saying I had cancer-induced anemia and used that to secure a steady supply."

"So you're rich?"

Sydney shook his head. "Not anymore." He once more indicated the surrounding destruction. "I think I can safely say our net worth is roughly equivalent about now."

She smiled and nodded. "I concede the point."

They both sat in comfortable silence for a few minutes. "You know," Allie said. "If I could find that Fritz guy, I'd gladly drive a stake through his heart. Being a vampire is the pits!"

Sydney nodded. "I really miss the sun. What I would give to have a beach trip. Laying out enjoying the bright warmth. All the people frolicking in the surf. I'd give anything to be normal again." He sighed. "It's been so lonely being a vampire. No one to *really* talk to. I quit dating, afraid I'd be tempted to make her my next meal."

"I know what you mean. I had my job to keep me busy. Without that, I would have gone crazy. I worked hard at being an excellent technician. No one could take blood as painlessly as I could." Allie smiled. "I guess being a vampire gave me a natural advantage."

Sydney chuckled. "I'm glad being a vampire is good for something." He got up on his knees and began to gather their stuff. They both reached for an empty cup between them at the same time, and their hands touched. It was electric. He looked up to find her on her knees and her face dangerously close. He couldn't stop himself. It was almost like she was drawing him in, and he couldn't stop. Not that he wanted to.

Sydney leaned forward and gently kissed her lips, finding them soft and receptive.

She jerked back. "Ouch! You bit me."

Sydney's eyes went wide in horror. "I'm sorry," he blurted out. "I didn't mean to! I've never kissed anyone before... I mean, kissed anyone as a vampire. I forgot about the teeth. Let me look?"

She waved him away. "I'm fine. It just took me by surprise." She snorted. "Sunlight and blood, I understand. But kissing? Vampires really have it rough."

Sydney took her hand and grasped it between his two. "I'm so sorry. Please don't hate me."

She softened. "Don't apologize. It's easy to forget we're

always armed and dangerous. We'll just have to be more careful next time."

Sydney stared at her in disbelief. *Next time!* She said next time! His face broke out into a thousand-kilowatt smile.

SARGE chose that moment to join them. Sydney groaned, and Allie chuckled. He was beginning to hate that robot.

"There you are," the robot said. "I thought you might have left me... again. I'm beginning to think you might not want me around."

Neither Allie nor Sydney made a comment.

SARGE put her hands on her hips. "OK, back to the problem you gave me to solve." the robot said. "I have to admit that I wasn't able to answer it. What *do* you want for breakfast?"

Surprised, Sydney and Allie glanced at the other. Sydney shrugged. "Nothing, really," he said. "We've already eaten."

SARGE gazed at them a moment, "Wow. I would never have guessed. You humans are more complex than I thought."

Sydney and Allie simply looked at each other in confusion.

CHAPTER EIGHT

Making Friends

Allie

TWO HOURS LATER, JUST ahead of a brewing storm, they arrived at Pleasant Oaks Hospital. The dark clouds cut off what little illumination the sky offered, making the night blacker and certainly more creepy. The storm's blinding flashes of lightning made the ruins of the once prestigious neighborhood seem ghostly and the old-fashioned stone building of the hospital appear haunted. The wind had begun to gather, moaning as it ripped through the broken windows. The hospital reminded Allie of a haunted castle out of some gothic novel. At any moment, she expected to see a ghost come running towards them. She suppressed a shudder.

With glass from the hospital's broken windows crunching

beneath their boots, the party climbed the few granite steps to the entrance. Sydney and SARGE went on inside while Allie paused to look at the building storm. She thought the nuclear blasts must have done something to the weather. They had been having a lot of thunderstorms.

As she watched, a glowing ball of reddish light dipped below the clouds. It looked like a giant bloodshot eye, hovering there, completely soundless.

She immediately turned and yelled, "Sydney! Come see this!"

The pair came running out.

"What's wrong?" Sydney asked.

Allie turned and pointed. "There's some kind of UFO over…." She trailed off, puzzled.

The object had vanished.

"I don't see anything," said SARGE. "Maybe you need to have your eyeballs adjusted. That did wonders for mine."

"It's gone now," said Allie. "But something was there a minute ago." She shrugged. "Maybe it was a trick of the lightning."

The storm decided it was time to unleash its downpour, and they hurried inside. Just before entering, Allie glanced over her shoulder at the sky one last time. She was sure she had seen something.

Neither of them were familiar with the hospital, so they took a few minutes to search the ravaged lobby for direction signs. As she expected, the blood refrigerators were downstairs.

Sydney led them down a corridor towards the stairs. He turned to say something to her when a sudden flash of lightning briefly illuminated the interior. Up ahead, silhouetted against a window at the far end, she saw someone standing.

She froze in place.

Seeing her expression, he asked, "What's wrong?"

She pointed. "I saw someone."

Sydney looked where she pointed. The flash came again, once more illuminating the window. She could make out drapes flapping in the breeze and what was left of a crosspiece.

But no silhouette.

Allie rubbed her eyes. First a UFO and now a person. Maybe she did need to have her eyes checked.

SARGE moved right up against Sydney and snuck an arm around his waist. "I better get closer in case I need protection."

Sydney frowned. "I thought you were supposed to be protecting us?"

"Welcome to the real world, pal."

He shoved her away.

Allie shook her head in disapproval. She was going to have to have a little talk with SARGE.

They went downstairs, emerging into a long corridor. They turned right, passing several doors. Allie perked up when they passed the morgue. This would be the perfect opportunity to see if there were more dead bodies in there. It might even provide a clue on what had happened to all the people. But maybe later. Finding blood came first.

Further down the corridor, they entered a room and discovered the blood refrigerators. They were perfectly intact. While Sydney held the light, Allie touched them. "They're cool."

Sydney smiled. "Maybe we got lucky."

She took a deep breath and opened the door. A waft of cool air drifted out—

But all that was inside were two used and empty plastic blood bags.

Allie sighed in disappointment. She picked one up by the corner. "These have been used and not too long ago."

"Another vampire?" asked Sydney.

She pointed to a rip on each bag. "Must be. Whoever drained them didn't use the bag for medical purposes. See how it's ripped along the top. Someone wanted these bags opened in a hurry."

Sydney shook his head. "This is bad. There is yet another vampire out there somewhere."

Allie consulted the sign-out sheet next to the refrigerator. "I think there were three bags inside. Two of them were drained, which means they took one with them."

"Well, whoever did it, they're not here now. We might as well move on."

Allie nodded.

Together they retraced their steps. When they reached the door to the hospital's morgue, Allie stopped. "Let's have a look in here," she said. "Maybe we can find a clue as to what happened to all the bodies."

Sydney hesitated. "I'd rather not." There was a slight tremor in his voice.

"Aren't scared, are you?" She said playfully.

Sydney frowned. "As a matter of fact, I'm terrified."

SARGE put her arm around him. "That makes two of us! Where there are dead bodies, there have to be ghosts. They kind of go together. You know, like peanut butter and jelly."

Sydney pried the metal arm away.

Allie touched his shoulder. "I'm sorry, Sydney. I can see you really are scared. I wasn't trying to be mean."

Sydney nodded. "I know."

"Why are you afraid?" she asked. "It's just someone's mother or father who has died. Not some monster."

Sydney shook his head. "You don't understand." It looked like he wanted to say more, but he hesitated. He closed his eyes and took a deep breath before continuing. "You'll think I'm an idiot, but I had a bad experience as a child." He related a story of his cousins locking him in with his Uncle Jimmy's body.

When he was done, he looked so ashamed. *Poor guy.* She guessed he'd had it rough growing up too, just in a different way.

Allie pulled him into a tight hug. He immediately stiffened but then relaxed into her embrace. "Don't feel ashamed, Sydney." She pulled back and looked into his eyes. "Psychoses like yours are more common than you would think. As for me, I hate spiders. They are just so yucky." She shivered.

"You don't think it's stupid?" he asked.

"Do you think my fear of spiders is stupid?"

He shook his head. "From what I've seen, you're very smart. As smart as you are pretty." His eyes went large as he realized what he'd said. His blush was almost bright enough to light the corridor.

Allie blinked at him in surprise. Smart? Pretty? *Her?* No way! She remembered standing just outside the kitchen as one of her mother's boyfriends voiced his opinion of her teenage daughter—dumber than a rock and just as plain. Of course, her mother had lit into the guy, and before the day was over, he'd been kicked to the curb. But Allie had heard. And she had sadly known it was true.

But while she might not be smart or pretty, she could at least be gracious. She smiled. "Thank you. I'm not sure I agree, but that was nice of you to say."

SARGE abruptly pulled them apart. "Hey, you two. This is a public building. Don't be getting too frisky." She stepped up to Sydney. "That's my job."

Allie frowned. Yes, she was definitely going to have a little girl-to-girl conversation with the robot.

Allie pointed to the morgue. "So, back to the original topic. I want to see if I can figure out where all the bodies went. You and SARGE wait out here, and I'll go inside. I'm a big girl. I can handle it." She grinned. "As long as there are no spiders."

Sydney frowned. "I'm not sure I should let you. The first rule of horror movies is to never split up."

She smiled and held out her hand for the flashlight. "I'll keep that in mind."

With the light in hand, she stepped into the morgue. It was a small room with body drawers directly across from the entrance. She left the door open, and Sydney watched intently just outside. SARGE covered her face.

She'd only taken two steps when Sydney called out. "Allie! What's that by your foot?"

She shined the light on the floor. "It's only water. There must be a leak in here, which is not surprising." She shined the light up at the ceiling. Strangely, there were no signs of dripping water. She suddenly grew uneasy but quickly dismissed it. What could possibly be down here to hurt her?

She went to the far wall and started opening drawers. She moved methodically down and across them, but they were all empty—except the last one.

A sheet was draped over the body. She folded it back to find a large man lying peacefully underneath. He was still dressed in his work clothes. She looked back at Sydney and smiled reassuringly. "See. There's nothing to it."

Suddenly, the man's eyes sprung open, and he grabbed her wrist. She struggled to pull away, but he was just too strong.

"Allie!" yelled Sydney.

The large man sat up, firmly grasping a wicked-looking axe in his other hand.

He gave her a big smile. "Are you my friend?"

CHAPTER NINE

An Axe
To Grind

Sydney

"NO!" YELLED SYDNEY. "SHE'S not your friend!"

Ignoring Allie's protests, Rip swung his legs off the edge and slowly stood. He regarded Sydney.

"I know you!" he said. "You're the friend who broke my chainsaw. It's good to see you again." Rip raised the axe, pointing it in Sydney's direction. "I couldn't get my chainsaw working again, so I had to switch out." He smiled. "Don't worry, I spent all day sharpening it. Now, if you'll just have a seat, I'll be with you in just a minute." He turned back to Allie. "I have to deal with her first. Especially since she escaped from the other morgue."

"It was you!" she yelled. "You locked me in." Allie started kicking him, but he just twisted her arm, forcing her to kneel before him.

"Leave her alone!" commanded Sydney. "She's not your friend." Sydney looked around for something to use as a weapon.

"She's not?" Rip asked. He bent to look at her more closely. Noticing the image on her shirt, he smiled. "Wow! I like your shirt. If I was good, the nurses would let me watch wrestling sometimes. Do you like Clare Montare?"

Allie looked up at him through her mussed hair. "Yes, she's my favorite."

Rip nodded thoughtfully. "She's my favorite too. She is so cool."

Allie nodded. "She is very cool. She's my idol."

Rip brightened. "Mine too! Did you see the fight where she jumped off the corner post and caught Bustier Betty off-guard? She had to have been airborne for at least five seconds."

Sydney whispered to SARGE. "Do something! I thought you were going to protect us."

"All right." The robot looked uncertain. She took one hesitant step forward and froze.

"SARGE?" he whispered. He knocked on the side of her head, which sounded strangely hollow. But the robot didn't respond, having apparently fainted. Robot style. Sydney threw up his arms in frustration.

He turned back to Rip. "Just let her go. She's not your friend."

"You're right." Rip nodded thoughtfully. "She isn't. Any woman that likes Clare Montare can't be a friend." He shook his head sadly. "No, she's got to be a special girl *friend*." He looked at me levelly. "I'll keep her head with me at all times."

Allie struggled harder.

"No, Rip," said Sydney taking a step into the room. "You don't want her. It's me you want."

"Naw," Rip shook his head and made a face. "I want to kill both of you. But she was here first, so you'll just have to wait your turn."

With that, Rip raised the axe over his head, and Allie, struggling helplessly, screamed.

In desperation, Sydney lunged, catching the axe just below its head and at the apex of its swing. Rip was pulled off balance. He jerked the axe forward, but Sydney wouldn't let him complete the swing. He staggered as Sydney dragged him off balance. He released Allie's arm.

"Get out!" Sydney yelled.

She scrambled for the door on all fours.

Sydney moved closer and snaked an arm around Rip's neck.

Rip fought and managed to get his other hand on the axe. He gave a mighty pull, jerking the handle out of Sydney's grasp. The freed blade flew forward and landed in the wall, traveling completely through the plasterboard. Sydney stumbled backward and fell, sprawling on the floor. Single-mindedly, Rip began trying to free his axe. Allie dashed back into the room carrying a broken piece of two-by-four. With all her strength, she hit him over his head. Rip collapsed, unconscious.

Dropping the board, Allie went to Sydney and helped him stand. "I take it you've met our friend before?"

Sydney nodded. "Yeah, I ran into him yesterday, and he tried to kill me with a chainsaw. I barely escaped."

Just then, SARGE unfroze. "Where did he go? I was going to destroy him!"

"Some help you were!" Sydney said sourly. "We could have been killed."

Strangely the robot didn't say anything. Instead, she just looked down and, for once, was quiet.

Rip groaned and began to stir. He reached an unsteady hand toward his axe.

Allie eyed him nervously, backing away. "Let's get out of here. I don't want to be around when he wakes up."

Sydney agreed.

They took time to block the morgue's door, hoping it would slow him down, and then hurried out of the hospital.

Sydney suggested they head to his shelter to resupply. But not before they made sure they weren't being followed. Thus, they turned easterly and backtracked three times.

After over an hour of travel, and no pursuit in sight, they stopped for a rest break. Thankfully, the rain had stopped, and the wind had calmed, leaving only a slight breeze tugging at their clothes. If not for the surrounding devastation—not to mention a deranged killer potentially chasing them—it would have been a pleasant evening.

Allie wanted to wipe off and change her clothes, so to give her a little privacy, he stepped around a mostly intact building. She had strangely requested that SARGE stay with her. The robot was delighted to be treated as one of the girls. But from Allie's expression, he thought there might be more than chit-chat coming.

Sydney used the opportunity to relieve himself. Not for the first time, he couldn't help but take comfort in this one thing.

While he had pointy teeth, a sunlight allergy, and a blood nutritional requirement, he still needed to water the flowers. It was a perverse reminder that he retained a bit of his humanity, and at this stage, he would take what he could get.

Just as he was zipping up, he looked up and saw a glowing eye-shaped object in the sky. It must have been the UFO Allie had seen.

Sydney called to the others excitedly, "Allie! Come see this!"

Allie came tearing around the corner, a worried look on her face.

"What's wrong?" she asked, coming to a halt beside him. He couldn't help but notice she had on a different shirt, but she had maintained her wrestling theme with another pose of the woman she was so crazy about. This shirt was more fitted than the other and showed off her figure and, well... other assets. He quickly turned away, blushing.

SARGE came around the corner to join them. She looked at them inquisitively.

He pointed in the direction he had seen it, only now it was gone. "Nothing's wrong. I just saw something strange glowing in the sky. It looked like a giant eye."

Allie nodded. "That's exactly what I saw. It was really weird."

Sydney looked to the robot. "How about you, SARGE? Can you detect anything?"

She put her hands on her hips. "What do I look like? A radar tower?"

Sydney grew frustrated. "Aren't you supposed to be military-grade hardware? Don't you have special laser optics or night vision?"

She shrugged. "The engineers didn't think I needed it."

"So let me get this straight. As you proved back there, you can't protect us, you don't have any special senses, and you're scared of everything. So tell me, what exactly are you good at?"

She looked at him indignantly. "Being sexy."

Sydney threw his hands up in frustration.

They went back to their packs, and Sydney shared the last of his sandwiches and thermos of blood.

He was just explaining to Allie about his experience with Rip and how the serial killer dealt with his *friends* when SARGE cocked her head to one side.

"I hear something…" She pointed. "From that direction."

Sydney held his breath and listened closely. He didn't hear anything at first. Just something rattling in the light breeze. Then he heard it faintly. His eyes went wide, and he glanced at Allie, who likewise met his gaze. Voices. And what sounded like breaking glass.

Allie stood looking in the direction of the voices. "We better investigate. It could be other survivors."

With Rip fresh in his mind, Sydney shook his head. "I don't know. It could be trouble."

SARGE scolded him. "Ah, come on. Where's your sense of adventure? Of course, we should check it out." She rubbed her hands together. "It could be a party!" The robot grabbed Sydney by the shoulders and spun him towards the sound. "You lead."

Reluctantly, Sydney agreed to at least check it out.

SARGE directed them around a corner and to a side street. About halfway down, a light emanated from an open door with voices coming from inside. Sydney paused to listen, making SARGE and Allie bump into him and almost knock him down.

He could make out two distinct voices—one high pitched and the other a deep bass, but both were definitely male.

"You stay here," Sydney whispered to the others.

Allie put a hand on his shoulder. "No, I'll come too."

He stared at her a moment and then nodded. Then together, with Sydney leading, they quietly approached the building. He froze at the sound of breaking glass and glanced back over his shoulder at Allie. She wore a stern expression. A couple of building lengths behind her, he could see SARGE. The robot shooed him forward.

He harrumphed. The stupid robot was scared of her own shadow but certainly wasn't afraid of sending *the humans* into danger.

The light came from the door of a red brick building in the middle of a closely packed row of similar structures. It had suffered from the destruction but was in by far better shape than those around it. The sign over its door was written in raised wood letters with a single 'R' missing from the word 'friends,' turning the bar into the *Midnight Fiends* Tavern. Sydney just hoped that wasn't a statement of its occupants.

Just beyond the door, the building had two normal-sized windows and, like every other window he'd encountered recently, was sans glass. Light spilled from them into the street, but from his position, Sydney couldn't see the occupants through them.

Inching forward carefully, Sydney peeked through the tavern's open door and froze in disbelief, completely forgetting to hide.

A fairy stood behind the bar unscrewing a bottle of beer. He spotted Sydney and held the bottle up toward him. "Come on in," he said. "We've got plenty."

He slapped the beer down in front of the room's only other occupant, who quickly lifted the bottle and drained it. Then with a flick of his majestic tail, the unicorn looked over his shoulder at him. "Well?" he asked drunkenly. "Are you coming in, or are you going to stand there all night?"

And then he belched.

CHAPTER TEN

The Unicorn
And The Fairy

Allie

"ARE YOU COMING IN, or are you going to stand there all night?" came a deep voice from inside the building. It was quickly followed by an impressively rude belch.

Allie leaned forward until she could see into the room. She blinked in surprise.

The tavern's interior was in excellent shape, considering what had happened. It retained most of its old English pub atmosphere with dark wood paneling and elaborate trim. It even had a brick hearth fireplace over to one side.

But it had not escaped unscathed. The polished wooden floor was littered with broken glass, no doubt from the front windows. Tables were scattered about, the force of whatever had broken the windows shoving them to collect along the walls. In one corner at the back, the ceiling had partially collapsed with wires, and a central air vent spilled out.

The interior was softly lit from a single chandelier hanging from the ceiling. *Odd. Wasn't the electricity off?* She blinked in surprise as she realized the light bulbs were moving.

A half-dozen tiny glowing figures reclined on the fixture's branches, watching the newcomers with wicked amusement. They were no larger than action figures and had rainbow-colored wings on their back resembling a dragonfly's. *Pixies!* Both male and female members were dressed in the bare minimum of brown clothing and armed with miniature swords belted to their waists. Allie had no doubt that they were deadly despite their size.

To her surprise, the pixie she had confronted the day before sat among them. He smirked and gave her an informal salute in recognition.

Against the wall opposite the door stood a highly polished but dusty mahogany bar that ran the length of the room. Surprisingly, the bar's stock of bottles sitting behind it in a decorative brass cage had suffered few casualties and was mostly intact. Only now the doors to the cage had been flung open, and a few of the bottles extracted and placed in a neat row on the bar.

A small man sat next to them with his feet dangling over the side. His exact height was hard to say, but he had to be no more than three or four feet tall. He was pouring what looked to be some type of bourbon into a shot glass. Nothing extraordinary about that, except the little man was nude, had two short antennae sprouting from his head, and two delicate butterfly wings on his back. *A fairy?*

The fairy motioned them forward. "Hi there," he said in a friendly tenor voice, his wings fanning gently. He took up his glass and saluted them. "Come on in and join the party!" He downed the splash of bourbon in one swallow and smiled.

While the fairy was unusual, he was nothing compared to the bar's other occupant, who was likewise nude.

But of course, that's expected of a unicorn.

With a horn of pure gold, a coat of pale yellow, and coal-black hooves, the equine was a regal sight. But from the way he swayed, he appeared to be well on this way to being hammered. Allie was convinced that if the unicorn didn't have four feet, he'd already be sprawled on the floor. As she watched, the unicorn grasped the next bottle in the row with his lips, lifted it, and in three gulps drained the contents.

Then with a toss of his head, the unicorn threw the empty at the cold fireplace. He missed, and the bottle shattered against the wall. The amount of glass around the fireplace was further evidence of the equine's consumption.

The unicorn once more belched rudely and glanced at them, lowering his head so that his horn pointed in their direction. "Don't just stand there staring. You're making me nervous. It's like you've never seen a unicorn before."

Allie broke her trance. She stepped around the stunned Sydney and into the room. "Sorry," she said. "But you're the first I've ever seen." She felt drawn to the unicorn for some reason. Her hands itched to run their fingers through his rich coat.

Sydney followed her inside while SARGE cautiously peeked

in behind them. He was just as shocked as she was. "You're a fairy, and you're a unicorn."

The annoyed equine snorted. "Whoopie shit! I'm glad someone finally told me. I hope it's not a revelation that you and the lady have the stink of vampires, and the tin can behind you is a mechanical!" The unicorn turned back to the bar. "Give me another! I'm going to be needing it."

The fairy slid another bottle in front of him. "Excuse Frank," he said, nodding towards his unicorn friend. "He gets irritable after a few."

"I do not, dammit!" Frank shouted. "You're the worst angry drunk I've ever seen." He softened. "I just get mellow."

The fairy nodded. "Whatever you say, Frank." He took another shot himself.

The unicorn gave his friend a withering glance before lifting his bottle and quickly draining it. Once more, he threw it towards the fireplace. It didn't even come close this time. Frank laid his head on the bar and closed his eyes.

The fairy leaned forward. "Now, what can I get you? Frank hasn't drunk everything… yet." He glanced at his friend.

"Give me time," the unicorn mumbled. "Avalon wasn't built in a day."

The fairy chuckled. "By the way, my name's Jacques."

Allie stepped forward, a hair faster than Sydney, and shook his hand. She introduced them all.

Jacques managed to find a couple more shot glasses and splashed some in each. "Both of you are of legal age, aren't you? I'd hate to lose my license." He snickered.

Allie pulled up a barstool in front of the proffered drink. Sydney likewise found a stool but slid it between her and Frank.

The young man glanced nervously her way then to the unicorn. It struck Allie that he was trying to protect her. She couldn't decide if she was pleased or annoyed. She was her own girl and could take care of herself. She seriously doubted the pair posed much of a threat. But she had to admit that it was kind of cute seeing him get all protective.

Frank's head rolled to the side, and he gave a loud snore.

Jacques spread his hands. "So what brings you people to this fine establishment? I know it couldn't be the exquisite decor."

"We saw the light and thought it might be other survivors," Allie said.

Jacques grinned at her over his drink. "You wouldn't by chance be the lady that protected a certain cat recently?"

Allie looked up at the pixie that she'd had to face down. He smiled back at her, very pleased with himself.

Sydney looked puzzled and Allie sighed. "I'll explain later."

She turned back to Jacques. "Yes, I did. He was going to hurt poor Schro, and I couldn't allow that. He'd already bloodied his ear."

"It was fair!" shouted the pixie. He flew down and lighted on the bar. "The evil creature jumped me."

Allie frowned. "Schro's not an evil creature. He's a cat. And when I stepped in, he was running for his life."

"I demand justice!" the pixie stomped his foot. "She interfered with my kill."

Frank opened one bloodshot eye and glared at the pixie. "Will you shut up? I don't care about justice. I want quiet." He shut his eye as if that was the end of the conversation.

The pixie drew back in surprise. "But he jumped me," he whined.

Jacques rolled his eyes. "I'll register with the guild that you drew blood. Would that suffice?"

The pixie grinned. "Double bonus?"

Jacques looked at him levelly. "Don't push your luck."

The pixie shrugged. "Can't blame a bloke for trying." He returned to the chandelier and received quite a few backslaps from his companions.

Sydney pointed to the pixies. "What was that about?"

Jacques sighed. "The guild has a strange incentive program for its members. Anyone successfully fending off an attack gets a bonus. It's supposed to improve everyone's readiness, but really all it does is drive bad behavior."

Sydney stared in disbelief.

Allie leaned forward. "Uh… Excuse me for asking, but what are a fairy and a unicorn doing in a bar?" It sounded like the beginning of a bad joke.

Jacques chuckled. "What one normally does in a bar? Consuming alcohol! We're consoling ourselves. Or at least Frank is. The barrier between the worlds became much weaker a couple of days ago, so we immediately came looking for someone special." He sighed. "But it appears we arrived just a wee bit late."

"Someone special?" Allie asked.

The unicorn sniffled a few times and then continued to snore.

Jacques nodded and refilled Sydney's glass. He held the bottle toward SARGE, who had come up to stand beside Allie. He gave her a questioning look.

The robot shook her head and tapped on her chest with her knuckles, making a metal-on-metal sound.

Jacques nodded and then filled his own glass. "It's a long story, kind of strange... and kind of personal. You see, Frank is the last male of his kind. For years now, he's been searching for a mate. We've crossed perilous oceans, blazing deserts, and soaring mountains. Not to mention some of the seediest pubs you've ever seen."

He took a sip and continued. "Then we heard rumors of a new queen in the faraway kingdom of Naelimag. To our surprise, she was a female unicorn."

Sydney nodded. "But she spurned Frank's love for another, and you came to the bar to console yourself."

Jacques shook his head. "No, actually they fell in love at first sight. Married too. In fact, it was a very regal wedding."

"Then what went wrong?" asked Allie. "Did they not get along?"

Unexpectedly, the unicorn sneezed in his slumber. He rolled his head to face away from them.

"Then what happened?" asked Sydney.

Jacques frowned. "The problems started on their wedding night. You see, Frank and his mate couldn't... you know." He blushed and took a sip of his drink. "Seal the deal."

Allie gasped. "That's terrible."

Sydney shook his head. "But surely they were able to later. I've heard there can be a lot of stress after a wedding."

The fairy took a deep breath. "It's not that simple. Both of them were aware of the problem and thought they could work through it. It was just stronger than they had anticipated." Jacques shook his head. "You see, millennia ago, unicorns and humans were at war. It had gone on for a long time, and the humans were quite sick of it. So a human king made a deal with the Dark Elves to do something about it. The Dark Elves put a curse on all unicorns which gave them a strange allergy. One where the males reacted to virgins of all kinds, even their own mares. And if that wasn't enough, the sick bastards made it so only a human virgin could provide relief by rubbing the nose of a male unicorn. This would impart a temporary immunity so the unicorns could mate without unpleasant side effects. This worked well for many centuries."

Frank sneezed violently and turned his head the other way.

Jacques eyed his friend briefly before continuing, "But when the universes split, human maidens grew short in supply, and the unicorns started to die out. When the barrier between the universes weakened, we were able to cross and came hoping to find one."

Allie's eyes went up in surprise. "So that's why unicorns and maidens have been associated together over the ages."

Jacques nodded.

Sydney sighed. "That's unbelievable...."

Abruptly, the unicorn raised his head and began to sneeze repeatedly and violently. "Dammit!" he yelled at Sydney. "You're a blasted *virgin*! Get away from me before I sneeze my brains out. I couldn't smell it before because of your vampire stench."

Sydney backed away and glanced nervously at Allie. She tried to suppress her smile. Likely his stupid male pride didn't want her to know that piece of information. Like it mattered to her. In fact, she found it more reassuring than anything. It was just another reason to like him more. *Get a grip, girl!*

Jacques laughed outright. "Yeah, except for human maidens, unicorns react to all virgins. Even the human *male* ones."

The unicorn got its sneezing under control. He must have

been listening to some of the story. "It's a damn paradox. How can you *be* with someone only after they're not a virgin? It doesn't make sense."

"Now you see the problem," said Jacques. "Unless Frank can find a virgin human female, he will never be able to consummate his marriage. And if that isn't enough, since his mate is queen, she *must* produce an heir. If they can't, then by law, she will be required to annul the marriage." Jacques shook his head sadly. "Poor Frank tried to do the job on his wedding night, but it ended in disgrace. He nearly sneezed himself to death."

SARGE started laughing—it sounded like a washing machine with an off-balance load and in need of repairs. "I don't believe it. I thought all unicorns were naturally horny!"

The unicorn turned to glare at the robot. "Listen, brass butt. I've heard all the *horny* jokes I can stand. So lay off, OK?"

The robot ignored Frank and continued to laugh. "A steer wouldn't have your problem—he's twice as horny!" Her mirth was so great, she doubled over and began slapping her knee.

The unicorn's eyes grew red. Sydney could swear he saw Frank blow a puff of steam out his ears. "I said to lay *off* Mac! Next person that tells a horny joke, I'm going to shish kebab!"

Allie felt bad for the unicorn. To finally find someone you love and not be able to have a family. It was terrible. For herself, she had always imagined it might be nice to have a couple of the little rug rats. But only if she found Mister Right. She refused to repeat her mother's mistakes, so it had to be someone that would be around to help raise their offspring.

She reached a decision. Allie pushed away from the bar and went to the unicorn's opposite side, where she put her arms around the unicorn's neck, digging her hands into his silky mane. She'd been dying to do just that since she had first seen him.

She glanced at Sydney, seeing what looked like surprise and maybe a bit of jealousy. This wickedly pleased her. Maybe he really did like her.

Allie had expected Frank to protest, but instead, he laid his head on the bar. She switched to rubbing his forehead. "You poor thing," she said. "Forced to be separated from your bride. And it's not either of your fault."

Frank's eyes suddenly got droopy. "That feels good."

Allie asked, "Is there anything we can do to help?"

"Well," he sighed heavily and spoke in a dreamy voice. "There is one little thing you could do."

"What?"

The unicorn yawned and closed his eyes. "You could…"

He broke off in mid-sentence and began to snore softly.

"Well, how about that?" Allie took a step back and placed her hands on her hips. "I put him to sleep."

Just then, a bright white light came from outside the door. It flared briefly, then subsided.

"What was that?" asked SARGE.

Sydney shrugged and watched the door curiously. "Lightning, maybe? Although it didn't look like it."

"There wasn't a storm," Allie said.

A jingling noise came from outside and slowly approached the entrance. A moment later, Allie could hear the unmistakable sound of footsteps. She immediately thought of Rip, that he had found them. But that didn't match up. No, these steps were closer together. *Someone smaller?* And there was more than one person.

Allie, along with the others, turned to stare at the door. Frank shifted to snoring loudly.

The jingling grew louder, and the producer of the sound stepped up to the door.

"What the hell?" exclaimed Sydney.

Standing just inside the bar's entrance were three little men—short and squat, wearing black leather jackets looped with large steel chains and dusty black boots with spurs. Their hair was done up in various styles of spiked mohawks. And their skin—well, to put it bluntly… it was green. It was obvious, they were not of this earth.

The alien smiled widely. He drew himself up to his full height and stuck out his chest. "Take us to your leader!" he announced. Then he turned to his comrades. "I've always vanted to say that."

CHAPTER ELEVEN

Alien Invasion

Sydney

THE GROUP'S LEADER, THE ugliest and fattest of the bunch, stepped forward. His many chains bounced on his belly as he walked, and a stomach-wrenching smell wafted from him. Had there been any flies left from the radiation, they would surely be circling him.

"Ve happened to be passing close by when ve see a big flash," he said. The alien spoke with a strange accent. "It looked like one super big party, and ve've come to join."

Allie grabbed Sydney's arm and whispered, "What *are* they?"

Sydney shrugged. "Damn if I know. They look sort of like punkish Martians."

The green punk alien with spiked hair took one look at

SARGE and grinned. He licked his hand and tried fruitlessly to get his spike to stay up. Sydney couldn't imagine what it was, but the little alien had a glint to his eye as he checked out the robot.

As his leader talked, Wilted-spike sidled up to SARGE. He was a little shorter than the others, so his head only came up to her mid-thigh. Lovingly he caressed her leg and gazed up at her. "Hi, beautiful," he said. "You look like my kind of female." He sighed. "I'm into heavy metal."

SARGE huffed. "Heavy? Are you saying I'm fat?"

"No, you just look like you're well put together." He ran his hand higher up her leg. "I'd love to run my fingers over your nuclear core. I bet there would be sparks."

SARGE shoved his hand away. "If you don't keep your hands to yourself, there will be a lot more than sparks."

The leader, followed by another alien, strolled into the bar. The second alien was the biggest of the bunch and wore a leather vest that exposed his well-developed arms. From his proud swagger, he obviously provided the group's muscle. He paused just inside the door and gave a smug grin.

The leader smiled. "I'm sure you von't mind if ve have a drink with you." He raised his hand and snapped his fingers.

The muscular alien suddenly punched a hole in the crumbling brick wall. He meant it as a show of force, but it lost some of its credibility when he turned his back on the rest and bent over to hold his hand, obviously in great pain. In Sydney's mind, this confirmed his suspicion that they were not an intelligent species.

The pixies lounging on the chandelier must have thought the

same because they snickered loudly. The well-muscled alien shot them a withering glance, but his leader just ignored them and strolled toward the bar.

With his eyes just clearing the top of the counter, the leader slapped the top. "Give me a drink. Something strong, and put it on the rocks." He grinned, very pleased with himself. "I heard that in a vid from your vorld."

Jacques grinned mischievously, "If you say so." The fairy hopped down on the opposite side of the bar. He disappeared below its edge. They could hear the sound of something hard going into a glass.

"Where exactly are you guys from?" asked Sydney casually. "You don't appear to be locals."

After a moment, Jacques popped back up with a glass full of what looked like bits of broken concrete. He cheerfully poured a can of soda over them and pushed it toward the alien leader. He grinned. "One soda over rocks."

The alien picked up the drink and saluted us. He took a sip. "Tis good!" He then gulped the rest and belched rudely. "My name's Veezott and ve come from Violespote. A planet from vhat you call Alpha Centauri."

They all stared in disbelief as the alien began to merrily crunch the rocks.

The leader continued, waving toward the alien who had just punched the wall. "He's Vese, my security officer." He then pointed to the one now hanging on SARGE's leg. "That's Vac. He's my engineer."

Sydney took a sip of his drink. "I thought they had proved there were no habitable planets around Alpha Centauri?"

In one quick motion, Veezott pulled a switchblade and pointed it at Sydney. "You calling me a liar?"

Sydney leaned back and held up his hands. "Of course not. Scientists don't know anything these days."

The leader continued to glare at Sydney. He leaned forward and sniffed. "You smell vorse than a damp *macupoodle*. I don't like you."

Sydney barely restrained himself from telling the alien that the smelling was mutual.

SARGE was getting irritated at Vac, who was sitting on her foot with his arms wrapped around her leg. She kicked at the pesky alien. "Leave me alone!"

Veezott stared at Sydney for a moment with the switchblade pointed toward his throat. But his attention was diverted by a shout from Allie.

"I asked you not to touch me!" She slapped Vese across the face.

The well-muscled alien was unfazed. He grinned evilly. "You look like a security risk. Vhat say ve do a strip search."

Ignoring her protests, Vese ran his hand up Allie's leg. She jerked away. "Will you quit!"

The pixies snickered and Jacques, eyeing the snoring Frank, motioned for everyone to be quiet. "Hold it down, guys. You don't want to wake him up right now."

Sydney frowned. He'd had enough. Interplanetary relations be damned.

"*STOP!*" he yelled as loud as he could. They all paused and looked at him, except Frank who just snored louder.

Sydney glared at the aliens. "I suggest you leave Allie alone."

The leader stepped over, looked Sydney square in the eye. "You don't order my crew around!" He punched Sydney in the stomach. The vampire doubled over, falling to his knees and gasping for breath. These guys were *strong!*

Allie moved to help, but Vese grabbed her arm. Brandishing his knife, leader Veezott stepped up to Allie. He grinned. "I'm curious too! Perhaps ve find out if human females are the same as ours. Hold her, Vese." The other alien grabbed her other arm and jerked both of them behind her back. Allie's eyes grew wide as Veezott waved the knife in front of her face. He grinned. He lightly ran the blade down the front of Allie's shirt.

Allie looked up at the pixies. "Won't you help us?"

The one closest to them shrugged. "Not my problem."

Jacques began to look more panicked. "Hey guys, you're being a little loud. You really don't want to wake him up."

Sydney groaned as he held his stomach. His every instinct was to run. But he couldn't. They were hurting Allie. And Carringtons never ran.

Clenching his teeth, Sydney rose and glared at the aliens. "I said to stop it!" he shouted.

Veezott swung his knife toward Sydney.

Allie yelled, "Don't hurt him!"

With a snort, Frank finally awoke. He opened one eye and looked around the room.

Jacques moaned. "Oh no."

Frank lifted his head. "What the hell is goin' on here?"

All the aliens stopped and looked at the unicorn, noticing him for the first time. Veezott broke into laughter. "It's a hue'nicorn! I thought you were a stuffed animal."

Already short of temper, this did nothing to improve the unicorn's disposition. Quickly taking in the situation, he said, "Leave the girl alone."

Vese joined his leader's laughter. "What? You want girl?" He shifted to hold Allie with one hand and stepped to the side. "You don't need her. You not horny enough!" He laughed harder.

Frank's eyes narrowed. That was apparently the wrong thing to say. He raised his head and glared at the alien—no trace of his previous intoxication present. His eyes turned bright red, and his breath became steam.

In one smooth motion, Frank side-stepped, aiming his back-side towards Vese. Then with deadly accuracy, he kicked the alien square in the chest, sending him flying through the air to forcibly strike the far wall. The alien slid to the floor and didn't move.

The alien leader shouted, "You got Vese! I'll show you!" He charged the unicorn with his switchblade, but Frank quickly wheeled and parried with his horn. Veezott drew back and tried again, but once more Frank easily blocked it.

Frustrated, Veezott drew back. The unicorn grinned. This was extremely unnerving, considering unicorns were not made to grin.

Infuriated, the alien lunged at Frank, and the unicorn, in one swift motion, disarmed the alien, knocking his knife away.

SARGE, finally tired of Vac swooning over her, lifted him up to eye level, turned him upside down and dropped him. The alien hit on his head, fell to his back, and smiled up at her. "I love it when you're rough." He passed out.

Veezott, the alien leader, glanced around the room and quickly realized all his men were down. Cautiously, he started backing towards the door. The unicorn tracked the alien's every move with his horn.

After taking three steps backward, Veezott turned and ran for the door as hard as his short legs would allow. But the unicorn quickly lunged forward, lowered his head, and—stuck the alien in a vulnerable spot. Veezott yelped and sped out the door.

The unicorn nodded and turned back to the bar. "That'll show him who's horny!"

Allie helped an embarrassed Sydney to his feet. He'd botched another one. He had wanted to protect Allie but instead had ended up endangering her further. *Would he ever do anything right?*

One by one, SARGE went about the bar gathering up unconscious aliens and tossing them out the door. "I can't believe a high-grade military, female machine like myself is reduced to taking out the trash." She shook her head. "What a waste of the taxpayers' dollars."

Allie gave the unicorn a hug. "Thanks for getting rid of those *things*. Bars just aren't safe for ladies nowadays."

The unicorn bowed his head. "My pleasure. It's always good to rescue a fair maiden in distress."

Much to Sydney's consternation, Allie blushed.

The unicorn glanced at Jacques, and Sydney thought there was some secret meaning passing between the two.

Frank cleared his voice. "Now that I've helped you. There *is* something you could do for me."

"Of course, but what can I possibly do?" she asked.

Frank gave one of his unnerving grins. "Accompany me to the Realm of Naelimag and help me get it on with my bride!"

CHAPTER TWELVE

Turning
The Corner

Allie

"HOW DID YOU KNOW I was... inexperienced?" asked Allie, slightly embarrassed to be discussing her personal life, and with a unicorn no less. Not that it mattered. She had made a life choice to wait for that special one. She refused to repeat her mother's mistakes.

"When you put your arms around my neck," replied the unicorn. "It made me drowsy. Not only does a human maiden's touch allow me to get near my mate, but as a side effect, it also makes one sleepy. Your touch, combined with the drink, put me out."

"But I'm not human," protested Allie. "I'm a vampire. Won't that make a difference?"

"Nope." Jacques shook his head. "Even though you've been magically altered, you're still basically a human."

Allie nodded. "The touch must work like an antihistamine, which would explain the drowsiness."

"I don't know what that is," said Frank. "But I do know it fools my allergy. Here, I'll show you. Just stroke my nose."

Allie did as he requested.

"Remember how I reacted to Mac before?" Frank pointed to Sydney with his nose. "Watch." Frank stepped up to Sydney and took a big whiff next to the vampire. "See, no more sneezing. You'll just have to do the same thing when we reach my mate. The effect only lasts for a couple of hours."

"So," observed Sydney. "That's why unicorns down through the ages have sought out human maidens."

"Yeah," SARGE piped in. "Human marital aids."

Frank glared at the robot.

"How do we get to this place?" asked Allie. "The Realm of Naelimag, I believe you called it?"

The unicorn pointed toward the door with his horn. "It's just around the corner. Of course, you have to know *how* to turn it." He grinned, which was kind of strange on a unicorn. "Just hop on my back, and I'll carry you there."

"You're from an alternate universe, aren't you?" asked Sydney.

Jacques smiled. "You might say that. But it's a little more complicated."

Sydney nodded thoughtfully. "That's how you escaped all the nukes."

Jacques considered him. "I'm not familiar with that word. Are these *nukes* what caused all this destruction? I've never heard of such magic, but it must be potent. Most advanced kingdoms outlawed magic that destructive ages ago."

Allie considered him, glancing from Frank to Jacques. She wanted to help the unicorn. The thought of such a magnificent species going extinct was terrible. However, going to another world did seem pretty big. Especially one as different as this Realm of Naelimag sounded.

Allie had a sudden thought. Maybe this was a solution to their blood problem. "Are vampires OK over in your world? Could we live there? Our world is a little messed up right now."

Jacques sighed. "That might be a problem. Vampires can only exist in Naelimag for a short time. They once were our guardians of the night. But a few centuries ago, one of them pissed off the wrong Dark Elf who magically banished the entire group from the realm."

Allie shook her head. "That doesn't sound good. Does that mean if I show up, someone will arrest me? Or even worse, try to kill me?"

Frank gave a vigorous shake of his head. "Nothing like that. It's a magical banishment, which means it won't let you exist there."

Allie frowned, puzzled. "Then how can I be there if I can't exist?"

Jacques grinned. "It does seem odd, but it's just how it works. The original caster allowed for brief visits in case a vampire was ever needed in the realm. However, it will gradually catch up with you and return you to this world. Nothing to worry about as long as we hurry. The advantage is there is no way you could get stuck over there since your return is guaranteed."

She sighed in disappointment. So staying there wasn't going to work. Which left them with their original problem. No blood. She glanced at Sydney and found him staring at her, his face a mask of concern.

He said hesitantly. "Allie, don't forget we're under a deadline to find a new blood supply. Not to mention, it's only a few hours to dawn."

That much was true. She turned to Frank. "How long do you think this will take?"

"Not long," Frank said, dipping his head. "If we leave now, you should be back before the sun rises."

SARGE stepped up and took Sydney's arm. "I think you should go." She glanced over at him and smiled. "That would give my man and me a chance to have a little alone time." Sydney tried to pull free, but the robot wasn't letting go.

Allie sighed deeply. "I'd like to help, but we are kind of short on blood. Since the destruction, our supply has given out, and we have to find a new one. The added complication is that we prefer the bottled kind. We don't bite." She shook her head sadly. "So maybe we can help a little later. I'm not planning on changing my... experience level anytime soon."

Frank cocked his head to one side and glanced briefly at Jacques. "Blood? Is that what's holding you back? I'm friends with a magician there, and as a favor to me, he might be able to help you. He's extremely powerful."

Jacques fluttered his wings in agitation. "Frank..."

The unicorn glared at the fairy as if daring him to speak. "What?"

Jacques stared back and shook his head. He took a drink

from his glass. "I was just going to say we had better hurry if we want to try this and also meet with a magician."

Allie took a deep breath and let it out slowly. *Should she? Could she let this species die out?* In her heart, she knew what she had to do.

Sydney opened his mouth. Shut it. Then opened it again. "Allie, can I talk to you for a moment?"

He stepped toward the far corner.

Allie turned a polite smile on the others. "Excuse us."

She joined him in the corner, and he leaned close. "I think this is a bad idea. It's just too convenient," he whispered, glancing over his shoulder at the others. "But it could give us exactly what we need?" she protested.

"It could also get you killed. We don't know anything about this other world, or for that matter, these... *beings*." He glanced again in their direction. "I don't think they're being completely truthful."

"And you're an expert in detecting unicorn lies?"

He blushed. "That's not..."

She interrupted. "We won't know until we check it out. Besides..." she glanced in their direction. "He's a unicorn. The last of his kind."

"Allie, don't..."

She poked his chest with her finger. "It's my decision. If I don't do this, it could mean the extinction of the unicorn species."

Sydney frowned and crossed his arms. "So you're going?"

She nodded.

Sydney considered her for a moment before finally sighing

in resignation. "I'm going with you," he stated. "You might need help." He softened. "Unless you don't want me."

Allie's heart fluttered. He wanted to protect her. That was so sweet. It would be nice to have someone else there. "You don't have to, Sydney. I'm a big girl. I can take care of myself."

He glanced at the floor and blushed. "I know, but..." he looked away for a moment before turning back. "We agreed to be partners."

Their handshake immediately sprang to mind. She remembered his big hands and how warm they had felt. *Get a grip, girl!*

She moved back to the others with Sydney in her wake. She turned to Frank. "Can Sydney come too?"

The unicorn gave a huge nod of his head. "I can carry both of you there." He swung the horn to point at SARGE. "But the mechanical will have to stay. Their kind won't work in Naelimag."

SARGE placed her hands on her hips and glared at him indignantly. "I'll have you know I'm designed to operate in every kind of extreme condition." She banged her chest with her fist producing a dull clang. It sounded hollow.

Frank shook his head. "Your making has nothing to do with it. The same would go for any machine operated by what you call electricity. Magic and electricity don't work well together."

The robot folded her arms across her chest and turned to Sydney. "I'm against you going without me. I won't be able to protect you."

Both Allie and Sydney gave her a skeptical look.

"Ahhh..." SARGE glanced at them nervously. "How about providing practical advice?"

Sydney put a hand over his face and groaned.

Allie smiled. "Great, then it's agreed. Realm of Naelimag, here we come."

Before leaving, the party had one more drink for the road and toasted to their success.

Once outside, they found the discarded aliens had left, evidently having awakened and retreated back to their ship. Frank snorted in satisfaction at their disappearance, but Allie had a funny feeling that they had not seen the last of the punk green men.

Since SARGE couldn't accompany them, the robot reluctantly agreed to take their packs and continue on to Sydney's shelter. But she wasn't happy about it. After receiving directions from Sydney, she stomped off, mumbling something about trusting bartending fairies and horny equines.

As soon as they stepped outside the door, the swarm of pixies surrounded them in a protective cloud. Not only did they provide illumination of their path, but they also were alert for any possible dangers. Allie couldn't help but think that if they had suits, they would be perfect secret service agents.

Being a city girl, Allie had never ridden before, so Sydney mounted first. In one smooth motion, he grabbed a handful of Frank's mane and threw a leg over to sit perfectly astride the animal. He held out a hand for her, not the least bit concerned about his balance. She gingerly took it. Allie yelped as he quickly pulled her up and swung her to sit behind him. Frank immediately shuffled to gain his new balance, which terrified

Allie. Afraid she would fall off, she clutched Sydney tightly around his middle until the unicorn settled.

Sydney placed his own big and warm hand over where hers fastened around him. "Don't worry," he said. "You're doing fine."

Allie had been simultaneously relieved and horrified. His presence was very reassuring, but dammit, he was right up against her! She quickly relaxed her grip and tried to shift back to put an inch or two between them.

Frank sensed they were ready and stepped forward, setting a steady pace. The fear of falling returned briefly, but as she rode, she began to feel a special joy at the power of Frank's muscles beneath her.

After they had traveled for a few minutes, she leaned closer. "You've ridden before, haven't you?" she asked quietly.

Sydney nodded. "My grandfather thought I should be prepared for anything and made me learn how to ride and care for many different kinds of horses. He even made me learn trick riding."

"Trick riding?"

He blushed. "You know, like standing on a horse's back while juggling rings."

"Wow," said Allie. "Your grandfather must have been really strict."

Sydney nodded. "He was." But the young vampire said nothing more. Allie sensed it was a sensitive topic.

As they rode, Allie became uncomfortably aware of her body pressing against his back, having gradually slid closer to him. She tried not to but found she enjoyed the contact.

She had to admit he was kind of cute. Considerate, too.

While her repertoire of male acquaintances was severely compromised by her mother's loser boyfriends, she had to admit she had never met anyone quite like him. A little klutzy, maybe, but definitely understanding and caring. And he even acknowledged she had a brain. She was really starting to like him.

She frowned. It had to be some kind of vampire reaction. Maybe the mind trick thing did work on other vampires, but differently. It had to be. Allie's resolve tightened. She was just going to have to be on guard. She remembered her mother's heart-broken sobs as yet another boyfriend *du jour* made his exit. She refused to have that happen to her.

After they had ridden for what seemed like a couple of miles, they came to a street intersection and stopped. Jacques was nowhere in sight.

"The Realm of Naelimag is just around the corner," Frank said. "Hold on to your stomachs. We might experience slight turbulence as we depart."

Frank carried them forward, turned to the right and...

Emerged on the shores of a lake, backed by a tall majestic forest.

Allie's heightened vampire senses were immediately assaulted with the strange sights, smells, and sounds of untouched nature. The large body of water beside them stretched into the distance, illuminated by a full moon and making it seem to sparkle with silver. Fireflies dotted the backdrop of trees, and the gentle sound of chirping crickets engulfed them. Off in the distance, she heard an owl hoot. The air, fresh and clean, was scented with the smells of a multitude of living things, both plant and animal. She could make out pine and some fragrant flowers, but the rest escaped her. There were just too many living things to pick out. It was such a contrast to the lifeless destruction she had left that her head spun.

Jacques was waiting for them, and the contingent of pixies spread out, searching for some sign of danger. Allie couldn't imagine there being anything in this beautiful world for them to worry about.

"Welcome to Naelimag," announced Frank. "I told you it was just around the corner."

Allie sighed. "It's so beautiful here. I bet you love every minute of it."

Jacques shrugged. "It gets boring as hell. Sometimes we have to stir up a war just to have something to do."

"Let's move on," Frank said impatiently. "We don't have time for this chit-chat. I figure we have about two hours before these two fade out on us."

Jacques nodded. "I'll fly over the trees and warn you if I see anything."

With that, the fairy flapped his wings and leaped into the air. Frank wheeled and took off at a gallop into the forest.

Fascinated, Allie looked behind them. With the full moon and the clear sky, she had no trouble seeing Jacques gracefully circle out over the lake to gain altitude. He looked like a giant butterfly. It was only a moment later that they plunged into the forest, and the view was cut off.

As the unicorn gained speed, increasing to a full gallop, Allie began to worry about hanging on. She tightened her grip around Sydney's middle and prayed she didn't fall off. He must have sensed her discomfort because he put a reassuring hand on the arms circling him. She tried to ignore his strangely reassuring presence but found she couldn't.

To distract herself, Allie turned her attention back to their path. She wondered how Frank managed to navigate through all the trees at a full gallop. But then she realized the unicorn was traveling a well-established route. Their contingent of pixies provided plenty of illumination as they flew ahead. Their path was also lined with what looked like luminescent mushrooms, which provided their own pale yellow light.

Allie marveled at their beauty. That is until she saw a moth, attracted by the light, fly too close to one of the mushrooms. The top of the mushroom suddenly split open, and a mouth similar to a Venus flytrap emerged, snapping up the moth. It retracted into the top and reclosed, ready for its next meal.

Allie blinked in surprise. It had happened so fast. As they drew away from it, she looked back over her shoulder at the deceptive mushroom and began to wonder just how strange this paradise really was. *Could there be more here than meets the eye?* She began to realize their pixie escort was for more than just illumination.

A few minutes later, the mushrooms and trees began to thin, with the mushrooms finally vanishing altogether. The trees became crooked and sick-looking, finally giving way to broken corpses of once tall and majestic hardwoods. A chill mist hovered just above the ground, making the path invisible and forcing Frank to slow his pace. She was convinced that if a haunted forest existed, this was it—a horror writer's dream come true.

Up ahead, Allie could see a group of stones in a clearing, which didn't appear to be part of the natural landscape. She grimaced. They were glowing with a green luminescence, reminding her of the glowing sky from her own world.

When they reached the boulders, Frank slowed and began to pick his way through them. Boulder-sized and greatly weathered, the stone's layout suggested they had once been arranged into some kind of pattern. A castle maybe?

"What is this place?" she asked.

"It used to be Weeping Mime Tree Keep," answered Frank, glancing back at her. "But it was destroyed a few hundred years ago."

"A war?" asked Allie.

He gave a nod of his big head. "Yes, the Second Whole Earth War. It was the last war that used destructive magic so powerful that the stones still glow even after a hundred years. As you can see, it's not a very healthy place. The Weeping Mime Tree is all that's left."

"Keep moving folks." Jacques swooped down out of the dark and circled. "We don't have all night." He soared back up.

"Why is it called Weeping Mime Tree?" asked Sydney. "That's an awfully strange name."

Frank stepped around the last of the boulders and stopped in front of what looked to be a large weeping willow. "This tree here is why."

A voice identical to Frank emerged from the tree. "This tree here is why."

"Is someone in there?" asked Allie

"Is someone in there?" responded the tree.

Jacques made another pass. "Hurry up down there."

"Hurry up down there," it mimicked.

Frank turned away and continued along the path. He called over his shoulder. "That was The Weeping Mime Tree. It mimics the sounds of any passerby, be it human or otherwise, in hopes of getting them to eat its fruit."

Behind them, a loud wail arose.

"Is the fruit good?" asked Allie.

"No, it's terrible," said Frank. "That's why it called a *weeping mime*."

As they traveled away from the tree, the vegetation slowly returned, and the forest thickened to its previous lushness. The path they traveled took a turn to the west and began to follow a wide, shallow river. At a clearing in the trees separating the path from the river, Allie could see a fountain in the middle of the water with ever-changing, multicolored lights illuminating its center.

"How beautiful!" she remarked. "The way the lights change is almost hypnotic."

Frank snorted. "Beautiful? You might not think it so pretty if you saw it up close."

"Why's that?" she asked.

Frank slowed to a stop, picked up a stone with his teeth, and tossed it towards the fountain.

The stone arched gracefully towards the fountain, looking to fall just short of its mark. But before it could reach the water, a green tentacle snapped from the fountain's center and grabbed the rock in mid-air. A gaping maw emerged from inside the glowing lights, and the tentacle popped the stone inside. Then, just as quickly, the fountain returned to its deadly deception.

"Wow!" exclaimed Allie.

Frank looked back and gave her a serious look. "Nothing is as it seems in Naelimag." The unicorn turned and sped on.

Abruptly, Frank slowed, and the pixies extinguished their glow, plunging them into darkness. Allie involuntarily tightened her arms around Sydney's waist. Frank drew to a halt just as the forest ended.

Her vampire eyes quickly adjusted, and she could make out a large pasture ahead of them. It appeared empty. In the distance, she could make out the gentle lights of a large town. Jacques landed beside him, and together they surveyed the area.

"I don't see the sonofabitch," said Frank. "You think he's out there?"

Jacques shrugged. "Hell, if I know. But this *is* his favorite territory."

"Who are we talking about," asked Sydney.

"Peggy," replied Frank.

"Is Peggy your wife?" It was Allie's turn for a question.

"No, he's my enemy. Queen Heather is my wife."

"Peggy's male?" asked a confused Sydney.

"He's more than male," Jacques chimed in. "He's a pegasus. Not to mention very upset that Frank came along and ruined his plans."

The unicorn snorted. "More like ready to kill me."

"But why?" asked Allie.

Frank scanned the sky. "Peggy has been trying for years to get Heather to marry him. That way, he would gain considerable power over the realm. Fortunately for me, she can't stand him. But his logic that it was best for the kingdom almost had her convinced. Then I showed up and swept her off all four feet. Peggy swore to do everything he could to get rid of me."

The unicorn sighed. "Then he found out about my problem, and he's started afresh. He's a real pain in the tail."

"Seems like he could solve your problem," observed Sydney. "At least for the first time."

The unicorn looked back and gave Sydney a look of utter disgust. "Unlike some *humans*," Frank stated flatly. "Unicorns mate for life. The thought of infidelity is unimaginable to us." The unicorn resumed scanning the sky.

Allie silently cheered. She could perfectly understand their mentality. Death do you part and all that. It was her ideal, too.

Frank sighed. "We've got no choice. We'll have to run for it. Jacques, if featherbrain shows up, fly ahead and get help. Don't try to fight him." He looked up at the pixies. "And you guys don't do anything stupid."

They all saluted.

The fairy nodded, and Frank took off at a gallop. Allie looked back to see Jacques launch himself skyward and fly just behind them.

They were halfway across the field when Jacques called out. "*Incoming!* He's found us."

Allie heard a splat right beside them, and it stank to high heaven. She covered her mouth. She glanced up apprehensively.

Where they being—

Bombed?

CHAPTER THIRTEEN

Aerial Assault

Sydney

"DAMMIT!" FRANK SHOUTED. "HE'S up there, all right!"

The pixies took a defensive formation around Frank while the unicorn veered hard to the left. Jacques put on a burst of speed and darted ahead in the direction of the town. He was soon out of sight.

Sydney looked up and saw a white form sailing over them.

In the moonlight, he could make out the flapping of silver wings above them.

"Incoming!" yelled one of the pixies. Frank immediately veered back right. Another splat came from where they had just been. Was the unicorn throwing some type of mud at them? A stink bomb, maybe?

"What's he dropping?" asked Sydney.

Frank dodged another falling object. "The same thing birds use. Only this guy's a lot bigger." The unicorn veered back in the direction of the town. "Try to avoid getting hit. The stuff is heavy and sticks to anything. It's especially hard on the pixies. If they get any on their wings, they can't fly."

I looked around and noticed we were indeed missing all but two of their pixie escorts.

"No!" screamed one of the remaining pixies as he and his partner dived in front of another bomb diverting it from Frank's head with their own bodies. They crashed with it to the ground.

Sydney marveled at their bravery. They really were like secret service agents.

"Hang in there!" yelled Frank to them. "Help is coming!" He cursed. "He's taken out my escort. Poor pixies will never be the same, so believe me. He's going to pay for this."

The lack of pixies also meant Frank had to slow. Without the illumination they provided, he ran the risk of breaking a leg.

This was evidently what was planned. A sudden rush of wind almost knocked Sydney and Allie from Frank's back as the pegasus passed just above their heads—his hooves coming so close it made the vampires duck. Then with a mighty flap of his wings, he circled in front of them to land directly on the path ahead.

Peggy faced them and spread his wings to block their path. "Halt!" he called in a vibrant voice, reminding Sydney of a British Shakespearean actor. "Halt, I say!"

The pegasus had a pure white coat and huge feathered wings

of the same brilliant shade. Sydney had to admit it was quite the regal sight. Too bad his sanitary practices were less than desirable.

Sydney was afraid the unicorn wasn't going to stop, but at the last moment, he skidded to a halt just two feet in front of his attacker. The unicorn lowered his head threateningly. His horn pointed at the pegasus. "If you know what's good for you, you'll get out of my way," he said. "I'm on royal business."

Ignoring the unicorn's request, the pegasus calmly took his time settling his wings against his sides. He didn't look up until they were to his satisfaction.

He frowned. "Royal business, you say. More like illegal business. If my intelligence is correct, those are a couple of vampires. You know that vampires are forbidden in Naelimag. I'll have to report you to the Council of Sages. They won't be pleased."

"The Council won't care," shouted Frank. "Vampires can't last here, so they're no threat."

Peggy's eyes narrowed as he sniffed the air. "Ahhh... Now I know why you brought them. She's a maiden." He shook his head. "Tsk, tsk, Frank. I can't let you do it. It's sick and perverted, making a human participate in your mating. Absolutely disgusting. Besides, while you've been gone, Heather's developed feelings for me. We could be really happy together if you'd just get lost."

"You've been bothering her again!" Frank took a step forward in agitation.

Peggy looked pained. "Courting her is a better word."

"She hates your guts!"

Peggy chuckled. "I'm not so sure of that. I'm confident I can win her charms." He smiled. "Unlike you, I don't need any marital aids."

"You don't care a thing about her. To you, she's just a tool to get power." Frank pawed at the ground with his right hoof, his eyes glowing red. "Now stand aside!"

"Never," the pegasus held his head high. "I must fight for the one I love."

Frank and Peggy squared off and began to circle one another.

"Hey," called Allie, tightening her grip around Sydney. "Can't we talk this over?"

"Yeah," said Sydney. "I'm getting dizzy." He was concerned that Frank had forgotten they were on his back. He put a hand over where Allie squeezed his middle as if to reinforce her grip.

Peggy charged. Frank thrust with his horn, but the pegasus countered, leaping aside and batting the horn away with his head. The two equines reared up on their back legs, swinging at the other with their front.

Staying mounted on a rearing horse while bareback was difficult, but Sydney managed it. Unfortunately, Allie did not. She slid off and landed hard on her back.

"Allie!"

Realizing he had lost one of his riders, Frank wheeled to protect her. But Peggy, unencumbered by a rider, moved faster.

Allie, stunned, was slow getting to her feet. Peggy seized the opportunity and charged at her from behind. Bending low, and with a flick of his head, he scooped up the surprised Allie onto his back. Terrified and completely off-balance, Allie grabbed at the pegasus's much shorter mane and tried to keep from falling off. Meanwhile, Peggy shot forward and galloped away with wings spread, trying to gain enough speed to take off.

"He's got Allie!" Sydney shouted.

Frank bolted after the pegasus. Remembering his training, Sydney leaned close to the unicorn's back and took a firm grip on his mane. They only had seconds before the pegasus was out of reach.

"Get me as close as you can," yelled Sydney.

Frank's gallop quickened. He was able to partially close the distance, but it was not enough. Just as they were only a few feet behind, the pegasus gave a mighty flap of its wings and leaped for the sky. He snickered in triumph.

From Peggy's back, a completely forlorn Allie looked over her shoulder at them. It broke Sydney's heart. All Peggy had to do was take her up a few thousand feet and conveniently drop her. He doubted even a vampire could stand up to that.

One of his grandfather's sayings came to mind—something about desperate times calling for desperate action. Sydney certainly thought this one qualified.

Trying not to think about how stupid this was, Sydney gathered his balance, and matching the rhythm of the gallop, he stood up on Frank's back. Then using Frank's neck and head to launch himself, he took two steps and leaped after the pegasus.

Adrenaline and vampire muscles carried him farther than he would have expected, but not as far as he wanted. He landed badly against Peggy's rump, and unable to find purchase, slid off. He barely managed to grab hold of a back leg. Sydney's toes brushed the ground, and the sudden weight on one side made the pegasus bank hard to the left.

Peggy tried to shake him off. "Let go!" he screamed. "You'll break it."

But Sydney was determined to hold on. The pegasus continued to climb slowly with every beat of his mighty wings, and the vampire felt his toes lose contact with the ground. Sydney suddenly had this vision of not one, but two vampires falling from a thousand feet.

Seeing Sydney's flying leap seemed to spur Allie to action. She tried to throw both legs over one side so she could jump off, but the pegasus nipped at her legs, forcing her back between his wings.

From right behind Sydney, Frank yelled breathlessly. "Whatever happens, Mac… don't let go!"

Sydney suddenly felt something take hold of the seat of his pants and pull. He glanced behind him. Frank had grabbed the seat of his trousers with his teeth. Sydney hoped his pants held and prayed they didn't come off!

Gently, Frank increased his pull, and the pegasus, unable to ascend with everybody's weight, slowly lowered towards the ground. His efforts to dislodge the vampire increased, but Sydney held on tight, refusing to let go.

As they continued to sink, Sydney realized that when the pegasus hit the ground, he would be in a bad position. He would have to let go to keep from being trampled.

Suddenly, the air was full of buzzing fairies. Jacques danced in front of the pegasus, dodging his bites, while two others avoided his flapping wings and took Allie's outstretched arms, lifting her safely off the equine's back. Peggy cursed them furiously.

With Allie free, the pegasus surged upward, and Sydney's pants ripped. Frank let go and veered to one side, while Sydney released Peggy's leg and dropped to the ground. The vampire fell on his face and scooped up a mouth of earth.

He sat up and spat dirt. So much for a graceful landing.

Peggy climbed into the sky and dropped one more bomb, which landed inches from Sydney.

"Sore loser!" Frank called after the pegasus.

The group of fairies landed around them, their wings buzzing in excitement. Allie tackled Sydney with a hug and nearly knocked him back down. She kissed him soundly on the cheek.

She leaned back smiling. "Thank you for saving me."

Sydney blushed and shrugged. "I just wasn't going to let him get away. We are partners, after all."

She gave him another hug. "Indeed we are."

Jacques landed beside Frank. "Are you all right?" he asked of his friend.

"Not even a scratch," said Frank. "And we kept our girl too, thanks to Mac's quick thinking." He turned to Sydney. "That was some trick you pulled there. Where did you learn to ride while standing?"

Sydney shrugged. "My grandfather made me learn."

"Well, that was one neat trick. I would never have guessed you had it in you."

Allie gave Sydney another peck on the cheek. He decided he could get used to this.

Without further incident, the fairies escorted the group to the town. The whole way, they chattered about the confrontation and the part each one had played. The stories grew with each telling. Their leader, a gray-haired fairy with silver-tipped wings, repeatedly apologized for taking so long to arrive. He promised nightly drills to improve the young lad's readiness.

Tired from carrying them, and not to mention the fight with Peggy, Frank asked if Allie and Sydney would walk the rest of the way. He indicated it wasn't that far.

The elder fairy rolled his eyes and snorted at the request. "More likely, he wants to save his strength for his big night."

Frank glared at the elder but said nothing. The two vampires politely looked the other way.

As they entered the outskirts of the town, Sydney was surprised at how primitive it seemed. The streets were packed dirt, with most dwellings constructed of straw, sticks, and mud. There were a few larger buildings that reminded Sydney of overgrown log cabins. While he couldn't be sure, he thought they were some type of government building or perhaps places of worship.

From glimpses inside the few houses still alight at the late hour, Sydney could tell that they had few furnishings. But this lack did not seem to come from poverty—the group which escorted them seemed happy and well-fed. It appeared the inhabitants lived well but simply.

Frank led the group to the center of town and toward a wide single-story stone structure. It was very regal, with banners flying atop the roof—not to mention the traditional mote, drawbridge, and guarded entrance. But it didn't look like any castle he'd seen before. In fact, it looked more like... well, an oversized barn.

Frank paused. "Welcome to Castle Steadfast," he said with obvious pride.

Sydney considered the structure. While he had expected

something grand for a kingdom's ruler, he hadn't expected a barn. Then he realized that his own human prejudices were biassing him. This was a kingdom of unicorns, fairies, and pixies, so their physical needs likely required something more suited to them. A barn would make perfect sense for an equine species. He had best watch himself to make sure he didn't come across as a half-cocked human.

Frank's shoulder gave a nervous twitch. He turned to Jacques. "How do I look?"

Jacques gave him a critical once-over. He flew up and raked his fingers through Frank's mane in a couple of places. He nodded. "Good enough to meet a queen."

Frank gave a big sigh and again headed for the castle.

On the other side of the drawbridge, two fairy guards wearing helmets and breastplates stood to either side of a highly polished double door. "Welcome back, Lord Frank," announced the one on the right. "Queen Heather awaits you."

They opened the doors, and Frank led them inside.

They entered a wide foyer furnished with only a few fairy-sized chairs around the edges. Sydney marveled at the lush green carpet under their feet. It was unusually soft and yielding. It took him a moment to realize that the carpet was actually a carefully manicured lawn. Looking up, he saw lots of windows in the high ceiling for the sunlight to enter.

The room was gently lit by several pixies that lounged on a small shelf just above head height. To Sydney's surprise, they were all female and naturally wore the barest of clothing. He tried not to stare, but a dark-haired pixie leaned forward and blew Sydney a kiss. He blushed. When he turned away, he noticed Allie watching with a frown.

Frank took them directly through another set of polished double doors and into a large hall. Occupying a raised dais at the room's opposite end stood another unicorn. There was no doubt the equine was female. She stood slightly smaller than Frank with a coat of dusty gray, a long, neatly combed mane, and a gold chain around her neck. She was quite beautiful.

"Welcome," said Queen Heather. "I've been expecting you."

Frank held back, approaching as close as he dared because of his allergy, and bowed to the queen, as did Jacques. Allie and Sydney followed their example.

Heather turned an admiring gaze on her husband. "I was worried about you, darling. You didn't tell anyone where you were going. I was afraid you had deserted me. But I *knew* you wouldn't do that, would you?"

"Never, love."

"Good," the queen looked towards the vampires. "And I see you've brought the solution to our problem. I knew you were resourceful."

Frank bowed again and introduced the pair. "Since my friends are vampires, speed is important. These two will return to their world in a matter of minutes."

"Very well." Heather nodded and turned to Allie. "Are you ready fair maiden?"

"What do I need to do?" asked Allie nervously. "I-I won't have to be in the room, will I?"

Queen Heather shook her head. "No worries, dear maiden. I realize you humans get embarrassed about such things. Simply rub Frank's head and especially his nose." She smiled and gave her husband a wink. "We'll take care of the rest in private."

Sydney could have sworn that Frank blushed.

Allie did as she was told, paying particular attention to Frank's nose. When she finished, he stepped atop the dais with his mate, and they nuzzled.

"At last," sighed Frank. He leaned up and whispered in his wife's ear. She giggled.

Heather looked over at them. "Thank you ever so much for your assistance. Now, if you will go with Jacques, he will take care of you while..." She glanced over at her husband. "We take care of each other."

The unicorns stepped down from the dais, and side by side, trotted through a wide door at the back of the hall.

Allie sighed enviously. "They're so cute together. To think we just saved their race from extinction."

Sydney nodded, relieved to be rid of the unicorn since Allie seemed to have a problem keeping her hands off him. It was no doubt that maiden-unicorn thing, but still.

Sydney paused. Was he jealous? It couldn't be. Allie was nice and everything, but he'd only known her for, what? Two days? He glanced at her. He had to admit she was not like any woman he had met before—intelligent, brave, and more than a little bit beautiful. He shook his head. There was no way she could see anything in him. All he did was mess up.

He blinked and looked at Allie more closely. In the bright lights of the hall, he noticed something odd about her. She seemed sort of—*blurry*. He held up his hand to the light. He could see a dim glow through it.

"Jacques, what's going on?" exclaimed Sydney. "I can see through my hand."

The fairy nodded. "That's what we were talking about when we said vampires couldn't last here for very long. The magic of this land gradually rejects your presence, returning you to your world."

Allie held up her own hand to the light to confirm the effect. "Too bad," she said. "I would rather stay here. Your world is so beautiful."

Jacques frowned. "Beautiful maybe, but it gets kind of boring after a while. We haven't had a good war in ages." The fairy pointed to the door and sighed. "We don't have much time, so let's go see the royal magician."

Maybe it was the late hour, or perhaps being tired, but Jacques didn't sound too happy.

He escorted them out of Castle Steadfast and back into the town. They went up the same street they had used to enter the city and then took a side turn. This section had large elegant houses, evidently the rich area of town.

Jacques directed them to the finest house on the block. "This is the home of Magician Rtyus," he said as he led them through an ornate gate and toward the richly carved front door. "He is the most powerful magician in all of Naelimag. If he can't help you, no one can."

Even though the house was dark, Jacques didn't hesitate to flutter up to the door and knock. When there was no response, he knocked harder, almost pounding. Presently, a light came on upstairs, and they heard steps from within. The thick wooden door creaked open to reveal a tall thin fairy with thick gray hair. He stood in the doorway, still in his pajamas, rubbing sleep from his eyes. Even though the man had obviously just gotten out of bed, not a hair on his head was out of place.

"Oh Jacques. It's you. What's going on?" asked Rtyus. "You

realize, of course, that I charge double for services after midnight."

Sydney shook his head. Somehow this person didn't strike him as being a magician, let alone the most powerful one in Naelimag. He more reminded him of his lawyer. The guy would drive Sydney nuts with his letter-perfect ways. He was always finding a piece of lint on Sydney's clothes.

"Sorry to bother you so late, but this is the queen's business," said Jacques. "These people have done the queen a great service. Lord Frank promised them you would grant their request."

The magician looked them over. He reached forward and picked a piece of lint off Sydney's shirt. "Forgive me."

Sydney just sighed.

"Who's paying?" asked Rtyus.

"The queen, of course," answered Jacques.

Rtyus grinned. "Then the price is triple. Government work always costs me more."

"You don't even know what they want?" protested Jacques.

He shrugged. "You wouldn't be here if it wasn't something near impossible." He stepped back and smiled. "Now, won't you come in? My workshop is this way."

They followed Rtyus through a tastefully decorated den and into what could only be an office or study. Sydney was disappointed at how little it resembled the magician's workshop depicted in the many movies he'd seen. The kind where a wizened wizard bent over a table cluttered with flasks and magic symbols while examining an ancient tome and usually illuminated by a candle atop a human skull. No, Rtyus's workshop didn't even come close.

A solid mahogany desk faced the door, with matching shelves lining the surrounding walls. A thick carpet in an elegant pattern of blues and browns adorned the floor, while several glowing pale yellow globes, strategically placed around the room, provided a warm glow. The desk and shelves were of such highly polished wood it put his old mansion to shame. It looked more like a lawyer's office than a magician's. He couldn't help but wonder if maybe the professions were related. Could it be the lawyers of his world were actually evil alchemists? His grandfather had lamented several times over the years that lawyers could make gold magically disappear.

The magician sat behind the desk in a high-backed leather chair. There were no other places to sit, so they stood across from him—or in Jacques's case, floated.

Rtyus clasped his hands and rested them on the table. He smiled. "Now, what request did you have in mind? I'm running a special this week on protection amulets—two for the price of one."

Sydney noticed that Jacques seemed troubled.

"Thank you," said Sydney. "But we're looking for something a little different. You see, we're vampires, and in our world, everyone has been wiped out. Needless to say, that leaves us with no blood supply. Lord Frank told us you could make us some."

"He what!" exclaimed Rtyus.

Allie repeated the request. "He said you could make us some blood."

The magician blinked at them a moment and then leaned back in his chair and laughed—a deep, hearty belly laugh. He began to slap the desk as he howled. "Now *that's* a good one!"

Sydney began to feel the same sinking feeling he got when he realized his cousin Martha had played a prank on him.

Usually a nasty one.

Rtyus calmed and wiped a tear from his eye. "I'm sorry gentle-folk, but I can't magically make blood appear."

He leaned forward.

"No one can."

CHAPTER FOURTEEN

The Truth Comes Out

Allie

"WHAT DO YOU MEAN?" asked Allie, a sinking feeling in her stomach. "Aren't you the most powerful magician in all the land?"

He nodded. "Indeed I am. But everyone knows that's impossible, even for me." He wiped a tear from his eye. "Who sent you? I haven't had a prank played on me in several years. Was it Klara? Oh, the little hussy, this sounds like something she would do. Imagine vampires coming to me for blood. Next, you'll tell me you want some sunscreen to go with it!" He laughed again.

Jacques sighed sadly. "This is no joke, Rtyus."

The magician stopped laughing and noticed that the others were frowning at him. He sat back and cleared his throat. "You're serious, aren't you?" He sighed. "I'm sorry, gentle-folk. I hate to disappoint, but someone has misled you."

Allie turned to Jacques. "What is he talking about?" she asked, anger in her voice.

"Yes," Sydney echoed. "What is going on here?"

Jacques refused to look at them and instead seemed to find something very interesting on the ceiling. "Why does Frank always leave the dirty work to me?" He finally gave a deep sigh and turned to the vampires. "OK, I admit it. He stretched the truth a little...."

The magician snickered.

Jacques gave him a sidewise glance. "OK then, he outright lied. I guess we shouldn't have deceived you, but don't be too hard on us. Frank was desperate. He would have promised you the moon to get you to help him out."

"And we trusted you." Allie folded her arms across her chest and glanced guiltily at Sydney. His warning about coming sprang to mind. *Would he hate her now?*

"Yes, it was dirty," said Jacques. "And I'm sorry about lying, but I promise we'll make it up to you. We meant it when we said the magician would grant your request. It only has to be within his power."

Sydney glowered at the magician. "I thought magic was, well, *magic*. That it could do anything. What you're saying is that it's of little practical use."

"Oh, magic can do a lot," said Rtyus. "But it does have its limitations." Rtyus leaned back in his chair and steepled his hands, assuming the air of one about to deliver a lecture, something he must love to do. "You see, magic can control energy and matter and the conversion of one into another. It's easy to say, turn lead into gold or make a blinding light from specks of dust since they involve the simple rearrangement of *quirkies*."

Sydney held up his hand. "Wait a moment. What's a quirky?"

Rtyus blinked at him in surprise. "They're the basic building blocks of matter and energy." Then he grinned. "That's right. Your world hasn't discovered those yet. I believe the closest you have is called quarks."

Sydney shook his head. "Quirkies? That's a strange name."

Rtyus shrugged. "And quarks isn't?"

Allie put a hand on Sydney's arm. "Let's not get distracted. You were telling us about making living things."

The magician nodded. "Magic involves affecting the quirkies which make up everything and persuading them to take another state. But making a living thing would involve combining *lots* of elements and getting them to react together *precisely*. Even down to their correct spins. There are just too many factors involved for this to be possible."

Sydney cocked his head to one side. "If all magic can do is move these quirkies around, then how did we get here? That's quite the stretch."

The magician smiled. "Once again, by the precise application of magic, we were able to convince the quirkies in your body that they belonged here and not there. It's a simple locality problem, which is why you're fading. The quirkies in your body are realizing they don't belong here."

Allie almost sighed in frustration. Sydney was getting

distracted again. While she appreciated his curiosity, they were on a bit of a deadline.

"Well, if you can't make us what we need," said Allie. "Can you at least remove our vampire curses?"

The magician leaned forward. "Let me see your hand, young lady."

Allie extended her right hand, and Rtyus examined it. Already it had faded to almost transparent.

The magician shook his head. "It's as I thought, I cannot help you. You have been injected with a type of dark magic that now permeates your body. This is what changed you to a vampire. In other words, the dark magic inside you has altered your quirkies to allow it to survive. I bet you've noticed that sunlight has an adverse effect. It's because it disturbs your dark magic, which in turn causes your quirkies to become unstable."

Allie frowned. "Can you remove the magic?"

The magician frowned. "It would likely kill you if I did. You'd have to simultaneously remove the magic and revert your quirkies back to their normal state." His gaze narrowed. "It would require a vast amount of energy."

Sydney frowned. "Like how much?"

Rtyus chuckled. "More than I can muster without seriously jeopardizing the whole countryside. I could lose my license for that."

Jacques sat over to one side, appearing quite bored. Allie realized this must be common knowledge to the inhabitants of this realm.

"You talk about magic like it was a living thing," said Allie.

The magician looked thoughtful. "In a sense, it is. Magic in our world envelops and inhabits everything. Here it is completely normal, and life here could not exist without it. But in your world, magic is an anomaly. Almost a wild thing. It alters that which it touches in a way it wasn't meant to."

The magician closed one eye and looked at Allie again. She felt like she was being x-rayed.

"But there *is* something strange about you two. The amount of magic that should surround you is slightly diminished. It's as if your magic has been damaged. It's strange, but the magic used to destroy the Keep of Weeping Mime Tree had this same side effect on some of the local inhabitants."

Allie uncrossed her arms and sighed. "So there is nothing you can do to help us?" A note of desperation crept into her voice. To her surprise, Sydney reached over and gave her hand a reassuring squeeze. His hand was so warm.

"You still have a gift coming to you," said Jacques. He eyed them. "Although you might want to hurry."

"What do you recommend then?" Allie asked, slightly irritated.

"How about a protection amulet?" He grinned. "They're on special."

"What else?" asked Allie.

"I have some love charms, some good luck bracelets, some lightning rods, and I think I still have a couple of infertility rings." He smiled. "That one is very popular with the young ladies."

"Infertility?"

He nodded. "For those wanting to do certain things, but not wanting children yet."

Allie considered. That last one might be useful someday. She blushed and couldn't help but glance at Sydney. Who likewise glanced in her direction and also blushed.

She looked down at her hands. She could see completely through them now, and beyond that, she could faintly see the destroyed city. A sudden thought occurred to her. "Will everything you've mentioned work in our universe?" That infertility ring did sound interesting, but a girl had to be sure certain things... *worked.*

The magician sighed. "Unfortunately, no. Only the protection amulet. Everything else requires a magic power supply. Only the protection amulet would work since it simply powers itself from whatever force is thrown against it."

"Oh, great!" Sydney raised his hands in frustration. "You mean all this magic stuff, and only one damn thing works!" He looked at Jacques. "This is one fine reward we're getting here!"

"Hey, don't blame me." Jacques pointed a finger at himself. "This wasn't my idea."

Ignoring them, the magician reached inside a desk drawer and pulled out two silver necklaces with large oddly shaped pendants hanging from them. He came around the desk and slipped one on each of the vampires. "These necklaces are the best you can get. Guaranteed to give a lifetime of service and will not tarnish. They've been tested against spears, swords, and even possession magic. I back each one personally, so if they ever fail to work, no matter what has been thrown against them, I will gladly refund your money."

Sydney snorted. "Some guarantee. If they don't work, it means we'll be dead!"

Rtyus continued. "Each one comes with my standard package of basic evil magic protection and the ability to contact your significant other. Perfect for those times you're captured by an evil wizard."

Allie picked hers up and examined it. "Mine's defective. It's got one end broken off."

Sydney held his up. "Mine's the same way!" His face was getting red.

Rtyus waved a dismissive hand. "Don't worry about that. It's the latest thing among all the couples. You see, the two pieces interlock to make the pendant whole."

"Let me guess," said Allie. "You have to put the pieces together for it to work."

"Not exactly. Just holding it will activate the evil magic protection and the ability to contact your better half. But to access the physical protections, you need to put the pieces together." The magician smiled brightly. "Isn't it positively novel? It's the perfect couple's gift. Not only will it keep you safe, but it will let you show your love even at a distance." He nodded. "And they both look so attractive on you. I bet you'll have all your friends wanting one." He folded his hands. "The special runs until the end of the week."

Allie just stared at him in disbelief. "Really? We're not even a couple. I can think of several other things that would be much better."

The magician snapped his fingers, and the world began to fade faster. "Whoops, I'm sorry. I must have accidentally sped up your return. Now, what were you saying? I'm having a hard time understanding you."

"Oh, Rtyus," said Jacques, shaking his head. "You didn't have to do that. It's not like you *had* to make a sale!"

As the fairies faded away, Jacques's voice came to them weakly, "Sorry about the blood! But it wasn't my fault!"

The world of Naelimag vanished completely to be replaced

by a rubble-strewn intersection. A lonely breeze plucked at their clothes and hair. Sydney sighed, and frowning, crossed his arms and looked into the distance.

Allie shoved a hand in her pocket. "I'm sorry I dragged you into this." She shook her head sadly. "If it hadn't been for me, we'd have avoided this whole mess."

Sydney looked at her in surprise. "It wasn't your fault." He stated firmly. "They lied to us. You held up your part of the bargain."

"You're... you're not angry?" She wasn't used to males treating her this way. Her mother's boyfriends tended to blow up at her least infraction. He was being so sweet about it.

Her eyes turned down. "Still, you almost got hurt."

He stepped near and gently lifted her chin to look at him. "But I didn't. Just a few scratches which have already healed."

Then he smiled. The unexpected kilowatts of his curving lips made her heart give a lurch. He was standing so close. Her vampire nose could easily pick out the faint scent of his cologne. And it was nice. That warning voice in the back of her head began to cry out. *Get a grip, girl!*

She blushed and quickly leaned back. His smile faltered, and he dropped his hand. "Besides," he continued. "It wasn't a complete loss. We did learn about why we're vampires." Sydney held up his amulet and grinned. "And of course, if we hadn't gone, we wouldn't have this wonderful jewelry!"

His smile was infectious. She couldn't help but return it. "I guess you're right. One can always use another piece of jewelry."

"*Magical* jewelry, on top of that." He shrugged good-naturedly. "In case we ever have to use it, we'll just have to stay close together."

He held out a hand to her.

Allie wasn't sure what to do. She didn't dare get too close to him. He was out of her league, and there was no way he could want her for anything more than a quick fling. She'd seen it happen to her mother one time too many. *Get a grip, girl!*

Allie looked down at his hand a moment. Still... She shoved that nagging voice to the back of her mind and took his offered hand. "Having to stay around you? I can think of worse fates."

He grinned. "So can I."

CHAPTER FIFTEEN

It's
Gone

Sydney

TAKING HIS BEARINGS FROM the area's layout and the few remaining street signs, Sydney realized they were still in the city but a good ways southeast of his mansion. From what he could tell, the distance they had traveled in Naelimag was roughly equivalent to the same in this world.

But other than it still being night, he had no idea what time it was. His watch said only thirty minutes had passed, but he wasn't sure if that was because the watch had stopped or if time ran differently there. It certainly felt like it had been much longer. They had been warned that electronic stuff didn't work the same there.

Allie had been momentarily mortified when she discovered her phone was not working. But a simple restart fixed it, and it too indicated only a half-hour had passed. Sydney resolved to keep an eye on the sky just in case. Still, if the time was correct, they might be able to make his mansion before sunrise.

While Sydney had tried his best to lighten the mood, some of the enthusiasm had gone out of them. Allie seemed to be preoccupied with something. He hoped she wasn't feeling guilty for their little side trip. It had definitely been interesting, and he didn't blame her for agreeing to it. In fact, he was sort of pleased that she had stood up to him. She had a kind heart too. She was definitely different from the shallow ladies he was accustomed to being around.

Their northwest direction took them directly past Cedar Grove Doctor's Hospital. This had been one of the hospitals on Sydney's list to visit. Since they were there, they paused a moment in their journey to check it out.

But it proved to be another disappointment. Despite being virtually untouched—except for broken windows—whatever had wrecked the area had also turned the refrigerator into an oven, spoiling the contents. They had been able to scavenge a few bottles of water, but nothing more. It was like the land was deliberately teasing them. Severely deflated, they resumed their journey

The horizon was just beginning to lighten when they reached the bottom of the hill leading to his mansion. As they started picking their way up, Allie froze in place. "This is Carrington Hill," she stated matter of factly.

Sydney nodded and resumed walking. "I'm a Carrington."

But Allie stayed frozen to the spot. "I had no idea you were one of *those* Carringtons."

Sydney stopped and wearily turned to face her. "Is there something wrong with that?" He smiled and tried to make light of it. "Don't worry, we gave up virgin sacrifices a few generations ago."

But it didn't faze her. "Your family earns more money than some small countries."

"Used to," he stated flatly. "And with the current state of the world, I don't think that's the case any longer." Sydney glanced up at the sky. It was definitely getting lighter. "We better get going. It'll be sunrise soon. I've got a spare casket you can use."

But she still refused to follow. "I haven't been in town all that long, but one of the first things I had pointed out to me was to stay away from Carrington Hill. That your family was part of the mob. Even the FBI was looking into you."

Sydney sighed. A sinking feeling over where this was going. "That was not me, nor my grandfather. I've been living here quietly since he died a year and a half ago." He glanced up at the sky again. "Can we discuss this later? I admit we do have a bit of a reputation, but none of the allegations are true. It was just my cousin Martha embezzling money from us, and when she was caught, she spread all kinds of lies to the media."

He looked away. Good old cousin Martha. She had maintained her troublemaker status even into adulthood. Grandfather had brought her on to help with the business. But she apparently didn't understand it wasn't *her* business and started transferring sizable chunks of money to a private offshore account. It caused quite the scandal. The media ate it up as his vindictive cousin lied about his family being connected to organized crime and other assorted evils involving trafficking people and drugs. Sydney was fully convinced that the stress drove his grandfather to an early grave.

Allie just stared at him. It broke his heart to see the indecision on her face. He couldn't blame her really. If she had heard half of what Martha had said in her lies, it was no wonder she was having second thoughts.

He sighed and pointed up the hill. "I'm not sure what you've heard, but I'm going to go to my shelter now. You're welcome to come, but I won't force you." He looked down and tried to keep the bitterness out of his voice. "I'll understand if you don't."

She considered him. He could almost see the gears turning in her head. He looked away. His family had done it to him again.

He turned to leave when she spoke behind him. "Is it really true that you don't sacrifice virgins anymore?"

Surprised at her comment, he turned to look at her, and she was smiling playfully. His heart immediately lifted.

"I'm living proof."

She stepped forward and poked him in the chest with her finger. "TMI... partner."

She brushed past him and walked on up the trail, leaving him standing in confusion.

"You mean it doesn't bother you."

She glanced back at him over her shoulder and gave him a mischievous grin. "What? That you're a virgin?"

He blushed. "No, I mean my family."

She shrugged. "Not really. I was just surprised that you're a quadrillionaire."

"My family doesn't have *that* much money," he protested.

"My mother was into rock stars, and she would always be at-tracted to the flashy ones. Especially those with lots of money. And they always took advantage of her." Her voice got softer. "And she always let them." She shook her head. "But you haven't done that. You're a little quirky, maybe, but you've treated me sort of nice, really. Even if you are a Carrington."

"So you're staying with me? My family…"

She turned to face him. "Listen. You don't get to pick your family. My mother and I have a weird relationship too. So, maybe one day, you can tell me about them." She looked into his eyes and smiled. "You do, however, get to pick who's your partner." She turned back to the path. "Now where is this won-derful shelter you keep telling me about?"

He smiled and followed.

When they were nearly there, SARGE came bounding down the path, breezing by Allie and stopping right in front of Syd-ney. "What took you so long?" asked the robot. "I've been waiting here for hours."

"Sorry," said Sydney. "But we got dumped a few miles away from here and had to walk back."

Allie paused and waited for them to catch up to her. "And Frank and Jacques lied to us," she said. "They couldn't help us after all."

The robot crossed her arms across her chest. "Well, it just goes to show you, don't believe anyone saying they're from a different world."

SARGE noticed their amulets. "Hey, where did you get the fantastic jewelry?"

Sydney held his out. "It's our reward for helping. It's their equivalent of glass beads."

Allie fingered hers. "And they're supposed to be magic."

SARGE cocked her head to one side. "Magic? And you believe that? From the guys that lied to you?"

Allie frowned. "Well, they could be. We saw a lot of magic there."

SARGE dismissed her with a wave. "Whatever." She bent forward and inspected the amulets more closely. "In any case, I think they're cute. And look, they each fit together. I wish I had one like that. I bet you might start a fad."

Sydney looked at Allie and both shook their heads.

Together they resumed their trek up the hill with SARGE prattling on nonstop. It had Sydney wondering if she had a mute button.

Reaching the shelter, he turned to Allie and indicated the entrance. "And here we are."

It was still clogged with debris with only a tiny path out, but the sight brought a sense of relief. He was home.

"SARGE, why don't you stay out here and guard the entrance." He really didn't want the robot wandering around loose inside while he slept. His lips were still chilled from her kissing him awake.

SARGE grabbed his arm. "Guard? You mean stand here at the entrance all day?"

Sydney eyed the brightening horizon. "Oh, I don't know." He waved his arm, indicating the wreckage. "You could also straighten up a little? It could certainly use it."

"Hey! I'm a robot, not a maid."

Sydney sighed. "Well, I really don't care what you do, just don't let anything near that door, OK? You're a high-grade military robot, aren't you? Surely you can do a little guard duty."

"All right," SARGE agreed reluctantly. "I don't think that was what my makers had in mind when they made a sexy thing like me, but I'll do it."

She leaned toward him and spoke in her sweetest voice. "But you'll have to reward me first."

"Like what?" The vampire eyed the brightening horizon.

"How about a little kissy-poo?"

Sydney grimaced. "Anything but that."

"What! You don't like my kisses? Well, mister, if you don't want a little snog, you don't have to! Go ahead and miss this once-in-a-lifetime chance, see if I care." She turned her back on him. "And I won't guard your door either."

He heard Allie chuckle behind him.

Sydney huffed. "Oh, all right." He leaned over and gave her a peck on her metal cheek. The contact was brief, cold, and his lips came away numb.

"Satisfied?" said Sydney.

"Not really," said the robot. "But it'll just have to do... for now." She placed her hands on her hips suggestively. "If you decide you want another, you know where to find me. I also have a built-in bed warmer for those cold, cold nights." She pulled her shoulders back proudly. "My makers thought of everything."

Sydney turned away and muttered under his breath. "I'd rather freeze." He tried to ignore Allie's snicker.

He quickly turned and led Allie down the steps to the shelter door. Sydney pulled out the key and went to insert it into the lock, but at the pressure, the door unexpectedly swung inward.

It was open.

Sydney stared in disbelief. "I know I locked it when I left."

He called over his shoulder. "SARGE, did you by chance open this door?"

"No," she called back. "I did notice it was unlocked when I arrived, but I didn't go in. It was dark inside." There was almost a shiver to her voice. "Ghosts like the dark."

Cautiously, he gently pushed the door open. All the lights were off. He always left at least one on. Sydney stood frozen, staring inside.

"Is something wrong?" asked Allie.

Sydney gave his head a shake. "I'm not sure." He paused a moment before stepping into the dark shelter and flicking on the basement's lights. But a quick glance around indicated that nothing was out of place. Everything was in order.

Sydney quickly checked through the shelter—in the closets, under the beds, and in the bathroom—but could find nothing wrong. He breathed a sigh of relief.

Then he remembered the one place he hadn't looked.

"No," he breathed. "It wasn't possible."

Allie watched him as he rushed over to the bar. "What is it, Sydney?"

Nervously, he squatted in front of the refrigerator under the bar. Slowly, he opened its door, and the interior light illuminated the inside—

It was empty. The blood was gone.

CHAPTER SIXTEEN

Strange Dream

Allie

"WHAT'S WRONG, SYDNEY?" ASKED Allie again. She could feel the approaching sunrise. It was not as strong inside the shelter, but it was still there.

She stepped around the bar to see him squatting in front of a little refrigerator.

"It's gone." Sydney shook his head and gently closed the refrigerator door. He looked like he was almost in a daze.

"What's gone?" she asked.

He stood and turned to her. "Our blood. It's gone."

She noted he called it *our* blood instead of *his*. It seemed he was taking this partnership thing seriously. And for a moment, she wondered if maybe he felt just a bit more strongly about her than just a partner.

He gave his head a violent shake as if trying to focus. "We don't have time for this now. We'll deal with it when we awake."

He took her hand and led her towards a bedroom with a huge casket inside. *Was that a double?* It was highly polished wood and brass. A work of art all by itself.

She eyed the bed. While she liked Sydney and all, she was *not* going to sleep with him. But he surprised her.

He went to a closet, pulled out fresh linens, and handed them to her. "I hope you don't mind sleeping here. And sorry for leaving you to make up the bed, but I'm a little short on servants at the moment." He raised the lid for her. It was perfectly balanced and held its open position when he stepped away. "I have a spare casket in storage that I'll pull out for me."

She stared at it in awe. It was the nicest thing she'd seen outside of furniture store windows. "Sydney, you don't have to give up your bed. If you'll just let me have a quilt, that would be fine."

He shook his head. "You're my guest. I couldn't do less for my... partner." He smiled and left the room.

She watched him leave in disbelief. Yep, he was feeling something just a little more than partnership there. She was pleased and nervous at the same time. She had seen those looks of interest before and had run screaming for the door when she saw them. She would *not* repeat her mother's mistakes.

She heard Sydney moving stuff around in the other room.

He gave a soft yelp and cursed. She smiled. He was quirky. Maybe even cute. Definitely not someone she would normally spend time with. But there was one thing she could say for sure.

Sydney didn't feel like a mistake.

Allie squirmed in the grips of an unpleasant dream. At first, it was her mother sitting on the other side of a tiny kitchen table. The scene came from her memory of when she had been seven or eight. Her friends were waiting outside in the sunshine, but her mother wouldn't let her join them until she drank her milk. It was good for her, her mother explained. Organic even.

But instead of white, the glass's contents were a deep red. The young Allie curled up her nose in disgust. Blood was so gross—

And then the dream began to change. Her mother, the table, the blood all faded. It felt different. Like someone was hijacking her dreams.

Allie's childhood kitchen was replaced with the image of a woman she didn't know. The woman looked to be just slightly older than Allie and had bright red hair. She was sitting cross-legged on a metal-framed bunk bed and dressed in some kind of blaze orange jumpsuit—something a prisoner might wear.

There was a loud metallic thud, and the woman looked up. She was in a jail cell, and the door had just been slid open. The woman looked up in anger as two men in military fatigues entered.

"*Help her,*" came the thought.

The men grabbed the woman's arms and hauled her to her feet.

Suddenly, Allie's vision was filled with the face of a black cat. The one that said he was looking for his mistress.

"Help her. Please."

Allie broke free from the dream and bolted upright to slam her forehead into the casket's lid. She rebounded back to her pillow and lay dazed, staring into the darkness and wondering where she was.

As the memory of being in Sydney's bed gradually crept back into her mind, she gently probed the damage to her forehead. That had hurt, but she didn't feel anything wet. At least as a vampire, she didn't have to worry about getting a bruise.

She could feel that it was near sunset but not quite complete. Normally, she would have hit the snooze button and gone back to sleep, but the dream bothered her. Not the part about her mother. That was a pretty normal dream. At least for her. No, it was the part about the woman. It had seemed so real.

She raised the casket lid a fraction and peered out.

All was quiet. The room's only light came from a tiny night-light just outside. She eased out of the casket and fumbled for her bag. There was no sunlight in the underground shelter, so she felt confident she could move around even though it was not quite dark outside.

She went to the bathroom to take care of her post-sleep business. It was not large, but it was upscale from what she was used to. Sydney likely thought he was roughing it. Allie eyed the shower. One sniff of her clothes told her she could definitely use one. And she didn't think Sydney would mind.

As she undressed, she shivered. It was cool in the shelter. On the wall by the door, she spotted a timer switch clearly labeled *Sunlamp*. She thought it odd since none of the other switches were labeled. But then again, it wasn't her shelter. She remembered a motel that she, as a girl, had stayed in with her mother. She had played with a sunlamp in the bathroom. Could this one be the same? It would be nice to feel the sun on her skin again—even if it was fake.

She tried to turn the sunlamp's timer, but it would not budge. After trying for a few minutes, she gave up. It must be broken, she reasoned. Not surprising, considering everything that had happened. Or for that matter, it could just be old, and Sydney never got around to having it fixed. He had said the shelter was several decades old.

Turning to the shower, she experimented with the faucet. Her mind drifted back to her dream which still bothered her.

Who was that woman? And why was the cat in her dream? Before her brief trip to Naelimag, she would have dismissed it outright as just a fabrication of her troubled mind. Being a vampire in a post-apocalyptic world certainly qualified.

But Rtyus the magician had told them they each had magic inside them. In fact, it was magic that made them vampires. So could someone else in the world have magic and be using it to reach out to her? It could certainly explain why the cat could talk. What had it said to her before? That he was a familiar? That implied belonging to someone magical. Could it be that woman?

As she stepped into the shower and luxuriated in warm water, she had the nagging thought.

Assuming the cat really was magical, then why was he

contacting her? She hoped she wasn't somehow attracting magical, talking animals.

The last one had lied.

CHAPTER SEVENTEEN

Wall Of Portraits

Sydney

SYDNEY AWOKE TO THE sound of running water. He lay in that half-asleep doze one gets just before you know the alarm clock is going to go off. He thought it was raining outside—the kind of early morning showers that makes one pull the covers up, hit the snooze button, and then stay in bed maybe just a little while longer. Then with a jolt, he remembered it was not morning, and he was not in bed.

And he was still a vampire.

Steeling himself, he opened his eyes and pushed open the casket lid. The running water came from the bathroom. Evidently, Allie was taking a shower.

Once again, Sydney thanked his grandfather for the shelter's preparations. Since the senior Carrington had dug a well and installed a pump, water was not a problem as long as the propane to run the generator held out. He needed to add that to his list of things to search for.

Of course, there was a larger problem.

He got up and pulled on a robe. Hoping he had been mistaken, he went to search the refrigerator again. But it was still empty. The blood hadn't magically reappeared. Just to be sure he hadn't misplaced it, Sydney checked his refrigerator in the kitchen, but no luck. Someone had definitely stolen it.

But seeing the moldy pre-apocalypse takeout containers inside the refrigerator reminded him he was hungry. And Allie likely would be too.

He set about making his favorite. Pancakes. The food God had intended to raise men's spirits. The comfort food of comfort foods. He had been eating them a lot lately. Even before the world blew up.

Allie emerged from the bathroom behind him, her hair still damp but combed out. And while he tried not to be obvious in his examination, he thought she was wearing some light makeup.

He smiled, remembering his grandfather's council about the fairer sex. "Beware," he had said one evening. "When a woman wears make-up. It's their war paint. And they are mighty warriors. No man can stand against them."

It wasn't until he was older that he understood what his grandfather had meant. And he had to admit they were a formidable foe. But so far, his walls had held as he fought off those with eyes on his family's money. That is until he met Allie. She breezed through all his carefully constructed defenses. Although, he couldn't decide if he really minded.

She smiled when she saw him in the kitchen. "Good evening," she said. "I hope you didn't mind me using your shower. I figured you'd rather have a clean partner than a stinky one."

He couldn't help but smile. "Yes, I agree. Stinky is bad."

She had changed into yet another black T-shirt bearing the image of a woman who looked to be a professional wrestler. It was the same woman he had seen her wearing previously. And the one that Rip had commented on. In this pose, the wrestler was leaping through the air.

He nodded toward her shirt. "You must really like wrestling. What is her name again?"

Allie broke into a huge grin. She pulled the shirt down to smooth it out. "This is Clare Montare. She's the best. I've been a fan of hers since she first appeared."

Sydney noticed that pulling the shirt taut highlighted Allie's feminine features. They were... breathtaking. He swallowed and abruptly turned back to the pancake he was frying.

"Oh, by the way," said Allie, nodding towards the bathroom. "I guess it's not surprising considering all that's happened, but when I tried the sunlamp in the bathroom, it didn't work. The blast must have knocked it out."

Sydney whipped back around and stared at her in disbelief. "You turned on the sunlamp!"

She blinked at him. "Well, I tried. But the knob wouldn't budge."

He relaxed. "Nothing else?"

She shook her head, clearly puzzled. "Just that. Did I do something wrong?"

He sighed. "It's my fault really. I should have warned you not to mess with it. When grandfather built this shelter, he was afraid we might be down here for quite a bit and would not be able to get our dose of sunlight. So he had a sunlamp installed. It's as close to real sunlight as he could get—full-spectrum light and even includes infrared and UV. Unfortunately for us vampires, it's the same as real sunlight."

Allie's hand went to her mouth. "I didn't even think about that. Is that why it didn't work? You disabled it?"

Sydney shook his head. "No, it works. You just have to know how to turn it on. Please for your own safety, just leave it alone." *And for my safety too!* He glanced up at the ceiling. *Especially with the modifications I made.* Being prepared was sometimes dangerous!

"I promise I won't touch it again." She sniffed the air. "That smells good."

He turned back to his cooking. "Pancakes and some canned ham," he said, trying to focus on his task. "I hope that's OK, and you'll eat some too."

She padded over on bare feet and examined his work. He could smell the scent of soap and shampoo. It was the same stuff he used, yet from her, it took on a whole new dimension.

"Are you kidding? I'd love to. Besides, how often do you get to eat breakfast made by a quadrillionaire?" She grinned at her tease. "And they're all coming out perfect. Oh, and coffee too." She looked around. "Where are your plates?"

He directed her to the cabinet. She took the plates to the table, thankfully not noticing that he'd just washed them.

They were both hungry and dug in, chatting lightly about the food and the shelter. But they were avoiding the one pressing topic before them. As they finished, Allie brought it up.

"Sydney," she said, resting her elbows on the table and holding her coffee cup in front of her. She took a sip. "Was your blood really stolen?"

He nodded. "I'm not sure how they got in, but it's the only explanation."

"You don't think SARGE..." she trailed off.

He shook his head. "While the robot is crazy, I don't think she did it. If she had, it'd be because she thought she was helping us and be bragging about it."

She nodded thoughtfully. "True."

"But who would want to steal blood?" She took a sip of her coffee and then her eyes widen as she came to the same conclusion he had earlier. There was only one explanation.

"There's another vampire," she said.

He nodded. "Who else would go to the trouble of stealing it? He or she likely has the same problem we have."

"Have you come into contact with one before? I haven't."

He shook his head. "No, but there has to be at least one more. After all, who turned us into one?"

She sighed and took a sip of her coffee. "You're right."

"I've suspected as much before. I even made contingencies in case he wanted to hurt me." He took a sip of his own coffee. "I don't know how your turning was, but from the way he left me, it was pure luck that I survived. I think that's how he keeps things secret." He looked at her levelly. "He usually kills his victims."

"But how did he know about the blood?"

He shrugged. "I'm not sure. It's possible he was just checking out a possibility. Or it could be he's been watching and
knows I haven't bitten anyone. And, more importantly, he
knows where I live."

They sat in silence for a moment, considering the implica-
tions. Allie finally spoke. "What are we going to do about blood?
We can get by today, but tomorrow we'll have to have some."

"I know," he said. "But they didn't get all of my supply. I keep
a spare."

"You do?"

"Sure, I'll show you. I figure my partner has a right to know
my secrets." He got up and led her towards the back of the
shelter—the drone of the generator became barely audible.
They went down a short corridor and entered a long, wide hall,
with paintings displayed along the walls.

Stepping inside, Allie asked, "Wow, is this a museum or
something? Who *are* these people?"

Sydney indicated them with a wave of his arm. "They're all
portraits of my relatives," he explained. "They used to be upstairs in the parlor, but I had them brought down here so I
could look at them." He led her to an elderly gentleman in a
powdered wig who seemed to start the progression. "This is our
founding father, Abraham Douglas Carrington. He fought in
the Revolutionary War with George Washington. And this..."
Sydney took her down the line explaining about each one and
telling of the heroic deeds each had done. Sydney drew up to
the last three portraits. "... And this is my grandfather Sydney
Ulysses Carrington Senior, my namesake. He was in a war and
received several medals for bravery."

"You certainly have some interesting ancestry," said Allie.

Sydney nodded slowly. "Yes, I guess I do." But instead of feeling proud, he felt ashamed. Would he ever live up to his family name? Not likely as a vampire.

"And these..." He pointed to the last two portraits. "Are my parents."

"What heroic thing did they do?"

Sydney smiled. "Nothing, really. They were killed in a boating accident when I was three. I never knew them."

Allie's eyes widened. "Oh, I'm sorry, Sydney. I wasn't trying to make fun of them."

"No offense taken." Sydney pointed to his grandfather's portrait. "He raised me and was the only parent I've ever really known. He died of a heart attack shortly before I became a vampire. It was kind of sudden. My grandfather and I weren't on the best of terms when he died. We'd had a falling out...." Sydney trailed off, realizing he had said more than he had meant to.

"It must have been rough on you, growing up like that. You know... without your parents."

"It wasn't too bad, but it was lonely at times."

Sydney led her to a cement block wall at the back of the room. He pressed firmly on one of the blocks, and it gave a soft click. A section of wall came loose, and he slid it to the side, revealing the cement blocks to be just a veneer over a wood partition.

He turned and smiled. "Every mansion needs a secret chamber."

Inside was some additional shelves of supplies, a rifle case with several weapons in it, and lastly, a small freezer. Sydney opened the freezer and showed Allie the contents—seven frozen bags of blood.

Allie gasped.

Sydney sighed in relief. "Thank goodness they didn't find these." He turned to his companion. "While it's not much, if we split each bag, it'll do us for fourteen days." He took one out and shut the lid. "Assuming we drink every other day, that will give us a little over two weeks to find another source."

She shook her head. "Sydney, are you sure you want to split this with me? Until two days ago, you didn't even know I existed. You'd have enough for a month without me."

Sydney ushered her back out of the storage area and reaffixed the door. He looked at her coolly. "Are you proposing I kick you out and make you starve, knowing that you'd gradually waste away until you became so weak you couldn't move?" Sydney gave a wave to the portraits of his ancestors as they walked past them. "What would they think if I did something so cruel? I'm a miserable excuse for a descendant. Incompetent maybe, but I'm not cruel."

Allie stopped with a worried expression. "Sydney, there is no way I can pay you back for this. I don't... I can't... I won't..." She seemed to have trouble finding her words. "This gives you life and death over me. I will not be your plaything."

He shrugged. "I don't want you to be. We're blood partners, aren't we?"

"Yes, but..."

Sydney shook his head. "I've been alone since Grandfather died. And mostly alone before that. But since I met you, I've felt something I never knew existed. Why do you think I showed you my secret stash? If you were going to knock me on the head to have it, then I wanted to get it over with." He sighed and looked up at the portraits. "We're going to have to trust one another if we're going to beat this. I fully believe it's going to take both of us to do it."

Allie stared at him a moment. Then she glanced at the portraits of his ancestors before turning her gaze back on him.

It occurred to Sydney that she was afraid of him. No doubt she was carrying a deep scar—something she kept hidden.

Just like him.

Allie suddenly smiled, and Sydney realized he had been holding his breath.

"Blood partners?" she said. "That really is a terrible name."

He shrugged. "I'm open to something better."

"Nothing comes to mind." She held out her hand to him. "Then blood partners we are."

He took it, and they shook, but Allie didn't let go. She resumed walking and pulled him toward the main room. She grew serious. "A week isn't much time, And the longer it goes, the odds of us finding something grow smaller."

He nodded. "I don't want to bite anyone. I'll die before passing on this curse."

She nodded. "I feel the same way." She glanced at the door. "Do you think our thief will be back?"

"They likely will. I assume he or she is watching us. And when we don't keel over in a couple of days, they will figure out we have more than what was stolen." He scratched his head. "I'll have to figure out something else to make sure they don't break in again."

She stepped closer and put a hand on his chest. "Thank you

for asking me to be your partner." She looked away. "I'm not good with people."

He smiled. "And neither am I. I guess we'll just have to figure it out."

Just then, a banging came from the shelter door. He could hear calling from the other side. They both smiled and pulled away.

When Sydney unlocked the door, SARGE burst into the room. "You guys have been in here an awfully long time." She looked at them suspiciously. "You haven't been doing stuff, have you? Cheating on me behind my back."

Allie put a hand over her mouth to hide her smile. Sydney shook his head in disbelief. "I'm not cheating on you. We were just talking."

SARGE nodded thoughtfully. "Finally breaking the bad news to her that you've fallen for me?"

Sydney rolled his eyes. "Hardly. We were just discussing who had stolen our blood packets." He narrowed his eyes. "You haven't seen anyone come in here besides us, have you?"

SARGE shrugged. "Nope. I was here pretty much the whole time, and I didn't see anyone."

Sydney sighed. "We'll..."

SARGE interrupted. "But I did see some tire tracks from a land vehicle leading north."

"Tracks!" both Allie and Sydney cried at the same time.

SARGE nodded. "From a lightweight military vehicle. Most likely a Humvee."

Sydney folded his arms across his chest. "And you didn't say anything about the vehicle?"

SARGE shook her head, seeming to be puzzled. "No, why would I?" Then she brightened. "Of course, I get it now. You want to do it in the backseat!"

Sydney groaned, and Allie laughed out loud.

A Difference Of Opinion

Allie

TRAVELING IN A NORTH-easterly direction, SARGE led them unerringly in pursuit of the thief. Even with his vampire vision, Sydney had trouble seeing the trail at times. But the robot seemed to know exactly what she was doing, finally performing a job she was built for.

SARGE insisted the tracks were from a Humvee. Allie couldn't tell if this was correct or not. She was no expert in vehicles. But whatever it was, it had big tires and a wide carriage. The robot also maintained that a lone person had entered the shelter. She couldn't say for sure how many rode in the Humvee, but from the single set of footprints going to and leaving the shelter, she thought the thief had been alone.

As they moved, SARGE kept up a steady stream of information of what she was observing. However, Allie and Sydney were quiet. Allie did her best to ignore his glances which had started out cool, but had recently shifted to ones of concern.

They had argued.

Allie sighed. It hadn't been Sydney's fault. Not really. She had been eager to follow the thief, feeling it was somehow connected to the dream she'd had. But Sydney... He weighed the risks a little differently.

"I don't think we should follow them," he had said flatly. "We don't know what kind of hornet's nest we'd be stirring up."

"But Sydney," she sighed in exasperation. "We have to get back what's left of your blood. From what you described, there are at least two packs left."

He crossed his arms. "It's too risky. There are too many unknowns."

"And we need to find out what those unknowns are. It might lead us to a supply we hadn't thought about."

"No, our time would be better spent searching the hospitals."

"Which has gotten us exactly how many bags?" She winced. She hadn't meant to sound so accusing.

His eyes narrowed at the implied slight. "We don't know if they're armed or even how many of them there are. It's just too dangerous. I forbid it."

She gasped at his proclamation. Sydney shut his eyes, seeming to understand he had stepped in it. Big time.

Allie's eyebrows pulled down, and her lips hardened. "Then I'll go by myself." She folded her arms across her chest in a figure of defiance.

"Allie…"

"I'll take SARGE with me. She can help protect me."

His frown deepened. "You're being unreasonable."

She poked a finger in his chest. "And so are you!"

Sydney shook his head. "I can't let you put yourself in danger."

She put her hands on her hips and glared at him defiantly. "I'm a big girl. I can take care of myself."

Sydney ran a hand through his hair, clearly frustrated. His eyes slid to her chest, and she thought he was checking her out. But no, his eyes were locked on the protection amulet she wore outside her shirt. And she couldn't help but notice he still wore his. In the back of her mind, she couldn't help but wonder how much longer he would be wearing it. How much longer before he tired of her.

He sighed. "If you're determined to go…"

"I am," she shot back.

He sighed. "Then I'll have to come with you."

She drew back in shock. *What?*

"Partners are there no matter what." He looked away. "Even when she does something stupid."

While Allie had won, the damage had been done, and a tense silence walked with them.

As they worked their way further north, Allie judged that the devastation was increasing. She found it hard to believe that total destruction could get worse, but it was.

At Sydney's insistence, Allie grudgingly allowed a deviation from the thief's trail and checked out a hospital along the way. Unfortunately, St. Benmorin's Hospital, like the others, had proved fruitless. Collapsed concrete had crushed the refrigerators. Allie had remained silent, but Sydney glanced at her sheepishly, no doubt remembering her retort. Allie wondered why she said it to him. It was totally unfair.

He shrugged it off, saying that you never knew until you looked.

Around midnight they stopped in the middle of what had been a golf course, now stripped bare of any trees or bushes. They settled on a metal bench, surprisingly untouched in the sea of destruction, for a quick rest and a bite of lunch, or a midnight snack, depending on how you looked at it. She never could figure out this swapping of day and night stuff.

Allie sat on one end of the bench, silently chewing on her peanut butter and jelly sandwich. She painstakingly examined the tips of her shoes while Sydney sat on the opposite end, staring into the darkness. SARGE stood between them, glancing from one to the other, afraid she would miss some piece of the action.

Allie took a nibble of her sandwich. Maybe Sydney was right. Maybe she was being a little too reckless. Her plan probably wouldn't increase their blood supply. And they really couldn't afford to lose any time.

Going their separate ways would have easily solved the problem. But he'd been determined they stay together, pointing out that in every horror movie, the line 'Let's split up' always preceded someone dying. And usually not the bad guy.

Allie looked up from her sandwich and broke the heavy silence. "I'm sorry, Sydney," she said, regret in her voice. "I shouldn't have lost my temper."

Sydney almost choked on his sandwich. "What?" he said. It was like he couldn't believe what she was saying.

"I said, I'm sorry. I was mean."

He stared at her a moment and then slid over to sit beside her. "Don't apologize. You're right. My way of doing things isn't working. Maybe I'm being too conservative. Being bold might be better."

She shook her head and gave a weak smile. "I don't know about bold, but I am hardheaded."

Sydney chuckled softly. "I never would have guessed." He took her hand and gave it a gentle squeeze. "We'll continue looking for the culprit. And if we pass any possible blood locations, we'll stop and have a look. How about that for a compromise?"

She nodded and then looked away guiltily. "I didn't get a chance to tell you because of our... discussion." She gave him a nervous glance. "There's another reason I wanted to look for this thief."

Sydney frowned. "It wouldn't happen to be related to what that pixie said back in the bar? That you had saved a cat."

She nodded. "It's related. Sort of. That pixie had blooded Schro's ear. So I stopped it from getting any worse."

"Schro? As in Schrodinger's Cat?"

She nodded. "That's what he told me."

Sydney looked confused. "He told you?"

Allie sighed. "Yes, I thought I was hallucinating at first. He mentioned that he was a familiar."

"But what has that got to do with searching for the thief?"

She looked at him pleadingly. "Please don't think I'm crazy, but just before I awoke, I had a dream about that cat, and he asked me to save his mistress."

"And you think this dream and our thief might be related?"

She sighed and looked at him levelly. "It sounds weird, doesn't it?"

Sydney looked thoughtful. "Well, under normal circumstances, I wouldn't believe you. But just yesterday, I rode a unicorn, fought with a pegasus, and was cheated by a fairy. That sort of thing changes your perspective."

She smiled, her troubled expression slipping away. "It does, doesn't it?"

"Did this cat give a hint on where his mistress was?"

"No, he didn't." Allie looked up at him earnestly. "But I somehow feel they're related to our thief."

Sydney shrugged. "We'll just have to keep an eye out for this mysterious mistress."

She leaned closer and smiled. "Thank you."

Sydney froze with a caught-in-the-headlights type stare. Allie's eyes flicked to his lips, remembering how good they had felt. *Get a grip, girl!* She ignored the ever-present voice in the back of her head and began to lean forward.

"Incoming!" SARGE yelled. "It sounds like an aircraft."

Their moment fled. Sydney blinked and jumped to his feet. He began to hurriedly repack their supplies. "We've got to find cover."

"Why?" she asked, not understanding his sudden alarm. "It could be rescue."

He shouldered his pack. "It could also be the guy that stole our blood. We have to be cautious."

"It's a helicopter," SARGE yelled. "Oh shit... it must have spotted us. It's turned our way."

"Hurry!" Sydney was already searching the area for somewhere to run.

Allie followed his example, shoving the few things she'd

pulled out back into her pack. He grabbed her hand before she'd even slung it over her shoulder and began running toward a distant uprooted oak.

The helicopter's beating continued to get louder until the wind stirred by its blades pulled at their clothes. It had to be flying very low. Surely the pilot could see them now.

Suddenly, the world burst into dazzling white. Over the top of the helicopter's noise boomed a deep voice from overhead, "STOP! STAY WHERE YOU ARE, OR I WILL OPEN FIRE!"

Allie blinked in the sudden glare. Her vampire eyes couldn't handle such bright lights. She shaded her eyes and tried to see what was ahead as Sydney pulled her forward relentlessly. From the shifting of the spotlight, she could tell the helicopter was coming closer.

A line of bullets ripped up the earth right beside their feet. The voice blared again. FINAL WARNING! STOP WHERE YOU ARE AND PUT YOUR HANDS UP!

Allie measured the distance to the fallen tree. It was too far. They wouldn't make it. To run on meant certain death.

Sydney must have realized it too. He drew them to a stop. "I'm sorry," he said. "I should have expected this."

They both faced the helicopter and squinted into the light as it lowered—its whirling blades throwing up dust and grit into their faces. Allie hoped this was just a misunderstanding, although the display of force did nothing to help her case.

The helicopter landed, its engine idled, and its rotor began to slow. Shading her eyes with her hand, Allie saw the silhouette of a man, armed with a rifle, get out of the craft and walk towards them. But the glare from the helicopter's lights prevented them from making out his face.

"All right!" he growled. "Put your hands on your head."

"We're not armed," Sydney called out, as he and Allie did as instructed.

"Where's the third one?" the man called.

"Oh, SARGE. She was right here." Sydney looked around, genuinely surprised not to see her.

The man stepped closer. "Well, you're obviously not military," he growled. Sydney heard him sniff the air twice. "Well, I'll be damned!" he exclaimed. "You're a couple of vampires!"

The man lowered his rifle and stepped to one side so they could see his face. Allie gasped.

Standing before them, dressed in a black flight suit and grinning a wide toothy smile, was...

A werewolf.

CHAPTER NINETEEN

Captured

Sydney

"SORRY, FOLKS," THE WEREWOLF growled. "I thought you were the people who kidnapped my wife." He paused. "She's a real witch, you know."

Sydney scratched his head. If she was a real witch, why was he searching? Seems he would be glad to get rid of her.

"Can we put our hands down now?" Allie asked.

"Oh, sure. I'm really sorry about that." He shouldered his rifle and extended a hairy hand, his lips curling back over numerous teeth in a semblance of a smile. The werewolf had pointed ears atop his head, an extended snout, and a mouthful of menacing teeth. But he still basically had a human form. A well-muscled one at that. He was broad-shouldered, with fingers instead of paws, and every inch of his exposed skin was covered in gray fur.

"Name's Kart Graw, or Quick, as my friends call me," he said, extending a hand. "Best damn 'copter pilot this side of Hades. Don't let my looks scare you. I may be a werewolf, but I don't eat people." He smiled. "Or even vampires, for that matter."

They shook. Sydney winced at the werewolf's crushing grip. He was strong. He turned and shook out his hand as the werewolf shook hands with Allie.

The pilot grew serious. "You haven't seen my wife, have you? A redhead, about five-five, real cute, knock-out figure. Although she has a hell of a temper." He held up a finger. "Wait, I'll show you her picture." He fumbled with the pocket of his flight suit and pulled out a mobile phone. It was almost comical watching his large hands fight with the small phone.

"Not that one," he mumbled. "Not that one either." He gave a wicked grin. "*Definitely* not that one." He continued to flip through them. "Here we go. Here's us at the beach last summer." He turned it around to display the picture of a large man and a woman with short-cropped red hair. She was petite and looked tiny next to the man. She was laughing and hugged up against him, while he held the camera out for the selfie.

He continued. "That's me in my human form, but the woman…" He looked up pleadingly. "Have you seen my Medorah?"

Sydney shook his head.

Allie stared at the picture a moment longer, and with a quick shake of her head, looked up at Quick sadly. "I'm sorry. She looks familiar, but I can't remember where I've seen her."

"How did you get separated?" asked Sydney.

Quick sighed and put the phone away. "I'm pretty sure she got herself taken prisoner while I was scouting for a new place to live. I don't know about yours, but ours got squished." He put his thumb and forefinger together to illustrate the point. "Probably would have been killed if Medorah hadn't reacted so fast."

Sydney had to ask, "How do you know it wasn't us that took your wife?"

"Two reasons. One, you seem... underequipped. And second..." He grinned. "You're not injured." He lowered his voice into a deadly growl. "And as I mentioned, Medorah is a *real* witch." He brightened. "Nah, from what I could tell from where they captured her, it had to have been army regulars. They've got a secret base around here somewhere. We'd had some trouble with them before, but this time, guessing from the tracks, they brought a tank. Imagine that. Bringing a tank to capture a lone woman. Must've been a sight. And from the looks of things, she gave as good as she got."

Allie seemed shocked. "How do you know she wasn't killed?"

Quick laughed. "You don't know my wife. She's one tough cookie and knows how to take care of herself. Plus, if she were dead, I'd know it. We've got this kind of psychic link. You know, ESP stuff. I don't understand it, but I know she's all right. I suspect she's being held captive somewhere. And when I find her, me and old *Demoness* are gonna *destroy* whoever did it. Demon-*nolish* them." He laughed at his pun and punched his fist into his left hand. Sydney had no doubt, this man—or beast—seemed capable of it.

"Who's *Demoness*?" asked Sydney.

Quick grinned and pointed a thumb over his shoulder. "Why, she's my bird. The hottest little woman ever made. She can fly circles around most other craft, including a lot of fighter jets. Military all the way, a lean, mean fighting machine!"

"Where'd you get her?" asked Sydney.

Quick hesitated. "I'd rather not say. It's classified."

Sydney understood completely. He'd stolen it.

Allie's eyes went up as if suddenly realizing something. "You said your wife was a witch. Does she have a cat?"

Quick nodded. "Schro? Don't tell me he's been bothering you."

"Well, I did save him from a pixie."

Quick sighed. "Yeah, that's Schro. Trouble magnet, that cat. He's my wife's familiar. Right after we were married, I found him in a parking lot. He was just a kitten then and must have gotten separated from his momma. Medorah immediately latched on to him." The werewolf looked thoughtful. "He must be looking for her too."

Allie's eyes went wide. "That's where I saw your wife," she said excitedly. "Schro showed her to me in a dream. She was being held in some type of prison cell, and there were guards in army uniforms."

Quick frowned. "It's what I thought. Now I just have to find their base." His frown deepened. "And when I do…" He slapped his fist into his palm, not leaving any doubt as to what was going to happen.

"We'll both keep an eye out for your wife," said Allie. Sydney nodded in agreement.

"I appreciate it," said Quick. "Well, I've still got a lot of ground to cover. I'd better go." He turned to leave.

"Before you go," interrupted Sydney. "Could you tell us if werewolves drink blood?"

Quick gave Sydney a puzzled grin. "Now that's a hell of a question. We generally don't, contrary to popular opinion. Werewolves are pretty nice people. Sure we get the urge to howl at the moon every now and then, but even humans do that." Quick scratched his head. "Damn fleas. Seems like I can never get rid of them. Anyway, what made you ask a question like that?"

"Someone stole our blood," said Allie.

"Stole it!" Quick scratched his head again. "But I thought that was how you got to be vampires, someone stealing your blood."

"Not that kind," said Sydney. "The kind we drink. We take ours pre-packaged. Someone stole it out of our refrigerator."

"You're kiddin' me!" exclaimed Quick. "What's the world comin' to? Right out of your damn fridge! That's as bad as someone taking your last beer."

Sydney quickly explained what had happened. "I've got a theory that another vampire stole our blood," he said. "You wouldn't know of another vampire, would you?"

Quick rubbed his snout. "There aren't any more that I know of. Hell, I didn't even know you two existed. Medorah might know of some, but I don't think so." He thought for a moment. "It might be connected with that army base near here. They have been acting strange."

"How so?"

"Capturing local citizens without a reason isn't exactly *normal* behavior, y'know." Quick slapped his leg. "Well, like I said, I still gotta lot of territory to cover. So if you hear of my wife, just get on a radio, tune to the flight frequencies—I monitor all of'm—and call ol' Quick. I'll be there before you know it."

Suddenly a shrill whistle broke the quiet, quickly followed by an explosion off to the left of the helicopter.

What the hell! Was someone firing on them?

"*DAMN!*" yelled Quick. "They found me!" He sprinted towards his craft, dodging the falling debris. He called over his shoulder, "Sorry folks, but I gotta run."

"Who found you?" Sydney called after him.

Quick made it to the helicopter and jumped inside. Immediately, the engine flared to life, and the propellers began to come up to speed.

There was a distant explosion as another shell took to the air. Sydney flung himself at Allie, knocking her to the ground. He shielded her with his body as the shell exploded and debris rained around them.

Sydney looked back at the helicopter. The last explosion had been really close and just slightly to the left, obscuring it with thick black smoke. Someone was finding their range.

Its propellers still building speed, the helicopter fired a missile. They ducked as the missile whizzed over their heads and exploded somewhere off to their right and close enough to feel its heat.

Looking back again, a cloud of dust and smoke had concealed the helicopter as another shell streaked toward it—dead on target. Then, just as the shell struck, the helicopter rose above the smoke, having exploded where the craft had just been. Sydney shielded his head from more falling debris and the wind-driven grit. The throb of the rotors drowned out all other sounds.

As the helicopter sped away and the drone of its propeller faded, Sydney could make out new sounds. Something with a powerful engine was rapidly approaching, accompanied by the squeak of what had to be metal treads. It sounded close.

He raised up, looking for somewhere to run, when a volley of machinegun fire cut up the ground nearby. Sydney threw himself back down and tried to decide if they should make a break for it.

He grabbed Allie's hand, ready to run, when a tank appeared out of the smoke and gloom. The machine gun on the turret was pointed right at them. At that range, the gunner didn't even have to be close.

A topside hatch burst open, and a man dressed in a yellow radiation suit popped up. He pointed his handgun at them and yelled. "DON'T MOVE, TURKEYS, OR YOUR ASSES ARE COOKED!" He looked down at one of his companions inside. "Get it? Turkeys? Cooked? Pretty clever, huh?"

Sydney had a bad feeling this was not going to turn out well.

The tank lurched, and once again, Sydney was sure he was going to be thrown off. Being tied to the outside of a moving tank was not the most comfortable mode of transportation. He glanced over at Allie tied beside him. She didn't appear to be faring any better.

They were tied face down just behind the turret but backward to the tank's direction. They could see where they had been, but not where they were going. Allie turned her head his way and gave him a weak smile. Sydney swallowed hard, trying not to appear too green, and managed to return it. Riding backward always gave him motion sickness. Add to that the rocking, lurching tank, and Sydney was just about ready to throw up. He tried to think about anything other than the swaying motion.

To his further dismay, Allie seemed to be unaffected by the movement. Instead, she would periodically strain at her bindings and try to see what was ahead, while Sydney just laid against the tank's surface and groaned. Some protector he was.

Their captors had bound their hands with zip ties and used those same ties to affix them to the tank. But other than their barked orders, their captors refused to talk with them, ignoring their protests of being citizens and that they had rights. The only response they had received was when one of their captors got tired of listening to him.

"Save it for the colonel," he had said. "Now shut up, or I'll gag you."

But while they would not talk to their prisoners, they would talk among themselves. After being secured, the three crewmen chatted amicably

"Too bad you missed the helicopter," said the one opening the driver's hatch. "The colonel's going to be mad about that."

The other was climbing into the hatch on the turret. "It wasn't my fault," he exclaimed. "All the advanced optics are broken on this thing, so there's no night vision, no laser ranger, not even radar. I had to do everything manually. I was lucky to come as close as I did." He paused and looked at his crewmate seriously. "Damn crazy, if you ask me. I think the colonel's got a screw loose, sending us out in a busted tank. It's just not like him."

"He's always been a little crazy," the driver called back. "But he's been especially bad since that new major arrived. That guy gives me the creeps."

The two then shut their hatches and started the engine.

That had been over two long and miserable hours ago. Sydney hoped they got where they were going soon. His motion sickness was about to get the best of him, not to mention sunrise was only a couple of hours away. He shuddered as he thought of what would happen if caught in the sun.

Once, as a child, Sydney had come upon his cousins—the same ones that would later lock him in the parlor—with their newly acquired magnifying glass. He was pretty sure they had swiped it from their elderly Aunt Betty. It was a bright day, and they were using it to focus the sun's rays on paper, wood, and various other objects. Then one of them got the bright idea to focus the rays on an ant. Without thinking, Sydney had commented that it would be cruel. It was the wrong thing to say. His cousins had just grinned and pinned him to the ground beside an ant trail. They then forced him to watch as they turned the focus on the unsuspecting ants. He watched in horror as each one had shriveled up beneath the point of light. He was pretty sure that was what would happen to Allie and himself should they be out when the sun rose.

Allie turned towards Sydney and shouted something, but he couldn't make it out over the engine noise. She spoke again, this time exaggerating each word. As she intended, he was able to read her lips. "Are... you... O... K...?"

He nodded. He mouthed to her. "Did... they... hurt... you...?"

Allie shook her head. "I'm... all... right. The... creeps...."

"Can... you... tell... where... we... are... going...?" asked Sydney. Allie didn't understand at first, and he had to repeat it.

She shook her head. "Every... thing... looks... so... different...."

Sydney nodded. He understood completely. The destruction on the far north side of the city was much worse than any they'd seen on the southern side. All the landmarks he knew had been crushed and swept away. He thought there was some kind of military base to the northeast of the city, but he wasn't sure exactly where or even what branch of the armed forces it was. All he knew was that a few years ago, the small base had briefly appeared in the local news with reports of experimental missiles being stored there. The stories were immediately denied by all levels of the military, and the whole thing quickly fell out of the news cycle.

Suddenly, the tank's front dropped, and they began heading down a steep incline. Overhead, silhouetted against the cloud's glow, Sydney could make out some kind of entrance. As they passed under it, the interior grew quite dark, even for his vampire eyes. But from the echo of the treads, Sydney could tell they were heading into a fairly large tunnel. It could only mean they had reached the base.

They traveled down the incline for several minutes when the tank abruptly came to a halt. It idled motionless in the dark for several minutes. Then a seam of light appeared before them as the two halves of a massive steel door slowly swung inward. A string of fluorescents mounted to the ceiling ahead flooded the chamber with cold white light.

When the doors were fully open, the tank rolled on.

From his rearward vantage point, Sydney saw the door start to close. The back of it read—*No unauthorized personnel beyond this point.* Sydney wondered if he was authorized.

The path leveled out onto an underground parking area. Several Humvees and trucks were parked in two neat rows.

The tank pulled into one of the marked-off places, and then the engines shut down. Sydney couldn't help but notice that there were no other tanks in the area.

Their captors got out and untied them. With flicks of their rifles, they herded them through a red door marked DECONTAMINATION.

Inside was a high-pressure shower which started automatically, rinsing them off with a cold, disinfectant-smelling chemical. The guards walked through unaffected—their yellow suits protecting them. But Sydney and Allie were both drenched and shivering in the cold liquid. After only a minute, the liquid turned off, and they were assaulted with a blast of very warm air, which sucked the excess moisture from them. When it clicked off, they were still wet but not dripping. Sydney felt like he had just been through a car wash.

They were then led to a changing area with a rack of yellow suits and a wall of lockers. The disinfectant smell was strong inside but was overridden by a different, very distinctive odor.

A bad one.

Sydney resisted the urge to hold his nose and tried to breathe through his mouth. He remembered the smell from somewhere. Not too long ago, either. But he couldn't recall exactly where.

As the guards took off their suits and hung them up, Sydney realized the smell was coming from the guards themselves. No doubt about it. But even five years of BO couldn't make a smell that bad. There had to be another explanation.

Two more guards entered—one male and one female. Both looked well-groomed but had the same smell as the guards. They all couldn't have missed their bath.

"Miss," said the female guard addressing Allie. "Come with me."

"No," Allie said defiantly. "I refuse to be separated from Sydney." She looped her arm through his to emphasize the point.

"I'm sorry, miss," the female guard answered coldly, placing a hand on her sidearm. "Either come with me peacefully, or I'll shoot you *and* your companion. I don't have time for games."

Allie hesitated, causing the guard to tense.

Sydney put a hand over Allie's. He eyed the insignia on the guard's uniform and tried to remember his ranks. "Where are you taking us, Sargent?"

The woman answered without a trace of emotion. "You will complete decontamination and be interrogated. I've received no orders beyond that."

Sydney nodded. He patted Allie's arm where she grasped his. "You better go with her. We have no choice." He gave her a weak smile. "I'm sure I'll see you later."

She looked at him sadly, having come to the same conclusion. She nodded and slowly released his arm. Sydney felt strangely naked without it.

The guard directed Allie through a door marked for her gender. She gave Sydney one last worried look before disappearing inside. He felt so helpless. He'd let her down yet again.

His own guard took him through another door to an open shower. He was instructed to strip, bathe, and put his clothes in the provided plastic bag. Sydney did as he was told, except he left on his protection amulet. He expected the guard to demand he take it off, but the fellow didn't say a word. It was almost like the guard didn't even see it.

Sydney smiled to himself. Their capture would have been the

perfect chance to test the power of their protection amulets—*assuming* they really worked. But in the heat of the moment, neither of them had thought of it.

When Sydney finished showering, the guard gave him some underwear, slip-on shoes, and a blaze orange shirt and pants. The clothes left no doubt of his new status.

They left the locker room and entered the complex itself—a maze of corridors that made one quickly lose all sense of direction. He'd asked his guard what kind of place this was and was curtly told that it was a research facility. The soldier refused to answer further questions.

But overshadowing it all was that ever-present stink. Everyone in the whole place had the same smell. *Where's a stuffy nose when you need it?*

A door marked DETENTION turned out to be their destination. Inside was what could only be called a jail, comprised of four cells, two on each side, and bars for a door. Currently, all were empty.

They locked him in the first cell and, without another word, left him by himself. But he was sure they were watching from the security cameras on either end of the row.

He plopped down on his bunk and put his head in his hands. Exhaustion settled heavily on his shoulders. He hoped Allie was doing all right. She had looked so worried as she been taken away.

What could the army possibly want with them? This just didn't seem like something they would normally do. He rubbed his face. And worse, he doubted they would give him any of his required beverage. He wondered what they would do when he started to waste away over the next few days. He snorted. For that matter, what would they think when he wouldn't wake up during the day?

A tugging at the edges of his consciousness pulled him out of his musing. The sun was beginning to rise. Even underground, he could tell he had only a few minutes before his vampire sleep claimed him. He looked around his cell—a bunk attached to the wall, a blanket, and a toilet. Not much to work with.

He didn't actually have to sleep in a casket, but being in an enclosed space while he slept just felt better. When he had first been turned, he had hypothesized that it was some sort of vampire survival instinct to hide while they were vulnerable.

Lying on the cold cement floor would give him a backache tomorrow, but it was the best he could do. So with no other options, he climbed beneath his bed and pulled his blanket over his head.

As he began to drift off, he worried what might happen during the day. Would it make them investigate further? Do some sort of test on him?

And what would they do when they found out he wasn't exactly human?

CHAPTER TWENTY

Tears Of
A Jailmate

Allie

AFTER ALLIE HAD BEEN separated from Sydney, she was taken into a large shower which reminded her of a girls locker room. She had hated high school. Detested might be a better word. Especially gym class and the mandatory showers afterward. And the room she entered impressed her even less.

She almost balked at the command to strip and shower. But one glance at the guard's hand resting on her sidearm made Allie realize that modesty was not an option. She kept her eyes down as she undressed. She had always been shy about her body and did her best to keep it covered.

Her mother had never been shy. Exactly the opposite in fact.

She loved dressing to kill. But, of course, her mother had a perfect body and could have easily been an actress if she had wanted. It was no doubt why she had no trouble finding yet another rock star boyfriend. That is until they tired of her.

Beauty can only take you so far.

This was a lesson she had learned well from her single parent and why Allie had preferred sweatshirts and loose pants throughout her school years. Even at work, she had worn the larger shapeless blouses. Her figure was nowhere near as beautiful as her mother's, so why bother? She didn't want the attention, anyway.

It wasn't until college when she discovered her idol, Clare Montare, that things changed. Allie had immediately ordered one of her T-shirts. The first time she had emerged from her room wearing it, with Clare proudly displayed across it, her roommate at the time had stared at her in shock.

Allie had at first thought she was surprised at Clare's picture on her shirt. But that wasn't the case.

"My God, girl!" the surprised woman had exclaimed. "You've got boobs!"

She had nearly fled back into her room. But then she stopped herself. Clare Montare wore these shirts all the time, didn't she? Then Allie could, too. And so she had stuck her chest out and continued to wear it. Of course, she had been forced to buy better bras, but that was a small price for the confidence it brought.

Which is the mantra she used to comply with the guard's orders. *If Clare can dare, so can I.*

Blushing furiously, she did as she was told, washing fast to try to minimize her girls' air time. Allie glanced at the woman guarding her, expecting some type of frown of disapproval. But instead the woman had crossed her arms and wore a half-smile. *Was she checking her out?*. Allie's eyes went up in surprise. Feeling more naked than ever, she hurriedly finished and dressed in the blaze orange shirt and pants.

She was then led out and through several corridors, finally reaching a door marked DETENTION. She was not surprised at the four holding cells, two on a side, separated by a wide central corridor. The bars on the outside gave an excellent view of the interior concrete slab walls, bunk, and a cold steel toilet. Her heart briefly lifted when she saw one of the cells occupied but quickly crashed when she realized it was not Sydney.

A woman with short-cropped red hair sat cross-wise on her bunk following their progress down the hall. She was a petite woman, almost skinny, dressed in the same orange uniform but with tattoos peeking out from under the short sleeves of her shirt. One bare foot was propped on the edge of the bed while the other hung off, swinging leisurely back and forth. She looked tired, with her hair mussed and the blanket rumpled. Their entrance must have awoken her. It was, after all, early morning for most humans. But she watched them intently, analyzing their every move.

Allie flinched as the cell door was locked behind her. The sound seemed so final and made her wonder if she would ever see the outside again.

The guard turned to the other prisoner who was in the cell across from Allie. "Be nice to your new friend, and maybe I'll let you have some breakfast."

The red-headed woman shrugged. "Don't put yourself out on my account. If yesterday's meal was any indication, I wouldn't be missing much."

The guard regarded the redhead coolly for a moment and then turned back to Allie. "And you too, sweetheart. Don't be picking on your jail mate here. She's been having it rough. I caught her crying yesterday." She smiled evilly. "Only she couldn't tell me why."

The redhead instantly launched herself at the bars reaching for her guard, but her fingers closed only on open air. She was barely out of reach.

Allie's eye was drawn to the ugly silver bracelet dangling from around the redhead's right wrist. It was a wide, gaudy piece—something her grandmother might wear. But for some reason, Allie found it repulsive. It reminded her of a prison manacle.

The guard smirked. "Now, now. Such behavior. I guess we'll just have to skip breakfast and see if that improves your attitude."

The redhead made a rude gesture and returned to her bunk.

The guard gave one final smirk to each of them and then left. The bolt of the door to the holding area slid home with a final solid thud.

Allie sighed forlornly and sat on her bunk. *What was she going to do?* And where was Sydney? What had they done with him? She never expected them to have his and hers holding areas.

She put her head in her hands and felt the growing dampness coming to her eyes. *She was not going to cry. No, she was not going to do it!*

"Hey," called the woman from the opposite cell. "Are you all right?"

Allie looked up and saw the woman was leaning on the bars of her cell.

Allie shrugged. "I'm fine, if you consider being in jail OK." She looked back down at her hands.

The woman indicated the door with her chin. "Don't let the bastards get to you. That guard is a bit of a bitch."

Allie nodded distractedly.

"My name's Medorah," the woman said. Allie looked up. Where had she heard that name? Somewhere recent. In any case, the woman was trying to distract Allie from her misery. While Allie really would have preferred to wallow in her despair, it was a nice gesture. It was the first kind act she'd encountered since arriving at the base.

Allie wasn't going to be rude. She stood and walked to the door. "My name's Allie," she said. "Allie Medley."

Medorah smiled deviously. "Something tells me Allie is a nickname."

Allie gave a weak smile. "You're right. My mother cursed me with the name Allegra."

Medorah looked puzzled. "Cursed? Allegra is pretty. What's wrong with it?"

Allie sighed. "She almost named me Allegro. But she did give me the middle name of Cadence."

Medorah thought about it. "Allegra Cadence Medley. What's wrong with...?" She grinned in understanding. "Musical terms. Clever, but I can't imagine why your mother stuck that on you. I imagine you were teased quite a bit."

Allie nodded. "I was. Mother has always loved music, and I guess she wanted to extend that to me." She added with a grin. "She did say I was the happiest note in her life."

Medorah smiled. "Sounds like someone I would like to meet."

Allie felt a sudden emptiness in her chest. Would she see her mother again? Not that she really *wanted* to see her. They fought like cats and dogs, but it would be strangely comforting to just hear her voice.

Allie shook it off. She couldn't go there now. "So, how long have you been here?" she asked.

Medorah gripped the bars and leaned on them. "This will be the start of the third day."

Allie couldn't help but notice the wedding band on her left hand. It wasn't silver. Platinum, maybe?.

"Three days?" Allie asked. "Have you talked to a lawyer or been in front of a judge?"

Medorah snorted. "I don't think they work that way. I've asked, but have been told..." She deepened her voice. "... Due to the extraordinary circumstances, you're being detained for your own protection." She smiled. But it quickly faded. "Except for the bitch queen, they've at least treated me well." She looked down. "I just wish they would let me go. I miss my cat..." she smiled weakly. "And... and...." She trailed off, staring blankly ahead for two heartbeats, then suddenly seemed to catch herself. "Yeah, I miss the little bugger."

Allie's eyes went wide. "Cat? He wouldn't be short-haired and all black, would he?"

Medorah blinked. "He is."

"And he…" Allie licked her lips. "Please don't think I'm crazy, but does he talk?"

The woman straightened. She eyed Allie suspiciously. "Not usually."

"I swear I wasn't on anything, but I encountered a black cat being chased by a pixie. The cat spoke to me and said he was looking for his mistress. And then later, he appeared in my dream asking me to find her."

Medorah looked shocked. "Schro spoke to you? You talked with my cat?"

Allie grinned sheepishly. "Well, I think I did. I've been under a lot of stress lately, so I might be having hallucinations…"

Medorah stuck her hands through the bars and leaned closer. "Let me get this straight. Schro talked with you?"

Allie shrugged. "Well, I think he did. Clever to name him after Schrödinger's Cat."

Medorah waved it off. "My… my…" She did that blank stare and pause again. She gave a tiny shake of her head. "Someone started calling him Schro because he was the improbable cat." She looked into the distance and smiled. "Schro was rescued from a busy parking lot. He was about to be run over when someone stopped traffic to save him. My…" she did that stare-pause again. "Someone brought him home, intending to take him to the shelter. But they made the mistake of showing him to me, and I fell in love with Schro at first glance."

Allie considered her friend. Medorah's story almost sounded like a badly edited video. Who was this *Someone*?

Medorah suddenly sniffed the air. Her eyebrows rose. "You don't stink."

Allie pulled back and frowned. "I certainly hope not. I just had a shower."

Medorah shook her head. "No, I mean all the other humans I've encountered have a foul smell coming from them. The room should be permeated by now. But it's not. In fact, it's been dissipating since Bitch Queen left. Which means you're not human and must have some magic in you." The woman straightened and squinted her eyes at Allie. "Yes, I can see it. You do have some magic. Although of a dark sort." She leaned forward. "Are you... a vampire?"

Allie stared at her a moment. She was going to find out in a bit anyway. Sunrise wasn't that far off. She nodded.

"What a coincidence." Medorah smiled. "I'm a witch."

Allie nodded. The cat had said it was a familiar. "It all makes sense now." She eyed the wedding band on her friend's hand. "Is your husband's name Quick?"

Medorah opened her mouth, but froze. She did the stare-pause thing again. Longer this time. Allie had time to wonder what was wrong when the redhead blinked at her. "No," she finally answered sadly. "I don't have a husband. I've never been married."

The statement didn't ring true. What was going on? Allie opened her mouth to ask another question but stopped. That familiar feeling started nagging at the back of her mind. The sun was about to rise. And if she didn't get to a resting place, she would just keel over.

Allie had to risk one last question. "Are you sure? We met a werewolf who was looking for his wife. He had a picture of you at the beach. He even said she was a witch. Don't you want to get out of here and see him?"

Again that awkward pause.

Medorah shook her head. "No, I've never had a husband. And why would I want to leave? I'm safe here. I have nowhere to go."

The witch almost sounded like a robot. But Allie didn't believe her.

Because there was a tear slipping down Medorah's cheek.

CHAPTER TWENTY-ONE

Where The People Went

Sydney

FOR THE THOUSANDTH TIME, Sydney paced the length of his cell and tried to burn off some of his nervous energy. He had no watch, but he suspected about two hours had passed since awakening. In that time, no one had checked on him. Had it not been for the tray left just inside his cell, he would have thought they had abandoned him.

And he had no clue where Allie was.

He had expected she would have been brought into the detention center, but he hadn't seen her since their separation the night before. They must be deliberately keeping them separate. The question was—*why?* He prayed nothing had happened to her.

And he missed her.

It was a strange feeling for him. Never before had a woman really *meant* anything to him. Sure, he'd had female acquaintances. Many fell all over themselves to gain his favor—not to mention his family's money. To their disappointment, he avoided them like the plague. But there had been a couple that had seemed genuinely interested—and sad—that he didn't try for more. The reason he didn't was quite simple—there was no connection.

But Allie was different. There was something between them—a feeling, a spark, a glow. Exactly what, he wasn't sure. But it was there. Maybe it was because they were both vampires, but he didn't think that was it. No, it was something much more basic. Something he wanted to feel for the rest of his life.

As he'd done periodically since awakening, he took the molded plastic cup from the tray, went to the bars, stroked the cup across them, and yelled. But no one came. He knew they were aware of his calling. They had to be. A camera watched, its unblinking gaze aware of his every move. Whatever it was they wanted with him, he wished they would just get on with it.

Resting his head against the bars, he tried to think of some way out of his cell. His grandfather would surely have found a way to get out.

Down the hall a door opened, followed by the sound of footsteps coming his way. "It's nice of them to finally remember me," he mused.

Presently a detail of three uniformed soldiers entered the jail area. They stopped at his cell, unlocked the door, and at gunpoint, cuffed his hands. Sydney was outraged. "Hey, you can't treat a law-abiding citizen like this. I'm a U.S. citizen. I have rights!"

One of the guards pointed a gun at Sydney's head. "Then I suggest you exercise the *right* of silence."

Sydney growled but said nothing more. Arguing would not gain him anything at this point.

They led him out of the detention area and through a confusing maze of corridors, finally stopping before a closed door. The leader of their group stepped forward and knocked. A muffled "Enter" came from the other side.

Sydney was escorted into a conference room and made to sit at the foot of an oblong table. Two men were waiting for him. Sydney racked his brain, trying to remember what his grandfather had hammered into him about their insignia. One was a major, and he was pretty sure the other was a colonel.

The colonel sat opposite him and projected an almost caricature of military perfection. He held himself rigidly erect with shoulders back and chest proudly extended, while his uniform was spotless and had creases so sharp they would cut you. His close-cropped hair was graying at the temples, and he held a thick brown cigar in his mouth. It was unlit and looked to be more for show than to actually smoke. It did look well chewed.

On the colonel's left sat the major. He was a sharp contrast to the colonel—painfully thin with a mop of long dark hair brushed to the side and a uniform that looked like he'd slept in it. But it was his eyes that unnerved Sydney. There was something about him. Almost evil. He shivered.

The colonel chewed on the end of his cigar and narrowed his

eyes. He turned to the major. "He doesn't look dangerous," he stated in a deep voice, one used to command. "Are you sure he's a vampire?"

The major leaned forward. "I assure you Colonel, he is." The man spoke with a vaguely Hungarian accent. "Don't be deceived by his innocent looks. He is a man-killer."

Sydney's eyes went up in surprise. He certainly didn't feel like one.

"And the other, the woman that was with him. She's a vampire too?"

"Precisely."

Sydney tried not to react, but it was clear their secret was out.

The colonel drummed his fingers on the table. "Vampires, witches, werewolves. What next? Unicorns?" He looked straight at Sydney and finally decided to acknowledge him. "I'm Colonel Thomas Beckette, and this is Major Fritz Van Vilkenberg. I hate to be the one to tell you this son, but you've been affected by the God-awful radiation nanos." He paused dramatically. "You've been turned into a vampire, an unfortunate effect of the war. I'm sorry."

Sydney was puzzled. *Radiation nanos?* Whatever that was, it hadn't turned him. He had developed his blood-drinking ways more than a year *before* the attack. He started to set Colonel Beckette straight on the matter. But when he glanced at Major Vilkenberg, the man's eyes seemed to flash. Sydney suddenly couldn't remember what he wanted to say.

"Now I know it's a shock," Colonel Beckette continued. "But we're doing everything within our power to perfect a cure for the radiation nanomachines. Unfortunately, it doesn't look too good at the moment. Even with the Twenty Minute War over, our resources are extremely limited."

Sydney's head was reeling. There was too much information being thrown at him. "Radiation... nanomachines?" asked Sydney.

The colonel leaned forward in a conspiring manner. "This is *very* top secret stuff, son. But you deserve an explanation. So, please keep this to yourself."

Sydney nodded. Like he had anyone to tell.

The colonel leaned back. "You see, in recent years, our enemies have been investing in increasing their firepower. But at the end of the day, there's only so much of the Earth to destroy, and we reached that point back in the sixties. So the president commissioned a secret project with a very unique goal—develop a way to have a war without destroying anything. Only people were to be eliminated. My team has been locked away in absolute secrecy for five years, developing that very thing. Naturally, in any research project, you can't achieve one hundred percent of your objective. But in this one, we came pretty damn close. We developed a nanomachine the size of a virus that would destroy only animals and leave everything else untouched." The colonel leaned forward and said in a patronizing voice, "Humans are animals, you know."

Sydney tried to keep his face impassive. This just seemed so ridiculous. The military couldn't possibly do something so bizarre. But then he thought about SARGE and began to reconsider his position.

The colonel leaned back in his chair and chewed on the end of his cigar. "The nanomachines would be released into the air, where they would take up residence in all animals, remaining dormant until triggered. Once activated, the little buggers would multiply so rapidly, their host would be completely consumed."

Sydney frowned. "Sounds like the perfect weapon. But something went wrong, didn't it?"

The colonel winced. "Well... yes, I guess you could say that. When developing the nanomachines, we ran into a *slight* technical problem. We found they required a huge power surge to get started. Light, electricity, it didn't really matter. It just needed to be something big. We discovered the perfect source was radiation from a nuclear explosion."

Sydney frowned. "Don't tell me. The perfect weapon could only be used during total destruction."

The colonel nodded. "You have a quick mind, son." He paused and sighed. "Unfortunately, we were hacked, and the nature of our work leaked out. But not the technical details. When the Russians found out what we were developing, they made a preemptive strike to keep us from releasing the nanomachines. The poor bastards didn't know that we had an accident in the facility a year ago, releasing the nanomachines into the environment. Why do you think the president has been negotiating so hard to get rid of all nuclear weapons?"

Sydney's eyes went wide in shock. "That's what happened to all the people! They turned into dust."

Beckette nodded. "But what we didn't know was that those who did survive would turn into vampires, werewolves, and witches. A most unexpected effect that didn't show up in any of our testing."

Sydney blinked. Even he knew that was a bit of a stretch. He once again tried to deny the vampire effect, but a look by Major

Van Vilkenberg somehow stopped him. A feeling of unease began to tug at the corners of his mind.

Beckette continued. "The only reason we survived is because we were testing an inoculation against the nanomachines. I'm sure you noticed the smell when you arrived. A slight side effect of the inoculation combining with the radiation. For some reason, it didn't show up in our initial testing on volunteers recruited from various prisons and mental institutions."

Sydney gasped in surprise. *Mental institutions!* That was why Rip survived and had the same terrible smell. He'd been one of the experiment's subjects.

The colonel sighed and shook his head. "More to the point, son. We don't have a cure for your condition, and until we develop one, I must isolate you and those like you. I'll be perfectly frank. We don't have the extra supplies for your... ah... *special* needs."

Sydney started to rise, but the guards on either side of him laid heavy hands on his shoulders. "But colonel! That's a death sentence! Just let us go so we can continue our search."

"I'm sorry, son. Major Van Vilkenberg here is working on a cure as fast as he can. But in all probability, you will die before we perfect it. We'll try to make you as comfortable as we can while you're here."

The colonel waved him away, and the guards grabbed him under his arms.

"What about Allie? The woman I was with?" Sydney asked as they lifted him to his feet.

"She's doing fine, but like you has become a vampire. It's terrible, I admit. We're doing all we can."

"Can I see her?" asked Sydney hopefully.

"No, that's impossible," answered Van Vilkenberg. *"Isn't* it, Colonel Beckette?" He turned to the colonel.

Immediately, a dreamy smile appeared on the colonel's face. But after a moment, he seemed to catch himself. "Why..." Beckette hesitated. "Why, yes. That's right. It's not possible. I'm glad you reminded me, Major."

The colonel nodded to the guards. "Take him away."

Immediately, the guards forced him to stand. Despite his protests, they hauled him out of the conference room and dragged him down the corridor.

Realizing that fighting was useless, he calmly walked with them to the Medical Department.

Inside, they gave Sydney a complete physical, poking into every orifice of his body and taking samples of hair, skin, and blood. Sydney cooperated with them, pretending to be meek and mild, but all the time looking for an escape. Unfortunately, there were always the watchful eyes of one or more armed guards.

When they had finished with him, the same group of three soldiers escorted him back towards the Detention Center. They passed through the main thoroughfare, clogged with the shift change crowd. Sydney briefly considered running, but even if he did, what about Allie? He couldn't leave her behind.

He looked up and noticed a large man coming towards him. His uniform was a bit snugger than the others, like it was a size too small. The man's face was familiar. Where had he recently seen a big, bald man with a strange grin on his face? The man drew no notice from his guards, and they passed without incident. It was only a minute that it came to him.

It was Rip! *What the hell is he doing here?*

Sydney tried to look behind him, but the guards didn't allow it and shoved him forward.

"Hey, that man back there," Sydney said to his guards. "He's a chainsaw killer...."

A soldier punched him in the ribs, "Stow it. Prisoners don't talk."

"I'm not a prisoner. Beckette said I'm just being held in isolation."

The man smirked. "You're being held in a cell. Right? You're in handcuffs, right? You've got guards, right?"

The guard shoved him forward. "Sounds like a prisoner to me."

Sydney couldn't argue.

They put him inside his cell and securely locked it. Once again, he was alone in the detention center.

Sydney sat down on his bunk and tried to take stock of his situation. One, they knew he was a vampire. Two, they didn't care. Three, he was going to die. Pure and simple.

And the explanation of him becoming a vampire *after* the nukes didn't even make sense. How could this colonel believe such a thing?

He remembered the nagging wrongness he'd felt in that room. And every time he'd looked at Van Vilkenberg, his thought processes had been scrambled.

Sydney looked at the floor and inspected his shoes. There could be only one explanation. Major Van Vilkenberg, if he really was a major, had some kind of mental ability. One that could not only control Colonel Beckette, but could also influence Sydney's own thought processes. He sighed. Getting out became more urgent.

And much more difficult.

Maybe he could trick the guard when they brought him his next meal. It was a long shot, but it was all he could think of. If one of them was a female, he might be able to influence her with his mental ability. He didn't have long to wait.

Shortly, he heard the center's door and then approaching footsteps. Sydney leaped onto his bunk and covered his head with his blanket, thinking if he pretended to be sick, they might come close enough for him to overpower them. Using his vampire strength, he was sure he could handle a single guard.

For good measure, he started moaning. "Ohhhh…"

He heard the door unlock and steps approaching his bunk. "Ohhhh…"

He waited until he was sure whoever was standing right over him. He threw back the blanket and lunged—

Only to freeze in place, finding his eyes locked with those of the deathly thin Major Van Vilkenberg.

He smiled. "Now Sydney. We can't have you hurting me, now can we?"

Sydney found himself nodding slowly in agreement.

"Sit up." commanded Van Vilkenberg.

Sydney did, but he couldn't understand why. *What was Van Vilkenberg doing to him?*

Van Vilkenberg produced a plastic cup filled with a red liquid. "I brought you something," he said, waving the cup beneath Sydney's nose. He knew exactly what it was, and his body was craving it.

"Take it," ordered Van Vilkenberg.

Robot-like, Sydney took the cup and held it with both hands.

"You don't know who I am, do you?"

Sydney slowly shook his head.

"Well, let me refresh your memory. I met you in a dark alley a year or so ago. You were quite drunk then, and your blood was so full of alcohol, I had to stagger away."

Sydney's eyes widened. "You!"

Van Vilkenberg smiled. "Ah, I see you remember now. Yes, I'm the one. That's why I have control over you. I made you a vampire, and therefore, I am your master."

"Yes," Sydney agreed. The words came out all by themselves.

He railed in his own mind, trying to break free. But he couldn't.

Van Vilkenberg continued. "I'm sorry it took me so long to get back to you. I usually kill my victims to cut down on competition, but in your case, I became so intoxicated, I was lucky to make it back to my coffin before dawn. As it was, I had a hell of a hangover the next evening. After that, you sort of slipped my mind. You didn't make a big fuss and draw attention to yourself like a lot of others do. But don't worry." He patted Sydney on the shoulder. "We're going to fix all that right now. In the cup is a specially prepared solution of blood. Unfortunately for you, it contains a potent poison which will kill you in a matter of seconds." He grinned. "It will be your last drink."

The old vampire leaned back and gave an evil laugh that any villain would have been proud of. Sydney was convinced the man had practiced. Talk about being melodramatic.

"'Why now?' You ask," said Van Vilkenberg, obviously enjoying every minute. "Because I fear you may, although it is a remote possibility, alert someone to my true nature. I do control Colonel Beckette, but I cannot control the entire base." He grinned. "And so now, you drink."

Sydney struggled but could not stop the cup's approach to his lips.

Just then, a door opened in the distance, and heavy footsteps came down the hall. Someone was entering the cell block.

Sydney felt the compulsion ease. Van Vilkenberg's eyes narrowed, clearly miffed at the interruption.

Presently, a lone uniformed woman came to stand in front of Sydney's cell carrying a food tray. Her head was bent down as she fumbled with the cell door.

Van Vilkenberg frowned. "I gave strict orders that I was not to be bothered while examining the patient. Now leave, Private."

The woman ignored the order and stepped into the cell.

"I said to leave!"

As the major's attention was diverted, Sydney felt the mental restraint loosen. He struggled to regain his will, and—

Broke free!

Van Vilkenberg wheeled on Sydney with narrowed eyes and exposed teeth. The woman behind him struck him hard on the head with the tray. Van Vilkenberg collapsed.

"Thanks, lady. He was going to kill me."

"How about a kiss, then?"

Sydney immediately recognized the voice and looked closer at his savior. True, the face had makeup applied, giving the impression of living eyes, mouth, and nose, plus the hair was a heavily styled wig. But there was no missing her true identity.

"SARGE!" exclaimed Sydney. "Is that you?"

"Sure is," said the robot. She put a finger to her cheek and cocked her head to one side. "This human female disguise worked better than I thought. Now, how about that kiss?"

Sydney swallowed. "Later... uh... We have to get out of here!"

SARGE stepped into the doorway. "You don't get out until I get my kiss."

"But SARGE...."

The robot leaned forward expectantly, and with a single finger, patted her painted-on lips.

He took a step back. "We should leave as quickly as we can. They've got to have seen us on the cameras."

SARGE shook her head. "Van Vilkenberg disabled them." She took a step closer. "Now for my kiss."

He sighed. *Will these humiliations never end!* "Oh, all right."

He stepped forward and pressed his lips to her painted-on mouth. It was as cold as dry ice.

She put her arms around him and hugged him close, sending frigid shivers down his spine. "See, that wasn't so bad. I think you're warming up to me."

"Unfortunately, you're not." He stepped back and looked at her more closely. "While I like your disguise, you can easily tell you're not human. How did you pull this off?" He rubbed his lips, trying to get warmth back into them.

"Easy." She touched her ample chest. "With babies like these, their eyes never go any higher."

Sydney blinked at her. He decided he wasn't going to approach that one.

"Where's Allie?"

"She's being held in the female compound. Just a couple doors over."

Sydney nodded. "So, what's the plan? What do we do next?"

SARGE shrugged. "Hell if I know. It took everything I had to get in here. Remember, I'm only a robot. You're lucky I saw this in a movie once."

Sydney thought for a moment. He bent over the unconscious major. "Here, help me undress him. I can use his clothes as a disguise."

Hurriedly—lest Van Vilkenberg awaken and use his mind control again—they undressed him and left him bound on Sydney's bunk. They covered him with a blanket in hopes that anyone checking on him would assume he was Sydney.

At the door leading out, SARGE whispered a word of advice, "No matter what happens, act important. If you talk loud enough and forceful enough, these flyboys won't pay you an ounce of attention."

That jogged Sydney's memory. "Hey, I thought you were Army. How come you're helping us instead of them?"

SARGE pulled back in disgust. "Are you kidding? Of course, I wouldn't help them. I'm a *Marine*. *Big* difference."

Sydney blinked. "Oh."

They went out the door leading out, but Sydney hesitated. SARGE was right. He needed to look and act important. His grandfather said that if you wanted to do something and weren't sure how to, think of someone who did it and imitate them. Who would that be?

Of course. His grandfather.

"Because I'm a Carrington," his grandfather had explained when a young Sydney had asked him about it. "And Carringtons command respect. We're the most important people on Earth."

Remembering those words, Sydney puffed up his chest and stepped out like he owned the world.

A short walk down the hall brought them to another Detention Area. A guard was stationed behind a small desk just inside the door. He looked up at their entry, and eyeing the major bars on the uniform, stood to salute.

Sydney did his best to look bored as he returned it.

"We're here to pick up a prisoner," announced SARGE.

"Yes, sir... uh... mam." The guard seemed puzzled. "May I see your papers, please?"

SARGE turned to Sydney, "The papers, Major?"

Sydney stammered, "The papers? Ah... yes, the papers." He didn't know what to do. The words 'act important' echoed in his mind. What would Grandfather do?

"Son, where are you from?" asked Sydney.

The man blinked. "Foss, Wyoming, sir."

"No kidding. I have a brother in Wyoming," Sydney lied.

"Really, sir?"

Sydney put his arm around the guard and took him to one side. "Listen, son. I seem to have forgotten my papers. But don't you worry, this little jaunt is kind of unofficial. We'll have them back in just a few minutes. You see, we need some dancers down in the CO club. Surely you understand."

The soldier grinned. "Yes sir, I understand." He opened the door and pressed a key into Sydney's hand. "Go right on in, sir."

"Thanks, son. What's your name?"

"Michaels, sir."

"I'll remember that. You show real promise, son. We'll see about promoting you."

They entered the cell area and looked in each of them. A petite red-headed woman with painfully short hair sat in one of the cells. She rose as they entered and came to the bars of her door. She pointed to the cell on the other side. "You might want to check on her. She hasn't moved in the last hour. I think she's bad sick. I'm not even sure she's breathing."

Sydney gasped. He turned to find Allie lying on her bunk with her eyes closed.

And she wasn't moving.

CHAPTER TWENTY-TWO

Silver Bracelet

Allie

ALLIE AWOKE THAT EVENING wondering where she was. She stared up in confusion at the underside of an unfamiliar bed. It definitely wasn't the one in her tiny apartment. But as her battered brain gradually began to work, the events of the last few days came flooding back. She closed her eyes, wishing it all away. But when she opened them again, it was the same unfamiliar mattress. She was still in some secret underground army base, in a jail cell, and underneath her bunk.

And no Sydney.

She scooted out and slowly stood, running a hand through her mussed hair. What she would give for a cup of coffee. And maybe a hairbrush.

Medorah saw her get up and came to lean against the bars of her cell. "Hey, you slept forever. You all right?"

Allie shrugged. "Yeah. Just part of being a vampire. You know, the whole sleep through the day thing."

Medorah nodded but seemed distracted. Not the smiling, bubbly person she had encountered before sleeping.

"How about you?" Allie asked. "Everything OK?"

Medorah looked at her strangely and then looked down. "I'm not sure."

"Did they hurt you?"

Medorah shook her head. "No, I don't think so. I just feel like crying all the time. And I don't know why." She waved a hand at her surroundings. "Probably just the ambiance of the place. It is a little depressing."

Allie went to the tray sitting on the floor in front of her door and looked at the contents. She scrunched up her nose. There was what looked to be some dried-out meatloaf and a congealed mess that had started out as mashed potatoes. These were matched with a rock disguised as a roll and a collection of green spheres and orange squares, which at one time must have been peas and carrots.

"This is breakfast?"

Medorah snorted. "The food's horrible. But it will keep the hunger away."

Allie picked it up and sat on her bunk with the tray on her lap. While it may satisfy one hunger, there was another that was starting to make itself known. She was going to have to have some blood soon.

Allie steeled herself and dug in, finding herself more hungry than she thought.

She wanted to dive into why Medorah denied she had a husband, but decided to ease into it and start with something light. "So what happened today? Are they letting you out?"

Medorah shook her head. "No, I had someone visit me today. It was just after you went to sleep."

"Who?" Allie shoved in a bite, chewed once, and stopped. It was so bland that it was almost painful. She wondered how they had managed to completely drain any flavor out of it. She grimaced and forced herself to chew. While her taste buds were screaming in agony, her stomach seemed to be quite pleased with the new addition. She took another bite.

Medorah pointed towards the door of their detention center. "That's just it. I remember someone coming in and standing in front of my cell door. I remember him saying something. Me standing. And then..." She shrugged and looked puzzled. "I found myself sitting on my bunk again. And no one was there. I've been wondering if it was a dream. I've had this feeling of dread ever since that happened."

Medorah leaned on the bars gripping them tightly. She looked tense and would periodically run a hand through her short hair. She was clearly unsettled. Allie's eyes were drawn to the silver bracelet on Medorah's wrist. That jewelry really had to be the ugliest piece of silver on the planet.

Allie took a few more bites of her food before her taste buds mutinied and overrode her stomach. She took her tray back over to the cell door and set it to one side. As she was bending over, her protection necklace slipped out from her shirt and dangled down. She grasped the cool metal in her hand and held it for a moment. It reminded her of Sydney. She tucked it back in her shirt, fearing one of the guards might see it and take it. It supposedly had protection magic in it. She smiled. Probably some snake oil too. She had a sudden thought and turned to Medorah. "Since you're a witch, do you have magic powers?"

Medorah nodded. "Normally yes, although I can only influence natural things." She spread her hands and indicated their surroundings. "Not much natural around here." She looked down. "But despite that, my magic has left me. I'm not sure what's gone wrong with it. I can sense it's there but just can't use it."

Allie sighed. "So much for an easy way out." She turned to the other woman. "I can't stay here any longer. If I don't get some blood soon, I will pass out and die. Want to break out together?"

Medorah looked at her strangely. "Why would I want to escape? There's nothing out there. I'm safe and protected here."

Allie gave her a puzzled look. "What about your husband? He's looking for you."

Medorah did her stare-pause again. "I didn't marry. I've been single all my life. There was this guy I was serious with but..." She trailed off and got a far-off look. "Nothing happened."

Allie became even more convinced that something had happened to her friend. "Then if you're not married, why are you wearing a wedding band."

Medorah looked annoyed. "I told you I don't have a husband." She stated emphatically. Her voice was almost shaking. And then she saw the tear slip down her friend's face again.

She could only draw one conclusion. Someone had been playing with the witch's mind, and while her brain might not remember her husband, her heart did.

Allie eyed the bracelet. It was just so damn repulsive. "Where did you get the bracelet?" she asked.

Medorah looked at her wrists. "What bracelet? I'm not wearing anything."

Allie pointed. "The silver one on your left wrist."

Medorah looked down. "They took all my stuff when I was checked in. Besides, I wouldn't dare wear silver. Silver is a magic metal and can affect me."

Allie shook her head. "It's right *there*. On your left wrist. Some kind of wide silver thing."

Medorah scowled. "Quit joking. It's not funny. I'm not wearing anything. First, you say I have a werewolf for a husband, and now I'm wearing a bracelet that isn't there. I think you've got some mental problem going on. You're delusional."

Allie blinked at her in surprise. There was definitely something strange going on here. She thought for a moment. Was there anything that Medorah had told her she could use to convince her friend? She looked up. "Do you have a cat?"

Medorah pursed her lips. "Of course I do. I told you that yesterday."

Allie smiled. "Where did he get his name?"

"Well, it was..." And then she paused. It was as if her brain was trying to access a piece of information but was being blocked. "It was..." Medorah looked up, clearly puzzled. "Someone."

Allie nodded toward her. "Look at the ring on your left hand. Where did it come from?"

Medorah slowly brought up her hand and stared at her fingers. She turned her hand over, inspecting it closely. She gingerly touched the ring. "I don't know," she said softly.

"What do you feel when you touch it?"

Medorah hesitated. "Warmth. Well-being." She looked up clearly puzzled. "I remember blessing them when someone and I..." She did the stare-pause again.

Allie pressed on. "You're a witch, so what would it feel like if someone had messed with your memory."

"Well, I wouldn't be able to recall certain things, or would recall them differently. I might even become angry for having the missing info pointed out. But I would still feel the attached emotions..." Her voice faded as she studied the ring.

She looked up, wearing a grim expression. "If someone hid a memory charm on me somewhere, that could cause it." She looked up. "But why would someone want to do that?"

Allie shrugged. "You're a witch, aren't you? I bet you could do some damage if you had your powers."

Medorah shrugged. "Not really. I can only affect things of nature. Like plant or animal, earth or sky, bindings or cleavings. Things like that. It's not like I can radically change things."

"So you can't unlock doors?"

Medorah smiled mischievously. "Actually, I can."

The vampire's eyes went wide.

Then Medorah continued. "With a key."

Allie's shoulders slumped.

Medorah looked away. "Magic is weird like that. Part of being a witch is knowing what will work and what won't."

Allie leaned her forehead against the bars. It seemed so hopeless. If she could reach her new friend, perhaps she could help her. So close and yet so far. As she leaned forward, she felt her protection amulet shift inside her shirt. Allie's eyes went wide. Could it work? Magician Rtyus had claimed it would.

She took off the necklace. She held it up for Medorah to see. "What about this?"

Her friend squinted in her direction. "I can tell it's got magic in it, but that's all. Where did you get it? The magic looks so... pure."

"I got it from a fairy magician as a reward for helping a unicorn."

Medorah gave her a funny look. "Are you serious? You really get around."

Allie leaned through the bars and tossed the necklace toward Medorah. It arched through the air to land in front of the witch's cell. She eyed it suspiciously. "It's silver. Witches should never touch silver since it is a magic metal. No telling what it could do."

"Please! It will either help you or do nothing at all. The magician who gave it to me said he was the best in the kingdom."

The witch shook her head. "I don't know."

"Please, Medorah. Trust me on this."

Her friend looked at it a moment, shrugged, and then reached through the bars to retrieve it. She stood and held it up. "It's pretty. Oh, and look, the charm looks broken. Like it has been split in two. It's pretty attractive."

Allie nodded. "My friend has the other half. Now slip it over your head."

Medorah nodded. "I think it's cute. I bet everyone will want one of these. It might start a fad."

The witch did as Allie asked, but nothing seemed to happen.

"Do you feel anything different?" Allie asked.

Medorah shook her head.

"I guess we were duped after all." Allie sighed. She looked up forlornly. "I was hoping it would help. It's just that it's so sad to see you not remembering your husband. Both of you looked so happy together in that picture he showed us."

Medorah frowned. "I told you I don't have a...."

Suddenly the necklace took up a bright blue glow, just as the ugly silver bracelet began an answering glow in deep red. Medorah's eyes went wide. "What's going on?"

The glow intensified, and Medorah's knees seemed to give out on her. She dropped to the floor. She held up the hand with the ugly bracelet, and suddenly, it snapped in two and fell off. The glow instantly disappeared.

Medorah's eyes went wide. She looked up at Allie in shock. "My husband, Quick! The love of my life. How could I have forgotten him?" She looked at Allie in awe. "You gave me my memory back. I... I can't thank you enough." Medorah quickly rose and kicked the remains of the ugly bracelet into the corner.

Grinning, she turned to face Allie and tossed the protection necklace back to her. "What say you and I get out of this place? My man is waiting for me. Besides, there is one thing you never do."

Allie returned the grin. "And what's that?"

"You never, ever, piss off a witch."

CHAPTER TWENTY-THREE

Breakout

Sydney

SYDNEY GASPED AT THE sight of Allie on her bunk, unmoving and with her eyes closed. She looked unconscious. He thought of the poison blood Van Vilkenberg had tried to give him. *Oh please, no.*

He ran to the bars of Allie's cell and looked inside. She lay stretched out on her bunk with the remains of her last meal, sitting on a metal tray just beside her.

The woman behind him spoke. "She said she wasn't feeling well and laid down. I've been calling for help, but no one's come to check on her."

In near panic, he fumbled with the keys, dropping them

254

twice in his hurry. He threw open the door and stepped inside—

When the lights went out.

Darkness enveloped him so thoroughly that even his vampire eyes couldn't penetrate it. It was as if every photon of light had been swallowed up. Suddenly he was struck hard on the head.

For a moment, that total darkness had stars.

He staggered and collapsed.

"Don't, Allie!" yelled SARGE. "It's Sydney!"

The lights came back on to find Sydney sprawled on the floor. He looked up as Allie knelt beside him. She was holding the metal tray with a suspicious skull-sized dent. "I'm sorry," she said. "We're trying to escape, and I thought you were one of the guards."

"See if I ever rescue you again," he mumbled in a daze, rubbing his head.

"You know this guy?" asked the redhead.

Allie helped an unsteady Sydney stand. "He's the friend I was telling you about. Sydney's a vampire too." She nodded toward the robot. "And that's SARGE. She's been following Sydney since we met. She's..."

The redhead finished for her. "Not alive."

Allie nodded. "She's a robot."

SARGE thumped her chest with a fist. "I'm the leanest, meanest, fight'n'est sex machine you've ever seen."

The redhead blinked at her. "I think I dreamed about you."

SARGE seemed to swell with pride. "I don't mind being your erotic dream partner."

"It was a nightmare."

Sydney found his balance, and Allie released him. He probed his head, checking for blood. His vampire healing ability sure was nice. "How did you make the lights go out?"

"I did it," said the redhead. "A simple darkness spell."

Allie grabbed up the keys Sydney had dropped and went to the redhead's cell. "Medorah is Quick's missing wife, the real witch."

"That helicopter pilot's wife?" Sydney asked in disbelief.

Allie nodded as she unlocked Medorah's cell. "We'd better hurry, or our friend outside will become suspicious."

SARGE pounded a fist into her palm. "So we're going to have to fight our way out. I'm ready. Bring it on."

Sydney wasn't too sure SARGE would be much use if it came to that. But he had a better idea. He quickly explained it to the others. The women looked at each other and then nodded in agreement. They quickly took their positions.

SARGE stood by the entrance with a hand on the doorknob.

"Everybody ready?" asked Sydney.

Allie blushed but nodded.

"Let's do it!" exclaimed Medorah, a grin on her face.

Sydney put an arm around each women's waist and strolled toward the door. They laughed as they exited, with SARGE bringing up the rear. Sydney winked at the guard as they left, "I'll be back in a couple of hours."

The guard saluted. "Hope you get lucky tonight, sir!"

Sydney looked back. "I do too, son!"

It only took a few turns to put them out of sight and in an empty corridor. But Sydney had no idea where they were or where to go. He turned to SARGE. "You found your way in without a problem. Any idea how we get out?"

"Not me. I just wandered around until I found a door and then used my top-secret clearance to get in."

Sydney was puzzled. "You have a clearance?"

SARGE looked indignant. "Of course. It cleared me after I broke the lock."

Medorah grinned. "Way to go, girl. I think we're going to get along just fine." She held up her fist, and the delighted robot gently bumped hers against it.

Sydney shook his head. "Please don't encourage her."

"Someone's coming," whispered Allie.

They paused at an intersection and listened. To their left came the lockstep sound of boots echoing up the corridor. Sydney peeked around the corner and saw a group of soldiers approaching. And they were armed. Sydney wasn't sure if they would be able to use the same bluff on these people. He needed something different.

They retreated and hurriedly ducked down a side corridor only to find it a dead end. He could hear the soldiers approaching. He opened a door to find a tiny utility closet with lots of mops and a bucket, but it was too small for all of them. And they couldn't stay in the corridor since their uniforms were a dead give-away.

Thinking quickly, he shoved the two women inside and asked Medorah if she could dim the lights, but not extinguish them. She nodded, and he shut the door. A heartbeat later, the surrounding area grew dimmer.

He then pulled SARGE toward him with her back to the intersection. Her clothes would get her past, but a closer inspection by those less distracted would reveal her robot features. Sydney pulled her tightly toward him. He could feel the cold radiating from her metal body.

She put her arms over his shoulders and brought her face close. "I think I might like this," she said, trying her best to plaster her body against his.

Sydney gritted his teeth and fought the urge to jerk away.

"Who's down there?" came a commanding shout. "Identify yourself."

Sydney looked around SARGE to see five men pointing rifles down the corridor. He leaned out further to make sure they could see his bars. "We're just having a discussion, Lieutenant. A *private* discussion." Sydney tried to interject as much irritation into his voice as he could. "Is there a problem?"

Sydney's eyes went wide as the robot snaked her hands down to his butt and pulled him tight against her. He tugged unsuccessfully at her hand to free himself.

The lieutenant snapped to attention. "No, sir. There's been an arms breach, and we're trying to lock everything down. You'll need to go to your station, sir."

Sydney tried to smile confidently. "I will, Lieutenant. We're almost finished. We'll be heading out shortly."

His eyes went even larger as SARGE gripped him tighter. "You've got a cute butt," she whispered.

The lieutenant blinked in confusion. "Sir..."

Sydney leaned further around SARGE, but the robot wouldn't lessen her grip on him.

"*Is there a problem, Lieutenant?*" Sydney used his most commanding voice.

The lieutenant immediately came to attention. "No, sir."

"Good. Then be about your business. This is an *important* discussion."

"Yes, sir." The man saluted and turned away. Sydney awkwardly returned it.

As soon as they were out of sight, he tried to push SARGE away, but she wouldn't budge. It was like shoving against a brick wall.

"Let go."

Her reply was filled with laughter. "Why should I? You've got my all-American made heart really going."

"You don't have a heart."

"I do so. Want to see it?"

Sydney just blinked at her.

"Now, how about a kiss...?"

The door they stood beside opened a crack, and Allie whispered, "SARGE! Leave Sydney alone."

SARGE's shoulders drooped, and she relaxed her grip. "All right."

The robot allowed him to move away from the door. Allie and Medorah slipped out to join them.

Allie stood in front of SARGE, hands on her hips and wearing a very disappointed look. "We had an agreement," she said, leaning towards the robot. "Remember?"

SARGE nodded and took a step back. "I'm sorry. You can't blame a girl for trying." She looked dejected.

Medorah gave Sydney a questioning look, but he just shrugged. *The two had an agreement?* An agreement concerning him? He was going to have to pay more attention to their conversations.

He led them back out into the corridor. They moved briskly down it and thankfully didn't encounter anyone else. Sydney paused in front of a door with a big sign on it. SECURE AREA— AUTHORIZED PERSONNEL ONLY. He couldn't resist and opened the door a crack to peek inside.

Although dark, his vampire eyes quickly adjusted. He could make out humvees, trucks, a mortar launcher, a tank....

It was the motor pool, their ticket out! He led them inside.

"Spread out everyone," Sydney said. "See if we can start any of them."

Sydney went to a humvee but saw that it had no key. He tried another with the same results. He glanced around. The keys had to be somewhere close.

"How about this one?" asked SARGE. She stood atop what appeared to be the very tank that had picked them up. Surprisingly, the gunner's hatch was open.

"How did you get in?" He couldn't imagine someone just leaving a tank unlocked.

SARGE dangled a broken padlock from her fingers. "I sort of broke it."

Sydney blinked. "You mean you're strong enough to break a padlock? And you were hugging my butt?"

SARGE looked indignant. "I wouldn't hurt you. I have like a thousand safeguards built into me to prevent me from harming anyone."

Sydney climbed up on top with SARGE. "Wait. You're a military robot, and you can't harm a human?"

SARGE looked nervous. "That's classified."

As the other two joined him, he studied the three hatches—

one under the cannon and two on top of the turret. From what little he knew of tanks, SARGE had opened the loaders hatch. Which meant the driver's was up front.

Just then, the alarm went off. A very loud one.

Sydney cursed. "Everyone get inside!"

SARGE shook her head. "It's a small space in there. Whoever is going to drive should go first and move to the driver seat." Sydney looked at his two companions, and they both shook their heads. No help there.

Sydney looked to SARGE. "How about you? Can you drive it?"

SARGE tapped her head. "I know everything about these babies."

"Good, then you drive."

"Hell no, I won't. I'm a soldier, not a bus driver."

"But you're the only one that knows how."

"I never said I could drive an Abrams tank."

Sydney waved his arms in frustration. "But you just said you know everything about them!"

"I do! But I'm not certified to drive one. They tried me in a simulator one time, and let's just say it didn't go so well."

"Enough!" Allie yelled. "SARGE, you go first. Both of you get to the front and figure this out. We're out of time!"

SARGE rubbed her hands together. "Hot damn! We'll have to share the driver's seat. It will be tight, but I think we can do it." She leaned closer. "You *really* have a cute butt."

Sydney groaned. It looked like he was elected. "Remember, I'm going to be driving this thing. I don't need any distractions."

"Yes, sir!" said SARGE, literally ripping off her clothes and wig.

"What are you doing that for?" asked Sydney.

"I've trying to make myself as small as possible by removing all unnecessary gear." She stepped closer. "You should do the same."

Sydney looked at her in disbelief.

Allie shoved him in the shoulder. "Would you two knock it off. We have to get out of here."

SARGE climbed in first, with Sydney on her heels. They made their way to the front and crawled through a tiny door to the reclining driver's seat while the two women came in behind them. Allie closed the hatch with a final thud.

SARGE adjusted the driver's seat as far back as she could, but it couldn't move that much. When Sydney hesitated, she patted her lap. "Come here, big boy. I think I'm going to like this."

"SARGE!" Allie shouted. "Our agreement!"

The robot's shoulders drooped. "Killjoy," she muttered.

"I heard that!" yelled Allie. "Why don't you calm yourself down a little so Sydney can work!"

Throwing caution to the wind, he slid in on top of SARGE. There was barely enough room to breathe, let alone drive. And the robot's hard curves didn't make for a very comfortable seat. He had two steel breasts pressing into his back.

SARGE shoved a helmet into his hands. "You better put this on. You'll need it to talk." She yelled to the others. "You two back there, find your helmets and put them on. Remember, safety first!"

As Sydney was trying to get his headgear in place, he heard a clang and movement in the compartment behind him. As he was fastening his chin strap, he glanced over the array of instruments in front of him. He had no idea what the collection of gauges and switches did. In front was a square column coming from the floor, which must be how you steer. It kind of reminded him of a motor scooter. He began to doubt the wisdom of their getaway vehicle selection.

Sydney heard someone cursing behind him. It was Medorah, and he was impressed. She had quite the talent for it.

With SARGE's help, he finally managed to get his helmet positioned and plugged in. But looking over the controls, he couldn't see how to start the engine.

"Where's the ignition switch?" he asked, exasperated. "I don't see a key."

SARGE pointed to a big red button. "It doesn't have one. Would you want to be fumbling with your keys while under enemy fire?" He guessed he wouldn't.

Feeling foolish, Sydney tried it. A low-level vibration filled the tank, but surprisingly there was little noise.

A moment later, he heard Allie through his helmet's earphones. "We've got company."

While Sydney watched the gauges through the warmup cycle, SARGE cautioned him. "Remember to take it easy with this thing," she said. "It's a turbo-diesel, so it's got some oomph."

Sydney snorted. "It must weigh a thousand tons. There is no way it can move that fast."

He grabbed the control handles and twisted the throttle hard. The tank hesitated a heartbeat, and then like a rocket, shot ahead, slamming him back into his seat. They clipped a humvee and crashed into a wall before Sydney could release the controls.

"Told you," SARGE said smugly. "Just like me, this is a top-of-the-line military vehicle." Then her voice softened. "Although I cost a little more."

"Hey!" Allie's voice came through the headset. "The exit's behind us!"

"Right." Sydney twisted the controls and put the tank into reverse while trying to turn. He backed *over* the humvee this time, crushing it.

"I bet you're hell on the expressway," said SARGE admiringly.

Sydney ignored the robot and tried turning the tank around. He slammed into both corridor walls eight times during the maneuver, managing to accidentally damage the rest of the vehicles in the motor pool. He never was good at three-point road turns.

"Hey! Take it easy," complained Medorah. "This thing may be armored, but my insides *aren't!*"

"To your right, Sydney," called Allie. The exit door is there.

Sydney began to figure out the tank's controls and aimed it toward the exit. They rolled up a slight incline, and without pausing, crashed through another door to emerge into the night.

"We're being followed," announced Allie. "And they're gaining on us."

"What are they driving?" asked Sydney.

"Don't ask," said SARGE.

Allie hesitated. "I'm not sure. But it's got a big cannon on it."

Medorah piped in. "It's a mortar launcher. A big one."

SARGE sighed. "I told you not to ask."

"Well, do something," yelled Sydney in frustration as he fought with the controls and crashed through a chain-link fence. "Do I have to do *everything?*"

He could hear the women talking to each other behind him. A whine filled the tank as the turret began to turn. He heard more discussion. Then there was a hum and then a solid thump.

"FIRE IN THE HOLE!" Medorah shouted.

Allie commented back. "I don't think you say that."

Medorah sounded puzzled. "Then what do you say?"

"Hell if I know. Just shoot the damn thing."

There was a loud explosion, and the tank rocked back on its suspension.

"Oh wow!" shouted Medorah. "I want to do that again! That was better than Tuesday nights."

"What's Tuesday nights?" Allie asked, clearly puzzled.

"It's when Quick and I spend some... ah... *private time* together."

"OK... explain it to me later. Why don't you go ahead and fire another," Allie said.

There was the sound of something sliding into place and then another explosion.

"I like this!" exclaimed Medorah. "Can I do it again?"

"That's enough for now. We knocked down both sides of the exit tunnel. That will make it more difficult for them."

"Ahhh..." said a disappointed Medorah. "That was fun."

Sydney was a little concerned that their friend had developed an addiction.

They climbed over a pile of debris and onto a road. "Which way?" Sydney asked in panic.

"South," called Medorah. "My husband is in that direction."

Sydney turned the tank onto the lane and turned in that direction. He gunned it.

"Damn," Allie said through the earphones a moment later. "They're still following us."

"A radio!" exclaimed Medorah. "I found a radio. I'll call Quick."

"We're in danger of our lives, and she wants to call her husband," mused SARGE.

"Quick!" Medorah yelled into the mike. "Your wife needs help. I know you're out there. We're just south of the Jennette Military Research Facility. And please hurry." Her voice switched to a deeper, sultry tone. "I've still got that nightgown. We'll pretend it's Tuesday night!"

Sydney's face turned bright red.

With a shake of his head, he focused on the road and pushed it to full throttle. Steering was difficult. He was trying to keep the tank on the road, but with all the debris, it was sometimes hard to tell which was which.

Medorah fired another round at their pursuers. "Damn! I'm out of shells, and they're still coming."

"Oh no," Allie said. "I've been eavesdropping on their transmissions, and I just figured out why they're chasing us." She paused to listen to the radio again. "They think we stole a nuclear device!"

"WHAT!" said Sydney.

"That's right. The alarm went out because they noticed a nuke missing, *not* because we escaped. We just happened to leave at the same time. They have orders to destroy us no matter what the cost!"

"Oh, that's just great!" moaned Sydney. "Who the hell would want to steal a nuclear device now? Everything's already been nuked."

Suddenly, a wind stirred in front of the tank, and a helicopter dropped out of nowhere, landing just a few yards ahead. Recognizing the craft, Sydney quickly turned the tank broadside to shield the aircraft.

"Let me out!" yelled Medorah. "It's Quick!"

She fumbled with the latch, and suddenly it slammed open. Her headgear went flying as a hairy hand descended and jerked her out. Sydney strained to see behind him and up through the hatch.

"Hi, honey," the werewolf said as he hugged her. "I missed you."

"And I missed you too, woofie, woofie." Medorah gave him a peck on his furry cheek.

Quick yelled down. "I'm going to get you all out of here, but I can only take two at a time. Medorah's going to be in the first run. Who's next?"

Sydney's Carrington blood refused to see a woman stay in harm's way. "Take Allie. SARGE and I will continue to run. But hurry."

Before she could protest, Quick jerked Allie out too. "Catch you in a few minutes." He slammed the hatch shut.

Sydney waited until the helicopter took off before pulling away. A mortar round landed beside the tank, and shrapnel splattered its side. Sydney floored it, running a zigzag course to prevent being hit.

Finally, he recognized where he was and turned down towards a freeway ramp choked with burned-out vehicles. He skirted the wreckage, crushing a guardrail and barely making it onto what was left of an interstate. Sydney opened her up all the way, hoping to get on the other side of an overpass just ahead. If he could make it, then the mortar launcher wouldn't be able to get a clear shot at him. He didn't know how far a lead he had, but he was sure it wasn't much.

Another mortar round landed just in front of them.

Definitely not far enough. He prayed Quick hurried.

Hardly believing his luck, Sydney dodged an upside-down SUV and started up the overpass. Maybe they were going to make it after all. They crested the top of the overpass...

And discovered the bridge had collapsed.

Sydney tried to stop but reacted too late. The tank went over the edge.

Sydney and SARGE both screamed as they fell thirty feet to the hard concrete beneath. The tank hit hard, smashing the front and knocking the treads off. It rocked to its side and lay smoking.

Sydney was momentarily dazed. SARGE shoved him to the side, opened the hatch, and pushed him out. The robot then threw Sydney over her shoulder and trotted away.

Gradually, the world stopped spinning, and Sydney realized he was once again riding backward and getting motion sickness. This was worse than falling *down* all the time!

"SARGE!" Sydney yelled. "Put me down!" He hadn't realized the robot was so strong.

"Gladly. You must weigh a ton!" The robot set him on his feet. "Have you considered going on a diet? It's never too late to start a healthy lifestyle."

The mortar launcher had positioned itself on what was left of the overpass. Unfortunately, there was no cover. They both turned and ran the other way.

"I don't think we're going to make it this time," said SARGE.

"What makes you say that!" asked Sydney breathlessly.

SARGE pointed a thumb behind them.

Sydney risked a look back. The mortar launcher had found them and was turning their way. He briefly wondered if vampires could be exploded. He imagined they could.

Amazingly, a helicopter dropped out of nowhere and landed five feet in front of them. Without hesitation, Sydney scrambled inside, and Quick took off with the robot just hanging on to the landing gear. They got no higher than fifteen feet when a mortar round exploded where they had just been. SARGE pulled herself in and shut the hatch. Quick angled off to the west.

Sydney climbed into the copilot seat and buckled up. He breathed a sigh of relief. "I'm glad that's over." He wiped the sweat off his forehead. "I didn't think we'd get away."

A cockpit alarm sounded, and one of Quick's displays started beeping loudly. The werewolf immediately toggled a switch and maneuvered sharply to the left. Not even a heartbeat later, a missile exploded in mid-air beside them.

"Who said it was over?" shouted Quick. "We've got company!"

Sydney looked behind him through a small window and saw another military helicopter of a different design in pursuit. "It's right behind us," he exclaimed.

"That's a modified air-to-air attack helicopter. I bet it's got heat seekers!" His lips pulled back into an evil grin. "This is going to be a *real* challenge." He hooted. "Come on, *Demoness!* Don't let me down!"

Quick began evasive maneuvers, and Sydney kept a constant vigil out the window. The ground's few night-time features were a blur beneath them. *Demoness* was slightly faster than the other helicopter and was slowly widening their lead. But if the other got a fix, they were doomed.

An alarm went off. Quick dropped into a steep dive, building speed. "Here it comes!"

Quick turned the craft hard to the left. The missile exploded right beside them. Quick jerked on the controls, putting the craft through a series of sharp turns—back and forth, up and down—finally going into a dive. To someone outside, it would look like Quick was fighting with the controls.

"Let's see how greedy you are," muttered Quick, eyes glued to his instruments.

The other craft fell for the ruse and came barreling in for the kill. At the last moment, Quick pulled up, did an impossible turn, and fired a missile, catching their pursuers off guard.

They exploded in mid-air…

But not before firing their own missile.

The explosion caught the tail of their craft. This time Quick fought the controls for real. They were falling fast towards an area that was without feature and totally black. It took Sydney a moment to recognize it was Lake Halawalnai. He hadn't realized they had come this far west. This area was well within a national preserve and was heavily forested.

Quick was managing to slow their descent, but it didn't look like he could pull it out. "Hold on to your hats! I'm going to have to ditch her!"

Sydney put his head between his legs and his arms over his head. With his voice quivering from the violently vibrating craft, Quick counted the seconds to impact, "Three… two… one… OH DAMN! I can't swim!"

At their speed, the water was about as soft as a brick wall. The craft skipped on the surface once, caught, and struck hard.

Sydney blacked out.

CHAPTER TWENTY-FOUR

Rolling In The Dough

Allie

SITTING ON THE CURB beside Medorah, Allie scanned above them for the returning helicopter. But the starless sky remained empty with just a layer of dark clouds high above. She glanced at her companion. The witch also couldn't seem to take her eyes off the sky. They were both worried.

Quick had said he would return for them as soon as he picked up Sydney and SARGE. Thirty minutes max. But thirty minutes had dragged on to an hour, and it was now close to a half-hour beyond that. Allie had a really bad feeling.

The werewolf had reluctantly dropped the two women in the remains of a shopping center parking lot about ten miles south of where they had been. Not far, but far enough to be out of the action. The women had taken refuge beside what had once been a drugstore and sat down to wait.

"What could have happened to them?" asked Allie.

Medorah picked up a pebble-sized piece of concrete and threw it at the collapsed building across the street. She shook her head. "I don't know, but it can only mean something's gone wrong. Quick is never late for Tuesday nights."

Allie glanced at her friend. "Do you think they're OK?"

"I'm not sure." Medorah threw another piece of concrete across the road. She looked worried. "I *do* know that Quick is alive, but I sense that something's not quite right." She shook her head. "Unfortunately, I know nothing about Sydney."

"Is it that psychic thing that you have with Quick?"

"Yeah. The big goon is always doing something dangerous, and if anything happened to him, I wanted to know. So I put a permanent binding spell on each of us to know when the other was hurt. It was a real pain to develop the spell, but believe me, it was worth it." Medorah looked down and began sliding the dirt around with her shoe. Allie could tell Medorah was concerned, but at least she knew he was alive.

"Couldn't you use your powers and bring them here or something?" asked Allie.

Medorah smiled weakly. "I wish it were that easy. Unfortunately, witches only have modest control over some things in nature. For instance, I can make it dark or bright like what I did in the jail cell. I can also control heat and cold or make animals come to me. I can even make the earth shake a little." She grinned wickedly. "But I generally reserve that for Tuesday nights."

Allie blushed and looked away.

Medorah sighed. "So I can't snap my fingers and make them appear. I wish I could." She looked down. "You see, you don't get something for nothing. It takes a lot out of me to do even those simple spells. Body movement and words help, which is why I make gestures and say..." she made air quotes. "*Magic words*. Specific words or gestures aren't necessary. It has something to do with generating the required kilowatts. The gestures generate additional power, and the words help me focus it. But the more I *bend* nature to my will, the more power it takes. I just don't have the kilowatts to say, make a seven-point-eight earthquake or stir up a category-five hurricane. Controlling animals require the least power, although I can only handle one at a time. And even then, it takes a lot of concentration."

"If you can only control nature," observed Allie. "Then how could you do that binding spell with Quick?"

"That was a modification of our love for one another. Remember, love is a product of nature, too. But for something like that to work, both parties have to *really* want it, and you have to come up with a lot of kilowatts to make it stick. Since Quick and I are married, and we care a lot for each other..." She grinned wickedly. "It was *no* problem generating those extra kilowatts, if you catch my meaning."

Allie smiled. "I guess I do. I might like to have one of those spells too..." she looked down and blushed. "If I have the occasion, of course."

"Well, the only problem is I would have to be present during your body motions." She nudged Allie with her shoulder. "And I doubt very seriously you would want me around for that."

The young woman blushed again, and Medorah laughed, patting her friend on the shoulder.

Allie sighed. "I guess witches have their limitations, just like vampires."

"You don't know the half of it," said Medorah. "Because of my witch's powers, I can't get pregnant. It's something to do with the creative power being channeled into the magic. Before I can even *think* of having a child, I must stop using it." She sighed. "Now, that might not sound too bad, but when you've been a witch all your life, it's hard to stop. Magic becomes a part of your life, and you use it unconsciously. I've tried now for several years to stop, and I'll manage for a few weeks, but then in the heat of the moment, I'll forget. Then I have to start all over again."

"That must be rough," Allie sympathized.

"Yeah, it's especially hard now that I'm older. I'm thirty-two, and I can't afford to put things off anymore. I want to have at least two brats, so I've got to get busy." She sighed. "Quick's been a doll the whole time—he's so understanding. Although he hasn't said a word, I know he wants a child badly. It's just so damn hard to stop."

Allie patted Medorah's shoulder. "I wouldn't worry about it. Right now is no time to bring another life into the world. No telling how the radiation and those nano things might affect it."

"Yeah," agreed Medorah. "You're right. I'm not as immune to all this crap as I thought. Since the big blast, my powers have been on the weak side—the radiation must be affecting them. I don't understand why."

"You know, when we were in Naelimag, the magician there said the magic that makes us vampires was weakening. I had just assumed that we'd be immune. But it looks like the radiation is affecting us, too." She thought for a moment. "I guess it only makes sense. Light is a form of radiation, and we're sensitive to that."

They lapsed into silence. It was only a short while later that Allie felt the tickle of her internal clock. She had no phone now, but she was sure that sunrise was less than an hour away.

"I've got to find a place to sleep soon," she said.

Medorah nodded. "I could use a few winks myself. I haven't slept much since I was put in that jail."

The witch turned to Allie and placed a hand on her shoulder. The normally upbeat woman became serious. "I can't thank you enough for getting that charm off me. It was horrible. If you hadn't come along, I might never have gotten out. And the worst part was I had this huge hole in my heart, and I never even knew it." She blinked, and a tear escaped down her cheek. "So if you ever need something. Let me know. I'll do whatever's in my power to pay you back."

Allie smiled. "You're welcome. I don't suppose you can make some blood appear. I could really use some about now."

Medorah looked at her sadly. "I'm sorry, I can't make something like that. But..." She pulled the collar of her shirt away, exposing the side of her neck. "I'll let you have some of mine."

Allie glanced at the patch of naked skin. It seemed to call to her. The desire to pull her friend close and sink her teeth into her throat was almost overwhelming. She unconsciously licked her lips. Her acute vampire vision could even see the throb of the witch's pulse. She'd never had warm blood before. She imagined it would taste so good in her mouth.

Allie leaned forward, the witch's pulse beckoning her. What

if she took just a sip? Just a little. Not enough to kill her. Only enough to take the edge off.

What if she couldn't stop?

Allie jerked her eyes off Medorah's throat. "No, I don't think I should do that."

Medorah released her shirt collar. "Are you sure?"

Allie patted her friend's leg. "Yes, I'm very sure." She gave the witch a weak smile. "I consider you my friend. And there's quite the difference between having lunch with a friend and having a friend for lunch."

Puzzled, Medorah stared at her a moment, but then her eyes widened in understanding.

Allie smiled. "But thanks for offering." She stood up and stretched, looking up into the sky over Medorah's head. "Come on," she said. "Let's find somewhere to sleep."

Unexpectedly, Allie caught motion out of the corner of her eye. Glancing in that direction, she saw a red glowing orb dip below the ever-present cloud cover. At first, Allie thought it was Quick's helicopter but then realized the object held no resemblance to an aircraft's running lights.

She had time to blink twice before it drifted back up into the clouds. It happened so fast. Like it was hiding. And she had seen it before.

"I saw something over there." She pointed. "Up in the sky."

Medorah turned to look. "I don't see anything."

"It's gone now, but it was there. Some kind of red glowing thing in the distance."

"A shooting star?"

Allie shook her head. "It didn't look like one." She shrugged. "In any case, it's gone now."

Together they left the drug store and walked up the street to a bank in reasonable condition. Inside it was too dark to see, so Medorah, with a wave of her hand, put a light spell on herself. She cast a dim orange light, like a halo, as they entered.

Carefully picking their way through the debris, they found the bank vault intact and, to their surprise, open. Medorah stepped inside and examined it in her orange glow. The interior looked untouched, free of rubble and dust, and no windows. Perfect for their needs, or at least Allie's. Working together, Medorah and Allie jammed the door's heavy lock to ensure it didn't trap them inside.

But her bed posed a problem. Although Allie didn't *have* to sleep in a casket, she took comfort in that closed-up feeling. And with no blanket or quilt to cover her, she needed a guarantee that sunlight didn't reach her from some unexpected source.

Searching through the offices, Allie found a large legal size filing cabinet that wasn't too badly battered. She emptied it out, drawers and all, and dragged it into the vault. Medorah brought over bags of money and emptied them in a pile next to the file cabinet. Allie took her share of the money and used it to pad her makeshift coffin. Medorah gathered all the cash she could find and heaped it into a large pile.

After closing the vault door, Medorah stood with her back against it, gazing at her pile. "I've got to do this," she said. Pushing off the door, she ran and leaped into her pile of money, sending all types of denominations flying.

She surfaced and pretended to swim on top of the pile. "Help me!" she giggled. "I'm drowning in money!"

Allie smiled and put her hands on her hips. "Need for me to call the lifeguard?"

"Hell no! I need a broker!"

They both broke up with laughter.

Allie pushed the open side of her makeshift bed against the vault's back wall and wormed into it from the open bottom. She sighed. It wasn't a real coffin, but it would do. It might not be the best money could buy, but it was the most expensive!

As Allie waited for the day's sleep to claim her, her thoughts drifted back to Sydney. She asked Medorah, "Does your psychic thing still say Quick's still OK?"

Medorah paused, the silence stretching between them. "Yes," she finally answered. "Quick's still alive. But..." her voice caught. "I think he's in trouble."

Allie awoke the next evening to the smell of cooking food and her rumbling stomach reminding her she hadn't had a real meal since their escape.

After worming her way out of her makeshift coffin and into the bank's lobby, she found Medorah gone but spotted a flickering orange glow out in the parking lot.

Cautiously picking her way over to it, she found both the source of the light and the smell of food. A small fire burned, fueled by what appeared to be packs of money, with two cans of stew simmering on rocks beside it. The food smelled wonderful.

"I didn't realize vampires slept so long." Medorah suddenly appeared beside her.

Allie jumped in surprise. She put a hand over her racing

heart and gave her friend an embarrassed smile. "It's the night-life that does it."

Medorah chuckled. "I don't know about you, but I was *starved*. I went across the street to what's left of a supermarket and looked for food. I managed to find some cans of chicken stew, apple sauce, and some soda right off the bat, but I had to search for over an hour to find a damn can opener!"

Intent on the food, Allie sat down on a rock, and Medorah served her a can of stew wrapped in a towel and a plastic spoon shoved in it. The witch then picked up a soda and held it tightly between her hands for a moment. When she handed it to Allie, it had ice forming on the outside.

"How did you get this so cold?" Allie asked as she popped the top.

"One of the advantages of being a witch. I could have done the same with the stew, but..." she smiled and swept her hand, indicating the collapsed structure. "I felt the place needed a little ambiance."

"I don't know. It looks like an expensive fire."

The witch tossed another stack of twenties into the flames. "It is, but I love throwing cash around."

They both laughed. Allie downed the stew quickly and was shortly scraping the bottom of the can for the last drops. She couldn't remember anything tasting so good. *Except maybe that breakfast in Sydney's mansion.* Sadness tugged at her heart.

She had to blink hard a couple of times. Allie put her can down. "Have you felt anything more from Quick?"

Medorah sighed sadly. "No. And I still believe he's in some kind of trouble."

"Think those army people caught him?"

She shook her head. "No, I don't think so. I'm not exactly sure what it is. The direction is different, and he's much further away."

Allie stared forlornly into the fire. "I hope Sydney's OK."

They sat in silence for a moment, each lost in their own thoughts. Allie suspected they needed to do something. She guessed heading toward Sydney's shelter would be the best bet. Surely he would go there first. Anyway, it had the only source of blood on the planet right now. Or, at least, it seemed that way.

Allie looked up intending to suggest this to Medorah, when she saw something move in the darkness outside the fire. "Something's out there," she whispered.

"Where?"

Medorah stood and turned to look where Allie pointed. "I don't see anything. The flickering light will sometimes play tricks on your eyes."

Allie went to stand beside her. She strained her senses to the max, looking and listening. It had been hard to tell from the quick look, but she thought it was some kind of animal.

Off to their right, they heard the crunch of gravel.

Allie pointed, zeroing in on the sound. "There!" She felt completely exposed in the light of the fire.

Medorah squinted into the night. "I don't see anything."

A few more anxious moments passed.

Allie licked her lips nervously. "Can you feel anything? Like an animal? The food could have attracted it."

Medorah shook her head. "Nothing. That's what's so odd."

They listened for a moment more. Allie shrugged. "Well, whatever it was, it's gone."

Then, there was another crunch of gravel off their left this time. They wheeled toward the sound. "Over there!"

They stared into the dark for a moment. Medorah turned to face her. "I think we better leave...." The witch froze, and her mouth fell open.

Allie felt something cold and hard poke her in the back. It felt amazingly like the business end of a gun barrel.

CHAPTER TWENTY-FIVE

A Midnight Swim

Sydney

SYDNEY'S FIRST SENSATION AS he awoke was that of being cold and wet. Very wet. He shook his head, trying to clear the cobwebs from his impact-addled brain. As awareness returned, he slowly realized that he was still strapped to the helicopter seat. But now, there was cold water up to his neck and quickly inching up his chin. He blinked in confusion at the aircraft's mostly submerged interior, wondering how he got there. Then the memory of their escape and the subsequent crash came flooding back. They were sinking in deep water. And he had to get out.

In panic, he jerked at his restraints. He only had a handful of seconds left before being completely submerged. He was going to die. He could feel a full-blown panic attack waiting to grab him.

He'd always had an uneasy relationship with deep water. But since becoming a vampire, his discomfort had increased to outright dread. Even going over bridges would give him pause. He suspected it was another aspect of his vampirism that he didn't fully understand. But now, he was not only in a huge lake, but *drowning* in it. He was totally unprepared for the panic coursing through him, threatening to blank out all rational thought.

Unbidden, a memory surfaced of his grandfather yelling at him for panicking, when as a youth, his cousin Martha had unexpectedly pushed him into the pool's deep end. His grandfather had plucked him out but had lectured him hotly.

"Fear," he had said, "will kill you faster than anything else."

Then he had thrown him back into the water.

Sydney curled up his fists. A vampire's respiration was lower than a human's. He'd proven he could last five minutes between breaths. Besides, he had been an excellent swimmer before his conversion. Despite his dislike of deep water, his grandfather had seen to it. So really, what did he have to fear?

With the rising water covering his mouth, he felt for the restraining belts across his chest and followed them to where they connected with the seat. He fumbled a moment and then found the release.

The craft's sinking was accelerating. In those few moments it took to remove his seat restraints, the water quickly climbed over his head. Holding his breath, he pushed himself out of his seat and floated out the side door, which must have sprung open upon impact. Sydney surfaced a few feet from the wreck and trod water while he scanned the night for the nearest shore.

Where's Quick?

Sydney called the pilot several times, but there was no answer. He looked back toward the sinking craft. It was within inches of being completely submerged. Quick had to be trapped inside.

Sydney steeled himself and swam back to the craft, diving down to check inside. His fears were confirmed. Through the cockpit's windshield and illuminated by a single emergency light, Sydney could see Quick—unconscious, still strapped to his seat, and water up to his chin. Only a moment later, the interior light shorted out, plunging the inside into complete darkness. He had to get him out.

The broken helicopter was turning on its side as it sank, forming an air bubble around the pilot. Otherwise, Quick would have already drowned. Sydney searched just beneath the water and found the hatch release. Bracing his feet on the side, he pulled on the door as hard as he could, but it refused to open. Sydney let go and floated, resting. He would have to dive under to the other door and enter the way he had left. Sydney shivered at the thought but could not let his friend die. He got a grip on himself and swam to the other side. He dove.

In the murky darkness beneath the water, even his vampire eyes could find no light to see. He discovered the door by touch and entered, carefully picking his way through the cabin. He swam up beside the pilot.

"Quick! Wake up!" Sydney shook the unconscious werewolf, but this had no effect. He splashed water on the pilot's face but only got a moan.

He gritted his teeth. The air space was almost gone. He had to get the werewolf conscious and fast. Sydney deftly unsnapped the pilot's restraints and dunked him in the water. Quick came instantly awake and tried to slug him, nearly drowning them both.

"Stop it!" sputtered Sydney. "Get a hold of yourself."

Although Quick didn't seem to come completely conscious, the pilot stopped fighting.

"Now do exactly as I say," instructed Sydney, trying not to show his own fear. "Take a deep breath, and don't panic."

The pilot inhaled, and Sydney didn't hesitate. He pulled them both down and out through the submerged door. Quick came up sputtering, but none the worse for wear. The vampire had the pilot float on his back, and Sydney towed him toward shore. As they swam away, the helicopter disappeared from sight.

"Goodbye, old girl," Quick said softly. "I'm going to miss you."

Sydney towed the werewolf in silence for a while, but when they neared shore, Quick spoke up. "Thanks," he said simply. "I owe you."

Sydney found the bottom and stood, stepping toward shore. "Not any more than I owe you."

Quick reached shore first and collapsed to sit on the bank. Sydney was just behind and fell in beside him. He wiped the dripping water from his face. "Sorry about your helicopter."

Quick shrugged, and they sat in silent thought for a moment. Then he looked around. "Hey," he said. "Where's that crazy robot?"

Sydney immediately felt a pang of guilt. He'd forgotten all

about her. Maybe because he *wanted* to forget. He sighed. It wasn't the robot's fault she was a pain in the ass. She'd just been built that way.

"I haven't seen her," Sydney finally said. He looked out across the dark water and saw nothing moving. "She wasn't inside when I woke up. I guess the impact threw her out."

Quick nodded. "I doubt she floated very well, so she's likely on the bottom with *Demoness*. She probably shorted out the moment she hit the water." He was silent for a moment. "What a way to go."

Sydney briefly wondered if he should go search, but quickly realized it was hopeless. He'd never find her. And even if he did, there was no way he could swim with the heavy robot.

Silently, Sydney rose and saluted his metal friend. Quick stood beside him and also saluted. It was the least he could do. Even though she had been a real pest at times, he would kind of miss her craziness. He shivered. But he would *not* miss her kisses.

After their moment of silence, Quick sat back down, and from a pocket of his fatigues, pulled out an obviously water-proof penlight. Sydney blinked in the sudden illumination, blindingly bright to his vampire eyes.

Quick used it to inspect a rip on his sleeve and the small cut just beyond. Sydney hadn't been gentle with him when they were exiting, and something had apparently snagged his arm as they left the wreck. The werewolf dabbed at the cut, and his fingers came away smeared with a streak of blood.

The wound wasn't deep. Bandaid category. But Sydney couldn't take his eyes off the red splotch. It glistened in the white light calling to him.

A sudden hunger gripped Sydney. And it wasn't for a cheeseburger and fries. No, this was for something unique to him. He could almost taste the blood on his tongue. All he had to do was lean forward...

Sydney looked away. He would die before preying on his friends. He had missed getting his regular dose of blood, and his prospects for getting some were now slim to none. Tomorrow, almost unnoticeably, he would begin weakening, but the day after that, the weakness would triple, making him sluggish and reducing his ability to concentrate. And then on the third day, he would hardly be able to move, unable to even feed himself. Sydney shivered. He had never gone more than three days, but he was pretty sure death followed after that.

His mansion, as far as he knew, was the nearest known supply of blood. And he needed to get back there soon.

That was also where Allie would likely go.

"How far are we from the city?" he asked.

Quick scratched his chin. "Not too far. Probably fifty to sixty miles. The dogfight took us further away than I had planned." He lay back and shut his eyes. "That swim took a lot out of me."

Sydney's heart sank. Fifty miles. Normally no more than an hour by car. Minutes if one was flying. But on foot? He did a quick calculation. Even if they started now, he was looking at twenty-some hours of walking. Plus, he was limited to just walking during the night. He was likely looking at two days minimum. More likely part of a third. And the longer he went without blood, the slower he would go. He severely doubted he would make it.

Sydney decided not to dwell on it and turned his thoughts to more pressing needs. He had to find shelter and soon. Sunrise was only an hour away.

Quick gave a loud snore. Sydney chuckled. Apparently, his friend really was tired.

Slowly standing, Sydney examined the area just up from the bank. It was dark, but to his vampire eyes, he had plenty of light to see by. Thick brush lined the lakeshore, and beyond that lay dense forest. He was surprised that it was still intact, especially considering the destruction he'd seen back in the city. Sure, the tops of some of the trees had been broken off, but not nearly as bad as he would have assumed.

Suddenly, there was a rustling from deep in the forest. It sounded like something large. He scanned the forest. But nothing came forward. Funny, he had not seen any animals since the apocalypse. He had assumed they had all been killed. He shrugged. Probably just a deer that had survived the disaster, nothing to worry about. But Sydney's imagination wouldn't leave him alone, reminding him of his grandfather's stories.

Frequently as a child, but less so as a teenager, his grandfather had brought him to this very same wilderness area—Lake Halawalnai, an old Native American name. It was one of the few things both he and his grandfather enjoyed. Although they had never strayed far from the public campsites, his grandfather had taught him most of what he knew of tracking, blazing trails, and starting a fire—the things normal kids learned in Scouts.

But the last time they had come, his grandfather had told scary tales around the campfire. The scariest had been about a monster that supposedly lived by the lake. It was at least a head taller than a man and only came out at night. According to the story, it had single-handedly wiped out an entire native village. But what sent jolts up and down Sydney's spine was his grandfather's confession that as a young man, he had *seen* the monster. That night after the fire was extinguished and as his grandfather lay snoozing beside him, Sydney stayed awake listening to every sound in the night.

He reined in his imagination. It was just one of his grandfather's tall tales, nothing to worry about. Besides, right now, he had other concerns.

Sydney reached over to Quick and shook his shoulder. "Get up. We need to...."

To Sydney's great surprise, the pilot came up swinging. His vampire reflexes narrowly saved him from getting decked.

"Quick, it's me! Sydney!"

The werewolf looked around, still in a daze. Gradually, understanding crept into his expression. "Don't ever wake me like that again! Tell me first. I'm not rational when I wake up."

"How am I going to tell you when you're asleep?" Sydney thought for a moment. "In fact, how does your wife wake you?"

"With a broom. Besides, you can buy them by the dozen."

Sydney frowned. "Thanks for the warning."

Quick stood and sniffed the air. He was gradually losing his werewolf features, becoming more manlike—teeth shrinking, hair vanishing. In his completely human form, he wouldn't look too bad. Sydney judged the transformation would be complete by dawn.

"The sun will be up soon," said Sydney. "I need to find shelter, or you'll have baked vampire for breakfast."

Quick made a face. "I don't even want to think about that."

He pointed up the ridge. "Being a werewolf has its advantages. I can smell some kind of animal up there... bear, I think. But the scent is stale, which means it must be a lair of some sort. I bet we could use that."

Sydney agreed. "But let's hurry." It was already getting lighter towards the horizon.

They took off in the direction Quick indicated, making their own path through the dense brush.

As they traveled, Sydney couldn't help but comment on Quick's changing appearance.

"Yeah," Quick sighed. "I turn back human when the sun comes out. Then when the moon rises, I'll transform back. It's a real pain in the butt. When I was first going out with Medorah, it made for some very interesting dates." He looked down. "I hope she's all right. I feel like I abandoned her."

And that reminded Sydney of Allie. He thought about her smile and quiet confidence. He had no doubt that she was doing all right.

Just up the hill, they encountered a faint path which they followed up a steep bank. Although the climb was rough—some of it over short stretches of almost vertical rock—they made their way to where the path ended at a clump of bushes.

Quick leaned closer and sniffed. "Yep, it's in there."

Sydney, his body now screaming for sleep and the dim dawn light hurting his eyes, parted the bushes. To his surprise, a cave entrance just slightly shorter than himself lay beyond. He marveled at his friend's ability. Without Quick, he would never have found it.

"Are you sure this cave is unoccupied?" asked Sydney.

Quick, who retained only vague remains of his werewolf

nature, sniffed the air. "It smelled that way down below, but now that I'm turning human, I can't say."

Taking a glance at the brightening horizon, where the light to his vampire eyes was becoming blinding, Sydney decided he didn't have much choice. But something about it made him uneasy. He stooped and cautiously entered the cave. Quick came right behind him.

The entrance led down to a short passage that turned sharply to the right, cutting off most of the light outside, and led to a room-size chamber. His eyes immediately fell on an enormous pile of clothes—shirts, pants, hats, and coats. Every piece of clothing imaginable. There were even a few rugs.

Sydney could barely hold his eyes open. He burrowed deep within them, praying there were no vampire sucking bugs in the bundle. No sooner was this done than he began to drift asleep. As he did, his subconscious pointed out that the pile of clothes had to be somebody's bed. *And*, he thought in horror, the bed was still warm from someone lying in it.

Which was his last thought before the vampire's sleep claimed him.

CHAPTER TWENTY-SIX

One Hot Time

Allie

STANDING IN THE RUINS of the bank's parking lot, Allie turned her head slightly to see who poked the weapon into her back.

"Don't move girl *friend!*" said a man behind her.

Allie sagged in disbelief. Only one person had a voice like that, and she remembered it well. Rip. The one that had tried to kill them in one of the hospitals. The guy really got around.

"I've been following you," he said. He was, surprisingly, dressed in military fatigues. "That helicopter ride almost threw me, but I caught up with you. Aren't you proud of me? As soon as I kill you, we can be friends forever."

Medorah took a slow step forward. Rip poked Allie harder

in the back. "Don't rush me, lady. I'm working as fast as I can. I'll get to you in a moment." He muttered to himself. "Everybody's always in a hurry."

"Don't hurt her," Medorah pleaded.

"Oh, I have no intention of hurting her. I'm going to *kill* her. Ever since I realized she was a fan of Clare Montare, she's all I've been able to think about. So, I've decided to make her my girlfriend. And my girlfriends always get special treatment."

Allie cut her eyes to the side to see what he was holding. "What *kind* of special treatment?" she asked.

She could almost hear the smile in his voice. "Turn around, and I'll show you. I think you'll be impressed."

Allie turned to find a grinning Rip with two tanks strapped to his back and holding a flame thrower. A damn big one too.

Her eyes widened in horror. "I don't deserve special treatment."

"Oh yes, you do! You're too modest. You made my heart burn for you, so I decided you should burn too!"

Thinking quickly, Allie got an idea. She looked Rip in the eyes, concentrating her vampire power on making him obey. "Rip, I like you too, and I really appreciate all the trouble you've gone to. So just for me, would you put down your weapon?"

Rip's hold on the flamethrower loosened slightly, but he blinked and then gripped it tighter, "Nope. I can't do that. You might run away again."

"I won't run away," she cooed. "How about if I hold it for you? I promise not to let anything happen to it."

Rip, staring intently into her eyes, slowly lowered the

weapon and held it out for her. But when Allie briefly glanced away to take the flamethrower... the spell broke.

"NO!" he yelled. "You're tricking me." He shoved her away. She tripped over some rubble and fell, landing hard on her butt.

Rip aimed the flamethrower at her. "Now, you'll forever be mine!"

Rip squeezed the trigger.

Quickly, Medorah mumbled something in that strange witch language and made some weird hand motions.

The stream of flames leaped for Allie.

But instead of burning her to a crisp, their path suddenly altered, veering away, circling around behind her, and then heading back towards Rip!

He released the trigger and took a step away in surprise. The stream of flame encircled the man, looping him tighter and tighter with rings of fire. He was forced to lower his weapon to avoid being scorched.

"What the hell is going on?" Rip yelled. One mischievous loop singed his belt, and his pants fell down. "This is as crazy as I am!"

Medorah laughed and went to help Allie up. "Are you OK?" she asked.

Allie took the offered hand. "A little overdone maybe, but otherwise OK."

As she stood, Medorah leaned close. She indicated the encircled Rip with a nod of her head and whispered, "Our friend there will be tied up for just a little while. I can't maintain the spell for long. So, I suggest we put some distance between him and us before the flames run out."

"Should we leave him free?" Allie whispered back.

Medorah frowned. "I don't know what else to do. My magic

won't let me kill him, and I'm definitely not going to get close enough to tie him up. Are you?"

Allie shook her head emphatically. "No."

Medorah turned toward Rip. "I advise you not to follow us. My husband doesn't like people bothering me." She held up a hand and wiggled her fingers. The flames squeezed him tighter. "And I don't like it either."

Allie and Medorah turned away.

"Don't leave me like this?" protested Rip. "I promise not to do it again."

Allie frowned and shook her head. "I bet you tell that to all your friends."

"Of course not," he said indignantly. "I only save that for my special ones."

Allie rolled her eyes. She was not too happy with being categorized that way.

The two slipped away, with Allie leading Medorah through the darkness. They didn't dare make a light since it would give Rip a way to follow them. While she wanted to get away as rapidly as she could, she also didn't want to lead him to Sydney's shelter. So she backtracked.

While the darkness was difficult for the witch, Medorah was a trooper and patiently followed. Allie was glad her vampire eyes made the night seem almost like day. But still, it slowed them down.

They weren't that far away from the shelter. If they hurried, they should be able to reach it by tomorrow. Allie didn't think Sydney would mind if she borrowed a cup. Besides, he was sure to return there for some himself. If he was still… alive. She tried not to think about it.

While moving carefully down a major thoroughfare, Allie noticed a military truck parked down a side street. She stopped. It was painted in camouflage and looked to be in serviceable condition. The vehicle must not have been there when everything blew up.

"What is it?" Medorah asked, gripping her hand and trying to see into the darkness.

"It's a military truck. I can't imagine how it got there."

"You don't think the army found us do you?" asked Medorah.

Allie shook her head. "I don't think so. There would be more of them about." She hesitated a moment. "Let's check it out. Maybe we can take a ride."

They walked to the truck. There were high walls on both sides of them, so Medorah risked putting a dim glow on her hands. Surprisingly, the keys were inside, and in the back, they found a boxed cargo marked with the universal radiation hazard symbol. Normally, seeing it would have given them pause. But Allie couldn't help thinking that at this point, a little more radiation wasn't going to matter.

But how did it get there?

Medorah placed both hands on the hood and glanced back over her shoulder at Allie. "I'm going to look into this truck's past. Before we use it, I want to make sure we're not going to bring the whole army down on top of us."

Allie nodded.

Medorah closed her eyes. She mumbled something to herself and went perfectly still.

After only a few moments, the witch opened her eyes and pointed with her thumb over her shoulder. "This belongs to that crazy bastard back there. He drove by while we slept, then stopped and camped somewhere over there." She pointed to their right. "He must have heard us talking and went to investigate."

"Where did he get the truck?"

"I didn't look back that far, but I suspect he stole it from that military facility back there."

Allie glanced at the vehicle. "Can you drive one of these?"

She grinned. "Of course. Quick wanted to be sure I knew how. He had one before he got that blasted helicopter. He'll be pleased to know...." She trained off with a worried expression and then looked away. She blinked at the sudden tears. "I hope he's all right."

Allie wanted to say something to reassure her friend but had no clue what it could be. *What would Clare Montare say?*

"Can you still feel him?"

Medorah wiped her eyes and nodded.

Allie put a hand on her friend's shoulder. "Then he wouldn't dare get hurt." She gave it a gentle squeeze. "He's probably trying to get back in time for Tuesday night."

Medorah looked at her, eyes still glistening, and then broke into a huge grin. "You're right. He wouldn't dare. He'd know I'd tear him a new one."

Allie returned her grin and hooked a thumb towards the truck. "What say you and I take a ride?"

"I don't have my license with me."

Allie patted her on the back. "Somehow, I don't think it matters."

An hour later, and with only twelve miles behind them, the

truck ran out of gas. The debris had made the going slow as Medorah maneuvered the vehicle through it.

But even though the drive had been short, Allie had found it very educational. Medorah could curse worse than a sailor. And in no less than three different languages! Allie was no stranger to foul language, but Medorah's profanity range was quite commendable.

So, leaving the truck behind, they started on foot again. The debris cleared up some, and they were able to make good time as they trekked southward. Lunch, or mid-night snack depending on how you were counting, consisted of some apple sauce and canned chili, washed down with an unbroken bottle of cranberry juice. Medorah just warmed up the chili and cooled down the juice with her hands to save time.

As Medorah was preparing their food, Allie happened to glance up and see that mysterious light hanging high in the sky again. The glowing orb repeated its previous behavior and drifted back up into the clouds. Whatever it was, it gave her the creeps.

After their short break, they were immediately off again. Allie grew hopeful that they would make Sydney's mansion before dawn.

After another hour of travel, they were walking side-by-side between two mostly intact buildings when Allie looked down and noticed something odd. She held out a hand to pause Medorah.

"What is it?" the witch whispered, suddenly tense.

Allie pointed to the ground. "It's a shadow."

Medorah looked where she pointed. A faint light came from around the corner, casting a dim shadow of the building's edge.

And it appeared to be a cool white, not the warm flickering glow of a fire. It looked artificial.

Allie crept up to the corner and cautiously peered around. In the distance was a single functioning streetlight in the middle of a large shopping center parking lot. The light was harsh to her vampire eyes after having been adapted to the dim glow from Medorah's hands.

Surprisingly, the lot was free from any type of debris. In fact, it looked like the debris had been pushed into a huge pile in the corner of the lot.

But that only highlighted the object just beneath the street-light—a single upside down shopping cart. The setup was just too artificial. It screamed trap.

Medorah came up beside her and surveyed the area.

"Doesn't that look odd?" Allie asked. "The power's been knocked out for days now. I wonder where the electricity is coming from."

Medorah shook her head. She opened her mouth to answer but then froze. She stared at the light.

Allie pointed. "It's got to be…"

Medorah immediately shushed her. "Listen."

Allie raised her head and strained for the slightest sound. And then she heard it. A very faint… meow.

Medorah immediately took off running toward the light.

"Wait!" she called. "It's got to be a trap!"

But Medorah didn't stop, so Allie had no choice but to follow. As they neared, it became apparent that a feline was trapped under the shopping cart—a solid black cat. It watched them approach with big green eyes.

"Schro!" Medorah shouted. "Are you all right?"

"I am fine, mistress." The cat rose and paced back and forth. "But you really shouldn't have come."

Medorah pushed over the cart and grabbed up her pet, pulling him into a hug. "I missed you so much." She gave him a gentle squeeze, which in typical cat fashion, Schro seemed less than thrilled about. "Why didn't you stay home? I was coming back for you."

Allie approached cautiously. She had picked up on Schro's warning. "And exactly why shouldn't we have come?"

The cat ignored her. "I'm sorry, mistress, but I had to leave. All the food was gone."

"Gone? I left you enough for a week...."

The cat lowered its head. "Unfortunately, the food went bad."

Medorah gave him a puzzled look. "Went bad? It was dry food. How is that possible?" Her eyes narrowed. "You didn't...?"

Allie felt completely exposed in the middle of the empty parking lot. The light's glare prevented her from seeing into the surrounding darkness. She surveyed the area nervously and repeated her question. "Schro, why shouldn't we have come?"

The cat looked at Medorah levelly. "I had no choice but to dump the dry food in the kitty box. I wanted a can of Feline Banquet."

Medorah sighed. "But you can't open the cans."

Schro started washing a paw. "Which is why I needed to find you. I needed my can opener person."

Medorah gave a deep sigh and looked over to Allie. "You can give a cat intelligence, but at the end of the day, it's still a cat."

Something in the sky caught Allie's attention. She looked up to see the glowing eye descending out of the clouds. It was the same one she had seen before. It hovered above the remains of a nearby building and sat there watching them. The hairs on Allie's neck stood up as it slowly started floating in their direction. She grabbed her friend's arm. "I think we had better run."

Schro glanced up at the descending orb. He seemed sad. "I'm sorry, mistress. Please don't be mad at me. I was so hungry. And I didn't have my can opener person." He took a deep breath and let it out slowly. "They had tuna."

Medorah looked puzzled at the sudden change in subject. "Tuna?"

Allie pulled Medorah harder. "I think we should go now."

The cat nodded. "With gravy. It smelled so good. You know how I love tuna. They said I could have all I wanted if I came closer. And I was so hungry."

The orb continued to float down. As it got closer and continued to grow in size, Allie could make out that it was some kind of flying craft. It was oval in shape with a large hatch built into it which, when combined with the pulsing red glow, gave it the impression of a giant bloodshot eye. It resembled no craft she had seen before, and it moved without a sound. Allie's eyes went large. It had to be a UFO.

And if it was an alien craft, then that meant they had to be aliens inside of it. And her last close encounter hadn't gone so well.

"Medorah!" Allie pulled hard on her friend. "We have to go now!"

But they only got a handful of steps away before a blinding white beam of light suddenly appeared right in front of them. They skidded to a halt and reversed direction. Allie felt the protection amulet bouncing against her chest and wished

Sydney was there. They could have put their pieces together and found out if it really worked.

The alien craft was in no hurry and leisurely floated directly over them. Suddenly, the blinding white light returned.

As the light washed over them, Allie felt a hot, pins and needles, prickling sensation all over her body—like every part had suddenly gone to sleep. She froze in mid-step, unable to move. Thankfully, she could still breathe, and she retained just enough control of her feet to remain standing. But another step or even moving her head was beyond her.

The angle of the light changed, and Allie could only assume the craft was landing behind them while still keeping them fully illuminated.

After what seemed an eternity, there was the sound of steps behind her, approaching slowly and deliberately. When the person was directly behind her, they paused. Allie had time to wonder what they were going to do. Kill her? Stab her? Or something worse?

But after only a few heartbeats, her assailant moved to stand in front of her.

She groaned. *Not him.*

Before her, with hands resting on his thick waist, stood a familiar alien, green in color with dark hair done up in a mohawk. The same creep that had been literally kicked out of the bar.

"So vhat do ve have here?" He stepped closer and grinned evilly. "I think ve're going to have some vun."

CHAPTER TWENTY-SEVEN

The Beast Laughed

Sydney

SYDNEY AWOKE IN A deep fog to what sounded like an animal making a deep growling-hoot while Quick yelled something unintelligible.

And it sounded like the werewolf was in trouble.

Groggily, Sydney tried to open his eyes. They didn't want to work at first, but he gradually pried his lids apart. Since he was able to at least partially awaken, the sun must be setting. But since he was still so out of it, the sun must not be all the way down.

Carefully, shading his eyes, Sydney peeked out from underneath his rather large pile of clothes. He flinched at the bright light, which made his eyes water. He quickly glanced around and saw no beams of direct sunlight, which would fry his skin as surely as a blowtorch. Actually, it wasn't all that bright by human reckoning, but for him, his vampire eyes could barely handle it. What he would give for sunglasses.

It wasn't difficult to see what had awakened him. Just outside the cave's entrance, Quick—still in his human form—was keeping a large hairy animal at bay with a hunting knife. The animal was big. It had its back to Sydney but looked to be a little larger than a grizzly. It had to be at least a head taller than Quick. But its fur didn't look bear-like, being long, thick, and dark. Definitely not a bear. But what?

As it circled Quick, Sydney got to see it from the front and was shocked to see a semi-human face and ape-like hands. It was too big for a monkey and not the right shape for an ape. And no way was it human.

Sydney's mouth fell open in disbelief. From drawings he had seen when he was younger, the vampire knew exactly what it was. A being of legend, something thought to exist but never proven. The Native Americans had called him Sasquatch. Or in more modern terms—

Bigfoot.

And Sydney was sleeping in his den. With evening falling, the large animal must have been returning home when he found Quick blocking the way.

Sydney cursed his luck. Out of all the acres of forest in the area, he had to find the one that had Bigfoot. Somehow this Mr. Sasquatch must have some magical properties like Quick and himself. Otherwise, it too would have been destroyed by the bio-nuclear virus thing that had gotten everyone else. And if it had some type of magic, that would explain its ability to stay hidden from the rest of mankind.

The being hooted again, and Quick gave another shout. Sydney needed to help Quick. He peeked out again, trying to judge if there was still too much light for him to join the melee.

The animal reached out with a large paw-like hand and batted at the werewolf. Quick lunged with his knife, but the animal, lightning-fast despite its size, deftly dodged and backhanded him. Quick went sprawling, while Mr. Sasquatch grunted repeatedly and bounced up and down. Sydney could have sworn he was laughing.

The animal gave the werewolf time to get to its feet, and then they were at it again. Obviously, Mr. Sasquatch had the advantage and could kill Quick at any time, but it appeared he was having too much fun. But what would happen when the monster got bored?

He had to help Quick. He had no weapon. Not even a flashlight since everything had been confiscated when he was captured. Except, of course, the accursed protection amulet around his neck. He wished Allie were there. Now would be the perfect time to try it out. Surveying the cave's interior, Sydney found it bare except for the pile of clothes he was in. Absolutely nothing he could use for a weapon. He didn't think just jumping up and waving his arms would scare the monster away.

Or would it?

He quietly sorted through the pile and pulled up a couple of pieces of fur-like material for inspection. One looked like an old furry bathrobe, and the other a once expensive fur bedspread. But both were too worn for his usage. He dug deeper.

Almost at the very bottom of the pile, he felt something *very* furry. He managed to get it up and was surprised to find a bearskin rug. He wondered what hunting lodge had donated this fine piece.

As quietly as he could, Sydney wrapped the bedspread around him and put the bearskin rug over his head. His plan depended on the monster's reaction. If the beast charged, he was as good as dead.

Sydney risked a peek outside. Quick and Mr. Sasquatch were fighting again. Only now, the monster was just batting away the knife thrusts. He was obviously losing interest.

Half-heartedly, Mr. Sasquatch swung at Quick. The pilot immediately took advantage of the opening and stabbed the monster with his knife. This was no more than a pinprick to the beast, serving only to anger it.

Roaring, the monster knocked the knife from Quick's hand, grabbed the front of his shirt, and threw him bodily against the cave wall. Quick hit hard and slid to the ground.

The monster roared and reared back, ready to deliver its final blow.

Sydney had to make his move.

Standing slowly, like dirty laundry rising from the dead, Sydney lifted his arms and began to concentrate his vampire powers on making himself appear larger than he was. He made growling sounds as loud and as ferocious as he could.

Mr. Sasquatch glanced over his shoulder and froze in midswing. He quickly turned towards Sydney, lowered his head, spread his arms, and growled back.

Sydney copied the beast and also began to growl. He eyed the unconscious man. "Quick!" he whispered. "Get up!"

But the pilot remained motionless.

"Damn! Can't something go *right* for a change?"

Sydney growled louder and started flapping his arms. "Grrr...! Quick! You better get up now! Grrr...! Time to wake up."

Mr. Sasquatch started flapping his arms in response to Sydney.

After what seemed an eternity, but was likely only a minute, Quick groaned and sat up holding his head.

Sydney began hopping up and down. "Quick! Get up! I think he's catching on to me."

The monster crouched and approached slowly. Sydney advanced, matching the approach and trying to look mean. The beast stopped only a few paces in front of him and roared.

Quick, now fully conscious, did a double-take on the disguised vampire.

"Get out of here while I distract it," Sydney yelled.

Quick, realizing retreat was the best option, regained his feet and fled out the cave entrance.

With the werewolf out of harm's way, Sydney began to make his own exit. He sidestepped and tried to work his way around the monster, being careful not to roar too loud or seem too ferocious. Mr. Sasquatch sidestepped with him, trying to keep Sydney squarely in his sights.

When Sydney had his back to the cave entrance, he backed toward it. But Mr. Sasquatch wasn't going to let him go that easily and matched him retreating step by retreating step.

Realizing now was his chance, Sydney roared and feinted a lunge toward the monster. Simultaneously, he grabbed his fur covering and threw it into Mr. Sasquatch's face. The surprised monster caught it, giving the vampire enough time to turn and run.

As Sydney disappeared into the forest, the beast behind him gave several hoots but thankfully did not follow. In fact, Mr. Sasquatch sounded disappointed, which was not the reaction that he had been anticipating. It was almost like the monster had enjoyed their little encounter.

Regardless, he prayed Mr. Sasquatch returned to obscurity and never showed himself again. After all, one never saw big-foot twice.

Did they?

When he was sure the beast wasn't chasing him, Sydney paused to lean against a tree and catch his breath. Realizing one of the fur bathrobes was still around his shoulders, he untied it and tossed it away. Unfortunately, its smell still lingered—and it wasn't a pleasant one. Sydney hoped it wasn't too noticeable.

Quick hailed him from up the trail, but as Sydney went to join him, the pilot made a face and held out his hand to stop him. "You smell horrible." He put a hand over his nose. "Worse than ten wet mangy skunks spending the whole night playing in rotten garbage."

Sydney frowned and stopped a short distance away. He had smelt it himself, so it must be absolutely horrible to the were-wolf's enhanced sense of smell. "Sorry, I had to dig pretty deep in that pile to find what I needed. If we pass the lake again, I'll wash off."

Quick waved a hand in front of his face. "I don't think all the deodorant in the world could get rid of that stench." He shuddered.

Sydney decided a change of subject was in order. "So, any idea on which way we need to go?"

Quick pointed to the southeast. "If I remember our crash co-ordinates correctly, the city should lie in that direction. If we push hard, we can walk it in only a couple of days. Three at most. And then maybe catch up with our girls." He shrugged. "Maybe we can get lucky and find a car or truck to get us there faster.

Three days. Sydney closed his eyes and rubbed the bridge of his nose. Whether it would take a month or a year, it wouldn't matter. He would be dead the day after tomorrow. That is, if he didn't get some blood soon. He was already weakening. Even continuing at a slow pace would be beyond him tomorrow.

He sighed, grateful he had shown Allie where to find his blood supply. At least she would be able to live on a bit longer.

He looked up at the canopy of trees over them. Perhaps it would be best to end it now. Surely there was a way that didn't involve a wooden stake. Neat, clean, and no suffering.

Sydney shook his head. No. Carringtons were not quitters. While there was life, there was hope. He would do the best he could. But either way, his friend should know.

"Quick," said Sydney. "I'm afraid I might not make it." He quickly explained his problem.

Despite the smell, Quick came closer and slapped him on the shoulder. "Don't worry, pal. We'll figure something out. In fact, I'll *carry* you if I have to. You've saved my ass twice now..." he stabbed himself with his thumb. "... and I never forget a debt." Quick turned away. "Well, let's get a move on. No sense wasting time talking about it." And he led off into the bush.

Sydney was genuinely touched by Quick's remark. Never before had anyone really cared for him as a friend. He felt unworthy of the other's company.

Quick set a grueling pace through the dense brush, which made the night seem thicker. The partial moon rose, and Quick made the gradual transition to a werewolf. He didn't even seem to notice. Sydney guessed that having this occur every day wasn't even notable anymore. He did notice that Quick had no problem with the darkness. Apparently, night vision was something vampires and werewolves shared.

Around midnight, Quick produced a couple of energy food bars from a pocket in his flight suit, and they munched on them as they walked. Sydney's feet began to hurt, something that had never happened since becoming a vampire. He guessed it was just another symptom of his blood hunger.

They did stop once so Sydney could try to wash off some of the smell. It partially worked. Quick said he still stank, but at least it was tolerable.

A couple of hours after midnight, they crossed a well-used trail heading in the direction they needed. Without a moment's thought, Quick adopted it, increasing their speed and easing their path. Sydney wondered what it led to.

Unexpectedly, Quick stopped, and with his arm, barred the vampire from proceeding. Sydney opened his mouth to ask what was wrong, when Quick held a finger to his lips, indicating silence. He then squatted down and pointed to the bare ground of the path. Sydney had to look twice before he saw the thin, almost invisible wire strung about two inches high across the trail. How had Quick seen it?

The werewolf carefully traced the wire's path. It was hooked under a stake next to the trail and then led up a tree to a long branch bent painfully far back. Several sharp sticks had been fastened to the limb.

Sydney's eyes went wide. It was a trap. If Quick hadn't stopped him, he would have tripped the wire, and the limb would have swung out horizontally over the path, plunging one of the sharpened sticks into his chest. If it hadn't killed him outright, he would have been seriously hurt.

Quick whispered to him. "We'll have to be careful. Someone doesn't want us on this trail."

"Who do you think set it?"

"Damned if I know. This is a deep forest in the middle of a national reserve. I can't even imagine who would want to." Quick shook his shaggy head. "We'll have to keep our guard up. There will likely be others."

Sydney pointed over his shoulder. "Should we go back?"

Quick considered him for a moment. "We don't have time to backtrack. We need to get you some blood."

"Not if it puts you in danger."

He patted Sydney playfully on his arm. "Danger is my middle name. Besides," He grinned expectantly. "I never miss a Tuesday night. She promised."

Sydney couldn't help but wish he had a special day of the week.

Quick immediately turned and carefully stepped over the trap, indicating that Sydney should do the same. After he was safely over, Quick again led off down the trail.

They had gone no more than a hundred feet when the werewolf again called a halt. This time he pointed out a chest-high sapling next to the path. Another almost invisible tripwire was attached to it and led to an eight-foot log suspended high over the trail behind them. The log had long, sharp spikes protruding from it. If they had just brushed against the sapling, the catch would have released, causing the suspended log to swing down and crash into them from the back. Sydney gaped in shock. They had passed beneath the suspended log, not suspecting a thing.

"Someone *really* doesn't want us here," mused Quick. "But for the life of me, I don't know why."

"Could the army be after us again?"

"Nah." Quick shook his head. "These traps are not their style. They're into overwhelming force, not trickery." Quick stroked his chin as he considered. He finally nodded to himself. "I think we should leave the trail. Maybe we can work our way around these traps."

Sydney nodded. That did seem like the safest move. He was just about to step off the trail when Quick suddenly grabbed his arm and jerked him back.

"What...?" Sydney asked in confusion.

But Quick ignored him and squatted down to examine the leaf-covered ground along the sides of the trail. He pointed to several patches, that to Sydney, looked no different than the others.

"Mines," Quick explained. "They've planted land mines on both sides of the trail. Apparently, they do not want anyone on this path." He pushed up on his knees and stood. "We'll just have to be very careful. Stay right behind me and step where I step."

Alert for a clear side trail, they continued forward. Twice more, they found traps, and each one they successfully avoided.

But they were the most clever and carefully hidden traps of any so far. Quick almost didn't see the last one.

Sydney drew even with Quick intending to make him turn back. The werewolf should not have to risk his life for him. Instead, they should find another way, even if it was slower.

Sydney opened his mouth to speak, when he detected a faint and vaguely familiar odor. He couldn't remember where he'd smelled the awful scent before, but he associated it with bad. Then it hit him. The military base that had captured him. The soldiers possessed the same horrible smell.

Suddenly, Quick squatted and pulled Sydney down with him behind a bush. The werewolf held a finger to his snout, indicating silence. He pointed up into the trees.

At first, Sydney saw nothing, but a moment later, he detected movement. Gradually, his brain filled in the details. High in the trees was a small wooden platform covered by camouflage netting. It blended in so well that Sydney would have never seen it had Quick not pointed it out.

The man, a rifle slung over his shoulder, wore camo fatigues and sported night vision goggles. He leaned against the railing around the platform and was whispering into a handheld radio—likely the reason they had been able to approach so close. The man no doubt thought himself safely hidden in the dark of night. The poor soul had no idea a vampire and a werewolf were watching him.

Quick leaned over and growled quietly in his ear, "Let's get closer."

Sydney nodded.

Silently they approached using the scant cover along the trail. When they drew even with the sentry, Sydney could make out the man's conversation. The party on the other end seemed to be annoying him. "... I don't care what your patrol found! I tell you George. It just isn't possible! I set those traps myself, and no one can get through them alive, or at least without getting injured."

Sydney held his breath. Did they already know about them?

The sentry listened for a moment to the other party, then continued. "Did you consider that maybe some animal set those off? I mean, what else could it be?"

Sydney breathed a sigh of relief. They hadn't set off any traps, so they didn't know about them yet. But Sydney was puzzled. If they weren't setting them off, then what was?

Quick, determined to power through, led them past the sentry using every possible patch of bush for cover. But they didn't go far before they again halted.

Up ahead, they discovered a wide clearing carefully hidden with camouflage netting hanging from the nearby trees. Some low, squat tents were beneath it. Despite the late hour, several men and women of various ages and sizes walked purposely between the buildings. Everyone wore camo fatigues and was armed to the teeth with guns, knives, and rifles. One of the men even had a sword. But while they were well-equipped, they didn't have that same disciplined feel he had seen at the army base. No, this group was different.

"What is this place?" whispered Sydney. "They're definitely not regular military."

"They're not." Quick sighed. "They're survivalists, and we've stumbled across their camp. They've been preparing for the zombie apocalypse for years."

Sydney frowned. "But there are no such things as zombies. The walking dead don't exist."

Quick nodded toward the camp. "Tell that to them. If they get you in their sights, you may be walking, but you'll soon be dead."

"But why didn't the nuclear virus get them?" protested Sydney.

Quick gave him a puzzled look. Realizing the werewolf didn't know about it, Sydney quickly explained.

When he was done, Quick nodded. "I'd bet my grannie's last nickel that they found out about it and stole it for themselves."

Inside the camp, two men had been standing talking to one another. With a laugh, they parted and moved away, giving them their first clear view of a large oak beside one of the buildings. A prisoner was chained to it—

SARGE!

Sydney jumped up, but Quick pulled him back down.

"That's SARGE over there," whispered Sydney, excitedly. "Even if she is a robot, I've got to get her free."

Quick frowned. "If we stop for her. We might not get your blood in time. Our trek back is already taking longer than I'd hoped."

Sydney glanced toward the robot and back to Quick. "Just as you owe me, I owe that robot. She helped break us out of prison. I just can't leave her stranded."

Quick sighed. "All right. But I don't know how we can possibly do it. They'll start shooting the moment we appear."

Sydney looked back toward the robot. There had to be a way to get her loose.

Just then, a twig snapped behind them. Sydney closed his eyes and silently groaned. He knew they'd been caught. They both slowly turned, expecting to see a man holding a gun on them.

Instead, standing behind them stood a shaggy, nine-foot bag of matted carpet, and Sydney suddenly realized who had been setting off the traps. Mr. Sasquatch had followed them.

He gave a toothy smile and roared.

Sydney and Quick both yelled and went in separate directions. Quick skirted the perimeter of the camp while Sydney took a more direct route. He charged straight into the clearing.

The vampire started yelling, "Don't shoot! Don't shoot!"

The bigfoot hesitated, looking first after Quick and then after Sydney. Deciding he liked the vampire better, he charged after him.

The sentries in the clearing grabbed their weapons and aimed at Sydney. But they quickly shifted their sights when they saw what was chasing him. But not by much. They were perfectly content to fire at the monster right *through* Sydney.

The vampire dove to the ground, while the shots zinged over his head. "Why are people *always* shooting at me?"

While the bullets didn't penetrate the bigfoot's shaggy hide, they did hurt. Sasquatch skidded to a stop, turned, and fled with amazing speed back into the forest. But the group seemed content to just keep on firing and did so for about five minutes more. Leaves and small branches rained down on him as their bullets cut through the foliage.

Then suddenly, the firing stopped. The complete silence was unnerving. Nothing *dared* move. Sydney uncovered his head and looked up. From the side, he felt a warm piece of metal touch his temple.

Sydney looked up and smiled. "Thanks. I appreciate the help."

In response, someone cocked a gun.

"It's nice to have company," SARGE said.

Sydney strained against his chains again, which both he and Quick shared with the robot. He relaxed back against the tree and watched the night sentries pace off their rounds. Sydney was on the opposite side of the tree from the robot.

"Be still, Sydney," said Quick on the other side of the vampire. "Quit wasting your energy."

Shortly after they had captured Sydney, Quick was brought into the camp by three armed guards. But the werewolf made a good show of himself—all three of them had black eyes and one a bloody nose.

Exasperated, Sydney asked, "SARGE, can't you snap these chains or something?"

SARGE shrugged. "I guess I could. But the way they have me chained, I'd have to pull straight out from the tree. And since tightening my end would also tighten yours, it would surely cut you in half. Now you wouldn't want me to do that, would you?"

Sydney sighed. He was beginning to feel the effects of his blood deprivation. The tiredness that had started off the evening was turning into full-fledged fatigue. And on top of that, sunrise was only about an hour and a half away. It seemed he'd fry before he died from lack of blood.

"Do you know what they intend to do with us?" asked Sydney.

"Well, tomorrow, I imagine they'll question you two," said SARGE. "As for me, they've decided to turn me into a pile of scrap. They even went out and found a cutting torch just for me. Wasn't that nice of them?"

"Aren't you scared?" asked Quick.

"Me, scared? Not a chance. After all, it's not like I'm *human* or anything," the robot's voice picked up a hysterical quality. "I'm not really alive, so how can I die! There will just be the hissing of seared metal and the sparks of severed wires... and I'll be gone."

"I'd be scared," commented Quick.

"OK. So I lied. I'm terrified. So hurry up and find a way out of this! You're the thinkers. *Think* of something!"

Sydney wished he could. But he was unfortunately coming up empty. He wondered what his grandfather would have said about this current situation. Probably nothing good.

A light breeze caressed his cheek. But instead of diminishing, the breeze quickly grew in intensity until the forest shook. Leaves and dirt flew on the wind, and branches were torn from the surrounding trees. The vampire could feel the mighty oak at his back moving in the wind. *What the hell's happening?*

A powerful throbbing sound came from above the camouflage net. Faintly at first, but it grew louder.

All three looked up.

Descending from the sky was an oval-shaped craft glowing a gentle red. The same one Sydney had seen several nights ago.

The ground below it suddenly erupted in blinding white light, and the camouflage net fell to the ground. A bright spotlight illuminated the clearing. The sentries sounded the alarm, and the entire camp turned out, taking up positions just outside the circle of light. They opened fire.

But the craft kept coming. A mortar fired from somewhere, but the projectile harmlessly exploded against some kind of force field. A beam of orange light shot from beneath the vessel, at first seemingly to shoot at random. One beam hit the oak they were tied to, and the top of the tree fell off.

"Talk about going from the frying pan into the fire. We're being invaded by Martians," shouted Sydney.

Gradually the beam became more controlled and fired at the tents, catching each one on fire. But the fourth must have contained the munitions, and it went up like a Fourth of July firecracker.

When the survivalists saw how badly they were overpowered, they turned and ran. Several bolts of light followed them into the forest to ensure their flight.

When all was quiet except for the craft's throb and the crackling of several fires, it extended landing legs and came to rest in the center of the clearing. It crushed one of the remaining tents in the process.

Sydney, tied directly facing the craft, held his breath as a large hatch opened and a silhouette showed in the doorway. The figure bounded down the steps and ran straight for him. As it approached, he could tell its skin was rough and caked like dry mud. An exoskeleton, he speculated. A bug-like creature, maybe? Two eyes peered out at him from inside the rough skin.

"Oh damn," yelled SARGE. "It's the invasion of the robot snatchers!"

He strained at his chains as the being approached. It walked right up to Sydney, took his head in its hands and...

Kissed him.

CHAPTER TWENTY-EIGHT

Wrestling Match

Allie

VALIANTLY, ALLIE STRUGGLED AGAINST the paralysis caused by the white light, but only her eyes were hers to command. Cutting them hard to the right, she saw that Medorah still held Schro and was likewise affected.

Veezott grinned evilly and leaned closer. "Remember me? I sure remember you." Allie noticed that not only was the alien's skin green, but his teeth were too. The sight made her feel queasy.

He then stepped over to inspect Medorah. The alien moved easily through the light. He must have a way to neutralize it. Although, Allie did notice he walked with a pronounced limp.

Evidently, his encounter with the unicorn had left an impression. A deep one.

He gave Medorah a close examination. "You're pretty too. A little thin, but you vill do. Vhat say we go have fun."

Allie could only imagine what Medorah was doing to the alien in her mind.

Veezott leaned in her face. "Vhat?" he said mockingly. "No answer. Has the cat got your tongue? Let me help with that."

With a chuckle, he plucked the cat out from Medorah's arms.

Allie was afraid he might hurt Schro, but all he did was tuck the paralyzed cat under his arm.

Veezott was soon joined by the other two crew members. They stared at the women with hungry eyes. Allie would have shivered if she could have.

"I could not find hue'nicorn," Veezott said. "So I settled for you. I vant revenge for having my *vogmog* punctured!"

Vese grinned. "Let's feed them to a *villmond*," he suggested.

Veezott popped him on the head. "You idiot! They don't have *villmond* here. They can't survive the journey, and besides, they a protected species."

Vac brightened. His wilted hair was flopping as he talked. "Ve could take them high up in the air and push them out. Then use the long-range scope to watch them splat!"

Veezott shook his head. "Not good enough."

"Ve could make them run naked on the moon," chimed Vese. "And vatch their..."

Veezott interrupted and pointed an accusing finger at the alien. "Naked? On the moon? You're a pervert, you know that? You better clean up your act. You'll get us all in trouble."

The alien looked down, ashamed.

"Ve could collapse their molecules one by one," suggested Vac. "The agony would last for centuries."

Veezott shook his head. "Creative, but not bad enough." He slapped a fist into his open hand. "No, I vant something vorse. I vant them to... to...." He paused.

The group drew closer. Allie squeezed her eyes shut. This had to be bad.

The leader grinned even harder—his green teeth gleaming. "I vant them to mud-vrestle to the death!"

The group gave a collective, "Ooooh!"

Vese whispered to Vac, "That's bad, real bad. And dirty. Veezott must be really mad." The other alien nodded.

Vese thought for a moment and gave his commander a puzzled look. "How do you vrestle to the death?"

Veezott wheeled on Vese and started beating him on the head. "Ve improvise!"

Vac looked apprehensive. "But isn't that *dangerous*? Vhat if THEY find out. Having their kind in the ship is forbidden."

The leader wheeled on his underling. "Are you going to tell?"

Vac shook his head vigorously. "No. But...."

Veezott poked his underling in the chest. "Then they won't find out."

Vac didn't look happy. Whatever the danger he was concerned about, the others didn't seem to share it. She couldn't help but wonder who this mysterious THEY were.

Veezot stepped to where both women could see him and took out a dull metallic cylinder from a pouch on his belt. Then pulling on both ends, he extended it to a rod of about three feet.

"Both of you vatch closely." He touched the rod to the asphalt, and it immediately exploded into fine dust. He grinned evilly. "See vhat happens if you try to escape. Think what this vould do to your body parts."

He waved a hand at Vese, and the alien touched some buttons on a wide wristband. The blue light extinguished. Both women stumbled before finding their balance.

The leader pointed. "Now, go into the ship."

Allie and Medorah glanced at one another.

"Now!" Allie yelled.

The pair took off in different directions. Allie glanced over her shoulder to see if the aliens were following. Unexpectedly, the blue light returned and once more froze them in place.

Veezott shook his head. He walked up to Allie first and then over to Medorah. After thinking a moment, he held up the paralyzed Schro and pointed his rod weapon at him. "Do I need to show you again? Vould leave quite the mess."

Despite being unable to move, the eyes of both women reflected horror.

Veezott waved a hand. "Let's try this again."

This time when the light was extinguished, the women stayed in place. Medorah held out her arms. "Can I have my cat back?"

The leader stroked Schro's head, and he purred contently. "I think I'll hold him for now." He looked at the cat. "He likes me."

Schro gave the alien a satisfied look and then glanced at the two women. "I really can't stand him. Honestly, mistress. But he's got tuna."

Medorah grew angry. "Tuna? You'd trade me for tuna? He was going to kill you."

Not having magic, the alien couldn't understand the cat. He looked puzzled by Medorah's sudden outburst.

"So?" Schro moved so the alien could scratch his chin. "He's got tuna."

Medorah rolled her eyes.

Veezott pointed toward the ship with his rod weapon, and they were marched inside. As the hatch began to close, Allie had time to glance behind them one last time. Would she see the world again? Would Sydney think she had abandoned him? With a soft hiss and a note of finality, the hatch irised shut.

The inside of the ship was larger than Allie had expected. Lights and instruments lined the curved walls, and there were several swivel seats positioned in front of the consoles. On one side of the ship, which Allie thought of it as the front, was a large video screen, which currently showed a detailed view of the parking lot outside.

Vese went to a ladder set against the opposite wall going down into a hole in the floor. He climbed down, which meant there had to be a lower deck.

A moment later, Vese returned with two bodysuit-type garments and gave one to each. He then led them to the back and to a short door. "Change into the traditional costumes in there."

Medorah glared at him. "What if I don't want to?"

Vese shrugged. "Then you do it naked."

Allie grabbed her friend and pulled her inside a tiny room. It was hard to tell from the fixtures, but it looked to be the alien version of a toilet closet. At least the smell matched. The clothing was some sort of short-sleeved bodysuit. It was dull brown and made of a material that Allie had never encountered before. Thin, very tough, extremely slick—

And way too small.

It looked like it was made for one of the aliens. However,

she tugged at the garment's material and found it stretched quite a bit.

She quickly stripped off her prison uniform and began to pull on the item. It was tight, but the suit seemed to adjust to her larger size. It had short sleeves and came to just above her knees. Overall, not bad. Her swimsuit would have shown more. Although, it did highlight every curve of her body. She wondered what Sydney would have said to see her in it. She couldn't help but grin wickedly. *Get a grip, girl!*

The protection amulet had swung free as she changed. She briefly considered taking it off but decided against it, tucking it inside the high collar of the suit. She smiled. She had begun to think of it as a good luck charm. Maybe someday, they'd be in trouble together and get to try out its protection magic.

When Allie looked up from changing, Medorah had not moved. She just stood looking at the suit and made no motion to put it on. Despite her earlier bravado, the witch looked ready to cry. She looked at Allie uncertainly. "They want us to fight to the death. Are you really going to kill me?"

Allie smiled. "Me? Kill you? You're the one with powers."

Medorah shook her head slowly. "I can't use them directly against another person. And everything in here is artificial. I can't manipulate it. Besides..." She looked up at Allie. "I can't hurt a friend."

Allie put an arm around her. "No one is going to die." She grinned, feeling a confidence she hadn't felt since the apocalypse started. "We're just going to do what Clare Montare did that time she and Fortney Daylor fought with Bustier Betty and Evil Earlie." Allie nodded. "But for that to work, I'm going to need your help."

Medorah shook her head. "I don't know how to wrestle. How can I help?"

Allie grinned. "Because you're the one with the hocus pocus."

They emerged a few moments later. As per Allie's instructions, they held their heads high. The aliens were waiting and hooted at their entrance. Veezott whistled, and Vese applauded.

Allie had to admit, the suits did make them look pretty good. Especially Medorah. The garment seemed to love her slender form, and it showed it off perfectly.

She had also learned something personal about her friend. She didn't wear underwear. It freaked Allie out a little. She could understand not wearing a bra since the witch didn't have a lot upfront anyway. But still, it just went against everything Allie had been taught. Medorah had explained it was a witch thing. Clothes separated her from the natural environment, and she tried to keep those to a minimum. From the conversation, Allie suspected that when Medorah was at home just hanging out, that she literally *did*. Allie made a mental note to always call before visiting.

While most of the aliens were clearly enjoying this, Vac looked terrified. "Boss, I don't think this is a good idea. *THEY'LL* know. Somehow they always find out."

Veezott smacked him on the back of the head. "No, they von't. There is no vay they vill know."

Evidently, he was still concerned about the vague *THEY*. But Allie needed them all to participate if her plan was going to work. *What would Clare Montare do?*

Allie drew her lips back in the brightest smile she could imagine and waved. She nudged Medorah, and the witch gave a weak smile and also waved. Allie felt sorry for the normally confident witch. She was completely out of her element. Allie just prayed she could do her part.

The aliens led the pair below deck to an open space where they had set up what looked like a large kid's blow-up pool. Allie cringed to see it was filled with a greenish-brown, sticky-looking... mud. It had to be six inches or more deep. Allie frowned. This was not going to be fun. She hoped there were showers close by.

Veezott, still holding the cat, pulled out his destructo-rod and waved it at them. "Don't forget. I have this. Once you enter the ring, only one can come out alive." He raised the rod high. "Now, go to your corners."

Vese looked puzzled. "But... it's round."

Veezott glared at him. "I know, stupid! But that's the ritual phrase!" He turned to his captives. "DO IT!" he yelled.

It was time to put their plan into action. Allie shoved Medorah to the side. "Don't touch me, you witch!"

Medorah stumbled and gave Allie a puzzled look. Then understanding spread over her face. "Who the hell are you pushing, you ugly... blond!"

Allie gave her friend a frown. Was that the best she could do? She shoved Medorah again. "Listen, you good-for-nothing witch. Just because you have magic powers doesn't make you special. I can beat your butt any day or night."

Medorah shoved her back, getting into the exchange. "I may be a witch, but you're a vampire bitch. You have no class, so I'll kick your ass!"

Allie was impressed. She made a rhyme. Not bad. "Oh yeah! Bring it on, witch." She shoved Medorah hard. The witch stumbled back, her legs catching on the edge. She fell back into the pool.

All the aliens roared with laughter. Enraptured by the exchange, they moved closer. Only an evil grinning Veezott held back. He stroked Schro's head. The cat could have cared less what was going on.

As Medorah picked herself up, Allie put her hands on her hips and laughed dramatically. "What's the matter? Feeling a little dirty?"

Medorah nearly slipped again. "So that's how you wanna play. Then so be it. You are so gonna pay, vampire girl. Now get your ass in here."

Allie lifted her chin defiantly. "Make me."

Medorah reached across, grabbed Allie's arm, and yanked her in. Allie jumped a little to amplify the witch's tug and landed face-first in the mud while the witch lost her balance and fell backward.

Allie scooped mud out of her eyes and looked across to Veezott. He was still hanging back, the destructo-rod hanging loosely by his side. She needed him closer.

Allie jumped up, gave a flying tackle towards Medorah. They both grappled, and Allie threw her down. She dramatically jumped to land on the witch, but Medorah rolled away, leaving Allie to belly flop where she had been.

The aliens went wild, hollering and pumping their fists.

Veezott raised his head and took a step closer.

Both women stood and lunged for each other. Medorah grabbed her around the waist and tried to throw her down, but with the slickness of the mud, she just slipped off and fell herself. Allie stepped back and tried to rake some of the mud off her face. She was covered from head to toe.

Veezott took another step closer. He was almost there. Allie glanced at Medorah and saw her breathing hard from the exertion. Moving in the mud was exhausting, and it looked like the witch was nearing her limits. It had to be now.

Medorah moved to a crouch, as did Allie. She gave a faint nod to the witch who returned it with one of her own. Then they immediately rushed at each other. Allie grabbed Medorah and threw her down. The witch pushed her off and then tried to crawl away.

"Oh no, you don't!" Allie grabbed Medorah by her ankles and stood. Drawing hard on her vampire strength, she began to swing Medorah around by her ankles.

The aliens went wild at the move.

Veezott took a step closer.

Allie smiled, taking note of exactly where he stood. He was close enough.

"NOW!" she yelled.

Medorah whispered, "Gravi, ruchis, nill illumious!"

Suddenly the inside of the ship was plunged into total darkness. Allie released Medorah low to the ground just barely high enough to clear the sides of the pool. A moment later she heard a collision and Veezott yell out.

After a moment of scuffling, the lights snapped back on. Medorah stood with one muddy foot on Veezott's chest, and the destructo-rod pointed at his head. "Go ahead," she said evilly. "Make my day."

Schro stood to one side, pacing back and forth. He appeared

agitated but unhurt. Allie reached to pick him up, but the cat hissed at her.

"Don't you dare touch me with that mud on your hands." Schro shivered. "I'd never be clean again." The cat promptly turned, stuck his tail up in the air, and strutted a short distance away. He sat down to glare at her.

Medorah held the weapon at Veezott's head. "All of you! Get out before I use this on your friend!"

"Actually, he's not my friend...." said Vese.

"DO IT!" yelled a panicked Veezott. He was looking a little pale, even if he was green.

Vac fell to his knees before them. "Please don't take the ship. *THEY* vill kill us."

Medorah glared at him. "You want mercy after all you were doing to us?"

Vac nodded hopefully. "Please. Ve vere just having a little fun. Ve vould have let you go." He licked his lips nervously. "But *THEY* don't mess around. A fate vorse than death avaits us."

Allie shook her head. "Sorry, but you should have thought about that before you took us captive. Now, do as my friend says. And take off your wrist bands."

Vac got to his feet, looking totally defeated. The two crew members did as instructed and then went out the door.

While Medorah held the rod to his head, Allie hauled Veezott to his feet and dragged him to the door. He balked at the hatch.

"Can ve talk? Maybe vork something out? Vac's right. *They* vill kill us."

Allie and Medorah considered each other.

"I guess we could," said Allie. Both women grinned. "But then, maybe not." She shoved the alien out the door.

He tripped down the steps and landed hard on his butt. He howled in pain and rubbed his backside. "My *vogmog!*"

Medorah hit the door controls, and the door irised shut.

Laughing and caked in the alien mud, Allie and Medorah hugged each other.

"You did great, girl!" said Allie.

"You did great too. And that was a lot of fun." She eyed the pool "I might set one of these up at home for Quick and I to play in." She grinned evilly. "It would make a fun Tuesday night. Especially if..."

Allie held up a hand and turned her head away. "Stop right there. TMI!"

Medorah grinned a moment longer and then looked around in alarm. "Where's my cat?"

Allie pointed to the animal sitting well away from them. Medorah took a step in his direction, but the cat immediately stood.

"Don't even think about it," he said. "I'll scratch your eyes out."

Medorah grinned. "But you want tuna, don't you? Surely a little squeeze is worth that?"

Schro huffed. "The tuna was just a clever ploy to help you capture them. I had them completely under control."

Medorah put her hands on her hips. "How many cans of tuna did you eat?"

"The jerk only had five."

Medorah stared in disbelief.

Schro started grooming a paw. "I was hungry."

Medorah rolled her eyes. With a look of disgust, she turned to Allie. "I'll never understand cat logic."

Allie looked down at her mud-covered self. Whatever it was, it wasn't true mud, but rather some kind of synthetic goo. And it was drying fast. She rubbed on it, trying to get it off. While there were a few flakes, for the most part, it didn't want to come off. That would just have to wait until she could get a shower.

Allie looked to the front of the craft. Through the screens, they could see the group of aliens outside arguing. She couldn't hear what was being said, but she could tell there was definitely a lot of heat in their words. As she watched, the normally calm Vac punched Veezott.

Allie nodded toward the controls. "Think you can fly this thing?"

Medorah smiled. "I drove the truck, didn't I?"

Allie rolled her eyes. "Yeah, but this is a spaceship."

Medorah shrugged. "So. Those idiots drove it, and I'm sure my IQ is at least a hundred points over theirs. Besides..." She grinned evilly. "There are a few more curse words you haven't heard yet."

CHAPTER TWENTY-NINE

Mud Monster's Kiss

Sydney

SYDNEY BLINKED IN SURPRISE as the strange being drew back from the kiss. It had been pleasant—not the horribly painful, deadly experience he had expected. And it was somehow... familiar.

"You're a hard person to keep track of," said the being using Allie's voice. She grinned widely, displaying vampire teeth just like Allie's. His mouth fell open.

"Is that you?" asked Sydney hesitantly.

In typical Allie manner, she put her hands on her hips. "I know I don't look my best right now, but I've had a rough night." She nodded towards the chains. "Looks like yours hasn't been going so well either."

Just then, Medorah, likewise covered in a layer of the black stuff, tore out of the spacecraft and ran to her husband. She jumped into his arms and kissed him all over his hairy face. When she pulled back, he was covered in mud smears. "You're all right!" She gave him another squeeze. "I was so worried about you! And from the looks of things, we arrived just in time."

Quick shrugged as best he could while bound to the tree. "I had the situation completely under control. I was just getting ready to make my move."

She kissed him again, leaving another huge smear. "Whatever you say, dear."

SARGE made a throat-clearing sound. "When you get through with all the lovey-dovey stuff, could you let us go? I've been chained here for quite some time. If I don't move my joints soon, they'll freeze up."

He and Allie exchanged a glance. A frozen SARGE? Now that idea had some appeal.

Medorah produced the alien destructo-rod and burnt out a link of the chain holding them. Then, with his arms free, Sydney pulled Allie into a hug. "I was worried about you," he said. And then he kissed her. Not a peck, but a *real* kiss.

They separated. Allie staggered. "Wow! I didn't know you could kiss like that."

Sydney smiled, likewise affected. "Neither did I. It must have something to do with the partner."

Quick looked around. "We better leave before those survivalists come back. They're going to be a little pissed that you squashed their tents." He pointed a thumb at the spaceship. "You're going to have to tell me how you got this."

Sydney nodded. "And how you got covered with that... stuff?"

The two women glanced at one another and exchanged a knowing look. Medorah smiled, her teeth looking brilliant white against the dark of the mud. "We got into a little bit of a fight."

Allie smiled. "But we'll tell you later. It's a long and *dirty* story."

Sydney looked from one to the other and then finally to Quick. The werewolf shrugged.

Allie looked down at the mud on her hand. "I wish I could get this stuff off. It's starting to itch."

Sydney pointed to one of the few remaining tents. "That looks like a shower over there."

Allie glanced in that direction and then at Medorah. The witch grinned.

"Do you mind waiting?" asked Allie.

Sydney chuckled. "You're the one driving."

Allie and Medorah took off for the shower. Only a few minutes later, they returned with damp hair and a towel across their shoulders but looking much cleaner.

But the suits they wore. They were... Sydney stared with an open mouth. He knew Allie had not been dressing to show off her figure, but damnation, she was beautiful.

SARGE came up beside him and gently pushed up on his chin to close his mouth. "You don't want to catch flies. Besides, her figure's nowhere near as sexy as mine."

Sydney looked from the robot back to the approaching Allie. "Are you sure about that?"

SARGE sighed sadly. "Are you telling me you'd rather have *her* than this wet dream of a body?"

Sydney didn't even look at her. "Yes."

SARGE looked down. "Does this mean we're breaking up? Use me and then discard me. Leave me for another woman without a thought?"

Sydney looked from SARGE to Allie. "But we've never..." He threw up his hands. "I give up." He walked away.

SARGE called after him. "Remember, I'll take you back."

Sydney just ignored her and went over to join Allie.

A breeze suddenly picked up and began to stir the trees. But instead of decreasing, it steadily grew stronger.

"Uh, sorry to be the one to break the news, but I think we've got a problem," announced SARGE unexpectedly.

Sydney immediately scanned the area. "Where? I don't see anything."

SARGE pointed up, and Allie gasped.

Looking to where the robot indicated, Sydney's mouth flew open in shock.

Directly above them was the largest flying object he had ever seen. It was huge, glowing with a pulsing pink light and dwarfing the spacecraft the women had arrived in. It gradually descended, completely filling their view of the sky, before hovering over them with its bottom nearly touching the tallest trees.

SARGE groaned. "They're going to make me their Martian love slave. I just know it. I'll spend the rest of my life wearing a collar and see-through skirts."

Sydney really had to wonder exactly what SARGE had been given to read during her programming.

He put an arm around Allie and protectively pulled her to his side. He had seen the firepower of the smaller craft. From the size of this one, it looked like it could take out everything on this side of the continent. But one thing was sure.

It was the aliens' mother ship.

Mother Ship

Allie

A BEAM OF BRIGHT pink light shot down in front of them, blinding them with its brilliance. Allie had to hold up a hand to shield her eyes. Gradually, the shadows of three figures appeared in the beam. Allie couldn't tell if they had floated down or just materialized there. Either way, it was unnerving. This had to be the mysterious *THEY* the aliens had been worried about.

Suddenly, the light vanished. Allie blinked at the unexpected change in illumination. As her eyes adapted, she could make out a small group of beings. They all were of short stature, had green skin—

And were definitely female.

There were three of them, and while they were not beautiful by human standards, they were not ugly either. Allie thought of them as being short and full-figured. The female leading the other two was dressed in a gray business suit. She looked very professional and didn't appear the least bit menacing. In fact, she reminded Allie of some of the salespeople that would frequently visit the hospital.

The second alien female was dressed in a T-shirt and jeans and held a small alien child on her hip. The remaining woman, wearing a blouse and skirt, held the hand of a young child standing beside her. It had a finger stuck in its mouth and stared at the humans in open curiosity.

The alien in the business suit stepped forward. "Greetings, Earthlings. We come from the planet Violespote. My name is Vibra, and I believe you have already met our husbands."

Allie glanced at those with her and found they were all just as stunned as she was.

SARGE unexpectedly shoved her, and Allie stumbled forward to stand before the alien female. "Take this one. We don't need her," called the robot.

Allie glared at SARGE as the robot grabbed Sydney by the arm and pulled him against her. "We have one woman too many, anyway."

Sydney tried to get away but was unable to break SARGE's grip.

Allie sighed. That robot. She was going to have a word with her about their bargain again.

She turned back to the alien. "Welcome to Earth. I'm sorry the place is a mess, but you've caught us at a bit of a bad time, with the apocalypse and all."

The alien nodded. "We did notice you had... ah..." she looked around. "Done some redecorating."

Allie nodded. "A little." She frowned. "So, what brings you to our planet?"

"We need to collect our husbands. I hope they haven't troubled you too much." She smiled sweetly.

Allie crossed her arms. "They only captured us, paralyzed us, and made us mud wrestle."

The alien eyed Allie's clothes. "I can tell," she said flatly. "I apologize for any inconvenience they may have caused. I assure you they will be punished." She looked pained. "You and Veezott didn't... you know." She gave Allie a knowing look.

"Hell, no," Allie snorted. "Not even close."

Vibra looked relieved. "So, I assume you have no objection to us collecting our husbands?"

Allie glanced back over her shoulder at her companions. SARGE was rubbing on Sydney as he tried to shove her away. Quick shook his head, and Medorah shrugged. They weren't much help.

Allie frowned. "Your guys I don't care about. We left them in a parking lot back in the city. I can tell you where."

"Are they all right? Is my Vac OK?" the one with the child asked, worry in her voice.

"They were when we left. We didn't do anything to them. Although they looked like they were fighting as we pulled away."

She visibly relaxed. The child holding his mother's hand plugged a finger in his nose and looked up at his mother. "Where's Da, Momma? Is he OK?"

She looked down at him and pulled out his offending finger. "He's fine, baby." She looked back up at Allie, the pleasant smile on her face vanishing and twisting into one of utter rage. "Or at least he will be until I *kick his ass* all the way back to Home Star."

Allie shivered at the woman's expression. Vac had been the one worried, and now she understood why.

The alien leader indicated the smaller craft behind her. "I hope you don't mind if we take our husband's vehicle."

Allie frowned. She was not going to let them get off that easily. "The ship would be nice to have around. After all, we did get captured."

The alien glanced behind her as the two others fidgeted. The child on the other mother's hip started to whimper, and the mother made shushing sounds.

"That might be difficult..."

"Oh?"

Vibra looked pained. "You see..."

Allie interrupted. "Let me guess. They're still paying for the last time they did something like this."

The alien grimaced.

The woman with the small child behind her stepped forward. "Please, miss. Our husbands are idiots. We know that. But please just let us have the ship back. He's still making payments."

The other woman piped up. "They're not bad guys. We love 'em, and they try to take care of us. They just lost their jobs and are having trouble figuring out what they want to do next. Downsizing, you know."

The woman with a small child nodded. "And don't worry. We'll see that they are punished." She had that terrifying look again. "Vac is going to be sleeping on the couch for a l-o-o-o-ong time."

Allie thought for a moment. These women were in a predicament. They couldn't help that their husbands were assholes. And they were asking nicely. Plus, she really didn't want to start an interplanetary incident.

Allie sighed.

"All right. But can you let us borrow it for a few days?" She pointed over her shoulder to her friends. "We need a ride back to the city, and Medorah needs to find a new home."

The alien woman smiled and stepped forward. She extended her hand. "You have a deal."

Medorah dropped Allie, Sydney, and SARGE in a clear spot at the base of Carrington Hill. Quick had been dying to get his hands on the craft's controls, but Medorah wouldn't let him, saying it was her ship right now. He'd have to find his own.

Medorah had invited the vampires to come along and search for a home with them, but they both refused. As Sydney pointed out, they needed to find a new source of blood, or they were doomed to die.

It was a tearful goodbye as they said their farewells. Medorah was especially reluctant to leave her new friend and pulled Allie into a final hug.

Medorah gave her a weak smile. "You know, I've never had a friend like you before. I'd even consider bringing one of those army soldiers over for you."

Allie shook her head. "Thank you, but no. I don't want to steal a person's blood. It's what someone did to me, and I refuse to do it to another."

Medorah looked at her sadly. "Even if you die?"

Allie held her gaze for a moment. She blinked as her eyes became moist. She nodded. "Even if I die."

With tears in her own eyes, Medorah pulled her friend into one last hug and turned away. Quick stepped forward and also gave her a hug and whispered in her ear. "Thank you. And let me know if there is anything I can do. Medorah doesn't make friends easily, and a friend of hers is a friend of mine."

She patted him on the chest. "Thank you."

Quick then turned to Sydney and pulled him into a bear-crushing hug. Sydney's eyes were bulging out. "And partner, thanks for saving my life. We're pack brothers now. And we never forget our debts."

He and Sydney fist-bumped. "Until we meet again."

Quick pulled Medorah to his side and rubbed her arm. "Just in case you change your mind, we'll stop by in a couple days to check on you. I should have a new *Demoness* by then."

Sydney smiled. "That would be nice." He didn't say more as he looked at his friend sadly. From his expression, you could see he had come to the same conclusion that she had. They likely wouldn't be alive when they returned. They only had three pints left. The math wasn't in their favor.

The couple turned, and arm in arm, went into the ship. Allie and Sydney watched silently as they disappeared into the sky.

Without speaking, the trio walked up Carrington Hill deep in thought. Allie had no idea what they would do next. Maybe they had overlooked something. Maybe there was a human out there that would be willing to donate. Maybe... Maybe...

Her lips twisted into a wry smile. *Right, pigs could fly. They were going to die. She was a poet and didn't know it.*

She glanced at Sydney and caught him checking her out. He

blushed and quickly looked away. She couldn't help the smile that came to her lips. The alien bodysuit revealed all her curves. She guessed she should be embarrassed. But she wasn't. He was just so easy to be around. She really liked him. Too bad they would only have a few days to be together. She sighed. *What would Clare Montare do?* As she always did, Clare would likely meet it head-on. And wouldn't stop until the bell rang.

As they crested Carrington Hill and walked toward the shelter, Allie instinctively knew only an hour of daylight remained. She glanced over at Sydney's profile. He was handsome, in a rich playboy kind of way. *Get a grip, girl!* came that unbidden thought.

She remembered all of her mother's boyfriends. And the heartbreak she had suffered. Allie cocked her head to one side. Perhaps her mother was more of a fighter than she thought. She might have lost all her matches, but at least, after every one of them, she had picked herself up and gotten back in the ring. Allie had never lost because she'd been afraid she would get hurt. And sometimes, you had to risk being hurt to be happy.

She looked over at Sydney. *Get a grip, girl!* came that thought again.

She smiled wickedly. *To hell with that!*

A sudden plan formed. If she hoped to put it into motion, she had best hurry.

At the entrance to the shelter, she turned to Sydney. "Why don't you station SARGE out here to guard. We're both exhausted and need a good day's sleep. I'll go in first and get everything ready."

Sydney put his hands on his hips and nodded. "That does sound like a good idea. I am sort of tired."

Allie then looked to the robot. "*SARGE*," putting a little force into the robot's name. "It's time. Our bargain."

SARGE slumped. "All right. I'll let you have this one, but the next one is all mine."

Allie nodded.

Sydney looked from one to the other but couldn't figure out what had just happened.

"Alright then," Allie grinned. "Show SARGE the perimeter you want her to walk, and I'll go ahead inside to shower. I really need to get all that mud off." She smiled. "I do have a few more nooks and crannies than you do."

Sydney blushed to an almost glowing red. She so loved to tease him.

Without waiting for an answer, she trotted to the shelter and went inside. Making plans on what to wear, she stepped toward the bathroom but paused at the scuff of a boot.

A cold cylindrical piece of metal poked into her back. Allie gasped in alarm.

"Hands up, miss," said someone behind her.

Allie almost cried. She knew that voice.

"Turn around."

She did as commanded and came face to face with Major Fritz Van Vilkenberg.

The evil vampire that had been behind their capture at the army base. And he could only want one thing.

Their remaining blood.

CHAPTER THIRTY-ONE

Thief Returns

Sydney

SYDNEY WATCHED ALLIE RUN into the shelter and scratched his head. "Why was she in such a hurry?" he mumbled to himself. But as she ran, he couldn't help but notice her beauty. He shook his head. No, there was more to it than that. No woman had disarmed him so thoroughly. He wondered what his grandfather would have said about her. Then he smiled. He would have liked her. Even said she had spunk. He nodded. The way she had handled those aliens? Yeah, she had spunk.

SARGE came up beside him. "You like her, don't you?"

Sydney nodded. "I do. Now, if only she liked me."

SARGE gave a snorting sound. "You males are so dense sometimes. The woman is smitten with you."

Sydney looked puzzled. He hooked a thumb over his shoulder in the direction she had left. "Her? No, she just views me as a friend."

SARGE looked at him a moment. "You have no idea what our bargain was, do you?"

Sydney frowned. "No. I've been wondering, though."

The robot put a hand on her hip. "We made a bargain that I could try to win your favors for two days. And if I didn't, I had to back off, because you were hers."

Sydney pointed to himself, and SARGE nodded.

"Not counting the time we spent apart, my time ended at midnight. She beat me." SARGE struck her sexiest pose. "I don't know how you could resist me, but you did. Which means there is only one explanation. And she is it."

Sydney thought the robot was a little off in her opinion of herself. He wouldn't have done anything with her even if she was the last woman, or robot, on Earth.

SARGE shoved him toward the shelter. "Now get in there and make me proud." And the robot stood at attention and saluted.

Sydney shook his head. Someone had really messed up badly on her programming. But then he smiled, stood erect, held his head high, and saluted her back.

The robot nodded. "Now get in there and give'm hell!"

"Yes, sir!" With a smile on his face, he turned and marched into the shelter.

When he entered, his smile fell. He immediately knew something was wrong.

At a muffled sound behind him, he turned to find Major

Fritz Van Vilkenberg holding a gun to Allie's head. Thankfully, she was OK. But she looked more pissed than afraid.

"Good evening, Sydney," Van Vilkenberg said. "I've been waiting for you."

Sydney glared at him. "Hello, Major. What brings you to this side of the city? I thought you were quite comfortable in your underground base."

Van Vilkenberg frowned. "I was. That is until *you* left me in that cell. The fools didn't find me until morning, and by then, I was fast asleep. When they couldn't rouse me, they became suspicious and ran some tests. They discovered I was a vampire and locked me up! I managed to escape, but I *will* find a way back in. I need their blood." He grinned evilly. "But now I need a quick fix. I knew you had some; otherwise, you would be dead by now." He pressed the gun to Allie's head. "So give it to me, unless you want to see her brains scattered all over your walls. She may be a vampire, but a bullet in her brain will kill her as assuredly as a stake in the heart."

"Don't do it, Sydney," Allie called. "He's going to kill us anyway."

Sydney sighed. "I have to."

In one quick move, Allie grabbed Vilkenberg's arm and pointed it up. A shot echoed through the chamber. In a swift wrestling move, she threw him over her shoulder onto his back. The gun went flying. She then planted a foot on his chest and savagely twisted his arm.

"You don't pick on a Clare Montare girl," she spat.

Sydney scrambled to get the gun. He leveled it at the old vampire. "Now who has who?" He smiled.

To Sydney's surprise, Van Vilkenberg just chuckled. "You really are stupid."

Against his will, Sydney swung the gun to point at Allie. "Release him, or I'll shoot," the words coming mechanically out of his mouth.

Allie looked at him in shock and betrayal. He motioned her to step back with the gun.

The old vampire slowly stood, rolling the shoulder of the arm Allie had twisted. "I haven't survived two centuries without learning the full extent of my powers. Did you actually think *you*, two neophytes, could capture me?"

He motioned to Sydney impatiently. "Give me the gun, and we'll find something to bind her hands."

Sydney stepped stiffly over to hand him the gun. Allie used the diversion to make a break for the door, but Sydney, grabbed her as she fled past and wrapped his arms tightly around her. He bodily lifted her off the floor as she struggled. "Sydney, you can fight it," Allie yelled. "You can overcome it."

Within himself, Sydney fought valiantly. But he couldn't win free. The older vampire's grip on his mind was too strong.

"Here," Vilkenberg handed Sydney the tiebacks from the shelter's fake draperies. "Use these to bind her hands."

Sydney pinned her to the wall and then tied Allie's hands behind her back.

Van Vilkenberg stepped over to Allie, gripped her by the scruff of her neck, and pointed the gun to her head. Sydney staggered as the older vampire suddenly released his control.

"I need your free will to show me where the blood is," said Vilkenberg. "After I have it, I will let you and the girl go unharmed. You have my word. But hurry!"

Sydney noticed the older vampire seemed paler than before and maybe a little weak. He must be overdue, which was why he fell easy prey to their brief physical attack. If they could think of a way to overcome his powers of control, they could get him. The shelter had a defense against other vampires—a contingency installed when he moved in. But it wouldn't work under the present circumstances. Sydney thought of the shelter's carefully prepared trap, installed just in case something like this happened. But he could think of no way to use it. It had all seemed so simple when he had planned it, but he had not counted on the other's mental powers. Sydney racked his brain, trying to come up with something.

He tried to stall, thinking he could perhaps run the clock out until sunrise. "I noticed you can control me, but not Allie. Is that because you can only control males?"

Vilkenberg smirked. "Unlike you fledglings, I have no such limitations. I can influence any human. But for vampires, I can only control the ones I've personally turned." He frowned. "But in a lapse of judgment, I let my traitorous protégée turn your young lady here." His voice drew deadly. "A decision I've come to regret."

"Who…"

Vilkenberg cut him off. "Quit stalling! I want that blood now!"

Sydney sighed. He was out of options. He turned toward his secret room.

Dragging Allie beside him, Vilkenberg followed Sydney into the interior of the shelter. They passed along the row of his ancestors' portraits. To Sydney, each one seemed to be frowning at him. "You disappoint us," they seemed to say. "You're a disgrace and a failure."

And then he passed in front of the portrait of his grandfather. His always angry eyes seemed to glare at him. He could
almost hear him. *And you call yourself a Carrington.*

He looked down. Carringtons never gave up. There had to be
something he could do.

He led them to the back of the shelter and paused at the hidden door. He glanced at Allie behind him, who gave him a weak
smile. How in the world could he have let this happen?

He thought of the trap he had prepared. The old vampire's
control would make it impossible to use. He would just take
Sydney over and use it on him instead.

Sydney blinked. Maybe, just maybe, there was a way.

He sighed dramatically and reached for the hidden latch.
The secret door opened, revealing the freezer.

"Open it," commanded Van Vilkenberg.

Sydney did and revealed the last three plastic bags of life.

The old vampire smiled. "Three bags. This was better than I
had expected! Give them to me."

He shoved Allie away as Sydney handed over the bags.

Vilkenberg motioned with the gun. "Back out."

"You said you would let us go!" protested Allie. "You gave us
your word!"

He laughed. "So sue me!"

He herded them back to the common room. "Well, it was
nice. So long, and thanks for all the blood."

Smiling, he raised the gun to point at them.

Sydney was racking his brain. This was the point he needed
to say exactly the right thing. If he didn't, they were dead.

Sydney took a deep breath. "It's a long way back to the base.
Don't you need to go to the bathroom?"

Both Vilkenberg and Allie drew back in puzzlement.

"Why did you say that?" demanded Vilkenberg.

"Oh, just wondering."

"You had to have a reason. Now TELL ME!" He raised the pistol to Allie's head.

"All right, but stay calm," said Sydney. "It's just that there's a sunlamp in there."

Vilkenberg laughed. "You've got to be kidding. You wanted to trick me with that? Did you actually think I would fall for something that stupid? No, I think instead *you* should go to the bathroom."

"But I don't have to go."

Van Vilkenberg frowned.

"All right, I was trying to trick you."

"Then the spider will get caught in his own web."

He motioned with his gun toward the bathroom.

Allie looked at him sidewise. She likely was trying to puzzle out what Sydney was doing.

They stepped inside and turned to face him. "Where's the controls," he demanded.

Sydney pointed at the timer switch inside the bathroom.

He grinned. "Excellent. A most fitting, not to mention painful, death. Bye, bye, suckers!" He shoved Allie inside and slammed the door.

Sydney only had time to catch Allie before the compulsion came. *Turn the sunlamp's timer dial.* Sydney reached for the knob.

"Fight it, Sydney! Fight it! You're stronger than he is. Don't let him win!" Allie tried to block his hand with her body and simultaneously tried to free herself. Gently, he pushed her aside.

"Don't do it, Sydney!" She jumped on him, trying to knock him down.

Sydney firmly gripped her shoulders and forced her to her knees. She struggled to stand, but her tied hands hindered her.

Sydney grasped the timer knob.

"DON'T, SYDNEY!"

Sydney paused for a moment. *Now why would he want to stop?*

He turned the knob.

Immediately, there was a scream from the other side of the door, and simultaneously, the control over Sydney was released.

Allie gazed up at him in shock. "What's happening? Why aren't we dead?"

Sydney smiled, helped her to her feet, and pulled her into a tight hug. "During one of my paranoid spells, I worried that the *other* vampire would come after me. So I arranged this little trap. The sunlamp controls are inside here, but the sunlamp is outside. Actually, about a dozen of them. Remember that first evening you were here, and you tried to turn on the sunlamp? That's why I was so upset. You could have accidentally fried me."

Sydney untied Allie's hands. She flung her arms around him and kissed him gently. Just then, the timer bell went off.

He grinned. "How do you like your vampire? Rare, medium, or my personal favorite?" He opened the door to a pile of bones and dust just outside. "Well done."

After reclaiming the partially thawed packets from the pile of bones and sharing one between them, they swept up

Vilkenberg's remains, and Sydney carried them outside. Just in time too. The sun had begun lightening the horizon.

SARGE watched him critically as he dumped the bones in a small hole and covered them with dirt. "Found a skeleton in your closet?"

"No," said Sydney. "Vilkenberg broke into my shelter and was going to steal my blood. But I fixed him."

"I'll say," said the robot. "That's the worst case of burnout I've ever seen."

"Now, keep a close watch for anyone trying to get in during the day."

"Right! No one will get past ol' SARGE." The robot thumped her metal chest. "You can count on me."

For some reason, this was not much comfort. Sydney went back downstairs.

Since Allie was already in the shower, Sydney got out the extra casket and set it up while he was waiting his turn. He hadn't had a bath in two days. He had just finished with the casket when Allie stuck her head out. "Sydney, you wouldn't have something a girl could sleep in, would you?"

"There are a few nightshirts in the storage area," he answered.

Allie wrinkled up her nose. "That wasn't exactly what I had in mind. Could you get me a robe, and I'll take a look myself?"

Sydney nodded. He went back into the storage room and brought out a long plain robe. He hoped it fit.

He handed it through the door to her, and a few minutes later, she emerged with a towel around her hair and wearing a much too large robe.

She smiled. "Do me a favor, Sydney. Don't buy me any clothes."

Sydney had to smile too. He blushed. "I never claimed to be good with women's apparel."

Allie went in search of sleeping attire, and Sydney went to take his shower. As he was undressing, he noticed she had thrown her clothes in the same corner he used for his. It seemed kind of intimate as he threw his own on top of hers. He tried to imagine a lifetime of sharing like that and found the thoughts pleasant. He sang in the shower.

Fifteen minutes later, he emerged refreshed and wearing clean pajamas. He opened the door and stopped dead in his tracks. His mouth flew open.

She was beautiful.

Seductively dressed in a long white-satin nightgown, she posed beside the extra casket. The gown fit her perfectly, clinging in just the right places and vividly emphasizing all her curves. Her half of the amulet still hung around her neck, and she somehow made the gaudy piece look excellent.

Sydney couldn't help but gawk, and Allie blushed.

"Do I look all right?" she asked shyly.

"E-e-excellent!" he managed.

She patted the extra casket and then pointed over her shoulder at his bedroom. "I hope you don't mind, but that casket in your room is so big, and so much has happened in the last few days, I-I wondered if you would like to share it with me."

Sydney smiled.

Allie held up a finger. "But to be clear, I do mean sleep." She took a deep breath. "This is a big step for me." She looked away, embarrassed. "And I'm hoping we can take this a little slow."

Sydney quickly closed the distance and swept her up into his arms. "I would consider it an honor and a privilege if I could share a casket with you. And as for the other, we can definitely take it slow. After all, we've got all the time left in the world."

And then he kissed her.

He carried her to his casket and placed her gently on the pink satin cushions inside. She giggled as he crawled in beside her and closed the lid. She snuggled up with her head on his shoulder and her scent teasing his nose. He could get used to this.

But as the vampire's sleep began to claim him, a nagging worry fluttered through his mind. He was forgetting something.

Something important.

CHAPTER THIRTY-TWO

Kidnapped Bride

Allie

AS ALLIE AWOKE, SHE wondered where that God-awful humming was coming from. It was terrible. Definitely not Sydney. It was just the same dozen notes over and over. It almost sounded like the beginning of the wedding march.

She opened her eyes to find she was no longer in the casket, but instead was laid out on a long table with her feet and hands chained to it. She still wore the white nightgown, and thankfully, her amulet.

What the hell?

She seemed to remember vague dreams of being jostled, covered in a plastic-smelling bag, and generally mistreated. And while she remembered trying to tell the person to stop, she hadn't been able to because of her vampire-enforced slumber. No doubt someone had moved her in the night. But who?

And where was Sydney?

She turned her head towards the sound of the obnoxious humming. The person had his back to her. He was dressed in what looked like a black tuxedo. And he was a big person. Strong looking. And familiar.

He was standing beside a table and seemed to be working on something she couldn't make out. A chainsaw, maybe. She wasn't sure. His bulk blocked the view. What looked to be a zippered body bag lay on the floor next to him. Likely it had been what blocked out the sun and saved her life.

Allie quietly tested her chains, but despite her vampire strength, were too strong for her to break. She was trying to be quiet, but the person must have heard her anyway. He turned and smiled when he saw she was awake. Allie groaned when she saw his face.

It was Rip. And whatever he was up to, it couldn't be good. After all, the deranged man had tried to kill her on multiple occasions.

"Ah," he said, grinning widely. "You're awake. I wondered if something was wrong." He leaned forward. "You're a pretty heavy sleeper."

Allie did not answer. Instead, she took in her surroundings, looking for a method of escape. Anything she could use against him.

But as her eyes searched, her horror grew. She was at the front of a partially collapsed chapel. Several strings of tiny white lights had been hung along the walls and softly illuminated the interior.

She was fortunate he had removed her from the body bag inside the building; otherwise, she would have shared Van Vilkenberg's fate. She shivered. Someone, or likely a certain protection amulet, was watching out for her. If she ever got back to Naelimag, she was going to have to apologize to the magician. His necklace really did work.

The table she lay on was positioned at the front of the chapel's altar. Beyond that, stretching toward the entrance, were at least a dozen rows of wooden pews, each decorated with a large white bow on the end.

But most surprising was that they were all occupied.

With dead bodies.

There were dead of all kinds propped in the seats, wearing their finest suits and dresses. Looking in the other direction, she saw a raised platform that served as the pulpit. But strangely, in the spot reserved for the clergy to deliver their message, was a mysterious object concealed by a red velvet covering. It appeared to be cylindrical in shape and about four feet tall. It didn't seem to be part of the normal furniture. Whatever it was, it gave Allie the creeps.

Why was he doing this? she wondered. And then it hit her. The tux, the chapel, the white ribbons.

There was going to be a wedding.

Allie's eyes grew wide in understanding.

She was the bride.

He left his chainsaw on the table and stepped over to grin down at her. "It won't be long now. I just need to finish sharpening my blades. I just want everything perfect for your special day."

He bent down out of her line of sight, and Allie could hear

him rummaging in something under the table. He popped back up a moment later, holding a short white veil. He carefully placed it on her head. "There now. Every bride needs a veil." He giggled in delight.

Allie shivered.

He patted her arm. "Now I have to finish up preparations for our big day." He paused, looking serious. "Do you need a sip of water, or do you need to go to the bathroom?"

The bathroom! Maybe he would release her for that.

However, before she could open her mouth, he bent down and lifted up a box of adult diapers. Extra heavy-duty. "I've tried to think of everything." He glanced at them. "It's the same kind they used on me at the hospital."

Allie paled. She shook her head. "I'm good," she said brightly.

He took her hand in his. "I'm glad we're getting married. I've never known anyone like you. When we first met, it was like something just hit me. I never expected it to be a two-by-four. And then we went on a hot date with real flames. I knew right then, I had to make you mine. You're one special lady."

Allie shook her head. "I'm not marrying you. I have a boyfriend."

Rip nodded. "Yes. Well, at least, you did."

Allie chilled. She closed her eyes and fought the tears that threatened her. *Please let Sydney be OK.*

Rip continued. "But your old boyfriend is out of the picture now. He wasn't worth your time anyway."

Wasn't worth her time? Now that pissed her off.

Allie jerked forward to the full extent of her chains. "You had better not have hurt Sydney! If you did, you'll regret the day you were born."

The man just chuckled. "I didn't kill him."

Allie sagged in relief.

Rip continued. "But I hope you're not expecting him to come to the wedding. I left several false trails. There is no way he would find you in time." He patted her arm. "Plus, I've been watching. It always pays to watch the competition. And I saw how he's afraid of the dead." He frowned. "He really shouldn't discriminate. They can't help that they're living challenged."

He rose and indicated the chapel with its throng of corpses. "With all my friends here, there is no way he'll come." He leaned in until his face was inches from hers. "I know a thing or two about irrational fears, so I know he'll be too afraid." He smiled. "Even for you."

He turned away. "So my dearest, please excuse me. I have much to do before our wedding."

Allie watched him walk away in dread. She'd noticed Sydney's phobia. And knew it was bad. And while he might be able to stand one or two of the bodies, what about dozens? A sick dread wormed into her heart.

But then she took a deep breath and let it out slowly. No, Sydney was brave. She would believe in him. It was time to use the amulet to call him. The magician had assured them it would work, and so far, it had done as billed.

She closed her eyes and focused on the protection amulet. She needed Sydney now more than ever. And in her mind, she begged him to come. To find her. She squeezed her eyes and tried to shut out the horrid humming. Tried to picture his face.

But nothing happened. The amulet remained quiet, leaving no doubt it was not working.

She felt a tear leak down her cheek. *What was she doing wrong?*

The magic protection had worked for Medorah, so Magician Rtyus had not been lying. So why not this?

She thought of Sydney and wished he was here beside her. Holding her. She loved his gentle strength. She regretted that she wouldn't be able to grow old with him.

But most of all, she wished she had gotten to kiss him one last time. She could almost feel his lips on hers.

"I love you, Sydney," she whispered.

Her eyes flew open, and she gasped.

The amulet had throbbed.

CHAPTER THIRTY-THREE

One Big Firecracker

Sydney

SYDNEY AWOKE SLOWLY AS he sensed the last rays of the sun slipping behind the horizon. He smiled, thinking of his bed companion and wondering if maybe they could have a little more snuggle time before getting up. He turned on his side and threw an arm over her. He frowned. She felt kind of cold. A nagging sense of worry crept into his brain. He hoped she wasn't getting sick.

He reached up and fumbled for the interior light, blinking in its sudden brightness.

Sydney's eyes stretched wide. Instead of Allie, he was cuddling a white-faced corpse. He shamelessly screamed in absolute horror.

Sydney shoved himself away from the body and pushed frantically on the casket lid, desperately trying to get out. But it wouldn't budge. He was trapped with a dead body—a nightmare that had haunted him since his cousins' prank.

He pounded on the casket's lid. "Allie!" he yelled. "SARGE! Anyone!"

No answer.

He beat on the lid with both fists. "Somebody! Get me out of here. *Please!*"

All his childhood fears came rushing back to him. He began to hyperventilate and thought he might throw up. He inched as far away from the corpse as he could, unable to take his eyes off the elderly man dressed in a gray suit and burgundy tie. His eyes were closed, and his arms were folded across his chest in silent rest.

Sydney squeezed his eyes shut and tried to take deep breaths. He strained his ears for any sounds outside, but he could hear nothing.

He was trapped.

Where was Allie?

Had she abandoned him? Had she locked him inside with his worst fear and stolen the rest of the blood? Had she betrayed him like every other woman he'd known? He thought she was different. A tear leaked down his cheek. How could she have been so cruel?

She couldn't. He knew it in his heart. The last few days with her had been a breath of fresh air. She was strong-willed, jumped to conclusions, and a bit quick to anger, but she was not cruel. It would be inconceivable for her to do something like this.

Sydney cursed. Then what had happened? He clenched his fists at his sides in anger and tried to think. Allie had the same daytime constraints as he did. So while she might have awoken a few minutes ahead of him, it wouldn't have been possible for her to find a body, place it beside him, and then lock him in as he slept.

Then who did it?

It was like some horrid sick joke. There weren't that many people left on the planet to pick from, and a normal human had other things to worry about right now. He grimaced. Normal was the keyword. Or better, someone that didn't think that way.

Rip.

His eyes flew open, and at the sight of the body, promptly shut them again.

He must have taken Allie. And whatever he wanted her for, it couldn't be good.

In frustration, he beat and kicked the lid to the casket, but it remained stubbornly unyielding.

He lay back, breathing hard from his exertion. His hands clenched. *What if she was dead?*

Another failure. He should have seen this coming. Should have made better preparations. He was so terrified he couldn't think straight.

A tear slipped down his cheek.

It was likely too late, and she was already gone. The one person in the world he cared about. He remembered holding her as they drifted off to sleep. He marveled at how close they had become in such a short time. He wished he had given her one last kiss before shutting his eyes.

I love you, Allie, he whispered.

The amulet gave a single quick throb. His eyes flew open. He was so startled that he didn't even see the corpse in front of him. He thought he might have imagined it, but then it did it again. And finally, once more.

Three times.

He remembered what the magician had said about being connected and the magic words. Allie was very much alive.

And she was calling him.

Sydney took a deep breath. Then another, steeling his nerves and building his resolve. He had to get free. There had to be a way out.

He turned off the interior light and took a deep breath. Bracing himself, he pushed up on the lid with all his strength. The cover rose fractionally, and a thin seam of light appeared where it met the base. There were also shadows where the latches were attached. He eased off and tried to visualize what they looked like.

The bed may have looked like a casket, but it was really just a piece of custom-made furniture. The latches were of simple design and intended to hold the lid in place while moving, not to seal it like a real casket. If he had something to poke through the crack, he might be able to release them.

Sydney felt up and down his pajamas. Nothing. Not even a piece of string.

Sydney glanced over at the corpse and shuddered. *What about him?* He nearly threw up at what he contemplated.

Keeping the light off so he didn't have to look at the body, he turned on his side and hesitantly patted the man's pockets. He immediately discovered a piece of paper pinned to the corpse's chest but ignored it for now. He stuck it in his robe pocket for later.

He continued his search and was rewarded with a lump under the man's jacket. Probing further, he found something metallic. Turning on the light, he found his prize to be a gold money clip. It must have been accidentally left in the suit.

After straightening the clip, he again forced the lid up and slid the flat piece of metal inside the exposed crack. To his utter amazement, the well-maintained latch easily slid aside.

As soon as the latch was free, Sydney threw back the lid and jumped out. He slammed it behind him. Putting a hand over his heart, he backed away from the bed and ran into the next room.

He drew up short when he caught sight of the shelter door. It had been sliced into several pieces, with parts of it lying on the floor. Someone wasn't messing around. Sydney ran outside.

SARGE nearly gave him a heart attack when she popped up from behind a pile of rubble.

"Did you see where he took Allie?" he demanded.

The robot pointed with her thumb back toward the city. "A big guy came along about an hour ago carrying something in a big bag over his shoulder. I thought he was going to make a delivery, but he came back out with the same bag. Although this one had a thermal signature inside."

Thank goodness she had been in the bag. The sun had been down less than an hour, so he must have collected her during the day. She had been separated from death by a thin layer of black plastic.

Sydney glared at the robot. "How come you didn't try to stop him?"

SARGE held up her hands. "Hey, I don't do chainsaws. If you had seen what he did to that door, you would have hidden too."

He thought for a moment. "Did you see which way he went?"

The robot pointed towards the city. "I can lead you to him. The guy left a trail a blind vacuum cleaner could follow."

Sydney shoved his hands in his pajama pockets, trying to think of his next steps. He found the note that had been on the body. Reading it didn't reassure him.

"*Here's a new friend for you,*" it read. "*I hope you enjoy his company. If you follow me, both of you will look just like him. Signed, Your Friend!*"

Further down, there was a postscript. "*P.S. I have dozens more like him guarding my place. Think carefully before you decide to come. You might get a little scared.*"

Sydney read the note again and wadded it up, clenching it tightly in his fist. Dozens? He had been almost incapacitated by a single corpse. What would a couple of dozen do to him? Put him in a coma? The guy must have heard them talking inside the hospital morgue. It was the only explanation.

Allie's disappearance, the dead body, and Rip's note—it was too much. A sudden wave of dizziness hit him, and he staggered, nearly falling.

Could he even get close enough to save her? His phobia would surely prevent him. And what could *he* do against a mad man like that? He eyed the door. He was severely outgunned.

He had no idea what to do.

Sydney stood up and stumbled back into the shelter. He went to the portraits of his ancestors and stopped in front of his grandfather's picture.

"I guess you were right," he said aloud. "I'm a coward."

The portrait showed a slightly younger version of the man Sydney knew, but the hint of a smirk on his lips was the same. It was like he was arrogantly saying, *I know something that you don't.*

He had hated the man. And yet, had loved him. Their last encounter had not ended well. Sydney had finally said he had had enough.

His grandfather had looked at him using the same expression as the portrait. "You haven't the balls to defy me. You're too much of a coward," he had said. "Now go on to your next lesson. You're nowhere near ready."

"NO!" Sydney had shouted, an unaccustomed resolve in his voice. "I will no longer play your games. I am *done!* You've destroyed my childhood and made a joke of my teenage years. Even my college days were stripped of their enjoyment, all because of your insistence I be ready for anything! You just resent having a grandson who isn't good enough. I'm sorry I'm a *disappointment!*"

He was quaking in his boots but remembered meeting his grandfather's gaze and refusing to back down.

To his surprise, the elder had just snorted. "Looks like I was wrong, and you did finally grow a pair." With a dismissive wave of his hand, he turned away. "My job is done. Your training is over. I hope you're strong enough to protect the ones you love."

His grandfather had taken two steps away and then looked over his shoulder at Sydney, giving him a sad smile. "And I never said you were a disappointment."

He had turned away and walked off. Sydney had been so angry he had never spoken to him again.

But that's because he had died three days later.

Sydney sighed. He hated that man. And sorely missed him.

He'd often wondered why his grandfather had chosen those last words. *To save the ones you love.*

The elder had never revealed why Sydney needed to be trained. He'd only responded vaguely, saying something about being prepared for anything.

To save the ones you love.

Sydney quickly reviewed the events of the last few days in search of fuel for his hope. Had he not defeated the chainsaw killer twice? Had he not jumped from a unicorn's back to catch a pegasus's leg? Had he not conquered his fear of water and saved his friend Quick?

Those were not the actions of a coward.

He scanned down the rest of his relatives. Had they done what they'd had to do? Had they been scared? Had they doubted themselves? He imagined they were more like him than he would have ever thought. He had indulged in ancestor worship to the point where he had become inferior to them.

Sydney pursed his lips. They were people, not gods. And if they could do it, so could he.

He walked back outside. SARGE was still standing where he had left her. With arms crossed, she seemed to be waiting.

"Did you finally pull out of your funk?" she asked.

He nodded. "I'm going to get Allie back. Can you track them?"

SARGE thumped her chest, and it gave a metallic clang. "Of course, I'm the leanest, meanest tracking machine you've ever seen." Sydney could swear the robot was smiling. "But it will cost you."

Sydney's eyes went large. "Not that."

The robot nodded. "Pucker up, big guy."

"Are you sure that's where they are?" Sydney peered around the corner of a broken brick building. A block down the street was a damaged chapel. The front had been completely knocked off, but otherwise, it seemed intact.

SARGE made a snorting sound. "You mean you can't tell."

Sydney had to admit, the dead bodies surrounding it were a strong indication.

Both dead men and women had been propped up as if they were guarding the place. It looked like they had been tied to rebar steel rods sunk into the ground. Some were dressed in police uniforms, some firemen, some in business suits, and some just ordinary people. It was sad and horrific at the same time. Rip must have robbed every funeral home and morgue in the area.

Sydney swallowed nervously. "I have to get past them," he muttered aloud.

In response, a chainsaw flared to life inside the building. It revved once, sputtered, and died. Well, at least he knew somebody was home.

A moment later, his necklace throbbed three times again. He was running out of time. But how was he going to get in quickly? He eyed the dead bodies nervously. Even looking at one would trigger an anxiety attack.

He pointed. "Let's move over there and see if we can get a glimpse of what's inside." SARGE nodded.

They circled the block and came back through a broken building across the street. It gave them an excellent view of the chapel's interior. But unfortunately, Sydney was not encouraged by what he saw.

The interior was lit by strings of miniature white lights hung randomly from the walls and pieces of furniture. They had to be battery-powered. To his horror, the first few rows of pews were occupied with more of the dead. Sydney shivered. He had to admit that Rip had outdone himself.

The man stood in the back to one side, leaning over a small table with a rather large chainsaw on it. Using a metal file, he looked to be carefully sharpening each blade. He obviously was in a good mood, indicated by his obnoxious humming.

Allie lay chained atop a heavy table in front of the chapel's altar. She was still dressed in the white gown she had gone to bed with, but she now also wore a bridal veil on her head. From her struggles with the chains, he could tell she was thankfully alive.

But the oddest thing about the interior was the unusually shaped object on the altar where the pulpit would have been. It was covered in a red velvet drape and was roughly cylindrical. He wondered what it was.

"Any ideas on getting her out?"

SARGE looked indignant. "Hell no. You're the thinker, not me. I'm just a sex robot."

Sydney frowned. He wished she was some heavily armed battle robot that could go in guns blazing. Or even some brave little robot that talked only in beeps and whistles. But no, he had to get stuck with a reject sex robot that thought she was seductive.

Sydney grinned. His grandfather had once said that everything had a purpose. And he had just found SARGE's.

He turned to the robot. "Can you distract him while I set Allie free?"

"What about your fear?"

Sydney took a deep breath. "I'll just have to keep it in check while I do it."

SARGE put her hands on her hips. "And just how am I supposed to distract that mother?"

Sydney smiled. "You're a sex robot, right? Well, he's a man. Just do what you were programmed to do?"

"You're kidding."

Sydney just looked at her.

She sighed. "You've got no heart."

"Neither do you. Now, get going."

The robot grasped Sydney by the arm, suddenly all seriousness. "Are you sure you want me to do this? You know I was headed for the scrap heap because I've never been able to complete a mission. I screwed up every time. What if I mess up again?"

Sydney put a hand on the robot's shoulder. "That's why I'm only asking you to create a distraction. Take it from me. You're very, very good at it."

The robot considered him for a moment, and if she'd had the ability, Sydney believed she would have smiled. "You know, you're right. I've done pretty well for a defective robot. And I *am* the sexiest machine money can buy."

Sydney nodded. "Let me get in place first. I'll signal you, and then you…" He swallowed. "Distract him."

She cocked her hip to one side and placed a hand on it. "I'll have him so distracted that he won't know which way is up."

Which meant he had to pass through them.

He steeled himself and stepped forward. Instantly, his heart rate jumped, and he broke out in a cold sweat. He was having trouble breathing.

He took a step back and looked away, trying to calm himself. He had to get through. Failure was not an option.

Not for the first time, he wondered why he hadn't developed a more *rational* irrational fear, like spiders or heights. Why did it have to be *seeing dead bodies*?

Sydney's eyes grew large. The solution was so obvious. Since seeing them was the problem, then all he had to do was just not look.

He got down on all fours, and keeping his head lowered, crawled toward the barrier of bodies. He was sweating as he passed the first and kept his eyes locked on the ground. He successfully passed the first row and was shocked that his idea was working. He smiled. Perhaps this was going to be easier than he had thought.

And then he ran smack into the dangling legs of a body, their stocking feet right in front of his face. He assumed it was a man from the trousers, but he resisted the urge to make sure.

His body began to tremble, and his breathing became erratic as panic nearly seized him. *I can't.* He wanted to run away in terror.

No, Allie needed him.

He closed his eyes and took a deep breath. By sheer force of will, he brought his breathing under control. Allie was depending on him, and he had no time for his phobia. *Yes, you're afraid, but you can do this.*

Carefully, he moved to the side and continued past the dangling legs. He breathed a sigh of relief as he navigated past the others and made it into the chapel, crawling down the aisle closest to the wall.

Once in position, he sat back and wiped the sweat off his forehead. He would never, ever do that again.

After catching his breath, he signaled SARGE. The robot immediately marched straight into the chapel, swaying her hips so widely Sydney was afraid they would break.

Striking a seductive pose, she called from the building's entrance. "Hi, handsome. Wanna have some fun?"

Startled, Rip jumped up and brandished his chainsaw. "What the hell are you?"

SARGE answered in a pouty voice. She stepped slowly toward him. "I'm just a lonely lady, dying for some male company. *Strong* male company just like you."

Now was his chance. Sydney crawled over to the table holding Allie and inspected the chains from underneath. They were secured using a hefty-looking padlock, and breaking it was not going to happen.

Allie's eyes grew large when he popped up beside her.

"Where's the key?" he whispered.

Allie shook her head. He glanced at Rip's worktable but only saw the tools he had been working with. Then he looked at Rip and noticed a set of keys hanging from his belt.

Damn! This would not be easy.

Rip had his back to the vampire, but SARGE had a clear view of Sydney's activities over his shoulder. He mimed a key and mouthed the words, indicating Rip's hip.

SARGE gave a slight nod.

Rip was none too pleased with the robot's attention. "You stay away from me, you creep!" he shouted. "I'll cut you to pieces!"

SARGE stepped forward. "You wouldn't hurt poor innocent me, would you? I'm sure we can help each other out on these long cold nights."

The robot quickly reached out, grabbing the front of Rip's pants. "How about a little kissy poo before we move on to other things?"

Rip struggled to get the robot's hand off his pants, a look of horror on his face. "No! Get away from me, you monster."

SARGE snaked a hand to the keys, and with the small rip of a belt loop, jerked them off. She tossed the bundle in Sydney's direction.

The vampire snatched them out of the air and looked at the bunch in frustration. There had to be a million keys on the ring. With no other choice, he immediately began trying them in the lock.

Rip squirmed out of SARGE's grasp and backed several steps away. He did a double-take when he noticed Sydney trying the keys. But the vampire didn't stop and frantically kept inserting them one by one.

"So you did come! I'm surprised you got past all my friends." Rip broke into a wide grin and jerked on the chainsaw's cord. It roared to life, and he revved it a few times. "Now, both of you can also become my bestest friends."

At full throttle, he stalked toward them.

SARGE tried to grab him again, but Rip swung the saw at her, and she had to dance back, tripping over the feet of one of the dead people. She sprawled on her backside.

Rip resumed his approach.

Allie's eyes grew large. "Any time now, Sydney!"

He kept trying keys. "Come on. Come on," he said to himself.

Rip came closer.

Click. Sydney heard it even over the roar of the chainsaw. The chains loosened, and he immediately jerked Allie off the table.

Hardly a moment later, the chainsaw came down where Allie's head would have been, leaving a long deep gash in the wood of the table. He looked up at them and grinned.

Sydney held Allie beside him and backed away.

Rip continued to advance, and they had no choice but to retreat until they reached the wall. They had nowhere to go.

Sydney had a terrible sense of déjà vu as Rip and his chainsaw approached. Only this time, he had no crowbar to save him. He was confident the chainsaw would kill him. Even his vampire ability to heal wouldn't be able to deal with that. And all he had to defend himself were his wits and two sharp teeth.

Sydney's eyes flew open. That was it!

He opened his eyes wide and laughed in his most sinister voice. "I'm glad you're my friend." He displayed a wide vampire grin, showing his razor-sharp, extended canines. He hissed and raised his arms menacingly. "Because I am a *vampire*! And I will so enjoy sucking your blood."

Allie quickly caught on and bared her own teeth. "Yes, you will taste so good. You don't mind giving us some, do you? *Friend*." Together they advanced.

Rip's eyes grew wide in horror, and he took several steps back. "Keep away from me!" he yelled. "I can't stand needles."

He turned to run, but SARGE blocked his path. Without hesitating, he swung at her with the saw, but she was ready with a length of the chain that had been used to bind Allie. She looped it around the spinning saw, and it immediately stalled.

Grabbing a nearby chair, Sydney whacked it over Rip's head. The man staggered, took one more step forward, and then collapsed in a heap. Allie scooped up the chainsaw and tossed it out a nearby window.

"You did it, SARGE!" exclaimed Sydney.

The robot looked at the chain she held in her hands and then back to Sydney. "I did, didn't I?" she seemed utterly shocked. "After all this time, I finally completed a mission."

Allie nodded. She hugged the robot. "That was pretty brave. I might even get you a Clare Montare T-shirt."

SARGE put an arm across Allie's shoulders and leaned close. "Since we just saved your ass, I think it's time you returned the favor with a little kissy poo?"

Allie pulled away. "Sorry. But I don't swing that way."

SARGE put her hands on her hips and sighed dramatically. "Not me, stupid." She pointed to Sydney. "Him. He's the one that should get one." Sydney could hear the smile in the robot's voice. "A nice, long and hot one."

Allie grinned and slipped her arms around his neck. "I think I can do that."

SARGE pointed to Rip. "What do we do with him?"

Sydney considered the chainsaw killer. "I'm not sure. But we can't leave him lying around loose."

Rip opened his eyes and sat up, blinking at them. "Are you going to put me back in the hospital?"

Sydney took the chain from SARGE, preparing to bind the man's hands. "I'm not sure that's an option."

Allie sighed and crossed her arms. "We might be able to get the army base to take him. He definitely needs some help." She turned sympathetic eyes toward Rip. "Wouldn't you like to be among friends again?"

Sydney groaned. *Please tell me she didn't just say friends?*

A look of horror passed over Rip's face. He shook his head emphatically. "No, not friends. Please!"

Suddenly Rip bolted for the pulpit. Before they could react, he had climbed the three steps to the raised platform and stood beside the mysterious velvet draped object.

"I was going to save this as a surprise gift for my bride. But since you've ruined everything, I'll just give it to her now."

He jerked on the red drape, and it spilled onto the floor, revealing a stainless steel cylinder. A bold yellow radiation warning symbol was displayed prominently on the side. Just below it, an access panel had been removed, and a thick cable snaked out, terminating in a small metal box hanging beside the access. A single red button and a digital display showing the number ten occupied the front of the box.

"HOLY CRAP!" yelled SARGE. "That's a ten megaton neutron bomb!" She put her hands over her face. "We are so screwed."

Sydney wasn't sure how Rip knew to do it, but he must have wired the bomb to explode, and the button was the detonator! He gasped. He must have been the one that stole the nuclear device from the army base. Sydney saw him there but never dreamed he was the one.

Rip reached for the button with a smile on his face. "I wanted to have fireworks at my wedding. But I could only find one really big one. I think it will do the job, though. I hope you enjoy it! Now let's all countdown together."

"*NO!*" Sydney yelled.

Rip slapped the button with his palm.

Then in digital accuracy, a synthesized voice counted to their deaths. "TEN... NINE... EIGHT..."

"OH SHIT!" yelled SARGE.

"Quick, Sydney! The amulet!" screamed Allie.

Sydney fumbled for it around his neck. *It wasn't there!*

"SEVEN... SIX... FIVE..."

He ripped his shirt open, and with probing fingers, found that the necklace had gotten twisted around. He pulled it out.

"FOUR... THREE... TWO..."

Allie held her half out, and Sydney leaned in with his. Their eyes met as they gently touched them together, and at that instant, the two pieces became one. A pale shimmer immediately appeared around them.

"ONE..."

Sydney reached out and jerked the robot beside them.

"ZERO!"

The room was filled with a blinding white light, a wrenching wind, and the feeling that they were flying through the air.

He had time to wonder if vampires were allowed into the afterlife.

CHAPTER THIRTY-FOUR

Sunrise

Sydney

SYDNEY PUSHED SOME DEBRIS off his chest and sat up. He was sorely disappointed. He had expected hell to look different than a war-torn Earth.

As his mind slowly began to work, he realized he was surprisingly still alive. It was hard to believe he had survived a direct nuclear blast. Glancing around him, he discovered the explosion must have thrown them a considerable distance from the blast site. And on top of that, the horizon was just beginning to lighten. Sunrise was only minutes away.

Remembering he was grasping something in his hand, Sydney looked down to find he still held his half of the amulet, apparently undamaged by the ordeal. He mentally thanked

Magician Rtyus. The protection amulets had worked after all.

But where was Allie? In a panic, he called her name.

"Sydney! Over here."

He got up and staggered over to where the sound originated. He started moving debris until he found her and pulled her up.

"Are you all right?" he asked.

She was covered with dirt and grime, and her now tattered gown was a dingy shade of gray. "Yeah, how about you?"

"All right, just a cut on my arm. It's still bleeding though. I wonder if the radiation affected my ability to heal."

She looked at him strangely. "Let me see." He held it out for her.

She looked at it a moment, then back at him with a puzzled expression. She hiked up her gown to her thighs and examined three scratches on her legs. They were bleeding too.

"Sydney, don't you realize what has happened? We're no longer vampires!"

He felt for his extended canines, but they were no longer there. His eyes went wide in amazement. "It must have been from the intense radiation. It undid whatever made us vampires. There were signs of this effect on us all along. Remember what Rtyus said about our vampire magic being sick? The radiation must have killed it!"

He pulled her against him. "Now we can be normal again!"

Just then, they heard a mechanical groan and a large pile of debris lifted up. SARGE peeked out.

"Hey! I'm glad you could make it," called Sydney.

The robot swayed and seemed a little disoriented. "I think I'm going to sleep in. I've got a terrible headache." She lowered the debris back on top of her.

Allie looked up at Sydney. "Do you think she's all right?"

He nodded. "I bet it was from the magic. Frank the unicorn had said mechanicals and magic don't mix. Just give her a little time to get over it, and I think she'll be as good as new."

Sydney saw Allie's eyes glance over his shoulder. He whipped around, expecting to confront another adversary. But nothing was there. Confused, he turned back. "What is it?" he asked.

She pointed to the brightening horizon. "The sun. It's coming up. I haven't seen the sun in…."

Sydney nodded. He took her by the hand and led her up a tall mound of rubble. Although they would have to move out as quickly as possible because of the radiation, they could take a few moments for a brief reprieve.

They sat down, side by side, on the top of the mound, facing east. Allie laid her head on his shoulder and sighed while Sydney put an arm around her waist. He wasn't sure what the future held. And surviving in a post-apocalyptic world was not going to be easy. Especially now that they were just humans. But at least he had someone special at his side.

Together, they watched their first sunrise in a long, long time.

Acknowledgments

Many people went into making *Monday After The Apocalypse,* and I am grateful to each and every one of them.

Thanks go out to Kelsey for her help with proofing and copyediting. She found the mistakes that flew right by me. I also need to thank Kasey, Callista, and Daniel for their wonderful advice and many corrections.

And once again, my wife deserves major kudos for putting up with all the time I spent glued to my keyboard. She also knew exactly when I needed a hug and a good dose of home-made lasagna.

Other Books
by Jessie D. Eaker

The Coren Hart Chronicles
Thief of Curses
Queen of Curses
Assassin of Curses

A Study of Curses (A series companion)

Other novels
Monday After the Apocalypse

About The Author

Jessie Eaker lives in central Virginia with his wife, son, their cats, and (her) parakeets. Originally a native of North Carolina, he's lived in Virginia so long, he's lost his southern accent (much to his wife's disappointment). When not writing, he watches anime, reads, and works on his ever-growing list of things to fix around the house.

Check out jessieeaker.com for his latest works and updates.

Made in United States
Orlando, FL
07 June 2022

18581437R10240